J L CASTEN

Published by Nightshade Publishing, LLC.

Cover design by Shay Stewart.

First edition

ADVISORY

Please be advised that some aspects of this work may be upsetting to some.

Themes in this story are listed at www.jlcasten.com

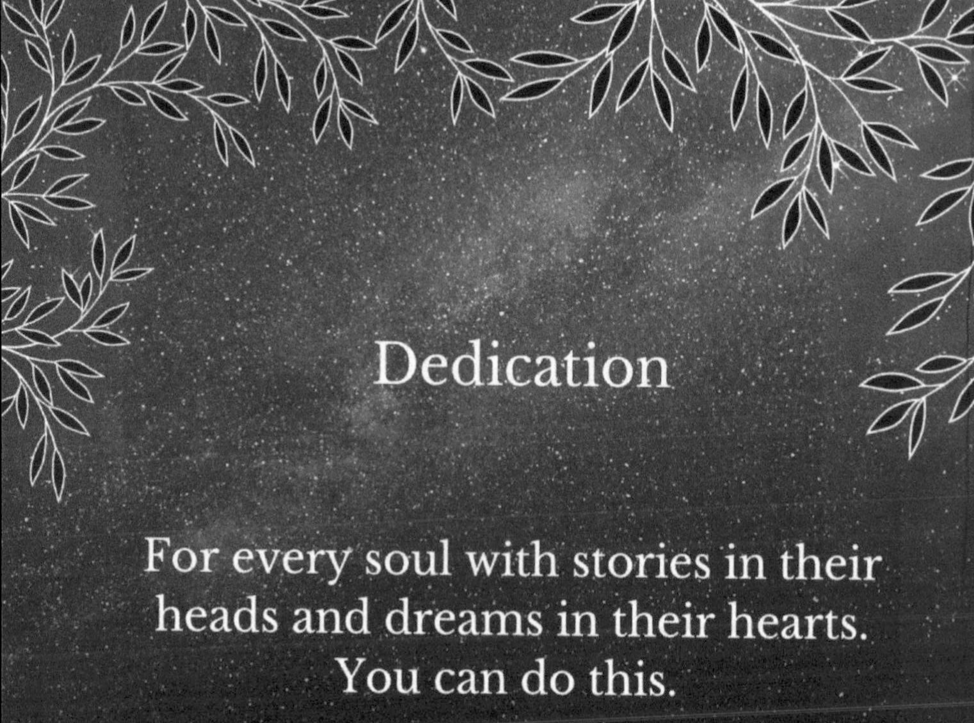

Dedication

For every soul with stories in their heads and dreams in their hearts. You can do this.

To my precious KimBee, I love you more than you will ever know.

Contents

1. Prologue 1
2. One 5
3. Two 19
4. Three 27
5. Four 37
6. Five 51
7. Six 57
8. Seven 65
9. Eight 75
10. Nine 87
11. Ten 99
12. Eleven 115
13. Twelve 129
14. Thirteen 145
15. Fourteen 157
16. Fifteen 169
17. Sixteen 181
18. Seventeen 185
19. Eighteen 197
20. Nineteen 207
21. Twenty 217

22. Twenty-One 231
23. Twenty-Two 241
24. Twenty-Three 245
25. Twenty-Four 257
26. Twenty-Five 265
27. Twenty-Six 271
28. Twenty-Seven 285
About Author 302
Acknowledgments 303

GLOSSARY

Spells/ Magic:
Accipio- I receive
Imperium Porta - gateway command
ignis- fire
voro- engulf, swallow
Annuo- give consent
In Aeternum- for eternity

athair- father
dinnae- don't (don't forget)
ken- to know
huad yer wheesht- shut up
mathair- mother
bràthair- brother
dachaigh- home
sàmhach- dormant
draoidheachd- magic
mo chridhe- my heart
saoghail- traitor
Fàilte- Welcome
mallachd- curse
damn e gu h-iomlan- damn it all

a bheil thu air chall? An urrainn dhomh do chuideachadh a 'lorg do shlighe? - Are you lost?

Prologue

May 10, 1999

Cadence stared, unseeing, through the window of the luxurious bathroom. The last few years she'd lived in Scotland with her new husband, she'd grown attached to the place. The Manor felt safe, felt like home in a way she didn't realize she had been missing in her life. Of course, the safety she felt would vanish quickly if that test came out how she thought it might.

She sighed, looking across to the stick lying on the counter. One minute left. One more minute living in this world, the world before she saw the result. She was struggling with how she felt about the possibility of bringing a magical child into this world, especially one with blood as powerful as they had running through their veins.

Choking back tears, she wondered how devastated Jasper would be to leave this behind. There was no question of staying, not if there was a child on the way. No, that would be a death sentence for Cadence, and a life of servitude for their child.

A baby meant a new life for them. It meant a life in hiding, a life they hadn't planned for. It meant a life removed from the battle, removed from everything they knew. It was the start of something unknown, something terrifying.

Make no mistake, they'd be hunted to the ends of the Earth if *she* found out about a baby. Their lives would immediately become about hiding that child, ensuring word never reached their enemies. Any child of theirs had too much potential, would

Her parents were gone, killed fighting *her*. She and Jasper's entire life now focused on helping to set things right, reuniting the family that had been ruptured.

Liam, her father-in-law, was a shell of his former self; gone was the robust and lively man she'd come to know. How much more damage would their leaving do to his already fragile state? How much further would he withdraw from the world, the family? Analyse being taken from him was just too much; he had been near to useless in the fight since. Not that there had been much fight. A skirmish here or there, one or two of *her* goons showing up to harass Guardians.

Wrapping her arms around her abdomen, tears falling despite her best efforts, she looked once more at the vibrant Scottish countryside. It was time. Turning, she walked over to the counter and lifted the stick, then collapsed against the marble edge of the bath.

Cadence sat stunned, holding the pregnancy test in her hand. Positive. It was positive. Panic, fear, and joy slammed through her, one after the other. She stood and called to her new husband.

"Jasper! Jasper, I need you!" She tried to keep the panic from her voice, but she knew he'd heard it anyway.

The door flew open, a wild-eyed Jasper scanning the room for threats before settling on her. Cadence held out the small stick with a shaky hand, knowing it would change everything about their lives. She should have told him her suspicions, better prepared him for this. All of their plans, every dream, every vow, shifted in that second.

"Ye'll haveta go on to the States. There'll be no stayin' here now. No' with everythin' as it is. I know ye were hopin' to have settled, but it'll no be safe fer the bairn," Liam said softly, barely able to get the words out. So much lost in so short a time.

He didn't know how he would manage, how he would continue day to day with such uncertainty.

"Aye. Ye know Da has the right o' it." Viv sniffed, tears flowing down her beautiful face freely. "If *she* knew, if she found out, ye know she wouldna stop huntin' ye. A bairn who could be the next Heir? No, she'd no' stop searching, hopin' to control that herself."

Cadence shot Jasper a covert look, one hand already cradling the child growing in her womb. She had known the moment that line appeared. Whatever plans they'd made to stay in Scotland, to help fight *her*, were over. Nothing was more important now than protecting their child.

They'd already decided the best course of action was to go back to Washington, make themselves disappear. Outside of immediate family, no one would know to search for them there. They had no ties left, no reason to go back there. It's what made it perfect; anyone on the outside would rule it out.

"Aye. We've booked a flight, an' have already spoken to the head o' the Order in Seattle. They're preparin' it all as we speak," Jasper admitted, shuffling his feet and keeping his eyes planted firmly on the floor in front of him. "We'll no tell the bairn. No' until we know this is'na permanent. The child'll be safer that way," Jasper blurted out, ignoring his sister's gasp of disapproval. It was cowardly, telling his family this as he and Cadence had one foot out the door, but it was the best he could do at the moment. Eventually they would come around, understand the decisions they were making to put the child first.

"What ye think is best, lad. I be certain ye have it right," Liam agreed, barely glancing at the couple. "Best ye be off methinks. Sooner ye free yerselves from 'ere, the safer ye'll be." The devastation and defeat so evident in his voice, so clear in his dismissal.

Viv gave one last indignant huff before storming out of the room. Liam sinking into a chair without another thought to his children, absorbed in his own grief. The toll exacted upon their family in this fight, yet another price to pay. It was simply too much for either of them to face.

As Jasper and Cadence left the Manor that day, no one waved from the steps. There were no bittersweet smiles, no promises to 'see you soon,' just the two of them silently driving away. A cloud of dread and foreboding fell over them all, the future unclear and unknown; a set of circumstances none of them could reconcile. A mix of grief and joy hung over each of them.

One

Present Day

Knock, knock, knock.

The door to my room swings open, and Mom's face fills the doorway, her smile beaming down at me in my plush queen bed. The light filtering in above my head from the window splashes onto her face.

"Lorali! It's time to get up!" she sing-songs at me as I groan and pull the covers over my face. I know she'll get annoyed with me, but I'm a little annoyed with her right now.

"*Mom!*" I complain. "Why do I have to go? I'd rather just stay home this year. I can even stay with Isobel!" Knowing exactly what is about to happen from the look on her face, I prepare myself. Pulling the covers up tightly in my fists above my head, I hear the door open fully, her footsteps approaching me atop the hardwood floors.

"Lorali. I will not have this argument with you again; now come on, up and at 'em, love." She grabs the comforter and yanks it off my head, out of my grip. "Or do I have to sing you the good morning song?" she asks.

"Oh God, please, *no*!" I sit up and glare at my mother, who continues to smile and remains completely unfazed. After a couple of seconds, I roll my eyes and move to get out of bed. It only makes her smile even bigger, give a nod of satisfaction, and leave the room. At least she closed my door behind her.

I know I could choose to ignore her. I could choose to stay home and do exactly as I please. I am an adult, after all. Except I still live with my parents, for the time being, and honestly I would rather not disappoint them. I want them to be alright with me making my own choices, my own plans. The fact that I *am* an adult somehow isn't as satisfying as my parents *seeing* me as one.

Today is the first day of Christmas break, except for me it's more than that. I am officially an early High School Graduate, with an early acceptance into the University of Washington. Most people about to turn 19 are halfway through their first year of college, but I got a later start than most.

Sometimes I think it makes me more eager to be on my own, which is why this trip is getting under my skin so much. Every year we fly all the way to Glasgow, Scotland, to visit my dad's family. The flight itself is brutal. Twelve hours on a plane cramped between my baby brother Toby and Mom, who sleeps through it.

Special thanks to the anxiety medication she has to have to even step foot on the plane. She hates planes. Like, *really* hates them—has a panic attack, and they once landed an entire plane for her kind of hates them. She'll drive across the country to visit her brother rather than take a flight. I guess it shows how much she really loves my dad, that she will fly 4,442 miles every year.

It's not just the ridiculous airplane ride though; we also have to drive to this tiny village my aunt lives right outside of. The house has been in the family since forever. I've never asked about it much because my dad has always acted kind of weird about our family history. He gets super awkward and strange whenever we've asked about anything involving our family. I think it must have been someone's castle at some point because it's completely made of stone and wood and very, *very* old.

Everyone calls it 'The Manor,' which always makes me laugh a little. Like there are no other Manors in the whole of Scotland. I think it is officially 'Galloway Manor,' but still; I find it funny.

Aunt Vivienne is married but has no kids, so there's absolutely nothing for me to do all break.

No malls or movie theaters. I don't even think they've heard of decent Wi-Fi. They have Wi-Fi, it's just horrible service. I don't think I have ever even met a neighbor out there, and the closest village is far enough it isn't feasible to walk to it. Driving is out of the question since I'm not licensed there. My grandfather lives there too, but he might as well not for as much as we interact with him.

I love my family so very much, but this trip is the thing I have been dreading all year. I've been trying to talk my parents out of making me a part of it. Isobel, my best friend, and I had planned to spend an eventful, fun break together. When I proposed our plan, Mom and Dad acted as if I had asked to move out forever. I thought they were never going to let me leave the house again after I brought it up.

So my perfect holiday break with Isobel was over before it ever had a chance. Isobel and I fought about it a lot over the past few weeks. She doesn't understand why I don't do what I want despite what my parents say. It's not as though they would cut me off or kick me out if I did, but it would upset them. This trip is important to them, it feels more important than any of the ones before, and so I will choose to respect their wishes. She doesn't understand why it is so important for me to stay close to my family when she can't wait to get away from hers.

I grab my favorite pair of comfy sweats and a long-sleeved shirt, slip on my fuzzy slippers. My suitcase has been packed for two days. I always knew I'd never win that battle, so I hid my suitcase behind my prom dress in my closet. I didn't want Mom to think I'd given up *all* hope. I also don't want to be in hot water for not being ready, though.

I walk over to my window and take a peek outside, hoping to glimpse Mt. Rainier. No matter how many times I see the mountain, it always fills me with awe and happiness. Every time I catch a glimpse, a joyful calm comes over me, and all is right with the world. No matter what. When we moved from Seattle to Tacoma, I was only five years old and absolutely *insisted* on this room because it faced the mountain.

You can't always see it because sometimes the clouds cover it—okay, most of the time the clouds cover it—but it is so worth it every time it peeks out over them. I am whole-heartedly a Washington girl. Sighing, I turn and head downstairs. It's time to face my family, no matter how much of me would rather not.

Dad is sitting at the breakfast nook in the kitchen, not eating breakfast but instead sipping his usual coffee as he scrolls through something or other on his phone. His tousled auburn hair is longer than he normally wears it, and he keeps flicking it off his forehead absently.

Toby is sitting next to him making a milk puddle on the wood as he "eats" his cereal. Whatever Dad is looking at must be pretty interesting for him not to notice the milk slowly creeping towards his favorite shirt. Mom is nowhere in sight.

This might be the perfect time to make one last plea to my dad. If I could even get one of them on board with this, I would feel better.

"Um, Dad?" I say as he looks up from his phone. "I was wondering if maybe we could talk about this whole trip again. I mean, it's not like I'm a little kid anymore. I'll be nineteen like next week. My grades are all great, I'm responsible. A few months ago you were both okay with me stay—"

Before I can even get another word out, my Dad raises his hand in the air, palm facing me—the international father symbol for "stop right there." He looks at me, almost as if considering for a minute, before he stands, walks around the table, and puts an arm across my shoulder. Uh oh. I know this move. I lift my head and look up at his face, and I see in his eyes that this will not go my way. This move never ends with words I want to hear.

"Lor, I know it's not the way you'd necessarily want to spend your break. I get that, kiddo." He sighs. "But, ya know...you're eighteen years old. You've already graduated early. You just took your last High School final. This is my last year with you. One year more than most parents get, and I'm grateful for it. I'm sorry, bug, but I can't give that up. I'm not ready." He kisses the top of my head and walks his cup over to the sink, then he walks out of the kitchen.

Great. Guilt trip city, party of one. Mom will smile me to death and tell me firmly 'no way!' But Dad? Dad makes me feel like the worst person on Earth for not wanting to be with them. He doesn't mean it as a guilt trip, but he is very good at making me feel the guilt. Toby laughs at me and between giggles, says, "Wow, sis, way to make Dad feel like crap. I thought I had the market on letting our parents down. Way to take one for the team!"

With that, he rises from his mess, leaving it there—as usual—and smacks me on the back on his way out. Toby is 14, but he will always be the baby. Even if he is 7 inches taller than me at 6'0". It's really hard to look at him as a teenager when he makes milk puddles simply trying to get the spoon to his mouth. When, like a toddler, he leaves a colossal mess whenever he goes. No matter how much he may *look* like a grown man.

I plop myself down on a chair at the table, realizing any appetite I once had is now totally gone. *Thanks, Dad.* Mom walks in as my head thunks down onto the wooden surface, stomach a jumbled mass of guilt and disappointment.

"Well now, still Ms. Grumpy Pants, huh?" she asks cheerily, cleaning up the cereal mess left by Toby. I watch, irritated that he's allowed to behave that way when I would get an hour-long lecture. It's like my parents failed to realize he is no longer four years old. Which is exactly why he does it—because he can, and because he *knows* how much it annoys me.

"You know this is probably the last family Christmas we're likely to have for a while, Lorali." Her tone takes on an edge of sadness. "It would be nice if you could find it within yourself to at least try to enjoy it."

She walks over and begins stroking my hair like she does when I'm sick or having a bad day. It's usually soothing, but isn't doing much for me this morning. "Now then, how about some coffee and a scone, huh?"

Just like that, Mom is back to her chipper self. She hardly ever allows anything to upset her for longer than 2.5 seconds. It's honestly a little creepy, if you ask me.

"Yeah, Mom, thanks. That'd be great," I mutter from under my hair, head still on the table.

They're not wrong. Next year I'm off to college, and I don't see myself willingly using my winter break to go to Scotland if I don't have to. Isobel and I are both early acceptance into UW, and we've already started planning our whole first year there.

It doesn't include me leaving the country for two or more weeks over Christmas. I think we all know living somewhere other than my parents' house will change the dynamics between us. Next year they won't be able to get my compliance by saying 'no.'

I decide to take a page out of Mom's book and 'choose to be happy.' I put a smile on my face and lift my head from the table. It's very close to the 'fake it till you make it' crap Isobel spouts.

Apparently I have perfect timing because she's pulling out the chair next to me with my coffee and scones for the two of us in hand. She's kind of magic like that. As much as it weirds me out that she never seems to let anything faze her, she also knows exactly what I need and when to show up with it.

"So, do we have plans while we're there or are we winging it?" I ask her, verbally conceding defeat. From the amount of crap they've given me, there *has* to be something planned in Scotland, but I have purposely avoided asking until now. Maybe my grandfather has decided he wants to make an extended appearance. I take a big bite out of the scone she's placed in front of me and watch her face visibly relax at my concession.

OMG. They're cranberry. Dang it, Mom. You're good. My eyes flutter a little as the pastry melts in my mouth and the cranberry bursts flavor across my tastebuds.

"Well, now. Viv is hosting a party while we're there. So that'll be fun." She smiles at me. "Your grandparents used to do that every year, but Dad and Aunt Viv haven't kept it going since your grandmother...well, they stopped the tradition."

My grandma died before I was born. My mom had only met her once, for a few days just after she and my dad married. Everyone tells me I look so much like her, and how wonderful she was. My grandfather lives with Aunt Viv, but he doesn't say much to us when we visit and barely comes out of his study. Mom says he wasn't always that way, and he used to be a lot of fun, before.

I wouldn't know; this is the way things have always been for me. He and Dad sometimes go off while we visit, and I don't see them again until the next morning, but other than that, I haven't seen my grandfather interact much. It's kind of sad, if what Mom says about how he used to be is true. I think I'd have liked to have known that grandfather. This one doesn't even come down for Christmas morning with the family, though there is always something from him under the tree for each of us.

Mom's parents passed away before I was born too, not long after they got married. So I haven't ever had a meaningful relationship with a grandparent, though I do have a close bond with Aunt Viv. Mom's brother, Zack, lives on the other side of the country, and we haven't seen him in years. We are still fairly close, though, and video chat often.

I always wanted one of those huge families that hung out all the time, but mine lives thousands of miles away from one another. So far, Mom and Dad are the only ones who've had children, too. It's always been one of the things that makes me melancholic, not having cousins growing up. I brush it off and focus on the party instead.

"What made Aunt Viv change her mind?" I wonder, curious now.

"I'm not sure, baby. Oh, but I'm so glad she did. I went to the last one your grandma held. It's something to see, let me tell you. You'll never see anything like it here, that's for sure." Mom is gazing out the window, smiling and looking as though she's a million miles away.

"What do you mean? It's just a party, right?" I ask, confused. "I mean. Who even comes to these parties, anyway?"

Mom chuckles.

"Oh, Lor," she smoothes my unruly hair behind my ear and pats my cheek, in my opinion, a little condescendingly. "Baby girl. I really wish we'd have been able to give you a bit more of your heritage than we have." She sighs, resting her chin on her hand. "This is a party unique to our family. Unique to Scotland. And while you may find similar soirees elsewhere, none are quite like this." She sips her coffee and stares out the window again, as if she were far away. "They're tradition. And people come from all over the country. Believe me when I tell you...this will probably be the first time you'll truly see what being a Galloway is all about."

"Okay, well, I'm going to go do my hair and throw my carry-on together then," I say, pushing out from the table, my mom's words leaving me more confused than when she started. To some, abruptly ending the conversation may seem rude or dismissive. Mom and I have an understanding, though, and she knows very well that when I get too out of my element, I need time to process the information.

I hate sounding ignorant and will often table a discussion until I can ask intelligent questions or learn more. There is just something...off...and maybe a little sad...about this conversation. Sometimes I let it go as something I don't understand and leave it at that, but that gets more rare as I get older and want to know everything about everything.

"Do you need help packing?" she asks innocently, though I have a feeling she somehow knows it's been done.

"No, Mom. I actually packed days ago..." I grudgingly admit. "I just didn't want you to think I'd given up. My suitcase is ready to go," I mutter, a little ashamed of my own behavior at this point.

Mom starts laughing uncontrollably at that, and I literally run out of the room with a groan and up the stairs to get ready.

"You have an hour, then we have to leave or we'll miss our flight!" I hear her yell behind me through the laughing as I close the bathroom door.

Locking the door behind me, I gaze in the mirror above the alabaster sink, taking in the disheveled state of my hair. *Oh, Lord. This is going to take some doing.*

Even with a day-long flight looming over my head, no way am I going out in public with my hair looking like something out of a horror movie. I set to work with my straightening iron, smoothing out the frizzy, tangled curls. I inherited my dad's deep red hue, as did Toby. I've wanted to dye it about a billion times now, but my parents absolutely refuse to allow me to touch my precious hair with chemicals.

They say it would be a sin to ruin such perfection. I say I'd like a little more of a subdued color on my head and to not look like a damned stop sign. They, of course, argue that it is absolutely not stop sign colored. Toby loves it; he says it makes him a "chick magnet." That always makes me roll my eyes, but he has always been too mature for his age mentally, even if he doesn't act it practically.

The enigma of creating chaos wherever he goes and yet somehow convincing us all he's mature is...well, it's just weird. He'll leave a half-eaten candy bar to melt all over the counter at the same time he is discussing physics. Accurately, and with my father—the physicist—I might add.

Hair finally tamed with my flat iron, I wash my face and start gathering up the last bits of stuff that need packing. I throw on some mascara and nude lipstick for good measure while I'm at it. Armed with a mountain of toiletries, makeup, and hair care products, I head back to my room to finish up and hear my Mom call out a 15 minute warning.

Crap. I took way too long on my hair in there. It really isn't my fault. Sometimes, the beast takes twenty minutes to tame, others an hour and a half. I really need to look into that hair straightening treatment again. Though my parents would probably cry if I actually had it done. The second I walk into my room, I start wildly throwing things onto my bed and begin a frenzied search for the backpack I use as a carry-on.

"MOM! Have you seen my backpack? The one I use for carry-on?" I holler over my shoulder, frantically searching for my shoes now. No matter how well I think I've prepared for something, I am always, *always* rushing at the last second. I could have made a dozen lists, with timelines, checked them off half as many times, and I would still be rushing at the last second.

"Lorali! You don't even know where your carry-on is?" Mom yells back, chastising. I can tell she's in her bedroom, down the hall from me. *Great. She must have some last-minute things to take care of too. Okay. Well. Not gonna get any help from her finding that bag.* I turn toward my dresser and see a strap peeking out of a bottom drawer. *Oh.*

Rushing over to the dresser, I yank open the drawer and grab the bag I've been tearing my room apart for. One day I will have to at least try to organize my stuff. Every time I attempt to do that, I get distracted, and it never gets done. I may not know where things are, exactly, but at least it's clean chaos. Maybe if I stopped trying to organize it every other month, things would stay in one place long enough for me to remember where that was.

"Never mind, got it!" I yell so she doesn't freak out on me. She is extremely calm, centered, and cheerful about 99.999% of the time. Except when something goes wrong on travel day. I think it's the stress of thinking about getting on a plane. Toby says it's because no one ever gets out of the house without her having to help them with one thing or another. The fact he has enough awareness to recognize that, but continues to do things like track mud from the door to the upstairs bathroom—it boggles my mind.

Honestly, both are probably true, which is why I am trying extra hard to get myself totally packed and out of the house this year. They'll never see me as an adult if I still need their help getting out the door.

Shoving everything I can into my carry-on as quickly as I can, I realize it won't all be able to go into the bag. I run over to my closet and drag my suitcase out from behind its hiding place. Heaving it up on the bed, I throw in my toiletries and such that I know won't make it through airport security.

Okay, now to find my tablet and headphones.

I refused to board that flight without some serious music and the movies I previously downloaded in case I ended up losing the battle to stay here.

"Gotcha!" I mutter, grinning to myself. Grabbing them off the nightstand, I throw them in the bag and close everything up. My timing could not be more perfect.

"Lorali, time's up! We gotta go, baby, come on!" Mom relays from the bottom of the stairs.

How did she even make it past my room without me seeing her?

I swear, my mom has superpowers or something.

"Okay, Mom, on my way down," I call back as I drag my suitcase toward the door. As I lug my bags down the stairs, I can hear my parents checking off everything to make sure nothing is forgotten, namely passports. I can hear the rustling of Mom pulling them out of her purse and checking each one to make sure everything is there.

Sometimes I wonder if I really am ready to be on my own. Here I am barely making it out the door on time, and my parents are standing there, car already packed, looking like they just stepped off a movie set. Their lists are complete, effective, and accurate. They are never late, and they look flawless doing it.

Seriously, though. Dad pulls off the auburn hair like nobody's business, and—

Is he really wearing jeans and a button-down shirt on a 12-hour flight? Are you kidding me?

Mom is no better. She has her long, gorgeous brown hair braided stylishly, and she's got on slacks and a blouse.

They are totally making me look like a bum in my sweats and sneakers. For a couple in their forties, they barely look twenty-five, which is a great indicator of genetics for me, but a little unsettling when your parents look barely older than you. I simply shake my head at them without comment and drag my stuff to the car, pretending not to notice the smirk they give each other as I walk by.

At least Toby is dressed somewhat in accordance with a *twelve*-hour ride in a tin can in the sky. He isn't wearing sweats, but he has his comfiest pair of jeans on and a plain T-shirt. It doesn't even look as if he bothered to run a brush through his hair. Of course, he doesn't really need to. He can pull off that Movie Star Heartthrob thing without even trying. Though I would never in a million years admit that to *him*, it has not escaped my notice that nearly every girl—and quite a few guys—within a few years of his age is interested.

As he is every year, I can tell Dad is excited about this trip as he gets in and starts up the car. He turns around with the biggest smile and winks. "You ready, guys?"

Dad emigrated from Scotland when he was 18 for college but stayed because of Mom once he graduated. She has made certain they've gone back at least once a year, over Christmas, since the day he chose to stay and marry her. The year they got engaged was the first time she went, and that's when she met my grandma.

It's really very sweet if I'm being honest, and it was always fun when I was little, having that big ole house to explore. Land to run and play on. Only in the past few years have I started resenting going. It's not that I don't enjoy it; I do. It's that I am ready to start my own traditions and trips. Dad says it's even more important for him to take us back than it is for him to go, because he wants us to know where we came from.

It always seems an odd sentiment for a man who doesn't like to talk about anything that happened before we were born. I'd be lying if I said I didn't appreciate it, deep down. Having had those experiences, it helps me feel connected to Scotland in a way I never would have otherwise. Besides, it has helped to foster a relationship with the remaining family we have, and that is a priceless gift when we've lost so many. The only grandparent left alive is my grandfather.

Shifting my thoughts from sadness and loss, I choose instead to focus on the joyous look on Dad's face, Mom's small yet anxious smile at seeing him so happy. My parents are adorable if I'm being honest, and I am lucky to have them. It doesn't take long before we are at the airport and on the plane, where I plug my ears with headphones and drift off to the sound of my favorite playlist.

TWO

The plane touching down in Glasgow jolts me awake, heart pounding at the surprise of it. I hate being woken up when the plane lands; it always scares me. Of course, Toby knows that and thinks it's funny, laughing quietly next to me. I should have set an alarm on my tablet rather than trust him to wake me. Smacking him on the arm in frustration, I shoot him the nastiest look I can muster over my slowly calming nerves.

I must have drifted off hard somewhere between hours 5 and 6, post layover. I tend to nap a lot on the plane ride. I think I was only awake for a grand total of 2 hours this time, and mostly only because I was hungry. *Good thing too, my tablet is totally dead*, I think as I roll my eyes. *Guess an alarm wouldn't have helped after all.*

I look over at my parents across the aisle and see them speaking animatedly to one another. They really look like two kids barely out of college on their first trip abroad together. One day, when I find someone I want to make a commitment to, I won't have anyone who doesn't look at me the way they look at each other. Even after nearly twenty years of marriage, they act like newlyweds.

Dad seems more excited about this Christmas than I can remember him usually being, and he is always hyped for Scotland, always animated and full of energy around this time of year. When he gets to go home. This year, something seems different. I can't quite put my finger on it.

Mom says our family has lived on this land for as long as people have walked it. I tried to ask Dad one time if that was true, and he almost looked sad when he told me it was. I think he really wishes we'd all move back here. I don't really know why he and Mom stayed in the States rather than move here, and they always hedge and redirect when asked.

I'm way too old for that now, though. If they moved here, they'd have to do so knowing I wouldn't be coming with them. I'm a Scottish-*American* girl, with roots and friends and a life planned back home. No matter how magical Scotland can be sometimes, and it really can be.

Wow. I haven't thought of it as magical since I was in Middle School. It's beautiful. I'll give it that, but it's *so very* boring. I need a big city close by, like Seattle. Glasgow is wonderful, but it is not an easy or close drive from the Manor.

I love all the hustle and bustle, and all the things to do in Seattle! Pike's Place and the zoo, the aquarium, walking along the pier. You could spend an entire week in Seattle and not see it all. For now, though, I need to at least try to have a good time here with my family. Or at least fake it so I don't ruin their holiday.

I know they really want to make lasting memories with me since this will be the last trip for me until who knows when. Looking out the window onto the tarmac, I can see it's snowed recently. I am happy about that. I *love* the snow, and there aren't many years I can remember we had snow on landing here. It's usually more like Washington, cold and rainy; which I love too, but there is something extra special about crisp snow. It makes me feel a lot like Mt. Rainier does, that deep down calm and peace, the joy of being in a place I can experience it.

I sigh and stand as my row is finally ready to exit this metal flying bucket. I know Aunt Viv will be waiting for us the second we get out of here, and I really am excited to see her. It always takes a ridiculous amount of time to deboard the plane, and my manners prevent me from shoving through first. Quite the contrary, I give every single person around me the opportunity to go first, but then again, so does everyone else in my family.

"Jasper, can you reach my bag, honey?" I hear my Mom ask as she stands up behind Dad, who is already opening the overhead compartment. She's all smiles again now that we're back on the ground. Flying is the one and only thing that rattles her. Like, really rattles her.

She can have a brief moment like the rest of us, but nothing really fazes her for more than a second. Except flying. Now that we are on the ground, though, you'd never be able to tell it ever bothered her. Even after a 12-hour flight, plus layover, she looks refreshed, flawless.

"Get a move on, Lor!" I hear as I get a nudge to the back of my knee from Toby, who is behind me. "And can you grab my bag too?"

He doesn't wait for an answer, pushing past me and walking right off the plane. I groan heavily and mutter some choice words under my breath. He's such a brat sometimes, I swear. I really should leave his stupid bag. See how much he likes that.

"He's just excited, sweet pea," Dad says as he reaches above me and grabs Toby's bag, ruffling my hair with his other hand. I want to be irritated, but the look on my Dad's face is so happy I can't be. Plus, his joy is making me feel really, really badly about my inner monologue right now.

I know Toby is only being contrary to pick at me and to cover up how he feels about me leaving home soon. Regardless of how we annoy one another, we really have a pretty good relationship. He isn't a little kid with an age gap so large we haven't bonded. I'll miss him like crazy when I leave.

"I know, Dad. Me too," I say, trying to assuage some guilt. I hug him quickly before grabbing my bag and heading off the plane. My parents following not far behind.

Toby is leaning against the wall opposite the gate when I finally make it off the plane, scrolling through his phone. I walk over and kick his leg to get his attention.

"Come on, brat. Dad has your bag." He doesn't even look up from his phone before following me towards our parents and Customs. He's probably playing some ridiculous time-killing game or something equally stupid.

Dad is anxiously shifting his weight back and forth like he's about to meet his idol, and Mom is cool as a cucumber as usual. Customs isn't a big deal mostly, especially since Dad is a citizen. Toby and I are as well, but we haven't ever actually lived here—not that Customs cares. Though I am sure it makes this process a little smoother with only one of us going through as a foreign citizen. Which is why Mom always grabs our UK passports instead of the US ones.

I know Dad is ready to get past this last checkpoint and be home again. It always feels kind of tense through this part of the trip; where we're there, but not there yet. Add to that, we've been cooped up in a stuffy airplane for a day. We all want to have the air in our faces and I, for one, would love a shower. I look over at Dad again, and my heart wrenches in my chest a little. He is never this at peace back home.

I know it isn't my fault he doesn't live here, but I think I'll always feel a little guilty for it anyway. Would my parents have eventually come back here if they hadn't had children? That's the question that haunts me whenever we come here and see him so happy.

Aunt Viv is running toward us as we step through the section of the airport she can't get to, and it's all hugs and smiles and everyone talking all at once. Okay, even I have to admit this part is great.

She and Dad are always hilarious together, and Mom acts like she's a kid again too when the three of them get going. It's a wonderful thing to see since my parents are so often serious and even keeled. I stand back a little and grin at their antics.

"Lorali! Ah, now then, lass, let's get a peek at ya." I'm totally obsessed with Aunt Viv's accent. She sounds like a Scottish fairy, and it's absolutely brilliant. I know, I know. I'm totally ridiculous and hating on Scotland one second, adoring the accent the next. I'm a mass of contradictions, okay? I'm complicated.

It's not that I dislike Scotland; it's that I *need* to love Washington more. I've never been one to jump into the unknown, take crazy chances, or cut ties with people I love. Washington is the plan; Washington is where my life is. Scotland has never been in the plan.

Plus side, Dad's accent will show up more and more the longer we're here. I only hear it at home when I'm really upset, or he is. He's tried really hard to suppress it as much as possible back in the States, especially if we're in public or around people we don't know. Which is a shame, really, because he sounds magnificent when he doesn't. He knows how much I love it, so when I've had a really hard day, or I'm upset about something, he'll drop the fake American accent and revert to cheer me up.

It's uber hard to stay sad or mad when Dad is talking to you in his normal Scottish way. I can't even imagine how difficult it must be, to always be aware of the way you're speaking, to be using a fake accent all the time. He even does it at home; it's become a part of Dad when we are in the States. Add in another point to 'reasons I feel guilty we don't live in Scotland.'

"My, but you 'ave become the woman now, 'aven't ye?" Viv grabs me up in the biggest hug, like she hasn't seen me for years. I can't miss the teary-eyed way she looks at us, and it makes me super uncomfortable. Everyone is so happy, but there is this underlying sadness that I can't shake, and I do not like it one bit. Mainly because I feel like it has everything to do with me being an adult.

"I missed you too, Aunt Viv."

I smile as she releases me and starts leading us out of the airport. She loops her arm through Toby's and whispers something in his ear, which has him immediately laughing. She's always had a way with him.

Mom and Dad are walking ahead of us all, hand in hand but deep in conversation and almost looking worried. I wonder if that nagging that everyone is just a bit sad is more accurate than I want to admit, and if so, why? If something had happened, surely they'd have told us by now. It isn't like anyone in our family to keep secrets, not really. So why do I feel like they're all putting on brave faces?

"Don't ye go bother'n Cadence with all that now, Jasper," Aunt Viv hollers towards them, while giggling at something Toby said. It wrests me from my odd train of thought, and I focus in on them all again. I've got no clue what she's talking about, but I wonder how she even knows what Dad could be saying. The nagging feeling something isn't quite right gets a little stronger. My parents are at least 10 feet ahead of her, and they aren't speaking loudly.

"Oh, ye know, Lor. I've known yer Da since I was born. I know when he's up to no good now, don't I?" Viv calls over her shoulder to me, causing both my parents to shoot her a mildly annoyed look. What—can she read minds now? I shake my head and notice she's brought the truck—excuse me, the lorry (that's what they call trucks here)—to pick us up in.

It's always a fun challenge to myself when we're here to use the right words for things. Like a little game I play to see how many times I can catch myself before I say the American word for something. I'm getting pretty good at it, honestly. Eighteen years of visits to Scotland and I've got two distinct sets of vocabulary: one for home, and one for Scotland.

Isobel always teases me when I come home and says I have an accent, but I don't believe I really do. As much as I'd love that. If I sounded like Aunt Viv or Dad, I'd never try to hide it the way he does. Besides, the Scottish words and phrases always sound funny when I say them. Like they don't quite belong.

"Alright, you two in the back, and no bickering!" Mom gives me a pointed look as she holds open the back door. Like I'm the one who starts those fights, anyway. Ugh. I settle in for the hour-long drive to the estate, shoving my bookbag between my brother and me to ensure he doesn't encroach on my space.

Mom and Dad climb into the front, and Aunt Viv slides behind the wheel, chatting away and joking the entire time. I can't help but smile as Mom settles in against Dad, his arm going around her casually. I used to think they were silly, all their little displays of affection, their absentminded way of touching one another in a million subtle ways. Now, I find it heartwarming and endearing, inspirational.

"Best ye try an' get some rest now, the both o' ye," Aunt Viv suggests, turning in her seat to make eye contact with each of us. I barely think to myself that I couldn't possibly sleep any more than I have before my eyes feel heavy and my eyelids flutter shut. Aunt Viv is pulling out of the parking lot as I melt into sleep.

Three

"She doesn't even know about any of this, Jasper. And I'm not certain she's mature enough to handle it, and even if she is...I don't know that she's ready for it all at once," I hear my mom saying as I groggily stir from my sleep. I don't move a muscle, because I can tell it's me she's talking about, and I want to know what *exactly* they are talking about.

"I was less'n 15 when I began this journey, lass. Our Lorali's near to 19 now. Stronger than ye think, too, I'd wager."

"Viv, life was different then, and ye surely know it." Whoa. Dad has lost zero time in reverting to that accent this trip. Or, well, or he's really upset about whatever they're discussing.

"Ye can ask her yerself; she's been awake at least a full minute now, hav'n ye, dove?" Viv calls over her shoulder from behind the wheel, amused. Okay. I'm really, really wondering about my aunt now. How could she possibly know I was awake? I haven't even moved. Maybe if I just keep pretending to sleep. She's probably guessing. No way can she hear a change in my breathing from up there, with the heat blasting and music playing, even softly.

A full five minutes of dead silence convinces me both of my parents aren't buying my sleep act. Damn it. Whatever it was they were discussing, I won't be let in on it right now. It won't stop me from trying, but I already know whatever is going on, they don't want me to know. Which is another cause of concern. My family doesn't keep secrets; my parents are almost brutally honest with us about everything.

"Yeah. Yeah, okay, I'm awake. Jeez." I straighten up in a huff, crossing my arms and glaring at my parents. "So? Is anyone going to tell me what the heck is going on?"

Aunt Viv takes a breath and opens her mouth, only for Dad to talk over her.

"It's nothing ye need t'be worryin bout right now, bug." Dad turns and squeezes my hand. "A nice cuppa and some rest, we've made the village now, and then we'll have a sit down, Lor," he says, glaring into the side of Aunt Viv's head, who closed her mouth but didn't even bother to glance in his direction.

She sighs heavily, shaking her head and saying nothing else. I can tell she wants to, though, which I will definitely try to use to my advantage as soon as I can. I do not enjoy being left out of the loop, especially when it is about me.

His transition in mid-sentence from Scots back to his American facade tells me whatever this is, it's bad news, and the discussion isn't open to debate from me. I may not know his reasons for hiding his original accent, but I am smart enough to know it's a defense mechanism. For him to do it now is more than a little hurtful, like he has to defend himself from *me*.

My parents rarely ever hide things from me. Like, ever. It's the only thought I can really focus in on. My parents do not lie to us. When I asked how babies were made in 3rd grade, I got the full picture during a "cuppa and a sit down" with my folks. They've always been super honest about things with both us kids, so this has me all kinds of concerned.

It must be obvious, because my mom looks worriedly at me before laying her head against Dad's shoulder in silence. Which is *her* defense mechanism. If she can't handle it calmly, she just doesn't handle it at all until she can. She's a bit of a control freak like that. Everything always has to be done in a calm, rational way.

She consistently says, 'Nothing is ever accomplished when people give an emotional response, Lorali.'

It's not like she's an emotional tyrant who discourages anyone from feeling how they feel. Absolutely the opposite. Honestly, she just won't attempt a serious discussion when emotions are running high. Productive communication is of utmost importance in our home.

That happens when your mom is a therapist. It might also have a thing or two to do with her immense emotional control personally and her image of being 'always cheery and calm.'

I stare out the window at the snow-covered ground, watching the last little house disappear from the village. The family estate is a good 6 miles outside the actual village and totally isolated. I'm not entirely sure exactly how much of the land my family owns, but I know I've never walked or ridden out to the borders of the land from the house without being in one of the family's vehicles. It's beautiful, lots of wooded land, some rolling hills, even a river running through it.

It's just in the middle of absolutely nowhere, and more than an hour out of Glasgow, too. The village only boasts a tiny little pub/restaurant combo, a gas station, an old bookstore, and a weekly farmer's market. I typically convince someone to drive me into the village at least once just to see other people, grab a book or two. Maybe buy a gift or two from the local crafters.

What they really need is a coffee shop. I'd be pushing to make the trip more often if they did. There are few younger people living there anymore. Most have moved closer to the bigger cities for work, leaving only a handful to help with family farms and businesses. It doesn't give me a lot of reasons to spend time there.

A cup of tea and a roaring fire sounds pretty damn good right now. My bones hurt from all the traveling, and the sun is almost setting. If we'd gotten in earlier, I'd have asked Aunt Viv to make a stop at *The Tome Stoop*. They always have the most amazing books.

We have an enormous collection at the Manor, but it's always fun to browse the shelves. As it is, I'm surprised we aren't picking anything up from Gallagher's (the only restaurant, also the local pub). Uncle Seamus must've done it while she was collecting us from the airport. It's basically family law that we have Gallagher's stew the night we fly in, which is wonderful because it is heavenly.

As Aunt Viv pulls up the long drive to the Manor, I can't help but press my face against the window. The place is magnificent; it looks exactly like what you'd picture an old Scottish Castle to look like. A minor castle, maybe, but nevertheless—a freaking castle. Even with the uncertainty hanging thick in the air, I can't help but marvel at it.

It's like being a little kid walking up to Disney, mixed with that first sip of coffee in the morning—both special and everyday joy all in one. I roll the window down, taking a deep breath of the air, letting it fill my lungs. It's crisp, cold, wonderful...and...snow. I can smell snow.

My face transforms into a grin, eyes closed to just enjoy the wonderful smells of home. I never want to make the trip, and then I'm here, and it's home too. Maybe that's why I fight it so hard every year, because I don't want to allow myself to see this as home. Not when I have my life planned out back in Washington.

I begin to make out the silhouette of the house and notice Uncle Seamus' car out front. He can't have been home long if the car is still in front of the property, and that means he came home with things to unload. Oh, I hope it's food from Gallagher's. Their stew is hands down, the best thing I've ever had. It will absolutely make up for the awful "meals" we got on the flight over here. Airlines are so ridiculous nowadays. Calling cheese and crackers with some fruit dinner. Psh.

I take in the thousands of lights decorating the massive structure, an eclectic mix of traditional colored bulbs and white twinkling lights. Aunt Viv doesn't allow inflatables and such. She says they are tacky, but there is a cute little family of deer and a huge angel placed strategically. She's added in some hanging snowflake lights on the entryway roof, and every window has chasing multicolored lights around the frames.

Every bush, tree, and plant is covered in ethereal fairy lights, and overall it just feels magical. We stopped decorating our house outside once Toby was old enough to not be upset about it. Which I secretly hate but won't tell because Mom stresses enough over the trip. We may not be there for Christmas, but it would still be nice.

The Manor sits on top of a subtle hill and is massive to be honest; much larger than 3 adults need to survive anyway. It's been updated over and over throughout the years, but the bones of the place are true to the original structure. It's all grey stone and huge wooden doors, wrought iron hinges, and there's even a chapel in the east wing. We used it when Aunt Viv got married, and my parents had a ceremony there as well, but mostly we don't use it much.

I can see the lights on inside the main entryway, through the windows, but the outside lights are all off to highlight the Christmas lights. They usually leave on the front lights in case someone shows up unexpectedly. Uncle Seamus must have turned them off to give us the full effect. It may not be entirely practical, but it makes a pretty picture.

I can make out the stone steps under the snow glistening from the light catching on it and the massive double doors (wood, of course) with the heavy wrought iron handles. Over all the years, they've never updated those doors or even put a modern lock on them. Aunt Viv says there's no need; 'Not a soul would dare come in uninvited,' she says.

The thought makes me smile as she puts the truck—*lorry*—in park and shuts the engine off, stretching her arms and sighing happily to be home. She loves to be dramatic and mysterious, and act like a Grand Lady. When we all know she spends most of her days neck high in muck with animals, and she would rather break her back helping someone in need than put on a ballgown. It's especially funny when she 'puts on airs' dressed in knee high wellies, muddy coveralls, and a wool hat with all her hair peeking out from under it.

"Out with ye. Go on now. I'll have Stuart grab your bags," she orders us all.

"Seamus'll 'ave dinner ready. Tell 'im I'll be along." Even I can hear the frustration under her cheery tone, and it renews my worry and confusion from before. I may have ventured off into happy land in my mind, but it is very obvious they have not. Aunt Viv refusing to even look in my parents' direction; and my parents trying desperately to pretend she isn't doing exactly that.

Even though I am still peeved about whatever the 'adults' were discussing as Toby and I slept, I know better than to make my stand right now. Besides, seeing the Manor has taken the edge off my anger, and I would rather enjoy the moment than dwell on what I can't change or control. I shove Toby to wake him and rush out of the lorry and up the steps. Before I can even get my hand on the handle, Uncle Seamus has the door open and is wrapping me up in a great big bear hug and swinging me around in the entrance hall.

"Aye, now what 'ave we 'ere?" He smiles down at me. "Intruders at this time 'o the night?" he proclaims, holding my face lightly between his beefy hands, eyes twinkling with love and mischief. It seems a permanent fixture of his appearance, those always crinkled in laughter or amusement, bright blue eyes.

He is a mountain of a man to Aunt Viv's waifish figure. His tawny hair is curly and unruly, like most of my family (and a wide range of people around here, if I am being honest), but he keeps it shorter than Dad does. I always think if he and Aunt Viv ever have children, they'd be the prettiest, happiest babies I've ever seen.

I giggle and stand on my tiptoes to kiss him on the cheek, though he still has to bend down slightly for me to achieve that.

"Oh, alright now, go on to the kitchen wit ye. Food's already on the plate, innit?" He blushes, always just a little off kilter whenever anyone shows him affection. He gives me one last squeeze around the shoulders, and then he is on to Toby, ruffling his hair and booming at him in that larger-than-life voice of his.

I take in the entrance hall for a second. It's always a bit intimidating, with its vaulted ceilings and archways, then walk into the sitting room beyond it. The fire's already been lit in the fireplace that I could fit half a soccer team in, and there's a book set out on one of the side tables by a sitting couch. I know Aunt Viv's put it there for me from the collection lining the walls of the room. *After dinner*, I tell myself.

I notice someone has also pulled out playing cards and assorted board games and stacked them neatly on the table on the other side of the room. That was almost definitely Stuart, the groundskeeper, maintenance man, and horseman that lives on the property in the guest house.

He earns his keep, but he has been around since before I was born, and Dad and Aunt Viv treat him more like a brother than an employee. I have no more time to explore the sitting room as my parents come in behind me, and I realize it is most absolutely time for dinner.

Just to get to the dining room we have to go through a series of rooms and hallways, one of which includes a massive hall that no one ever uses. I guess originally it was the dining hall, but back then this place had a host of people and servants and residents.

We don't really need a room almost the size of our entire house in Washington to eat in now. I still secretly enjoy it, often walking through the room with a hand trailing along the stone walls, musing about the history of it all. The meals that were eaten here, the parties and daily life of the people who used it regularly.

The actual dining room—the one we use—is just off the kitchen. Mom once told me it used to be some sort of stock or supply room or something, but now it's the perfect size for a decent dining table, with buffets along the walls. Honestly, it is still probably larger than most Americans' living rooms.

It too has stone walls, though some of them are made of wood, like someone added onto or renovated the space. There is even one painted wall in here. It's not something I ever wondered about before, but I did just complete my AP World History course, and now I'm curious to put that knowledge to practical use. It's not like people get to live in historic spaces often, and I don't think I have ever truly appreciated that we do.

The mahogany table sits smack in the middle of the room, with a beautiful chandelier above it, and a whole buffet station along one wall. My favorite part of the room, though, is the almost wall length window that looks out over the river. You can't see it at night, but breakfast is amazing in this room...unless it's pouring rain, which actually happens a lot. Even that is really a beautiful backdrop for a meal, though. The windows stretch almost as high as the ceiling and run from one wall to the other, with only a few inches on either side.

Uncle Seamus wasn't lying when he said the food was already on the table. We all had 'our' seats we'd grown accustomed to using over the years, and each one had a bowl of stew in front of it. There were also rolls in a basket on each end of the table and butter and honey out as well. Be still, my heart—my family sure knew how to welcome us home.

I can't help the massive grin on my face as I close my eyes and just inhale that blessed stew. The smell alone would make a person drool, and just sitting there innocently in a bowl, it looks like an ad for an upscale restaurant. Gallagher's may be a small village establishment, but their food could compete with anyone.

"Oh, Vivienne, Seamus! This is amazing! You know this is one of our favorite meals!" Mom said, beaming over at my aunt and uncle as she sits down next to Dad. She always acts like no one expects this to be our first dinner here, when we all know that's not true.

"'Course we do, why d'ye think it's on the table?" Aunt Viv teases her with a huge grin. Either Uncle Seamus managed to calm her down, or she's decided not to let her irritation show. For now.

Toby and I sit on opposite ends and sides of the table. It was better we have some distance between us during meals. His lack of composure and ability to get food into his mouth and *not* onto the table especially drives me nuts here.

I love home, but I live for the food here. It was just disrespectful, the way Toby would waste half a plate on the table or the floor. Not to mention, just totally gross.

"Well, 'ello!'" Stuart came striding in, drying his hands and stopping to kiss my mom's cheek and shake my dad's hand before making his way to ruffle Toby's hair and then to his seat next to me. Stuart was my favorite 'uncle' before I had an uncle.

When Seamus came along a few years ago, we all loved him to death, but I was always a little sad Aunt Viv hadn't married Stuart when I was younger.

Stuart is also a large man, topping 6 ft easily, with a mass of tawny curls and sparkling blue eyes. Honestly, physically, he and Uncle Seamus aren't too dissimilar. He's also got the most laidback personality of any person I have ever met. Even Mom.

I have never once seen the man even slightly annoyed. He's like what you would picture Santa Claus' personality to be, ever jolly and serene. I know he has to have his moments like any other person; I have just yet to see it.

Stuart sits down, leaning over to kiss the top of my head before digging in to his meal. He'd never been big on talk. I knew he was in trouble the minute I heard Aunt Viv clear her throat and saw his spoon stop halfway to his mouth.

"So, we don' give thanks now, do we?" she asks pointedly at Stuart, her brow furrowed and eyebrow raised, mouth puckered in dismay. He had the decency to look slightly embarrassed before putting his spoon down and looking around the table. I knew he would not be offering to lead the prayer, like ever.

Prayer at meals started with Uncle Seamus—the rest of us not being overtly religious people.

"Seamus," Aunt Viv said.

Uncle Seamus said a beautiful prayer, ruined by Toby's 'Amen, let's *eat*.' How he got away with that one is beyond me. If I'd done that, we'd be having a 45-minute lecture on manners and respect before we took another bite at that table. It's like no one expects him to act any older than five, ever.

I just sigh and dig in. It is seriously the best stew. Not worth arguing Toby's manners if it means I have to wait another second for my dinner.

The conversation drifts between Mom's work, Stuart's latest equestrian find, and Toby's newfound love of anime, before winding around to my plans next year and UW. Even that can't keep my eyes open tonight.

"I honestly think I might just head to bed for the night, guys," I say "Dinner really made me realize how bad I am feeling the jet lag."

"It has been a really long day for us, Lor. We understand if you want to get some rest," Mom says, smiling sweetly at me. "I think we should head that way as well soon," she adds, getting a nod of agreement from Dad.

Aunt Viv, standing up to hug me, says, "Oh, Lor, we've plenty 'o time for catching up. Sweet dreams, lass."

I make the rounds of goodnights and hugs around the table, and find my room with my suitcase already in it. A little difficult since it's not my usual room here. I don't even change before crawling into the enormous bed and passing out.

Four

The sun shining in the window of my room wakes me early the next morning. I lay there, thinking of the day before. The strange conversation between my parents and my aunt—that I still don't understand—on the way here. The fact that no one addressed that Grandfather didn't even bother to show up to welcome us this time.

It's not unusual for him to be antisocial, but he at least shows up to say hi when we arrive. Well, that's not entirely true. He shows up, and every once in a while he will speak—but usually he at least is physically present.

I sigh, sitting up and taking in the room. I didn't take the time to turn on a light beyond the table lamp when I got in here last night, so I didn't notice what it was like. Normally I stay near my parents' room, closer to the sitting room. This time I'm further apart from everyone else.

I can't help but wonder if that's so I don't overhear more of whatever it was they were discussing before, or just because I'm grown now and this room is more suited to an adult. The bed is certainly much larger than the twin bed in my other room.

This one looks like it came off a Hollywood set, a huge four-poster thing with draping on three sides and enough pillows to build the best pillow fort ever. The linens and mattress are an upgrade, as well. It was like sleeping on a cloud covered in satin and silk last night. Can't complain about any of that, now

The armoire against the wall looks straight out of 'Beauty and the Beast' too. I've even got a real-life vanity, and an attached bathroom. There's a long dresser and a recliner, as well as one of those posh end-of-the-bed padded benches.

Just because it would be *too* much, I check and—yes—the bench opens to reveal a storage of plush blankets and throws. I run my hand along the silky fleece of one and revel in the decadence of it all for a moment. Peeking my head into the attached bathroom, I am dumbstruck by the elegance of it.

A stand up shower takes up an entire wall, complete with bench and multiple shower heads (including a waterfall one! Eek!). There is a beautiful tub big enough for three people, massive double sink vanity and mirrors with backlighting. There are even two upholstered chairs tucked against a wall.

In case you tire of standing while you do your hair and makeup?

The thought makes me laugh a little to myself. It's like a luxury bed-and-breakfast suite, and I must admit I'm kind of in love with it.

Though there is a nagging in the back of my mind. Wondering why everyone was acting so weird last night, and just how my upgraded room might play into whatever conversation is coming. I know my family well enough to know, with hard conversations comes a lot of passive aggressive pampering too.

It's like they know they're about to make you have a significant emotional event, so they try to cushion it with anything they might think of. I'm surprised there isn't a display of chocolates and snacks on the side tables.

Both of my parents are gainfully employed professionals, but they don't really need to be. Dad and Mom both come from money. Mom's family made a fortune in the early days of the United States of America, something about the Gold Rush. Dad's family money is so old I don't think even he knows how it was originally made.

He and Aunt Viv co-manage a massive stock portfolio (with the help of a team of brokers), and they own a fair bit of real estate around the world—mostly in Europe and the States. I could just as easily take control of some of that instead of pursuing medical school, but I think it would bore me. Instead, I will be very thankful for the cushion that allows me to focus solely on my own passions.

I quickly unpack my things into the armoire and onto the vanity. Taking the world's speediest shower while longing for the massive tub opposite it the entire time, I dress and head off to find some breakfast and much needed coffee. I find Dad sipping coffee at the dining room table and discover an assortment of breakfast pastries and coffee on the buffet. Guess I missed family breakfast, then. *Oops*.

Maybe I should have saved the unpacking for later. Grabbing a muffin, coffee, and a banana for good measure, I sit across from Dad. I am immensely thankful Stuart puts out so much food and leaves it out for us to munch on until lunch. If he didn't, I would be a super grouch until then.

"Morning, sunshine. Sleep well?" Dad asks over the county paper he's reading, with a stack of other local and international papers on the table in front of him. I bite my tongue against the argument I want to start over the waste when he could just read them on his phone or a tablet.

"Yeah, the new bed is kind of amazing," I say, letting my suspicion seep into my words and raising an eyebrow at him in query.

"Mhm. Viv said she thought it was about time you moved to a bigger room. I told her we moved you out of a twin bed when you were 10." He chuckled, ignoring my unspoken accusation directly, but giving an excuse anyway.

"Well, it was nice. I love the room," I admit, dropping any hope of getting information out of him right now. I take a bite of the muffin and realize it's cranberry, my favorite. I can't help but make a noise of gratitude.

"Cranberry?" Dad asks, grinning at me.

"Yes!" I mumble, and he laughs, nodding.

"Lorali, I know you're upset...about the ride home last night..."

I'm mid-chew and can barely swallow my muffin now. I didn't think he was going to address this at all this morning. My dad is not a man of few words. The opposite—he always knows exactly what to say. His hesitation is troublesome.

I put my muffin back on the plate and watch the river outside and the sun peeking through the clouds, making the snow sparkle. I'm honestly afraid to say a word right now. Afraid anything I say might stop this conversation from moving forward, and I want to know what's going on.

"Lor...you know we love you."

Um... that's not freaking me out at all, Dad. What is actually going on, I think. My eyes snap to his. I'm truly panicking now. The worst thoughts running through my mind.

Am I adopted?

"Truth is, we have'na told ye everythin...about our family, lass."

And now he's slipping into his Scots—this cannot be a good thing. It means his mind is too busy with what he's saying rather than how he's saying it. I sit up straight, all attention on him. My hands are shaking, and I almost wish he'd realize he should wait for Mom, after all.

"And I shouldna be sharin this without yer Mam, either," he sighs heavily.

Anxious tears are forming in my eyes, and I can't imagine what is coming next, but he hasn't seen them because he's staring at his own hands by now. The tension is so palpable it feels hard to breathe. I wonder if he's about to tell me he's not my biological father, or that some ancestor was a murderer, or a thief, or some other terrible thing. I bite my lip to try and stop myself from breaking down in hysterics.

Oh, stop dreaming up the worst things you can think of! I chastise myself.

"To be tellin' ye truth—" He looks up, noticing my distress. "Oh, Lor," he reaches over and grabs my trembling fingers, "Lass, come now, is'na that bad. Please dinnae cry, *mo chridhe*."

I look at my dad, and I break down. I don't even know what he's just said, what those words mean. He's saying something as I start to cry, but I don't hear him. I am so confused, I can't even hear the words.

It is at that moment my mom walks in and all I hear is, "Jasper! What on Earth!"

Which just makes it all worse. I'm not even sure exactly why I'm crying, other than the fact my parents have never kept secrets. So finding out they have been, well, it's more than a little surprising. I feel more than a little betrayed right now, and I don't even know what the secrets *are* yet. I'm overwhelmed, and I'm frightened, and it is not a wonderful combination.

Bless Aunt Vivienne. I have no idea what brought her back in, as she is usually out with the horses this time of day, but she came right up behind me, pulled me out of that chair, turned me to face her, and said, "Lorali Brigit, what's this now, lass? Tears before tea?" and suddenly I was giggling through my tears.

She shot Dad a reprimanding look, hugged me with one arm, and told me there was a book in the sitting room for me. I look down at my half-eaten breakfast. I wasn't in the mood for food anymore, not even a cranberry muffin.

Aunt Viv may have broken through the overwhelming emotions swirling around inside me, but they didn't just go away. She just helped to ground me a bit, enough to realize I needed to calm down. If I am crying and laughing, it is a definite sign I can't process what's going on, much less anything more.

"I'll clean that up, bug. Just go on, take your coffee, and curl up by the fire," Mom coaxes, already moving to clear my spot at the table, giving me the space she knows I need.

I look over at her and am surprised to see a forced smile on her face. Dad looks pale and shaken, Aunt Viv angry and defensive. I wasn't even sure exactly what it was Dad had been about to say, but I had felt like it was going to be something I would not be happy about. Even thinking about it is making me want to cry again.

I decide the sitting room is a good idea. Yes, it was cowardly, but I wasn't feeling particularly brave at the moment. I decided to take advantage of the fact *they* still saw me as a child and walk away from this. For now... I wouldn't be able to just walk away from situations I didn't like for much longer. Before I know it, I'll have to deal with things head on, no matter how much I may not want to. I won't always have my family to cushion me from life.

As I walked away, I could hear the three of them arguing in hushed tones. I couldn't make out a word of what they were saying, but Aunt Viv seemed to be the angriest, followed by Mom. That alone—my Mom being one of the angriest people in a room—should have made me turn around, act like an adult, and deal with this.

I felt like I was a little kid running away from something, and just then, I was perfectly fine with that. All I wanted to do was curl up by the fire in my favorite chair with this cup of coffee and read a book.

That's precisely what I did for the next hour or so, forcing the morning's events to the back of my brain until Toby comes bounding into the room and flops down across from me with an exaggerated moan. I do my best to ignore him, wanting desperately to lose myself in the book—but he keeps shifting in the leather armchair, groaning and sighing with every new position.

He's being intentionally annoying, knowing I won't be able to ignore him forever and wanting me to start the conversation. He does this type of thing often, like he needs reassurance that I still care enough to ask what's bothering him.

"Okay, *fine*. What is it, what's your problem?" I snarl at him as I snap my book shut and toss it on the table next to me. I notice he's got his arms crossed, and he's staring me down like I've done something wrong.

Perfect.

"Why don't you tell me! Dad came to my room and said it was time for a sit down. You got here before I did!" Crap. I wonder if it's too late to go hide in my room.

"I've been here for over an hour. I don't know what's going on any more than you do, so chill out," I snap back at him.

I should probably try to calm him down, but I'm a little too on edge after this morning to worry about how he's dealing right now.

"Oh, good, yer both here." Aunt Viv walks in with a large tray, complete with a steaming teapot, mugs, sugar, and cream.

Uh oh. It's the "cuppa and a sit down."

"Aunt Viv," I start, my voice already a little shaky, "um...I think I'm just a little tired—"

"Lorali, calm down, lass!" She laughs as she sets the tray on the table in the middle of the seating area. "I know yer Da did a poor job of it before. Never was very good at gettin 'is point across when he was nervous. But it's jus' that. Nerves." She smiles at me warmly and sits down on the couch closest to me.

My parents walk in, and they both look worse for wear. Dad looks defeated, while Mom looks like she's been up with a particularly difficult patient all night.

"Did I miss something?" Toby chimes in, the attitude leaving his body as he sits up properly, eyes darting from person to person.

"Always, Toby, always," I say, rolling my eyes.

I really am usually better with him, truly. I simply do not have the capacity to deal with his antics today. This ability to be mature, like flipping a switch after acting like a child—it's too much for me.

Mom and Dad sit on the couch with Aunt Viv, and no one speaks while she pours everyone a cup of tea and we all add our cream and sugar. It gets even more awkward when we have all taken at least a sip and we're just sitting there, staring at one another, waiting for someone to start things off. I stare into the fireplace that's just embers now, afraid to make eye contact with anyone.

I hear Mom clear her throat. "Lorali, Toby." We both look at her; she's using her serious voice. "There are certain things that your father and I haven't been entirely forthcoming with you about. Regarding our family, and where you...that is to say—"

"What yer Mam is tryin t'say is we've lied to ye, children," Aunt Viv blurts out.

"Um, excuse me?" I'm trying to be polite, but I'm angry. "Exactly what about?" I say a little too loudly, jumping to my feet and crossing my arms.

All of the worst case scenarios running through my head again.

"Mom, Dad, what the heck is Aunt Viv saying; you guys never lie," Toby pipes in, his voice full of concern and disbelief. I look over, and his eyes have gone wide, his feet drawn up underneath him in his chair.

Oh boy. This is going to be a fun conversation. Toby may take this harder than I do. All eyes are on him, and everyone has gone quiet. At least I am not so naïve or young that I think my parents are infallible.

I really, really should've been nicer to him. I sit back down, hugging my arms to my chest and leaning toward my little brother.

"I'll take it from here, ladies." Dad stands and moves to the fireplace, running a hand through his auburn hair. He takes a second, then turns to face us all. "I'll ask that no one say anything until I've finished what I've to say. Can I get agreement on that?"

Nods all around, though I think he was really only talking to Toby and me. Mom and Aunt Viv seem only too happy to sit back and let him tell us whatever thing they've been hiding from us.

"Alright. 'Spose I should begin by saying Grandfather didn't welcome ye last night because he isn't here. He'll be back, tomorrow, for the Gathering. He won't be alone, either. He'll bring people with him. People important to us, who we have'na seen for a long time..." Dad's eyes water, and I notice Aunt Viv reach up to wipe her own eyes.

Mom gets up to stand by him, winding her fingers through his, leaning into him and resting her head gently against his arm. I have never in my entire life seen my parents so unsettled.

"The both of you should know that the things we didn't tell you, we did to keep you safe. And the things we told you that may have been untrue, were for the same reasons. We never thought we'd see a day come when this would happen again. I want you to know that before we go further; do you understand?" Mom speaks firmly.

Uh, no, I don't understand any of this at all, Mom, but thanks for clearing all that up.

Instead of saying that aloud, I nod my head along with Toby, although I'm almost certain he is thinking the same thing I am. I shoot him a look, and I can tell we are both wondering what the hell is going on, and really struggling to stay patient. Just to calm him, I reach out a hand and, to my surprise, he takes it.

"Ye best get to it 'for these two lose it," Aunt Viv chuckles, shaking her head and hiding her smile behind her hand. I swear I love her more than life, but she gets more and more odd by the second.

"Yes. Right. Okay then. Here goes. Your Grandmother—Analyse—is not dead. She's in fact alive and...well...in the past—and your grandfather has gone to get her through a Portal that has been on this property for centuries and was sealed until two weeks ago," my mother says, somehow with a perfectly straight face.

"The Portals can facilitate travel through Time, and Space...and they've been sealed for twenty years, until now."

My mouth is hanging wide open, and I can't hide my shock anymore. Toby is laughing hysterically across from me, rocking back and forth and slapping his leg. I am beginning to wonder if they've hidden a camera somewhere, and this is all an elaborate prank.

"Cadence, ye really have a way," Aunt Viv manages while doubled over, laughing and holding her stomach.

I really don't know if she is making fun of my mom or not.

"Lorali, I do'na make fun," she says between the laughter.

"Aunt Viv has Psychic and Empathic abilities," Mom says. I sit up totally straight, muscles tight, and look at Aunt Viv with wide eyes.

"What?" I'm absolutely serious now.

I think back on all the strange things going on with my aunt this trip. I already know it's true. It's not just this trip, either. There have been other times she seemed to know what people were thinking or feeling.

Granted, this trip she has definitely been a lot more brazen about it, but I guess if she knew we were going to be told that makes sense. Mom's pulled this one out of her hat to make me see that *every*thing she is saying is true.

Suddenly I feel sick to my stomach. I've thought something was up with Mom on more than one occasion. I don't want to think about what she might have 'overheard.'

"No, yer Mam is'na Psychic, dove. Empath. She can tune in to yer emotions, but no' yer thoughts."

Oh, Aunt Viv is going to have to stop that. It's just creepy now that I *know* she's doing it. And why on Earth is Toby being so damn quiet, anyway? I look over to him, and he's just sitting there, calm as can be. No longer laughing hysterically, but not visibly upset or off kilter in the slightest.

"Toby. Come on! This doesn't freak you out? Like, at all?" I practically scream at him. He shakes his head as if to snap himself out of a daze, looking over at me.

"Huh? Oh. Sorry...um...nah. I mean—it sounds kind of cool, doesn't it?" he asks, then glances over to our parents, face lighting up. "A Time Portal? How does that work? And why was it sealed? Grandma is alive? And what's a Gathering? How did it get unsealed? Am I Psychic or an Empath or whatever? Could I be? Am I a superhero? Are you, Dad? Are your parents?" he spews out at the speed of light, now teetering on the edge of his chair with excitement.

"Okay, buddy. Slow down," Dad says, chuckling and walking over to put a hand on Toby's shoulder. "All good questions. But let's take this one at a time, aye?"

He and Mom sit back down, more relaxed now that Toby has lightened the mood in the room for everyone, it seems, except for me. Aunt Viv reaches over and gives my hand a gentle squeeze. I feel like an outsider in my own family right now. Shock is an understatement.

"First, yes, my Mam is alive and well. It's been 20 years since I've had any word from her. Since anyone has, as that's when the Portals sealed. How and why that happened isn't important right now. We don't know why they are'na sealed now." Dad sighs and picks up his tea, settling against the couch.

"Dad...this morning, when we were talking, you said something to me. Something I didn't understand..." I stutter. It feels silly to be upset by words that were obviously just a language I don't understand, but—well, none of this feels normal. It's overwhelming.

"*Mo chridhe,*" Dad interjects, nodding and gulping his tea down to answer. "It's Gaelic. I didn't mean to scare you, bug. I'm so sorry I did. It means '*my heart.*' It's just a phrase, something you say to people you love."

"Oh." I look down into my tea, ashamed. "Well, that's kind of sweet."

I feel stupid now for getting so bent out of shape about it, but I don't know how to explain why it was so upsetting. I don't even really understand why myself. I just keep circling back to 'my parents don't hide things' over and over in my mind.

"They ought know what t' expect at the Gatherin," Aunt Viv chimes in, and my parents both look at each other worriedly.

"The Portals 'ave been active for centuries. Guardians from far an' wide, and 'cross generations will gather for the first time in twenty years. It means they will'na only be from this time, loves." She smiles at me.

"They won't all be from this Portal, either, but from ones all over Scotland," Mom speaks without looking at either of us, hands clasped on her lap, eyes focused down.

"*This* Portal? There's more?" I blurt out before I can think, causing the adults to laugh.

Well, Aunt Viv laughs. Dad chuckles while Mom manages a weak smile.

"Now is'na that wha' I said when ye told me, Jasper?" Aunt Viv asked, to which Dad nodded vigorously. "A girl after me own heart, our Lor." She beamed at me.

"Let's hope not, Vivienne," Dad jokes and sets his now empty mug on the tray.

"We'd hope the Portal seal would'na hold. Mam did'na show up in the grave, an' as long as she was'na there...hope lived." I'd never seen my dad so serious and somber before in my life.

Much like Mom, he was typically level-headed, a calm in the storm. Not as chipper as Mom, but still steady, rarely showing anger and serious only with a hint of humor. This wasn't like that. This was true gravitas.

"The grave? You mean the old cemetery out by the woods?" I asked him, picturing her tombstone in my head. A tombstone we placed flowers on and visited often.

He nodded grimly. "Aye. If she had ever shown there, we'd know the seal would'na open again. At least na' before her death. My Da has'na been the same since it split them; he went nearly e'ry day to see if she were there."

"You mean her remains. You mean if there'd ever been a body in that grave," I accuse, horrified and confused.

"Aye," is the only response I receive.

"Is that why he never spent time with us, Dad?" Toby asked, and for a second, it was very apparent that he was still very young.

Some wounds, even those unavoidable ones, are the worst to see. I felt protective of my brother just then in a way I hadn't for years. The desire to shield him from this softens my own anger. I brush aside understanding my family's motives in doing the same—protecting us in the way they knew how.

"Toby, your grandfather loves you very much. I think you'll find him a different man when you see him again. But to answer your question...yes. It separated him from the love of his life, and it caused him great pain. He had a hard time connecting after that." Mom's arm was around Toby's shoulder as she sat on the arm of his chair.

By the time she finished speaking, it felt like a very heavy weight was in the room.

I want to stand up and shout that it's the worst excuse I've ever heard. That being separated from our grandmother didn't give him the right to push us all away. That they're dismissing something that has caused us all pain.

Instead, some softer part of me understands how awful the pain must have been for him, to cut off everyone he had access to. How deep does the pain have to be to deny love from all other sources? It doesn't erase my anger, but it tempers it enough to stay silent.

The conversation drifted, and we didn't talk anymore about Portals or Empaths or Psychics. Toby asked to play a board game, and we obliged him. I think we all felt the need to comfort him. Mom has always been amazing at understanding when even the most important of topics must be set aside. *Being an Empath makes that easy*, I muse to myself.

The rest of the day passed by in uneventful, mind-numbing bliss, though monitored. The adults didn't seem to want to leave us to our own devices after the revelations of that morning, and my mind was full of questions. Questions I knew, without being told, would not be acknowledged with Toby around.

He was processing the major stuff in a way many well beyond his years wouldn't have accomplished. It was the personal, the emotional, that he was struggling with. It was Grandfather. Toby had always been the type of person who needed everyone to love him. He thrives on making connections with others. Never having had that with our grandfather, it had always been more difficult for him than for me.

It felt odd to me every time I would get a worried or furtive glance from my mom or aunt when a troublesome thought or emotion crossed my mind, knowing they knew exactly what I was thinking and feeling. They knew how much I wanted, *needed*, to ask more. But we all knew we needed to protect Toby too, and so we said nothing more.

Isobel called me twice, and I let it ring through to voicemail. As badly as I wanted to word vomit all of it to my best friend, I knew I couldn't breathe a word of it. Not only would she not believe it, even if she did, I didn't understand enough of what was going on or what it meant to share it with anyone yet.

When that specific thought went through my head, I got an admiring nod of approval from Aunt Viv, which creeped me out and sent her into a fit of giggles again. All this, and one thing I can say: my aunt is still a giant child. That thought had her tossing a throw pillow at my head, so I thought *child* at her really, really hard. Can I get a lecture for disrespectful thoughts? That seems unfair.

Five

Dinner was uneventful, if more quiet than a usual family affair. I was fairly certain that Stuart must know about everything with how long he'd been around, but I wasn't so sure if Uncle Seamus was in the loop. Stuart kept glancing at me like he knew I had found out, and that's why I was so uncharacteristically quiet. He doesn't speak much himself, but it probably helps him to have others doing enough for him to remain unnoticed.

Uncle Seamus was his normal chatty self and didn't seem to notice a difference at all. He and Toby joked and laughed like nothing had changed, and part of me wished I could be a little more like Toby. Compartmentalize the information, truly put it out of my mind for a while. That's not me, though. No, I am a dweller, an overthinker. I need answers and for my world to make sense.

Alone in my room, I got into a cozy fleece pajama onesie and curled up on the bed, knowing sleep would not happen for me anytime soon. Which was really just as well because Aunt Viv chose that moment to pay me a visit with her usual 'knock and enter without waiting for a response' routine.

"Brought ye some cocoa." She smiled as she handed me a piping hot mug of peppermint hot cocoa, complete with tiny floating marshmallows. She sat on the bed next to me and leaned against the headboard, sighing as she settled in. "I do love this bed, 'tis one of me favorites."

I can't help but grin. She's still one of my favorite people. Even if this has been the most concerning 24 hours of my entire life, and she's acted as if it's been *fun*.

"Thanks, Aunt Viv." I take a swig of the cocoa. "It's delicious," I say as I snuggle my way into the headboard under the heavy blankets.

Cupping both hands around the mug, I take a moment to just close my eyes and enjoy the sensations. The smells, the warmth, the simplicity.

"So, I figure we've some things t' discuss. Some questions runnin' through tha' head o' yours?" She interrupts my peaceful moment, finally a serious look on her face.

I peek over at her over the top of the mug. "Just exactly how Psychic *are* you, Aunt Viv?"

This elicits a minute-long belly laugh before she answers. So much for seriousness.

"Well, now. It's impressions mostly t' be tellin' ye true. But strongest wi' family. When emotions are high, then from time t' time I get whole thoughts. It does'na happen often, lass." She runs a hand over my hair and smiles sweetly at me. "O'course sometimes a person is projectin' so fiercely, I can'na help but pick it up. Like a certain someone callin me a child?" She grins, elbowing me gently.

Grinning back at her despite myself, I dodge the topic by taking another swig of cocoa. It also allows me to think about her answer before continuing.

"My Mom? How much do you know about her?" I ask.

"Yer Mam's a special gift all her own, as no two are ever quite the same. She feels what ye feel, and I've a mind ye've a touch of Empath in ye as well. Ye've nev'r felt a way ye knew was'n yer own?" Her brow raises in question as she gazes at me. "Maybe went from happy to sad an did'na understand the why of it?"

"Like a mood swing? But everyone gets those, Aunt Viv." I attempt to dismiss her claim, not really wanting to delve into it.

"No, dove. Ye know ye've felt another's pain. This morn when yer brother asked after me Da. Ye felt what 'e felt, did'na ye?"

"I...I'm not sure." To be honest, I'm really *not* sure.

I felt very sad and very protective of him in that moment. Did that make me an Empath? I really didn't know.

"It's alright, lass. All in good time. Ye don' ave to answer all yer questions t'night."

"Well, there is one thing that doesn't make much sense to me."

"Wonder'd when ye'd get to't. Go on then, let's hear it."

"If the Portals go through time, and Grandfather has gone to get Grandma, how does he know he'll get to the right time? And how does he get back to the right time?"

"Ach, knew ye'd be a smart one!" She smiled and hugged me fiercely. "I can only tell ye tha' some o' the Guardians have the pow'r to travel the Portals. No' all do, n' if ye don'na have it n' ye to travel, ye'll end up who knows when, or where. We learned that in the begin'n of it all."

Her face takes on a sadness I've glimpsed only a handful of times before.

"Wait. So, how do you know if you can safely travel or not? Do you just go and hope for the best? What if you get lost and can't get home?"

"Mercy, no! Ye ne'er travel if ye don' have the pow'r to control the Portals. Can ye trust me?" she asks and waits for my tentative nod before continuing. "When yer near a Portal, ye feel it in yer bones, Lorali. Ye're not t' go near one now, d'ye hear me? Not 'til we've got the feel of ye."

"But—"

"No, lass. Ye must swear to me this. Ye've no idea the danger ye cou'd be in should ye go through a Portal without know'n what it is yer doin, if ye can control em or if they'll overtake ye." She's adamant, concern and authority etched into her features. It is entirely unlike her.

"Yeah, okay, Aunt Viv. I swear. I won't...but how do I know? Can you see them? Is there one here?"

"Aye, there is...ye'll feel it 'fore ye even get close...just stay clear the river 'til I say not to."

A shudder goes through my whole body, and I'm not sure why, but I'm genuinely afraid.

"Yer no' afraid, lass. I am. An Empath ye are, jus' like I said. A good thing too. Tha' fear is real jus' the same, dove. Let it be a warnin' to ye. Stay clear o' the river."

"I will, Aunt Viv. I promise. That's the only place I need to be careful of, right?" She nods an affirmative. "Okay, then." I scoot down, empty mug in hand, and lay my head in her lap; we sit quietly for what seems like forever, it's been an unbelievable day.

"Aunt Viv?"

"Hmm?"

"Thanks."

"O'course, lass. I love ye to the moon n' back. Surely ye know that. I'll always be here for ye."

"I know. I love you to the moon and back, Aunt Viv." I smile and glance at the almost full moon outside the window.

We sit there quietly, resting and being in each other's company for a while.

"Does Uncle Seamus know about all this?" I sit up on an elbow, wanting to see her reaction to the question as much as I want to hear the answer.

She lets out an enormous sigh, and I can feel the sadness coming off her in waves. This Empath thing is actually really obvious when I know what I'm looking for.

"Lorali, I may be awed by yer ability t' focus on yer gift as quick as ye are, but it really is a'bit personal jus' now." She shakes her head and smiles sadly.

I open my mouth to apologize, ask how to not feel what she's feeling, but she cuts me off.

"No, Seamus does'na know. I did'na think the Portals would open, an' there's a'lot to explain. Somethin' I'll hav'te do now. Tonight in fact."

I can tell she fears how her husband will react to all of this, and there is sadness as well. I wonder if it's because Stuart really does know—as I suspected, and Uncle Seamus doesn't.

"Ye really are perceptive, aren' ye? Aye, Stuart has known for a long time now. Was'na a poin' in tellin' Seamus when the Portals were sealed now, was there?" Sighing heavily, she melts against the headboard again, looking up to the ceiling.

"I never planned to marry anyone. An' when I found Seamus, well, they'd been sealed over a decade, had'n they? We don' make a habit of runnin' round tellin' people, as a rule." She sips at her cocoa, quiet and reflective.

I stay silent, knowing she isn't done.

"As religious a man as he, how would I explain it to him? An' will he accept me once I have? There've been many in the past who'd do us harm. I do'na believe him to be one of those, but ye don' ever really know, do ye? So I admit to takin' the cowardly way out, hopin never to have to tell him at all."

Standing, smoothing the covers back over me and kissing the top of my head, she looks unsure, unsettled.

"Uncle Seamus loves you more than anything. Nothing will change that, especially not finding out you're a badass, Aunt Viv." I smile up at her from my cozy bed, half asleep.

"But how will 'e feel 'bout a wife who can read 'is thoughts from time t' time?" she says sadly as she leaves the room. Staring at the ceiling, I try to drift off to sleep without dwelling on her anguish.

Six

A rare occurrence in the area, nice weather, drove me outdoors the next day. I was also admittedly trying to avoid most of my family. Now that I was fully aware that most (if not *ll*) of the wild emotions I felt weren't even my own, I needed to get away for a minute and just be alone with my own thoughts.

I really need to sort through how I felt about it all, without all the others clamoring in on me for my attention. Until I could learn to tune them out, finding space to contemplate how I was feeling was going to be kind of important. Even thinking back on yesterday was insane to me, how easily I was affected by all of it. That wasn't me; I didn't lose it like that.

Sure, I have my own quirks and instances where I've been overly emotional. Or have I? I don't even know for sure. I needed to find a solution for that, and fast. I sighed and walked further away from the house, along the river but keeping my distance after Aunt Viv's warnings the night before.

The sun coming through the sparse clouds was lovely on the snow, glistening and sparkling. Like white glitter, covering the ground as far as I could see. A blanket to cover everything. Out here, in nature, the crunch of the snow under my boots—I feel at peace.

I have always felt peaceful and fulfilled in nature. Almost like connecting with nature somehow allows me to truly be myself. It's a difficult thing to describe, how I feel when I'm in the middle of a forest or on a mountain trail.

I try to clear my head of all thought, focusing on the sounds around me instead, the water flowing, the sound of the breeze rustling the branches on the trees nearby, the crunch and crackle my footsteps make with every step in the snow. I turn a bend in the river, knowing I'll be out of sight of the house by now, and frankly thankful for it.

I love my family, but I really needed the quiet. I didn't want anyone spotting me and trying to come make conversation or see what I was doing out here right that second.

Of course, just as I had the thought that I'd rather *not* have company, I barreled right into the solid chest of a man I'd never met before. A guy at least a foot taller than me, with dark brown hair, bright green eyes, and the weirdest clothing I'd ever seen in my life. All I can do is stare, dumbfounded.

"*A bheil thu air chall? An urrainn dhomh do chuideachadh a 'lorg do shlighe?*" His voice is deep, and I suddenly realize not only do I not know him, we're still on my family's property, and now he's speaking a strange language. One that sounds similar to what I've heard snippets of around my family and in the village, but I can't be sure.

"Um, excuse me?" I start to back up quickly, realizing this guy is definitely stronger than I am, and no one even knows where I am. He suddenly grabs my wrist and puts a hand on my forehead, moving a thumb across it quickly.

"*Accipio.*" He lets me go, and I back up quickly, puzzled and not a little frightened. He doesn't try to move towards me, though, and I'm about to bolt back towards the Manor when he speaks again.

"Are ye lost?" he asks, in English.

"*No.* Are you?" I ask, feeling more brave now I've put some distance between us.

"I do'na believe so," he says, grinning. "I've only arrived, but I believe it t'be the twenty-first o' December 2018? Or did I land all wrong?" he teases, obviously very sure of himself with his arms crossed and head tilted at me like *I'm* the oddity.

My eyes have to be huge as I stare at him, mouth gaping, managing to stutter out, "Yeah, yes, it...it's...that's right...but, I mean. Do you know where you are, who this place belongs to? Like...um." I frown, trying to figure out what I'm even trying to say at this point. He's put me off balance, unsure. I don't like it.

"Aye, Galloway Manor, as I'm tol' there's a Gatherin'. Are ye here for tha' as well?" He smiles at me like this is all perfectly normal.

Which, in all fairness, maybe to him it is. Maybe his parents didn't lie to him his entire life. Maybe he's known about these things all along, and I am the only one scrambling to catch up.

"Not exactly," I answer as I gesture back toward the house. "I'm here for Christmas. This is my family's home. I'm Lorali, and you are?" I say as I stick out my hand to him, my best attempt at hospitality.

I'm always just a little awkward around new people. Unlike the rest of my family, I need to get a feel for a person before I open up. Sometimes that comes across as snobbish or rude, but it's just me being me. I don't mean any offense by it.

"Ah, Wesley. Tha' should 'ave been first, I think," he said laughing. "Do ye think ye could show me where te go from 'ere, lass?"

"Uh, yeah. I can..." Brow furrowing, I'm not a fan of him calling me lass. My family can do it, but it's weird coming from someone who looks to be around my own age. It feels condescending from him. Besides, I barely had two seconds alone. Now I have to go and entertain? Ugh. This day just took a turn for the worst.

"What's this now?" He cocks his head to the side and studies me for a second "Ye do'na wish t'go back?"

"No, no. I do. I mean, eventually. I'm trying to clear my head. It's been kind of crazy." He's perceptive. Or an Empath, maybe?

Anything is possible at this point. I really have no clue why I am telling a perfect stranger this. I should just shut my mouth and escort him to the rest of my family. Let them handle guests.

"I see." He puts his hand on his chin for a moment, then takes his cloak off his shoulders (I don't know how else to describe it, cloak seems accurate), throws it over the snow, and sits.

"Come now, have a sit, an' talk 'bout what's botherin' yer wee head. Usually helps t' have a friend."

After a couple of seconds, I decide it can't hurt to talk it out. At least if I vent my thoughts out to a stranger, it won't hurt his feelings any. Though he is really going to have to adjust his language around here. He's obviously from a time when this is how you spoke to a woman. Well, it won't fly with me, that's for sure. With a groan of pent-up frustration, I plop down on the space he's left for me, throwing up a cloud of snow around us. He chuckles under his breath at me and shakes his head.

"Now, Lorali, would ye be of Clan Galloway? Ye say this is yer family home, an' as I know, this is Galloway land far as can see." He turns, leaning back on an elbow and looks up at the sky waiting for my reply.

Man, is he cocky as all hell.

"Yes, my dad's family. We don't live here, but we visit once a year. We live in Washington. That's in the States," I explain, unsure when and where he's from. For all I know, Washington wasn't a place then.

"States?" He looks genuinely puzzled. His head tilts, his hair falling behind him, his bronzed skin a lovely contrast to the snow under us. *Just how far back is he from*, I wonder.

"Uh, yeah, like the United States of America? You know, the...colonies?"

"I do'na know what ye mean, lass. Far from 'ere I gather."

"Yeah, across the ocean. Really far. Anyway, we come here once a year. And before yesterday I didn't even know about this travel stuff or the Portals or...any of it." I sigh, looking down at my hands.

"Yer Da did'na tell ye of yer power?" He looks at me and seems to be shocked now.

I tamp down my satisfaction at the break in his composure. It's really not fair. It isn't his fault I didn't know, or that I'm exceptionally unsure of everything.

"My power? You mean the empathy thing? No. He didn't tell me anything."

"Empathy? No, lass." He shakes his head, confusion on his face. "Yer an Empath as well? 'Ave ye known *that* yer whole life then?" His brow furrows, and he isn't as carefree and sure of himself now.

"What do you mean, an Empath *too*? No, I haven't known that my whole life. I just found out yesterday; I just found out *everything* yesterday. I'm just an Empath. What are *you* talking about?" I jump up, pacing and wringing my hands while glaring at him accusingly.

I can tell he is about to tell me something my family left out yesterday, and it is pissing me off. The relative calm I'd found with a good night's sleep and a little space chipping away. He sits up and stares at me intently for a few moments before he speaks.

"Ye say yer an Empath; try n' focus on my emotions, feel tha' I'm not lyin' to ye, lass. Ye need to believe I will'na lie to ye. Can ye try tha' for me?"

I think about it for a minute and nod my head, still not sure why I am talking to this guy I don't even know. Except that now I am absolutely certain he has information I should know. Information my family hasn't deemed necessary to tell me themselves yet. I hate being uninformed.

"A'right. Tha's good. Empaths can control tha' ability by focusin in on a certain person or by groundin' themselves. Did anyone tell ye tha' yet?"

I shake my head, unable to speak without letting loose my fury at the situation.

"They should 'ave. Controllin' an Empath's pow'r is important so ye don' become overwhelm'd. Ye may have done tha' already."

I huff angrily, the look on my face clearly an admission. I knew I should have pressed for answers on how to do that.

"I'm sorry ye have'na been taught tha', lass. Tis no' a difficult task, truly. No' for one with so much pow'r as I can feel comin' off ye." He waves a hand toward me, as if I would think he was talking about someone else.

"Wait, what? Power? Off me?"

He nods solemnly, not quite hiding his underlying amusement. "Aye, lass. Power. Focus on whether I be lyin to ye. Clan Galloway has passed down powerful magic for ye. Ye need it t' travel, it's how ye can control the Portals, how we all do. Yers is mighty pow'rful. Ye'll need trainin, bu' tis there I swear it."

His green eyes lock onto mine, and as much as I want to deny what he is saying, I can feel that he is being honest—or at least that he completely believes what he is saying. Simply because *I* believe what he is saying, and I have no reason to do so. Which means he must believe it. I sink back down with a sigh, collapsing against the ground.

"Lass, I do'na even speak yer tongue. Even now I speak in the tongue I always have. When ye could'na understand me, I cast a spell. Ye'll hear yer tongue now from any who don't speak yers. One o' the first I learned as a boy."

"Oh, *come on*. This can't be real!" I yell as I jump to my feet up again, totally convinced this guy is legit bonkers.

I cross my arms and shake my head. Part of me is waiting for the orderlies to come lock us both up, or to wake up and everything has just been some crazy dream.

"Is it proof ye be wantin?" he asks, smirk on full display now.

Oh wonderful, he's challenging me. I have an awful feeling I may regret this in a minute, but his demeanor is too much for me to ignore.

"You bet, psycho," I snap at him, my violet eyes cold as ice.

Hell with it. At least he's not treating me like I don't deserve to know or have to be slowly spoon fed information. He may be condescending, and having entirely too good a time with my not knowing what's going on, but at least he isn't acting as though I'm a child who can't handle it.

Wesley seems completely unimpressed by my show of anger and incredulity. He stands, picks up his cloak, shakes it out and puts it back on. Closing his eyes, he says a few words I can't quite make out under his breath and holds his hands a few feet apart. Before I can blink, right there between his hands is a bolt of lightning, flashing back and forth, contained between his palms.

I gasp and back up quickly. My hand flies up to my mouth. A more reasonable person would probably be scared. I was intrigued, after the initial shock of seeing it. I notice his eyes are still closed, like he is having to focus on holding it there. I take a step toward him, reaching a hand out, and he claps his hands together.

"I would'na go touchin pow'r ye do'na know ye can handle, lass," he says before he laughs.

"That was real, wasn't it?" I ask.

"Aye, real an' pow'rful. An' with trainin' ye can do the same an' more. I do'na doubt tha."

"No. I would know if I could do stuff like...like..." Trailing off, I shake my head. "Wouldn't I?"

"Ye say ye did'na know yerself t'be an Empath until yesterday."

"Yeah, but that's different. If I had real life magic, wouldn't I know that?"

"Do ye wish t' know, lass?" he asks, leaning towards me, one brow raised.

His voice is soft, but the question feels like an ultimatum somehow. His eyes intense, his question holding more than what appears at the surface; the 'lass' at the end doesn't feel so much condescending as provocative.

"I...yes. Yeah, you're damn right I do." I look up at him and challenge him to deny me. He grins, like he's been waiting for me to take the bait, like he knew I wouldn't be able to resist it.

"Ye've fire. Good. Now, hold yer hands out like so." He motions for me to put my hands palm down in front of me, and

I mimic him. "Good. Now picture the energy flowin' through ye. Picture it flowin' into yer hands. Ye got it? Ye feel it in yer hands?" I nod, eyes wide as I feel a tingling sensation traveling through my body. "Good, good. Close yer eyes."

I look up at him.

"No, lass, close 'em."

I close my eyes reluctantly, afraid I'll miss some vital piece. Like it's a test I didn't study for and now am flailing around for direction.

"Now, take tha' energy and push it out through yer hands. Jus' focus tha' energy. Tha's it now." His voice is like velvet, with an impatient edge to it.

The weird, tingling, warm sensation intensifies and moves through my arms and into my hands, focusing all my attention on that, and tries to force it out through my fingertips. It's like a current, gathering from within me, pushing through my fingers to my nail beds and lingering just out of physical reach, but still a part of me just the same.

"Tha's it, lass! Open yer eyes!" The excitement and adrenaline in his voice is palpable.

I open my eyes and see a strange purple glow flowing from my fingertips. I focus on it for a second, and then I get so excited I look up at Wesley and lose concentration, and it's gone.

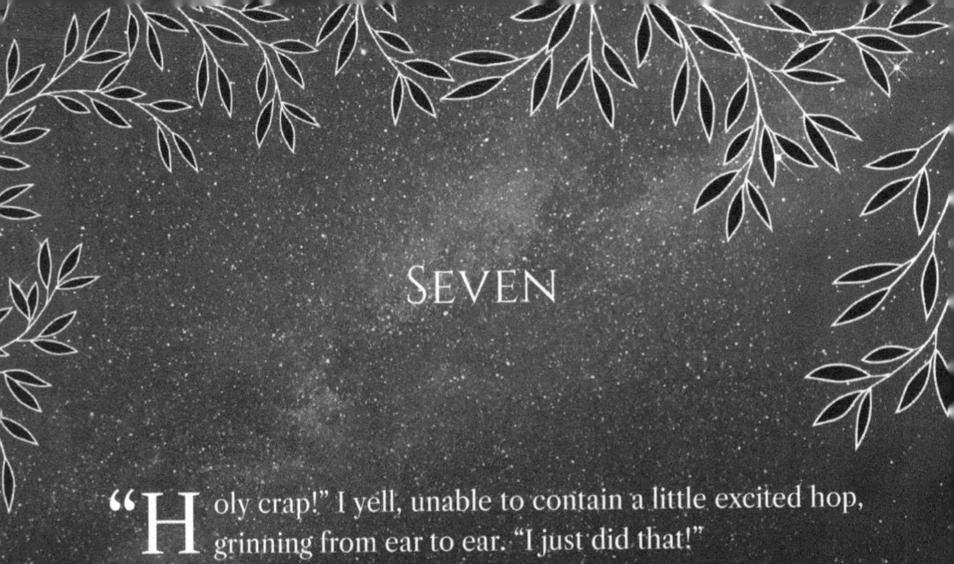

Seven

"Holy crap!" I yell, unable to contain a little excited hop, grinning from ear to ear. "I just did that!"

I jump onto Wesley and wrap my arms around his neck, planting a huge kiss on his cheek before doing a victory dance around a tree. Pumping my hands in the air, whooping and wiggling, I am certain I look ridiculous; and I don't care.

"If tha's me thanks, I will teach ye any thin' ye need," he says, laughing as I dance around.

"That was incredible! Wesley! I have freaking *magic*!" I yell, grabbing his hands in mine and spinning him in a circle. This sends him into another fit of laughter, which gets me going too.

Finally, I calm down and fall to the ground. Collapsing against the snow, not caring that it's going to soak through my jeans. I stare up at the sky, lost in my own head. This is a game changer. Magic is real, and I have it!

I don't know what I can do with it, or how it's useful in any way, but it's real and that is the coolest thing in the world. I roll onto my side and face Wesley, who has pulled his cloak off again and is laying on top of it.

"Does everyone have magic, then?" I ponder. It doesn't seem so ridiculous when considering I didn't know I had it until now.

"Ach. No, no' many do. I could feel yers, an' you said yer family was Galloway. Ye may be many generations down the line, bu' yer bloodline is strong." He pats on his cloak, beckoning me off

I climb onto the cloak to avoid hypothermia or having to end this little escape just yet. The thought is sobering, knowing my family wasn't forthcoming the night before.

"So, you traveled through the Portal. The one here on my family's estate...but in the past...and landed in the future on this date...right?"

He nods.

"Okay, and you knew, or I guess you know, my family, my ancestors...Clan Galloway, from when you...came from?"

Again, a nod.

"Right. And you came alone? For the Gathering, from your time?"

"No' exactly. I travel'd on me own, tha's true. Bu' others from tha' time will travel here to the Gatherin'. From yer own clan even, lass."

"Seriously?"

He grins at my enthusiasm.

"I mean, I know people can travel from other times in my family, obviously. My grandparents can...they were separated when the Portals—"

Wesley shoots to his feet and kneels in front of me, head bowed in the middle of my sentence. His frame is stone still, all the jovial teasing and cockiness from before melted away.

"Um—Wesley?" What the actual hell is this guy doing now? I stand up, feeling very uncomfortable with this turn of events.

"I did'na know. Ye have'ta believe...if I had known...forgive a lad 'is ignorance." He lifts his head and looks at me, his eyes pleading, but for what I do not know.

"Wesley, what on *Earth* are you talking about?" I lean forward, grabbing his bicep and trying to pull him up, but he won't budge.

"Yer Granda. *Liam* Galloway, tha's yer Granda, lass?" he asks, looking up at me with a mix of fear and awe in those emerald eyes of his.

"Um...yes? ...why?" How does Wesley know my Grandfather's name? Above that, why is he acting so strangely about it? I chew my lower lip, crossing my arms and looking around to ensure no one else is seeing the absolutely ridiculous situation.

"Oh, lass. Yer family has'na told ye who ye are. Or *when* ye come from." He shakes his head, standing up and taking my hand in his. "Yer Granda is from the same time as I, lass. I heard stories of 'im growin' up—from yer Gran." His gaze is searching my face, for what I am unsure.

"You...what? But—but that means...my dad—"

"Trapped on the oth'r side when the Portals sealed, lass. Yer family were all trapped in the wrong time when me Mam sealed the Portals," he said, looking very sad and ashamed. He backed away from me then and looked down at his feet.

"Your mom? But...they said we didn't know how..." I'm starting to get truly angry, not at Wesley, but at the family who has kept so much hidden from me my entire life.

"Aye. Me Mam sealed the Portals, took one last jaunt through 'em...t' leave me where she was born, an' locked 'em up tight. No one knows how she has the pow'r, or why she sealed 'em as she did."

I'd only known him for an hour, at most, but my heart broke for this man. I walked over to him and wrapped my arms around his neck again, almost leaving the ground to reach him. I am not normally this friendly with strangers, but he feels nothing like a stranger, really. Chalk it up to sharing my first magical experience, maybe, or simply his honesty with me when so much feels like a lie. Pulling back, I look at him from arm's length.

"If my grandma told you stories, she must have liked you...and you've been more honest with me than my entire family has my whole life. It's not your fault your mom did what she did." I close the distance between us and wrap my arms around him again, mostly because I don't know what else to say.

He wrapped his arms around my waist and pulled me into a warm hug, and we stood there like that for a few moments before he pulled away. I'm just thankful the proverbial ice has melted again, and he isn't acting all weird toward me because of who my family is. I should probably ask what the big deal is, prepare myself, but I ignore the thought.

"Yer a kind woman, lass. Yer Gran will be proud," he said with a smile. I smiled back and shivered; neglecting wet jeans for too long has its consequences. "Ye've caught a chill. Will ye take us in now, or have ye not got yer fill of quiet yet?"

"Yeah, my family is probably wondering where I've gone by now. Come on, follow me," I say begrudgingly and turn to head back.

We walk back to the house in silence, both lost in our own thoughts. He'd given me enough to think about. The toughest part was going to be hiding it from my parents. There'd be no fooling Aunt Viv. I knew that now. She'd pick up on at least some of what I knew at some point and call me on it.

Mom would only be able to tell I was feeling all the things, but I tend to be slightly emotional, and had already had a lot dumped on me, so she might not suspect I'd learned even more. There really has to be a way of protecting myself from anyone with the ability to just pick up on everything I feel, but no one has deemed it important yet. I just wondered if I knew all there was to know now—or if there was even more, just waiting around the corner for me.

It wasn't a very long walk back to the house, but it was long enough that it gave me some time to brood and study my newfound friend a bit. He was at least a foot taller than my 5'4", which seemed odd. Weren't people shorter than us in the past? Then again, Grandfather and Dad were tall, and they were from the past, too, apparently.

Even Aunt Viv was a little taller than I was, though not by much at 5'6". Still, I distinctly remember history class (my favorite subject), and historically people were much shorter on average. At least, that's what we'd been taught.

Wesley's hair was long and in clumps, I guess sort of like dreadlocks...but not like a style you'd see today. I blushed a little as I realized he was actually kind of hot, like—really hot. I forced myself to look away and tried to think of anything else.

Of course I couldn't and glanced back at him out of the corner of my eye, and caught him staring at me. Uh oh. I flicked my eyes forward, embarrassed at being caught. The low chuckle he let out wasn't lost on me.

Thankfully, the house was coming into view, and I could see Aunt Viv walking our way. She waved at us, and I could tell she yelled something, but we were too far away to make it out. I waved back, and Wesley straightened a bit.

"That's my Aunt Viv; she lives here with my grandfather and her husband, and a guy who helps around here, Stuart," I explained.

"Vivienne?" he asked in awe, becoming more serious by the second.

"Yeah, the one and only." I laughed. "Please don't make a fuss. She will totally take advantage if you do."

"Ye can'na understand, lass. Yer family is the head o' the Guardians. Clan Galloway brought the land out o' darkness." He looked at me seriously, a hint of disbelief in his eyes at my ignorance.

Vivienne was almost to us, and I thought I had better drop the subject, though I filed away the term Guardians for later discussion. I knew I wasn't going to win the argument at any rate. Whatever authority my family seemed to have had too much an influence on him.

My thoughts are interrupted as we reach her, so I simply smile and hug her, then turn to introduce Wesley. I shouldn't have been surprised to see him kneeling; I was anyway.

"Tis an honor, Vivienne. I pledge fealty to ye this day, an' always. My life, sword, an' all I 'ave an' ever will 'ave in the service of Clan Galloway."

He bowed his head and didn't speak or move a muscle. I looked incredulously from him to Aunt Viv and back again.

"Thank ye, the Clan accepts yer gift an' will honor an' serve the people always," Aunt Viv says, and without even looking at me, Wesley stands.

The two of them grasp forearms then pull each other in and clap each other's back before releasing one another. It is the oddest thing I've ever seen in my life, yet they looked so natural and at ease doing it.

"Um...Aunt Viv, Wesley—Wesley, Aunt Viv? ...Not that you two seem to need introductions at this point," I say, gesturing to each in turn.

Aunt Viv looks over at me and throws an arm around my shoulders, pulling me in close and kissing the top of my head.

"Oh, dove. Tis naught but tradition. Yer Da or me will do tha' with every guest tha' comes for tha' Gatherin'."

My ass it's tradition, I think.

For the first time in my life, I am actually one step ahead of them this time. I may not know exactly what a Guardian is, but I know our family leads them.

"Well now, tha *is* a twist, is'n it?" Aunt Viv asks, laughing. "So, how much do ye know, then?"

I barely manage to bite my tongue. Lashing out at her will do no one any good. I do, however, give her a very icy look. She knows I'm angry; I don't need to tell her. Not that it seems she would care if I did.

"Tha' would be my doin', Vivienne. I had no idea she did'na know who she was," Wesley explained, obviously apologetic, eyes firmly on the ground.

"Oh, don't you dare be sorry for it, Wesley!" I glare at Aunt Viv. "They should have been honest with me a long time ago." There goes my restraint, but I give myself points for not losing it completely.

"Now, lass, tha' was'na my choice," Aunt Viv tries to explain, most of her amusement fading as she becomes defensive.

"I don't care whose choice it was, it was the *wrong* damn choice. None of you had the right." I'm pissed now, and I don't care who knows it, but I still don't want to lose control of myself.

They already obviously think of me as a child, a perception I desperately need to change if I have any hope of learning the truth.

"I do'na deny tha', dove." Aunt Viv has the decency to look ashamed, which takes the wind out of my sails.

It's really *not* her fault, and it isn't fair for me to punish her for a choice she didn't have a say in.

"Fine. Whatever. Do you know where Toby is? I'd like to talk to him. You can show Wesley to wherever he needs to go, right? I don't know where you've got people staying." My response is dismissive and a little mean-spirited, which I instantly regret when her face falls further.

"Aye, lass. Toby is out with yer Da. Won' be back for a bit," she says, looking at me with sad, violet eyes that look just like mine.

"Of course he is," I sigh. "Wesley, I'll catch ya later. It was really nice meeting you. I really hope we get to spend some more time together. Not many people my age around here. You are my age, right?" I hadn't thought of the possibility he might not be. He looks to be about my age, but I could be wrong.

"Tha' is possible, lass. Twenty years. Ye appear to be about the same," he says with a smile. I can tell he's trying to lighten the mood, and that makes me like him even more.

"Yeah. I'm almost nineteen, so close enough, Wes," I say with a laugh as I walk away towards the house.

His deep laugh at my nickname makes me grin wider.

It's about time the giant bathtub in my room and I had a date, I think as I walk inside. It will ensure no one bothers me and chase away the chill of traipsing around in snow-dampened clothes.

Finally alone in my room, I draw a steaming hot bath and grab two bath bombs from a drawer, throwing them in. I add in a large glop of the bubble bath sitting on the side and light the candles in the room. Climbing in, armed with my wireless headphones connected to my now fully-charged tablet, I turn on my favorite playlist and sink in up to my neck. I have no problems indulging after the last day and a half.

Turning over all the events of the day in my head, I can't help but wonder how all of this will alter the course of my life. Just a few short days ago I had it all figured out. A neat little roadmap in my head on how it was all gonna go. Today I can't even answer my best friend's phone calls.

She'll know something's up and frankly, I'm not a great liar. Never have been. Especially not when it comes to Isobel. It will only lead to an argument about why I'm not telling her things, and honestly I'd just rather not. It's a copout and I know it, but how much can one person be expected to take on at once?

My heart aches a little, knowing our friendship may well be over. Isobel isn't one to accept being ignored or shoved aside, and I don't blame her. I would be hurt if she did this to me. It's worse that I don't know *when* I'll be able to even take a call from her. Not without hurting her more.

I yank my headphones out of my ears and dunk my head underwater, hiding from the entire world—if only for a few seconds. Staying under as long as I can, I come crashing through the surface gasping for air, gripping the sides of the tub and angry.

I pull the plug out, toss it over the side of the tub, and grab the towel off the radiator. Wrapping it around my body and another around the hair that reaches midway down my back before stomping back into the bedroom in search of clothes.

Sitting on my bed is a woman I've never seen before. I stop, gripping my towel firmly, scowling. She's older, but her hair is still a dark auburn. It's long and pulled up in a chignon.

She's got a few age lines, but not many, and she's thin but looks like she works out. Just as I'm about to ask her who she is and what the hell she's doing in my room, I notice her eyes. They're the same violet color as mine and Aunt Viv's.

"Are you...Grandma?" I ask hesitantly, shocked.

"Aye, lass." She smiles warmly. "Would ye tha' I did'na be here just now? Until ye've dressed?" Her voice is melodic, full of life.

"Oh!" I look down at my towel, having forgotten that's all I had on after realizing who she was.

"Um, no, no. I'll just...um...I'll grab some clothes and get dressed in the bathroom real quick. If you don't mind waiting?" My head feels a bit scrambled, too many conflicting emotions swirling around at once.

"Waitin' is no' difficult for me, dove. Go on, now," she says softly, a little sadly, but her eyes are full of warmth.

I rush over to the armoire and grab the first pair of sweats and long sleeve shirt I can find and return to the bathroom. I can hardly believe the woman I've grown up hearing about, the woman I thought long gone, is sitting on my bed. Waiting on me.

Eight

My Grandmother had been dead my entire life, or so I had been told. I understand why, I guess. No one knew when, or if, the Portals would open again, and she was stuck in another time. How do you explain that to your children? Especially when you don't tell your children Portals exist.

Now she was sitting on my bed, 10 feet away from me on the other side of the door. I pulled my clothes on, towel dried my hair, ran a brush through it, and put it in a simple braid down my back. A huge part of me wanted to just bolt back through the door the second I was dressed, but I needed to take the time to center myself. Taking a deep breath, squaring my shoulders, I opened the door and walked into my room to face the woman I'd heard so much about.

She looked up at me as I walked in and smiled, then stood and crossed the room, pulling me into a hug. We stood there for a moment in each other's arms before she pulled me over to the bed and sat next to me, but never let go of my hand. I could see there were tears in her eyes, just like there were in mine. Without even saying a word, it was like a piece of myself I didn't know was missing had snapped back into place.

"Ye do'na know the joy in me heart," she said, the faintest tremble in her otherwise steady voice. "I did'na know if me own children lived, an' here ye are, a grandchild o' me own blood!"

I smiled at her, but said nothing. I honestly didn't know what to say. It only hit me in that moment that she didn't even know we existed, Toby and I. She would only have found out after the Portals opened, and she and Grandfather were reunited.

"Ye're as beautiful as yer Mam, an strong like yer Da," she sighed, "I wish I had seen ye grow." The regret and pain clear, hanging bitterly in the air between us.

"Oh, Grandma. You're here now! I never thought I'd have that! That's a miracle!" I blurt out.

I have always felt the need to 'fix' things for people, and this was no different. Honestly, the need to comfort her was stronger than most.

"They did'na tell ye, I know," she said sadly. "I'd have done different."

Oh, I like her, I think to myself, picking up on the irritation of knowing her grandchildren thought her dead.

"Grandma, it's okay. You're here now. That's what matters."

"Aye. Yer right." She smiles and shakes her head as if to banish unwanted thoughts. "Vivienne tells me ye 've met Wesley a'ready," she states, and I nod enthusiastically.

"I ran across him earlier. I wanted some time away, to think. He'd just gotten here," I explain.

"Aye, well. A good friend ye'll find there, him an' Malakai," she says. "Glad I am ye met him."

"Malakai?" I ask, confused.

"His brother, lass. Ye'll no' have met 'im yet. But ye will tonight." She stands and walks to the window. "Took 'em both in, I did. Raised 'em meself. Good boys. An' good friends to ye they'll make." She nods, looking wistfully out onto the mountains in the distance.

"You took them in? You mean they didn't have any family at all?" I ask, remembering what Wes said about his mother leaving him before she closed the Portals. I had just assumed she'd left him with his dad or something.

"They had me." She sighs, turning toward me and resting against the window. "And each other."

"Wesley said his mother sealed the Portals...is that true, Grandmother?"

"Call me Gran, dove," her gaze fixed on me now, "Aye. Their Mam sealed 'em. Though none knows how."

"No one else can do it? Did she make them too? The Portals?" I ask, my need for information getting the better of me.

"No." She sits next to me again, patting my hand. "We dealt with him long ago, the maker o' the Portals."

Her tone tells me further questions on the subject will go unanswered, and I don't want to push it. I'll have to get those answers another time. We sit in silence for a moment, just being together, neither of us really knowing how to proceed, I suppose.

"Gran?" I finally ask, "If they're open now, can't we just go back and get you from earlier on, so you don't have to be gone so long?"

She looks very sad and takes a while before she says, "We can'na travel to any time when the Portals were sealed, dove. Tha' time is lost forever".

"Oh," I say and rest my head on her shoulder, and she puts her hand on mine again.

"Ye've used yer magics," she says.

It's not a question.

"How can you tell?" I ask, sitting up, shocked.

"It lingers on yer skin, lass. Any who 'ave the pow'r will feel its presence. Yer Da will no' have shown ye." She looks at me for a moment, waiting for an answer to the question she didn't ask.

"Wesley. I wanted to know, Gran. He showed me. I don't even know what it means, but...I just—" I hesitate, not knowing how to explain.

"That fool boy," she says, standing. "He should'na meddle in pow'r stronger than 'is own." She shakes her head, crossing the room and pacing.

"Gran, he was only trying to help," I try to explain, feeling the need to defend us both.

"Lass, ye can'na understand," she says. "An yer Da did'na prepare ye. That'll change. Has to. For now, jus' do'na try usin yer pow'r without yer Da or meself. It can and has been dangerous in untrained hands."

"You know, if all of you *adults* would let me know what the hell is going on, I wouldn't be potentially putting myself or anyone else in danger," I spout off, frustrated and disappointed in the situation.

Gran looks at me for a second and starts laughing so hard she doubles over. I stand there, looking at her, wondering what it is she finds so damn funny. I see nothing funny about any of this at the moment. She and Aunt Viv both seem to find my reactions hilarious. Right now, I'm actually pretty angry.

"Oh, lass," she laughs. "Yer a force, ye are," she says, wiping a tear from her eye as she starts to calm down. She walks over to me and puts a hand to my cheek. "Ye're right. Ye should know the truth, an' the whole o' it. An' ye will. I feel ye should 'ave known all along." She kisses the top of my head. "I did'na mean to offend ye, not used to anyone tellin me off, now, am I?"

She shakes her head and stands, brushing her hands down her clothing.

"Now I need to find yer Granda, an' we will speak again soon. I do love ye," she says, a small smile on her face. "Never doubt it, or think for a secon' not havin seen ye grow could change it."

"I'm so happy you're here, Gran," I say and stand to hug her.

She leaves the room, and I sit down on the bed, awed by the genuine connection I feel to her. She's right, it doesn't matter that we've only just met, or that I thought she was dead. That family bond is there. It's palpable and strong.

At least she seems to be on my side. Everyone else wants to treat me like I can't handle the truth. Maybe with Gran here, I'll stop getting curveballs thrown at me every five seconds. Although, to be fair, Aunt Viv acts like she would have told me everything from the start too. I throw myself back onto the bed, flinging my arms out to the side and turning my head to look out at the clouds rolling in.

I knew the weather wouldn't hold.

I sit there for a moment, stewing over my family and the choices they've made to 'protect' my brother and me from the truth. I'm frustrated that even now Gran and Aunt Viv are holding back, respecting my parents' wishes and waiting for them to say what we can know and when. Gran seemed to be more of a mind to override their wishes, but it isn't like she really told me anything new.

I bolt upright, realizing there is one person who hasn't tried to hide a single thing from me. I need to find Wesley. I grab my fuzzy slippers and do a check in the vanity mirror. Ugh. Okay, well, maybe just a little bit of makeup would help the situation.

Sitting down, I pull out my go-to eyeliner and mascara. I'm not ashamed to admit I like to accentuate my eyes a little. Not that they don't stand out on their own. I've met no one outside my own family with violet eyes, but the makeup really makes them pop. People always used to ask me why I wore contacts when I'd meet them, and it took a lot of convincing that I didn't. Other than Aunt Viv, I have never met anyone else with eyes the same color. Mom once told me it was a genetic fluke. Now I wonder if it isn't more.

I grab my rarely used highlight for good measure and throw on a nude colored lipstick, sitting back to assess my work. That's better. I think about doing my hair for a second and then am a little disgusted with myself. No. I will not get all dolled up for some dude. I wipe away the lipstick for good measure and push myself away from the vanity, satisfied I haven't gone to any further lengths than I would've done if I were just going down to dinner with my family.

I don't have any idea where Aunt Viv is housing any of the people coming for the Gathering, and I don't want to waste time tracking her down to ask, or deal with her interfering. I'm a little worried she might have done that already. I should have stayed with them instead of going to my room to make sure she didn't try to warn him off telling me things. Well, it's too late for that now. Besides, I got some quality time with Gran I might not have had otherwise.

I stand in the middle of the long hall outside my door, looking first one way and then the other, trying to think which way would be most likely. This wing is part of the older structure, boasting stone walls and glass windows with iron framing. The floor has been updated, at least within the last couple hundred years, with beautiful natural wood floors. I decide to head toward the sitting room, thinking that it's possible Wesley has settled and might be there by now.

I don't want to go around knocking on every door, and I don't feel like I can just go lumbering into every room now that I know we'll have visitors. For all I know there's a stranger in every room, though the empty hallway and lack of noise suggests otherwise. The walls are thick, and every room has a solid wooden door as well, but surely there would be some ambient noise if people were occupying them.

I should have asked Aunt Viv where she'd be putting these people, I think to myself in frustration.

The sitting room is probably best anyway. Showing up at his bedroom door is sending a message I'm not entirely certain I want to be sending. I've been told (repeatedly) in the past that I come across kind of flirty when I'm really just an open, affectionate person in general. No, we should absolutely be meeting up in communal spaces. I've had my fair share of guys getting upset with me for 'sending signals' I wasn't aware I was sending.

"Lorali! Where have you been?" Toby jumps up off his favorite chair and comes barreling at me, speaking a million miles a minute as I walk into the room.

"Me and Dad got back and there were people here, and they're so cool! They're not even from here. Well, not from 2018, they're from here, but not *here*. And the Gathering is tonight and—"

He's grabbing me by the hand and dragging me toward the seating area where Wesley has now stood from where he'd been sitting, talking with Toby.

Well, at least I've found Wes.

"Yeah, Toby, I know," I say, laughing and letting him drag me along. "I met Wes when he got here." His enthusiasm is endearing, and I can't find it within myself to be annoyed.

I smile and tilt my head at Wesley.

"Nice to see you again. You settle in okay?" I ask.

"Aye, Vivienne 'as made sure t' sort it all. I've 'ad lively talk wit' the lad here," he says, smiling at Toby, who looks like he's just met his favorite superhero.

He's always craving more adult male company, since most of the year it's just Dad. That isn't to say Dad isn't great for him, but he's missed out on having an extended male family around. Although, it's not as if I have anyone but Mom around eleven months out of the year, either. Another pang of guilt courses through me that we live so far away.

"Lorali, Wesley lived with Gran! Isn't that so cool? He can do magic too! The fire went out, and he just walked over and started it with his *hands*! I couldn't understand him when he came in, and he just said something and touched my head, and now I can understand what he's saying! He said he doesn't even speak English, Lor!" Toby's eyes look as big as a five-year-old on Christmas morning, and I can't help but chuckle a little.

I know how he feels. It's all a little fantastic.

"I know, bud. He did the same thing to me when I met him," I say, shooting a grin at Wesley, who is looking just a little embarrassed.

Toby shoots me a disgruntled look, and I know he has taken offence to me 'talking to him like he's a kid' again. It's an argument we have often.

"Ach. 'Tis no' a big bit o' magic, truly," he says to us, and I can see a tint of a blush forming.

I am ashamed to admit to myself how much pleasure I take in seeing him off kilter. I'm glad he's not as self-assured as he seemed at first. People like that are always insufferable, never willing to admit fault within themselves and always feeding their own ego.

"Well, it is to us!" Toby says, beaming at him like a puppy dog.

Before Wesley can be bombarded any further, Dad walks in with another guy. He looks so much like Wesley that I figure he must be Malakai, and they're deep in what looks like a very serious conversation. Wesley stiffens the second they come in the room, and they stop speaking as soon as they realize we're there.

Wesley's happy, carefree demeanor that I've come to recognize is gone. In its place is a quiet, stern face that I can't read at all, but the tension in the room...you don't have to be an Empath to feel that. It isn't like when he got serious before. This is a bomb waiting to explode.

The room feels as though one wrong shift in the wind and all hell could break loose. Toby is looking from Wesley to Malakai and back again, and I can see the confusion on his face. I wonder if mine is as clearly written for them to see.

"Lorali, Toby." Dad clears his throat, looking uneasily between the two brothers. "This is Malakai. He's a guest for the Gatherin'. Malakai, my children, Lorali and Toby." He smiles, but it seems forced, and I think even the two strangers in the room can see that.

"A pleasure, t'be sure," Malakai says and nods his head towards us. "Wesley," he snaps curtly, accompanied by a sharp nod without actually looking in his direction.

Screw this mess, I think, walking over to Malakai.

"Hi, nice to meet you." I say, holding out my hand.

He cocks his head to the side for a moment and frowns before taking my forearm like I'd seen Wesley and Aunt Viv do earlier that day.

I back up a step and look to Dad, trying to divert the tension while making clear I won't acknowledge it openly.

"Have you met Wesley yet, Dad?" I say, turning and holding an arm out to Wesley, who walks up to stand next to me.

"Aye, our paths 'ave crossed already, lass." Wesley smiles and nods at my Dad, who smiles at him. I smile sweetly in approval, thankful he is at least pretending his brother's presence isn't bugging him.

"How do you know Malakai? You look alike, but I don't think he likes you very much, Wesley," Toby spouts off, plopping down in his chair, clearly bored with the formalities.

An awkward silence fills the air as my dad glances between the brothers and the two of them stare each other down. I clear my throat, annoyed, causing Wesley to glance over at me.

"Gran tells me you're brothers, isn't that right?" I said with a smile, hoping to lighten the mood a little.

Wesley's eyes darken, and I can tell my attempt didn't work at all. So much for him trying to hide his aversion.

"Twins, m'lady," Malakai says, but offers nothing more on the subject.

I can't decide whether he's being sarcastic in his 'm'lady' or trying to diffuse things. I should have guessed they were twins, really. They look the same age. They're obviously not identical, but they've got the same piercing emerald eyes and dark brown hair. The resemblance is startling, if not exact.

"Malakai, let's have a look at that horse before the Gatherin'. Time enough for talk then." Dad smiles and steers Malakai out of the room, a master of diplomacy, Wesley staring after them.

He stands there, not saying anything for a few seconds, just staring at the doorway, before he mumbles, "I've some things t' see to," and walks out of the room.

I think about going after him for a second, but decide against it, and sit down across from Toby instead. I don't know him nearly well enough to get involved in a dispute between him and his twin; I have never been that great at keeping the peace.

"And I thought *we* had issues." Toby looks at me seriously, then rolls his eyes, causing me to laugh.

"Right?" I look at my crazy little brother, thankful we can always get over a fight in the end. I'd be beside myself if we ever got near the level of animosity apparent between those two.

"I mean, did you *see* that?" he guffaws, shaking his head. "Crazy!"

"Yeah, I know." I pull my legs up and tuck them under me, getting comfortable.

"I wonder why they're like that. Wesley was so nice to me; I can't imagine him doing anything that would make anyone that angry with him."

"Well, maybe it's the other way around. Malakai didn't seem all that friendly, he barely said two words."

Toby leans in, putting his elbows on his knees, and I feel my heart squeeze a little in my chest at our bond.

We fight, we argue, we annoy one another, but we have always been thick as thieves despite any of it. It's more poignant after watching the twins. That would break my heart.

I rest my head in my hand, thinking about the possibility of Malakai being the cause of their enmity.

"Yeah, but he was talking to Dad, so he can't be that unlikeable either," I point out. "Plus, Gran said they'd both make good friends, and she seemed to like both so..."

Toby frowns, realizing I've pointed out a fatal flaw in his argument.

"Besides, maybe he just didn't say too much because it was tense. Wesley barely spoke after they walked in, either." I sigh, settling back against the chair and looking up at the ceiling.

I can't really believe either of them to be instigators, based on Gran's praise. Which leaves me flustered as to why there's such an obvious rift between them.

NINE

"Are ye decidin' on whether or no' I'm fit t' be friend or foe, then?" Malakai says from the doorway, arms crossed and a look of amusement on his face.

Toby and I both have the decency to look at least a little ashamed to have been caught speculating.

"Um..." I sit up in my chair. "Hi...sorry, we didn't mean—" I stammer, embarrassed.

He holds up a hand, halting my apology, and walks over to an empty seat by Toby, settling into it. He crosses his arms, stretches out his long legs, and looks first at Toby, then at me before resting his gaze on Toby again.

"I will'na apologize for before," he says pointedly. "My brother an' I do'na get on well together." He sighs, softening a little. "Tha' does'na mean I can'na be a friend t' ye both."

He doesn't look at either of us, but stares at the fire instead.

I'm not sure exactly if that is his way of trying to make friends, but I have a feeling it's the best we are going to get from him. I look over to Toby, who is studying Malakai intently. I kind of wish I could read minds like Aunt Viv right then. Which gives me a thought. ...I wonder if I could try to focus in on Malakai's emotions like Wesley said earlier.

I settle back in my chair and close my eyes. No one was talking yet, so it made it easier to focus on him. I try just picturing him

A wave of sadness and anger washes over me. Definitely not my emotions. Almost as quickly as I felt them, they were gone, and there was nothing. I try to reach out again but can't. I open my eyes, frustrated, and see Malakai staring me down, eyes angry.

Uh oh.

"Has none ever told ye how rude tha' is? How invasive?" he snaps at me.

I shrink back a little in my chair. He's right, and I don't know why I didn't think of it.

Because you didn't think anyone would know you were doing it, I accuse myself.

The shame and disgust of that hits me, and I feel sick.

Toby looks at me, confused, then at Malakai, then back at me. "Hey, buddy, don't you yell at my sister!" he shoots off angrily at him, standing up and placing himself between us. He has no way of knowing I am the one in the wrong here, and that somehow makes it worse.

I stand up and put a hand on Toby's shoulder, warning him silently to stop. "No, it's okay, Toby. Thank you. He's right, though."

Toby turned to me, confused, disbelieving.

"I'm sorry. I didn't mean to offend you. I didn't even know if I could do it," I say to Malakai, almost pleadingly.

"An' ye thought I would make a nice plaything?" he responds, still seething.

"No! I just—" I begin to defend.

He doesn't give me time to say more, storming out of the room.

Toby turns to me, looking at me with a billion questions on his face. Questions I'm not certain I have answers to, but I know I have to tell him something. I'm certainly not going to keep him in the dark like our family has been doing to us.

"So ya know how Mom is an Empath? Like she can feel emotions or whatever?" I ask him, dreading admitting my own arrogance.

"Yeah, Dad explained how that worked more today." He nods, still not connecting the dots.

"Well, I guess I am too. Aunt Viv told me. Wes tried to teach me how to focus it this morning when we met. I was trying to do that with Malakai just now, to like...I don't know—get a sense of him?" I sigh, sinking back into my chair and hiding my face in my hands.

"Lorali! Why would you do that on *purpose*?" He looks at me in shock. "Malakai's right. That wasn't cool," he admonishes.

"I know." I look down at my feet so he doesn't see the tears forming in my eyes.

I feel terrible. I should know better. Which is exactly why I don't want Toby seeing my tears and feeling sorry for me. I wasn't the one hurt—but the one who did the hurting. If I feel like it's a violation of my privacy to learn my family has been doing it to me, what gives me the right to make someone else feel the same?

"I mean...it's pretty cool though...if you can actually zoom in on one specific person. Did you say you just found out?" he asks, already having forgiven me.

"Yeah—" I sniff, barely holding back tears, angry at myself.

"Lor! That's kinda badass!" he laughs, and I can't help but smile a little. He loves me no matter how much of an idiot I make of myself. "If you can do *that* in such a short time...remind me not to get on your bad side," he jokes, trying to cheer me up.

I punch him playfully in the arm, and he drops to the floor, teasing me. I put on a smile for his benefit. Suddenly, he sits up, an epiphany hitting him.

"If you can do that, I wonder if *I* have a cool thing..." His eyes go wide, I can see the wheels turning in his head at the prospect.

"Well. About that...there is something I wanted to talk to you about. We should probably sit down, Tob." I help him to his feet from the floor, and we sit back down.

I tell him all about that morning with Wesley, how I ran into him, and how our family is from the past. All about the Portals and Wesley's mom sealing them. How he showed me his magic. That I didn't believe him at first and how he showed me I had magic just like he did.

I tell Toby that Gran warned me not to mess around with it unless she or Dad were there and that it was dangerous and could hurt someone if I wasn't careful. I tell him they *must* have magic too if they don't want me using it without them around.

"Toby, I don't think I'm the only one. I think you've got it too," I finish.

His eyes go wide, and he jumps up from the couch, pacing around the room. He stops, looks at me, then goes back to pacing. I know this routine of his, and I let him do his thing for a minute. He's working through it, figuring out which questions to ask next.

"Lor. Do you think Dad wants to go back? Now that the Portals are open?" His eyes fill with tears, and he trembles a little.

I jump up and wrap my arms around my baby brother. I'm surprised that is where his thoughts jumped to. It hadn't even crossed my mind.

"Oh, Toby! *No*! Dad would never, ever leave us! Not ever! How could you even think that?" I hug him even harder as he starts to sob.

I'm beginning to think maybe I shouldn't have told Toby, when Aunt Viv walks into the room, and she gives me a sympathetic look.

"Now then, wha's all this fuss about?" She puts a hand on Toby's shoulder, who is still crying into my hair.

I look up at her with wide eyes, begging her to help me fix this. I have no qualms about admitting when I'm out of my depth.

"Ye know yer thoughts are fairly screamin' at me, lad. I can'na help but to come an' tell ye what a fool yer bein'."

Toby turns, eyes rimmed red and cheeks wet with tears. "Aunt Viv, I can't help—" *hiccup* "—it. What if Dad wants to go back?" He stares at her, all childlike innocence.

Toby is sitting, so he has to look up at her just slightly, and it makes him look like a little boy even more. I know these moments are ending, him seeming little. It feels wrong to focus on it now, but soon he'll just be grown. My baby brother won't be so little, won't need me as much. Silly, I know.

"Oh, lad. Yer Da would'na leave ye for all the world." She smiles and grabs his hands in hers. "Nor yer Mam either, for all that. He loves the three of ye more 'n life itself."

"Do you promise?" Toby sniffs and wipes his face with a sleeve.

"On all tha' is good in this world, *mo chridhe*." She smiles at him again. "Now enough with all the tears, lad. We can'na have a Galloway lad a weepin' mess in fron' of our guests, can we?" she says, making us all laugh.

It doesn't take very long for Toby to gather himself, feeling better after her repeated assurances.

"Aunt Viv, do I have magic too? Like Lorali and Wesley? And do you? Who has it other than Gran and Grandfather?" Toby asks her, a flash of excitement in his eyes. "You all must have it, 'cause you came here through Portals, right? Isn't that how it works?"

She is quiet, and her face is very serious for a moment. I can tell she is considering her words before she speaks. It's a departure from her typical off-the-cuff responses and flippant disregard toward adult attitudes.

"I do'na know for certain if ye have the pow'r or no, lad. I did'na know yer sister had it." She casts a knowing glance at me, and I know we are going to have words later. "Yer Da and I carry the pow'r, tha' much is true. Along with our parents. 'Tis passed down in families." She sighs, and it seems like she is weighing how much more she should say.

Just then, Dad walks in with our grandfather. It's the first time we have seen him since we learned all of this, and he seems different from the way I remember him. He's carrying himself differently, less fiercely, like he's been relieved of a heavy burden. He isn't as shut off, as distant. He even looks, dare I hope it, *happy*.

"Tha's enough, Viv. I can take it from 'ere," Dad says as he crosses the room.

Grandfather follows behind, but stops at the fireplace, gazing into it for a second before turning to face us. "Before yer Da begins, I believe ye deserve an apology from me," he starts, and a gasp escapes me.

I can't help it. My grandfather has been a stern, unmovable force my entire life. Intimidating, even. For sure, *not* the apologetic type. My aunt laughs. She must have picked up on that thought.

Grandfather glances at me and then begins. "Ye should both know it was my decision t' no' tell ye anything. When yer Mam were expectin' ye, Lorali, that was when I made the decision," he says solemnly.

Anger immediately fills my chest, and I look over to my father, who is looking down at his feet, then to my grandfather, who is looking right at me. Our eyes lock, his grey eyes filled with sorrow and searching mine, asking for forgiveness, it seems. Forgiveness I was not anywhere near ready to give. To him or my parents, who'd so readily gone along with it all.

"I asked yer Da as soon as I knew, to never reveal any o' this to ye. When Toby came, I asked of 'im the same. Had my Vivienne ever had a child, I'd have made the same request," he said, straightening his back and folding his hands in front of him as if awaiting our judgement.

Just before I opened my mouth to let him know just what I thought of his decisions, my dad spoke instead.

"It may have been me Da's decision as well, but yer Mam an' I had already made up our minds that we'd no' tell ye before he came to me," he says quietly, never lifting his head or looking at either of us.

Shame radiates off him.

I look over at Toby, who looks sad and confused and just as hurt and angry as I am feeling. Aunt Viv's face is unreadable, but she reaches over and takes Dad's hand in hers.

"Neither one of you had the right to keep all of this from us!" I rage at them both, standing. "Or to make Aunt Viv go along with it!" I spin towards the window, looking out towards the rolling hills in an attempt to calm myself for a second before continuing. "We lived our whole lives thinking our grandfather hated us...or at the very least was apathetic." I sighed, turning back to face them, my voice barely a whisper now. "I thought I had a damn mood disorder! Do you have any idea what it's like being an Empath and not knowing it?" I glare at the three adults angrily, all of whom are looking at me in shock.

It's something I wasn't sure I was going to admit to anyone, but I know they need to truly understand the effect this had.

"Lorali, why did'na ye tell me? We've always been close, we would've figured it—" Dad gets up to walk over to me, but I hold a hand up, and he stops, looking heartbroken and defeated.

"Nuh uh. You don't get to do that right now!" I huff, my body shaking, teetering between anger and defeat equally. "What was I supposed to say, exactly?" I demand, glaring at each of them in turn. "Hey, Dad, I randomly have these crazy mood swings that go as quickly as they come, and I can't control myself." I begin pacing back and forth. "Why? So I'd end up in therapy? No thanks, Dad!" I shoot him an icy look, righteous anger coursing through my veins like poison. "What *good* could any therapist have done? What could anyone have done when it wasn't even *me* in the first place?" I demand, hand splayed across my chest, eyes glistening with unshed tears.

"Lor, do ye no' think yer bein' just a wee bit unfair?" Aunt Viv asks, and I shoot her a withering look for good measure before continuing my tirade.

"Dad, all these damn secrets! And what good does it do?" I yell, furious. "Not five minutes ago, I was holding my hysterical little brother who thought you'd leave us all and go back to your own time!" I stop and cross my arms, glaring at him accusingly.

Dad gasps, turning to Toby and gathering him in an enormous hug, relief apparent on his face when he doesn't shove him away. I try not to feel betrayed by it. He's allowed to react how he wants.

"Toby!" He kisses the top of his head. "I'd never leave ye, no' ever!" I can hear my Dad's voice shaking, and I feel just the slightest bit bad.

Aunt Viv looks over at me, and her eyes are all kinds of judgy.

Wonderful.

"Hey, *I'm* not the one who did this!" I say to her, throwing my arms wide in a gesture of innocence.

She shakes her head, gets up, and walks over to me. Putting an arm around my shoulders, she whispers in my ear. "Yer anger will'na do a soul any good, lass. Ye've got to let it go now."

I look up at her, still angry. I know she's right, but I'm not happy about it.

"Dad, all I'm saying is..." I think about my next words for a second, desperately trying to calm myself. "We need the truth now. Maybe you all thought you were making the right decisions before, but they obviously did some damage." I sigh, walking over to the couch, collapsing and pulling my hands through my hair, defeated.

My dad looks at me, still holding onto Toby, and takes one of my hands in his. He nods, his eyes still watering with unshed tears. I know he had no way of knowing what their choices did to me. I never said anything. It doesn't shake the feeling that it wasn't my job to make sure we were alright.

My grandfather still hasn't moved from the fireplace, and I look over at him now. He has tracks of tears streaming silently down his face, and he's made no move to wipe them away. He's still standing stiffly, perfectly straight, and as if he's made of stone, waiting for the judgement to be cast.

Toby gets up from the couch, walks over to him, and takes his hand. "I forgive you," he says. "I don't know why you chose to hide it all, but I love you. I can't imagine what it must have been like to be away from Gran all that time. I forgive you for not being there for us while you had to deal with her not being there for you."

And damn it if Toby doesn't suddenly seem like a grown man in that moment. He's more adult than I can manage right now, for sure, and it humbles me.

Grandfather's lip trembles, but he still doesn't move, other than those grey eyes—which look down at Toby, causing more tears to course down his weathered cheeks. I feel my dad squeeze my hand and turn my head to look at him.

He nods towards my grandfather and Toby. "Yer go, lass. Ye do'na have to forgive if ye do'na believe ye can yet. The stubborn ole man will'na move until ye've had yer say, though," he says, his eyes sad.

I'm not used to seeing my dad like that. His eyes are a bright green, instead of their typical forest green, always calm and serene. Right now, though—it's more like looking at the sky right before a tornado; turbulent, unsettled. I sigh and stand, squeezing my dad's hand one last time before walking over to my grandfather and Toby.

I stand before my grandfather for a second, looking at Toby, who is still holding onto his left hand. Toby looks older than his years standing there, comforting our patriarch for all the poor decisions he's made. It's a far cry from the little boy I usually see in him. He smiles at me and nods, then reaches over and quickly squeezes my arm with his free hand.

I take my grandfather's right hand in both of mine and wait for his eyes to meet mine before I begin speaking. I want to be certain he takes in every word I say to him. His eyes meet mine after a moment, and I study them, reading all the pain and regret behind the facade he's worn my entire life.

"I won't lie to you and tell you that I've forgiven you right here and right now." Another tear rolls down his face. "But I do love you, and I can't imagine all the factors that went into the decisions that you and my parents made." I can feel him relaxing just a little bit. "I can't even say I don't sympathize with having to miss Gran all those years. She's amazing, and I've only met her once."

I smile at the way his eyes light up when I mention her.

"I guess what I am trying to say is that I think we should wipe the slate clean from here. From this point and this moment. No more lies or secrets or half-truths. If we can all agree to that, if we can work together and not shut one another out, I think we'll be okay." I notice the shift in his eyes from despondent to hopeful. "Can you promise me that? Can you promise me that you won't make any more decisions to purposely keep me or my brother in the dark?" I ask him, searching his face for sincerity, for the openness that seems so foreign on him to me.

"Aye, lass. No more secrets," he agrees, keeping his eyes locked on mine, an open book. "I can make tha' vow to ye, an' so can yer Da," he says and looks past me to Dad.

"Aye, tha' I can do," I hear Dad say.

"Okay, then I think we're good. Or on our way to being, anyway. You think we're good, Toby?" I ask, looking over at him.

"I said we were good before you did, Lor," he says, chuckling.

Grandfather suddenly pulls us both in and hugs us tightly, and I think it's the first time he's ever really hugged either of us. "Well now, ye should both have a seat. Ye need to test yer magics before the Gatherin'. An' we do'na have much time," he says as he pulls us both away at arm's length, looking at both of us intently.

The promise of transparency being made, he seems ready to jump in with both feet.

Ten

"Vivienne, will ye find yer Mam an' Cadence? I think they'd be wantin' t' be here for this," Grandfather says, as Toby and I sit on the couch and I grab his hand.

Neither one of us says a word as Aunt Viv walks out of the room, but we exchange glances of disbelief. Dad has already gotten up to go stand with Grandfather, and he doesn't look entirely thrilled about the whole thing. He shot some serious side-eye at Grandfather before moving off to stare out the window.

"You think I've really got magic, Lor?" Toby whispers to me.

I look at him, feeling a mess of excitement, fear, sadness, and anxiety coming off him in waves. I smile at him and nod.

"Yeah, I really do, Tob," I whisper back, trying to relieve some of the anxiety he was dealing with. It had to be scary, not knowing for sure.

My mom walks in with Gran and Aunt Viv, looking pale and clasping her hands in front of her. She walks straight to Dad, obviously upset.

"What do you think you're doing, Jasper?" she says in a high-pitched voice.

I could tell she was struggling to control her volume.

"We agreed that we weren't going to do this." Her voice went up another octave.

"Cadence," Dad began, putting his hands on her shoulders. "I know ye do'na want this path for 'em bu—"

"*I* don't want this path?" she yells, indignant. "What happened to *we*?" She glares at him angrily, and I'm taken aback by it all.

My parents have never, in my entire life, fought. This was the first honest argument they'd had my whole life, at least that I'd seen, and it was downright eerie to witness.

"Jasper. This is *dangerous*," she accuses. "Not to mention, they're still babies!" She turns to face us, finally.

Even if I couldn't already feel the terror coming off her, her face laid it bare for all to see.

"The Portals are open, *mo chridhe*. There is'na time to be coddlin' em now." My dad sighs, grabbing Mom's hand in his.

She shakes her head, looking at him for a minute, then nods her head once, a tear rolling down her cheek.

"They'll be called for the Gatherin' no matter what we'd prefer," he whispers, wiping her cheek with a finger.

"I know. I know, it's just..." She looks back at us. "They're our babies, Jasper," she says, pleadingly.

It's gut-wrenching to see. Even if I wasn't now aware that the anguish coursing through me was coming from her, I think I would recognize it on my own.

"*She* will'na care whose babes they are, love," Dad whispers; Mom's eyes wide and horrified, accusing. "Ye knew it would come t' this before we left home. No more puttin' it off."

I didn't know who 'she' was, but Mom didn't say another word or argue anymore about what was about to happen. Simply gathered herself up, wiped her cheeks, and faced us.

"So, where do we start?" Mom asks Grandfather.

He hadn't said a word during the entire exchange between my parents but stood quietly in the background, taking it all in with his arm around Gran. Mom's signature 'make the best of it' approach making me feel so uncomfortable with this after her outburst.

"Can we start with who the hell '*she*' is?" I say angrily, at the end of my rope with all their secrets.

I might also be feeling slightly protective of Mom as well. I know she's a therapist, but this cannot be healthy.

They all go silent, exchanging furtive glances. Mom looks like I just ran over her dog. Guess that protective streak didn't do anyone much good.

"All in good time, dove," Dad says, taking a step toward me. "We do'na have the time t' discuss it now, truly. An' I am no' just sayin it to put ye off."

"Me Mam," declares Wesley as he walks into the room, "ye must be speaking of me Mam. No' a soul can cause a mother to look like *that*," he says gesturing to the look on Mom's face, "when talking' bout her babes unless yer talkin' bout mine bein' near 'em."

He stops and stands by the fireplace near my grandparents, arms crossed, with a very unpleasant look on his face.

"As I said, we do'na have the time to be discussin it now," my Dad reiterates.

My mom is looking away, almost ashamed. Every person in the room who knows what's going on looks uncomfortable.

"Whatever," I huff, giving up, "later then."

"Aye, well, Lorali. Why do'na ye show us wha' ye can do then?" asks Gran, clasping her hands in front of her.

My parents shoot me a look, and I blush, knowing they won't be happy about this, either. The look on Gran's face as she glances toward Wesley, the concern, drives me forward despite them.

"Um, okay..." I stand, "It's not really anything, really."

"Ye let us be the judge o' that now, lass," says Gran.

I stand and repeat what Wesley showed me that morning, closing my eyes and focusing on the energy he showed me. When I feel it flowing down my fingertips, I don't open my eyes as quickly, not until Mom gasps loudly. When I do, I see the same shimmering purple light flowing from my fingers. I'm able to hold it just a little longer before I get too excited and lose it again.

I look up at Gran, and she's smiling at me. Grandfather is looking at me in awe. Aunt Viv is giggling like a child, and Dad has his mouth gaping open. Wes is leaning against the fireplace, arms crossed with a cocky smirk across his face. I turn to look at Toby, and he looks half ready to faint dead away, which makes me giggle a little. I turn back to Gran, who seems to be the least surprised.

"I told you it wasn't much—" I begin.

"No' at all, lass. It was quite a lot." She nods her head in thought. "Tha's raw pow'r, ye did'na even have a spell t' guide ye," she explains.

"I...what?" I ask, confused.

"Never ye mind jus' yet," Grandfather says. "Toby, come 'ere, lad. Come, stand an' see what ye can do."

Toby stands and looks at me with huge eyes, then looks at Grandfather. "I...I don't think I can do anything, Grandfather," he admits in a small voice.

"Ach. 'Course ye can," he snickers. "Close yer eyes an focus, tha's it. Now, focus on feelin' the energy in yer arms, feel it coursin' through yer body, lad. Now focus tha' energy. Put yer hands almost together now, but don' let em touch. There ye go, focus on tha' energy and put it right there between yer hands. Good! Ye got it, lad!"

A bright purple ball of energy is swirling between Toby's hands, small, but there.

"No, do'na open yer eyes, lad! Ye have to focus!" Grandfather admonishes him. "Try an' focus a little more energy, jus' a little now."

The ball of energy grows just a little, almost enough to fill the space between Toby's hands.

"Alright, lad, ye can open yer eyes, but stay focused!" Grandfather warns.

Toby opens his eyes, and for a split second the ball is there, swirling. Toby, like me, loses focus, and the ball vanishes. His excitement is infectious. He jumps up and down, pumps a fist in the air with a loud 'whoop,' runs over to our parents. I look on, beaming, so proud of him.

"Did you see that? How amazing was I!" he asks them, grinning from ear to ear.

They both nod, and I don't think he even recognizes that both of their smiles are forced. He runs all around the room, congratulating himself and stopping right in front of me. I give him a big hug and ruffle his hair.

"I knew you could do it," I whisper to him, hoping our parents don't overhear me.

"So, what does this mean? We've got magic. What now?" I ask. "It's not like we can do a whole lot with it as it is."

Mom groans and sits on the couch, putting her head in her hands. Dad follows her and places a hand on her shoulder. Wesley laughs at me and shakes his head.

"Ye do'na waste time, do ye?" he asks me.

I shake my head, a little confused. I fail to see what reaction they think I should've had. Aunt Viv is trying not to laugh, but she isn't doing the best job at it.

"Lorali, ye might go a step at a time, lass," she manages to tell me.

"I don't get it!" I mutter, exasperated. I look to my grandparents for some help. "You said you wanted to see what we could do before this Gathering thing, right? You had to have meant more than shoot colorful light out of our hands!" I look from one to the other, demanding any clarity at all.

"There is'na much we can show ye, lass." Gran sighs, looking at Grandfather. "Yer magic is a part o' me, in that it comes from my clan." She walks over to my brother and me, looking a little sad. "But it is magic I do'na 'ave. Ye'll need one that does, an' ye'll no' find that here." She sighs again, frustrated. "None with the level o' expertise ye should truly 'ave for trainin."

"What does that mean?" I ask.

"The twins each 'ave the same Affinity, an' they've been trained. Like you, they're learnin' still. Ye need someone well versed in it to train ye as well, an there's no one that can do such here," Gran tries to clarify.

Mom finally breaks her silence. "It means you'll have to travel, Lorali." she says, her voice cracking. "The only person with that magic is Gran's brother, and he's bound to his own time." She rubs her head like she's got a migraine and looks up at Dad.

"You mean, like through a Portal?" I blurt out, and Dad only nods in response.

Toby and I share a look, and we both start hysterically laughing. We can't help it. The past few days have been so unbelievably bizarre. Why not top it all off by having our parents tell us we have to travel through a Portal in time? Sure, makes perfect sense.

Our parents, however, look nowhere near amused by it.

"The Gatherin' begins in a little over an hour," Aunt Viv begins, "almost all our guests have arrived, why no' talk about this another time?" She tries to smooth over the situation. "We know they've magic, an' will know more at the Gatherin soon enough."

Toby and I are still laughing, holding onto each other and sitting on the floor at this point. We may very well be having a mental breakdown, who knows. I feel someone locking their arms under my elbows, lifting me up off the floor. I don't even look to see who it is, but I see Dad hoisting Toby up the same way.

"Aye, Analyse an' I've got last-minute preparations t' make," I hear Grandfather say and hear he and Gran leave the room. I don't miss the disapproval in his voice, but I am too overwhelmed to really care about it.

Slowly, I'm calming down, the energy of those around me tempering my reaction. I'm standing, but I'm leaning up against someone, not supporting my own weight. I take a deep breath, getting the laughter under control, and turn slightly to look behind me.

Oh, fabulous. Wesley.

I roll my eyes at the irony. Just what I needed, the complicated hot guy to see me lose it. I pull away, walking over and sitting in my favorite chair, shooting him daggers with my eyes. I don't really have any reason to be angry with him, but I am anyway. At the very least, highly annoyed.

"Toby, let's get ye to yer room an' cleaned up for the Gatherin', lad," I hear Dad say, trying to calm my brother down. "Lor, are ye alright? Do ye need me to stay? I can if ye do. Or yer Mam, one of us can stay with ye," he says to me, stopping after just a few steps.

I shake my head. "No, no. I'm okay, Dad." I force a smile, trying desperately to hide my irritation. "It's okay, go on. It'll probably take both of you to get him under control. I'll see you in a bit. It's in that big ole room we never use, right?"

He nods his head, putting an arm under Toby's shoulder and walking toward the door.

"You come find me if you need to, bug," Mom says as she gets up, kisses the top of my head, and follows them. She pauses at the doorway. "I love you, Lorali," she calls, turning enough to glance at me, and then rushes to catch them.

Wesley is standing a few feet from me, staring. I refuse to even look his direction. I'm more than a little embarrassed.

My family should have kicked him out. I can't believe they let him stay for all that. It should have been closed to spectators, for goodness' sake. All of a sudden he's next to me, and I'm being picked up.

"Hey! Put me down!" I yell, smacking him on the shoulder. "What the hell do you think you're *doing*?" I demand, affronted.

"I will'na. Ye need to change, an' ye need a bit o'rest," he chastises, not even flinching when I smack him again. "An' ye'll be havin' both if I have to stand an' watch ye."

"I swear to God if you do not *put me down*, Wesley!" I scream, flailing my arms and legs like a toddler, furious.

Nothing I do or say seems to make any difference to this caveman, and we're getting closer to my room. How dare he! Who does he think he is?

"Wesley! I *mean* it!" I yell again, horrified and thoroughly pissed off.

Not a foot from my door, I hear a deep, booming voice. "If ye do'na put her down, this second, *bràthair*, ye'll regret yer next step." His words echo through the hall, making the windows shake subtly.

I lift my head to peek over Wesley's shoulder and see Malakai barreling down the hall at us.

Oh, shit.

I have a feeling this isn't going to be good. Wesley stops and turns but doesn't put me down, which further feeds my embarrassment and anger.

"Mind yer own, *bràthair.*" Wesley sneers at Malakai, challenge in his voice evident.

Nope. Definitely not gonna be good. I'm torn between wanting to beat Wes up myself and wanting to escape.

"Uh...you think maybe you could put me down before..." I beg as Malakai gets closer, a little afraid I'll be caught in the middle of a brawl.

"Wesley! I'll no' think twice about teachin' ye some manners." Malakai is in Wesley's face now, leaning over me.

"Would ye not?" Wesley smiles at him, taunting. "Can I put the lady in her room first? Or would ye like to do it while I've got her in me arms?"

I shove Malakai back with both hands, then push at Wesley again. Neither seems to be bothered by it in the least.

"Damn it, Wesley! Put me the hell down!" I scream, jamming an elbow into him.

He looks down and seems to finally realize I am furious. He sets me down, and I cross my arms, glaring at both of them. I refuse to allow either of them to make me look any more weak than the entire damn display already has.

"What the *hell* is wrong with the two of you?" I say, shooting daggers at both of them.

They both look at their feet and start to talk over one another.

"I did'na do anythin, I was tryin' to save ye—" Malakai begins.

"Ye needed a rest, lass. I was only tryin'—" Wesley tries to explain.

"No!" I stop them both, raising my hands and pushing them each back.

"Listen. I don't know how things work whenever the hell *you're* from, but here, in 2018? Women do whatever they want, whenever they want, you got me?" I demand, poking a finger into Wesley's chest and glaring up at him.

Silence.

"I *said*, you got me?"

"Aye, lass," they say in unison.

"Now. I am *not* tired. This Gathering starts in less than an hour, right?"

They both nod, glaring at one another over my head.

"Okay then. Do either of you need to prepare for that?" I ask.

They both shake their heads. I'm not sure if they're being honest or if neither one wants to leave the other alone with me.

"Then, why don't the both of you come keep me company?"

They both start to speak, obvious arguments against the other.

"Uh uh! None of that noise. I don't give a damn how much you two don't get along. Gran said you'd *both* make a good friend to me. Are you telling me my gran was lying?"

They both look shocked I'd even say that. Exactly the reaction I was hoping for.

"I didn't think so. Now, follow me." I feel better now, on my own feet, in control of the situation.

I turn and walk into my room, not checking to see if they're coming or not. I would bet money they are at this point, though. Honestly, I'd be just as happy if they both left me in peace. Under normal circumstances, I'd have never spoken to Wesley again after that display.

I do not, and never have, taken kindly to anyone making decisions for me—much less manhandling me while they do. I am trying desperately to give him the benefit of the doubt, and give him a chance to respect my boundaries.

He'll only get this one overstep, I vow to myself.

I open my armoire, rummaging through my clothes. After a few minutes I holler out over my shoulder to the room, knowing they are both inside now without having to look. "Can one of you please close my door? I hate it when people just come walking in because it's open. Now that we have strangers here, especially."

I hear the door close and after a few more minutes of rummaging and the boys not saying a single word, I peek my head out from behind one of the doors. Wesley is standing just on the other side, and Malakai is standing just inside the room.

The both of them look as awkward as can be, and it's absolutely hilarious. Stifling a laugh, I walk around the armoire door and pull out the vanity chair to the middle of the room near the bed.

"Alright, one of you sit here and the other on the bed; you're making me nervous standing there like that."

They hesitate for a second, glancing at one another, then Wesley sits on the bed and Malakai in the chair.

"I will say this a total of *one* time, and expect absolute compliance if either of you want anything at all to do with me," I proclaim, glancing between the two.

Each of them eye me nervously but listen intently.

"Do not, ever, for any reason, manhandle me like that *ever* again. I am more than capable of making my own decisions. Do not ever attempt to make them for me, or this will be a very short friendship. Understand?" I cross my arms and wait for agreement.

"Aye, I did'na mean—" Wes starts, but when I fix him with a warning look, he changes tack. "I am sorry. It will no' happen again, ye have me word."

"Not somethin' ye'd find me doin in the first place, lass," Malakai boasts, looking self-satisfied.

Instead of feeding into their rivalry, I decide to change the subject and let it lie. I do, however, roll my eyes at Malakai first.

"So, can either of you tell me...what exactly is the dress code for this thing?" I ask. "No one's really filled me in, and with everything going on, I haven't even thought to ask."

"Dress code?" Malakai asks, clearly puzzled.

"Um, yeah. Like, is it formal or casual? I can't really tell if you guys are dressed up or not. Your clothes are just strange all the way around, at least to me," I try to explain.

"I think ye would say formal?" Wesley answers, "But I could be wrong on this."

I almost feel bad for him, so clearly trying to appease me. Almost. He did act like I couldn't think for myself, after all. I go back to my armoire and pull out a silver dress that goes to my ankles, with a peekaboo sleeve and a semi-modest neckline. I hold it up for inspection.

"So, this would be fine, then?" I ask them, hoping I don't have to pull out every dress in here. I only have a few, but I don't want to try them all on either.

"Ye wish us to choose yer gown, lass?" Malakai scrambles, his face going red.

"I mean, a little help wouldn't hurt," I admit, blushing a little myself. "Ya know what, just hold on."

I walk into the bathroom, kicking the door closed behind me. Quickly changing into the dress before walking back out to ask if it's an acceptable choice again, I glimpse myself in the mirror. It better be, it's the most modest thing I own. It's this or jeans. I highly doubt a plunging neckline or illusion back would be a wonderful choice, considering some of these people could be from 1800 for all I know.

Opening the door, I step out to see the guys looking at me like they've never seen a girl in a dress before. To be fair, maybe they haven't, at least not a modern dress.

"So, what do you think? Will this work?" I ask, a little self-conscious.

Neither one of them answers me, instead staring at me with really weird looks on their faces.

"Um, yeah, okay, maybe not." I turn to go take the dress off.

"Lass, 'tis perfect." Wesley stops me and grabs my hand. "Please do'na be upset. Ye look like a Goddess, truly. Forgive me brother and I. We've never seen the like."

I blush and grin like an idiot. "Oh, well. Guess I'll wear it then," I say, walking back towards the room, a strut in my steps.

"Ye wear these things all the time, lass?" Malakai asks me.

"Um, yeah, I guess. I mean, I prefer jeans. But yeah, I wear dresses too."

He just nods and studies me for another minute.

"Do ye know what the Gatherin' is? Did yer Da prepare ye for it?" Wesley asked me then, taking my focus off Malakai.

Likely an attempt at trying to garner my attention for himself. I tell myself it isn't conceit to notice the way they both look at me, or to appreciate it.

"No, actually, no one really told me anything about it. We've been a little busy catching up on all the other crap they haven't told me," I reply bitterly.

It's no secret I am less than thrilled with the way my family handled things, so why bother trying to hide it?

Wesley and Malakai share a concerned look, and Wesley takes a breath before continuing. It is probably the first time I have seen them look at each other without it seeming they could rip each other's throats out.

"The Gatherin' is for those charged with the protection o' the Portals, lass. They're called the Order o' Guardians. I've no' been to one, since I was born after they were sealed. The way I understand it, this Gatherin' will be when each of us is formally admitted." He looks over to Malakai again, as though waiting for approval.

"They cover all manner o' duties at a Gatherin'," Malakai gazes at me intently, "includin' welcomin' the next generation into the fold."

"Yeah, okay, like you two and me and Toby?" I ask. "Why do you look like that's a bad thing?"

They are both acting strangely, though I'm not upset to see them speaking civilly to one another.

"Lorali, ye need to know," starts Malakai. "Once ye've been accepted as a Guardian, yer life is'na yer own. It can'na be." He sighs, stretching his arms over his head and avoiding eye contact. "I did'na come in the room when yer family was testin' yer pow'r, but I heard yer Mam say ye'll travel."

"Yeah, so? She said I can't learn here. No one here has my magic. What does that matter?" I ask, but then it hits me like a semi-truck. "They intend to make us formal Guardians," I say, sitting on the bed.

Both Wesley and Malakai nod their heads slowly, neither looking directly at me.

"They've decided for us, without even telling us everything." I look at them, and they're now watching me quietly, assessing my reaction. "But what about our lives? Our home back in Washington? Our friends?" I ask.

I watch the sadness on both of their faces, but I could have felt it without having looked at either of them. It was like an avalanche coming from them, crashing into me, smothering me.

"What does this mean, what are you not telling me?" I demand softly.

"Yer lives changed course soon as the Portals unsealed, Lor," Wesley said quietly, gaze fixed on the floor at his feet.

"Evangeline would no' 'ave left ye in peace, even if yer parents had tried to keep ye from it," Malakai said, his emerald eyes staring into mine, face a firm mask of disgust.

Wesley shoved himself off the bed then, storming to the window and grasping the ledge with both hands. His knuckles white, the fury falling off him in waves.

"Evangeline?" I ask, turning back to Malakai's intense gaze.

"Aye. The one who sealed the Portals," he snarls, rage dancing behind his eyes.

"You mean, your mother?" I ask, and it was like flipping a switch. His gaze turned icy and harsh, boring into me.

"She is no' me Mam, lass. Tha' woman abandoned her sons, her family." He stood, pacing the room, voice a low growl. "A *saoghail*, a traitor, an' nothin' more," he says venomously.

Wesley comes flying across the room, grabbing Malakai by the collar and pinning him to the wall. I didn't even see him turn he was so quick, like he had been waiting to pounce, gathering himself for the strike.

I stood and put a hand between them, pushing against Wesley, trying desperately to separate the two.

"Whoa! Hey!" I say softly, trying to get Wesley's focus off his brother. "Enough! That's enough, please," I beg, watching his eyes soften slightly. He pulls back, letting go of Malakai, but the anger, ever-present, seething under the surface.

"Don' ye ever!" Wesley yells at his brother, poking a hand into his chest roughly.

Malakai says nothing in return, turning on a sharp heel and leaving the room. His footsteps slow and measured, echoing as they retreat.

"Hey!" I say, putting a hand against Wesley's chest.

I could feel his heart pounding against my hand, feel the war inside him to go after his brother, to fight this out.

"What the hell was that?" I ask. "You don't think that was a little much?" I look up into his eyes and see so much anger there, so much frustration.

"Ye could'na understand," he says, then sits down in the chair, putting his head in his hands. "He thinks she's beyond savin'." His voice now soft, muscles relaxing as the fight leaves him.

"Who? Your mom? Evangeline?" I ask, kneeling down in front of him, trying to peek under his bowed head to make eye contact.

He looks small somehow, defeated, sad. I feel like I am getting a glimpse of the little boy whose mother ran away, abandoned him.

"Aye," he says, scrubbing a hand down his face, "But I can'na give up on her, Lor. No' without tryin'. Don' ye see?" he begs. "I have to try, an' he will'na let me."

I don't know what to say, so I just take his hand, rocking back on my heels.

"If I can'na convince the Guardians to try an' save her, the order will be to hunt her down, an' they'll no' show mercy," he chokes out, the emotion bubbling toward the surface.

"I'm so sorry, Wes," I tell him, and I am.

I can't imagine what it must be like to be in his position, or Malakai's. And I don't want to give a lot of thought to what 'hunt her down' might mean. My heart feels like someone's placed it in a vice grip, and with every word he speaks, it squeezes a little more tightly. I feel nothing but heartbreaking sadness for them both.

"Ye have to help me make 'em see," he pleads with me, eyes wildly searching my face, frenzied and anxious.

"Wes..."

Oh, this is the worst.

"I can't do that," I admit, slowly, quietly.

He wrenches his hand out of mine, throwing his back straight, and looks at me like a wounded puppy, like I've hit him.

"I know nothing about what's going on here," I explain, trying to calmly reason with him. "I don't know anything about your mom, or the Portals, or what she's done...or...or any of it." I sigh, knowing this next part will make or break our friendship for good.

No matter Gran's opinion, I can't be close to anyone who'd ask me to do anything I'm not comfortable with. Anyone who would refuse to see how a situation could affect anyone but themselves.

"Please don't ask me to do something I have no business doing, Wes." I look up at him and see he's hurt, mouth hanging open in shock, a look of betrayal across his features.

I stand up, clasping my hands in front of me, and wait for him to say something. He stands, composing himself. His face goes blank, no emotion visible at all, his eyes deaden, and he looks at me finally.

"Aye, ye're right. I've no right to ask of ye things ye've nothing to do with." He turns to walk out the door, but turns back to me before he leaves. "Can ye forgive my askin' it?" he mumbles, the question an afterthought.

"Yeah, I can," I say, and I mean it. "I'll see you soon?" I question, hoping for any sign this won't be a lasting rift between us.

"Until then," he responds, giving a curt nod, and walks out the door.

I can't help but think to myself that this has to be the root of the animosity between the twins. The way they view their mother, the hopes each of them has pinned (or not pinned) on her.

I can't relate, on any level, and I don't know how to handle the knowledge. I can only hope Wesley meant it, and truly understands my stance, my refusal of help. If he doesn't, this will get much more complicated—very quickly.

Eleven

Someone absolutely transformed the Hall that had always been completely barren for the Gathering. I'm so used to seeing this room as a massive, vacant place on my way to our family meals that it takes me a moment to adjust to what I'm seeing.

To be completely honest, I don't think I could have described this room other than to say it was huge if someone had asked me to. I'd spent a lot of time imagining what might have happened in this room, but not making note of its beauty at all. There wasn't anything remarkable about it or any need to study it and commit anything to memory before tonight.

I see now that was ridiculous, that I had taken for granted the towering stained glass windows, the massive wooden beams along the twenty plus foot high ceilings, the fireplace you could fit a small army into. All of which were adorned with garland, symbols, ribbons, and flowers. A crackling fire spreads warmth throughout the entire room, the smell of cedar and pine wafting through the air.

This time, walking into the room, it was spectacularly noteworthy. I stood there, just taking it all in for what seemed like forever. Along the two sides of the room were four massive tables. On the left side, one was made of stone and the other a deep mahogany, and each of them had enormous, ornate glass jars on them.

The jars were wide at the base and curved into a narrower opening with a glass lid, they had beautiful turquoise designs along the bottom etched into them, runes I think, and they were literally glowing, a faint but beautiful light emitting from them.

The jar on the stone table had fire swirling around inside, but nothing else. There was no wood or paper to keep it burning, and the jar was sealed. I wondered how the fire even existed at all. Putting my hand gently on the surface, no heat escaped it, just those dancing, twirling flames with no fuel to maintain them.

On the wooden table the jar was filled almost to the top with dirt, and it too was slowly swirling around, undulating as though some unseen hands churned it over and over again. Both jars had intricate lettering on them, perfectly centered, in a language I didn't understand. It too was etched into the glass itself, faintly glowing.

On the right side of the room, two more tables stood. The first looked like it was made of marble. It was pure white, with not a single crack or joint visible, and the glass jar on that table had nothing at all in it, just an empty jar in the center of the table. It, too, had the same gold writing and turquoise runes inscribed along the sides and around the bottom.

The fourth table was an almost shimmering blue granite. I knew it had to be granite because we had a similar color in one of our bathrooms back home. The jar on that table had what looked like water in it, not quite full, and it was swirling around like the others had been, even though the jar was sealed and that table was not moving.

I stood there quietly, entranced in whatever magic was making this happen, feeling like I was in a dream.

At the back of the room, facing the door I'd entered from, was another table. It was purple, and I'd never seen anything like it. The jar on the table had a shimmering, swirling energy in it that was very similar to what both Toby and I had conjured up.

It was a light, pale purple and filled the jar completely and yet still had a movement to it that was visible. Every jar was identical, it was just the contents that were different.

What really caught my eye were the five pedestals in the exact center of the room, and each had a jar that was a match to one on a table, down to its contents. Each pedestal also matched one of the tables, and they were arranged in a straight line from end to end, perfectly spaced apart. I walked to them to get a closer look and realized the gold writing was slightly different on each one.

Standing in the center, I studied each for a moment, working out what it could be or mean.

Earth, Water, Fire, Air...I thought to myself, slowly spinning and looking at each jar. The one I couldn't place was the one Toby and I had seen before; the purple energy we could wield.

Lastly, there was the table at the head of the room. This table was raised, sitting on a platform and made of unfinished oak. There was no polish on it, nothing fancy or theatrical about it, no jars with magically swirling materials or gilded languages I couldn't understand or pretty runes. Just a simple table with eight chairs, with the four in the middle slightly larger than the ones on the outside.

I wondered why the only table that didn't seem all that special was the one on a dais. As I studied it, I could just make out a faint carving along the edges of the table, in the same language as whatever was on the jars. My best guess was that it was maybe Latin or Gaelic.

"A sight t' see, aren't they?" Aunt Viv asks, pulling me from my musings.

She was smiling at me, but there was a sadness to her. She was wearing a beautiful sleeveless green dress that almost touched the floor and an odd sash like I'd seen in a movie once across her chest. It was plaid and the ends of it reached to her knees, held together with a big, ornate golden brooch in the shape of a dragon made of intricate knotwork, with two perfectly cut emeralds for eyes.

She was stunning, but I wondered why she was alone.

"Yes, but...what is all this, Aunt Viv? And where's Uncle Seamus?" I ask.

"Time for tha' later, dove," she says, walking over to me. "These are Affinity jars. They tell ye where yer magick draws from." She nods her head, gently placing a hand on the jar holding Fire, as if I knew exactly what she meant.

"Um...okay?" I look at her, confused. "What does that mean exactly?"

"Well, ye have t' know where it comes from t' use it, don' ye?" she asks, a mischievous smile on her face.

"I...guess so?"

"Aye, ye do," she quips. "An' the jars do tha' for ye. Yer brother and ye will do jus' that tonight. An' then you'll join yer brothers an' sisters in magic," she says, gesturing around the room at the tables.

"So like, people only mingle with people who have the same magic?" I ask, taking in the tables in a new way, more than a little annoyed at the idea.

"No, lass," she says, laughing. "But at these Gatherin's we take the time t' learn from those who have the same Affinities. Is no' every day ye have so many in one spot now is it?" She looks at me seriously, ensuring I am paying attention. "Ye mus' take advantage o' the opportunity when ye can, lass. Is no' like the old days when magic was common. Forgotten now by most, sad t' say."

"So no sitting down yet, is what you're saying?" I ask, a little perturbed, and maybe a little more sarcastic than was necessary.

"No' yet, lass. Do'na worry. Testin' yer magic will be first order o' business tonight."

"Didn't we already do that?" I counter, feeling resentful of not being given any information on what would happen tonight.

"No' like this." She gives me a pointed look, turning to see the rest of the family walking in.

My dad and grandparents are all wearing the same sash as Aunt Viv, Toby talking animatedly to Dad. They look regal, decked out in formal wear, and the sash only adds to it.

It looks like a picture one might find in a book, or a photo in a news article on some hoity toity event. Except no one will be covering this for the papers, there won't be any news stations running the story.

"Lor! Dad says we get to test our magic tonight! We'll find our...um...Affinity?" Toby grins at me, closing the gap between us with an excited bounce in his steps.

He has on an impressive suit, complete with tie. I look over at Mom and Dad, wondering how long ago they bought it. I know it wasn't hanging in his closet back home a week ago. It only serves as a reinforcement that they knew what was coming long before we ever left home.

They knew, and they did an amazing job of hiding it from us. I do my very best to tamp down the resentment building over the fact.

Now is not the time, Lor.

"Yeah, that's what Aunt Viv was just explaining. Something to do with these jars here," I reply, waving at the row of jars on pedestals over my shoulder.

He sidesteps me, and I realize I've lost his attention for good now. Just as well. That cheery reply was about all I could muster, anyway. If Toby is living in ignorant bliss, I am content to let him stay there for the moment. No sense in worrying him with things I don't fully understand yet myself.

"Lorali, you're stunning. I'm so sorry I didn't get a chance to come and chat before all this. Some things came up with a few guests that needed tending," Mom says, hugging me.

She's absolutely gorgeous, as usual. Her hair is pulled up into an extremely elaborate updo, her gown an off the shoulder, shimmering magenta. She doesn't have one of the sashes the others wear, but she is sporting a large brooch pinned to her dress.

It's an elegant phoenix, tail dripping with jewels, made of exquisite rose gold with two sparkling sapphires for eyes.

"It's okay, Mom. I managed well enough." I smile, thinking she'd have spent too much time fussing with my hair if she had made it to my room. "Do we have much time before this thing starts?" I ask, but quickly realize I shouldn't have bothered. People are starting to come in.

Mom gives me a look that implies regret and turns to greet people. I notice every person that comes in is dressed in clothes from a different era. It's like watching a fashion show over time, and it's more than a little weird. People are walking straight toward the tables after they say hello to my family; Toby and I hanging back near the middle of the room, just taking it all in. I notice Malakai walk in, and he makes straight for us.

He stands next to me and nods, not saying a word. I'm relieved to see him, especially after he walked out earlier, but I had hoped he'd be in a better mood.

"Well, hello to you too," I say, with quite a bit of attitude.

"Apologies, I was'na aware ye needed a formal greetin'." He smirks, bowing slightly.

"Oh stop. *Hi* would have been just fine," I huff, crossing my arms in front of me and scowling.

I do my best to ignore the beat my heart skips. For someone who has been utterly confusing toward me, I am entirely too attracted to him.

"Are ye cross with me, lass?" he asks, his brow furrowed, but the smirk remaining.

I roll my eyes, uncross my arms, and look back out at the room, choosing to ignore his baiting. I can't get any sense of what he's feeling, and his demeanor isn't giving much away. It's leaving me feeling on edge, wondering what to expect from him next.

Wesley comes in with the last few stragglers, and I can feel Malakai stiffen next to me. I glance over at him quickly, wondering exactly what it is about his twin that causes such a reaction in him. Is it just their differing views on their mother?

Or is there more? I don't have long to wonder about it as Wesley reaches us.

"Lorali, Toby." Wesley nods and stands on the other side of me.

"Wesley." I smile, trying to ease a little of the tension. If the twins' defensive stances and refusal to look at one another are any gauge, I'm not succeeding.

Oh boy. This is going to be a long, long night if these two don't back off a little. The last of the guests are taking their seats, and my family is going towards the table at the head of the room, where four people I don't know are already sitting.

Of course they are, I groan inwardly.

Right up to the table on the dais. I really, really should not be surprised, especially not when they take the four larger seats. Mom is the only one who doesn't sit there; instead she walks to the Air table.

Everyone is sitting now except my brother, me, and the twins. I feel very exposed and totally on display, which makes sense as everyone in the room is studying us. They're studying us—and then discussing us, even worse. I can do nothing but stand there, watching them watch me.

Most of the men present are wearing kilts or plaid pants, complete with a fancy jacket on top, Dad included. Many of the women have a sash or plaid material of some kind worn in a variety of ways as well. It looks and feels surreal, like an elaborate costume party.

I grab both Wesley and Malakai's hands on either side of me. If I have to stand here and be stared at like some sacrificial lamb, I could use the support. I close my eyes, take a deep breath, when I open them again I focus on a spot on the wall above everyone's heads.

Clink. Clink. Clink.

I turn my eyes toward the dais and most of my family. Gran is standing, her glass and fork in hand. I take the time to study her, in a voluminous dress—something you'd see in a museum, except this looks new and crisp. She makes a striking figure, hair in a mass of delicate braids and loops, thick gold chain dipping below the neckline of her dress. A much simpler brooch than Aunt Viv has reflectes light around the room. Hers is circular, a design on it I can't quite make out.

It hits me that I don't actually know how old she is, but she looks much younger than Grandfather sitting next to her. In all honesty, she only looks to be in her mid-forties, while he is more like sixty-something. I file it away to inquire about later as she speaks.

"*Fàilte*! Welcome! It has been t' long since we've 'ad the pleasure of each other's company." She smiles out over the crowd, scanning the faces. Her voice is loud, strong, and full of authority. "For too long the portals 'ave been sealed, closin' off family from family. Our duties goin' undone. Our magics lost. Our greates' threat gone free, out o' grasp." She addresses the room, serious and focused, and everyone hanging on her every word.

"No more! The Gatherin' begins again!" She raises her glass in salute, and everyone around the room does the same, cheering loudly.

The sound is deafening, feet stomping under tables, fists pounding, voices raised.

"The Guardians will no' fall." She steps down from the dais and walks over to where we are standing, arms outstretched in front of us. "Tonight we gain four new Guardians. Let 'em be tested an' let 'em no' be found wanting."

She turns to face us as the room eruptes in applause and yelling.

"Ye will each turn toward the Affinity jars before ye, an' ye will loose yer pow'r on 'em," she instructs, gesturing toward the pedestals. "Ye will focus yer pow'r until I tell ye, do ye understand?" she demands, meeting each of our gazes.

We all nod, and I can feel the nerves coming from each of the others. At least I'm not the only one who isn't feeling like this is the best idea ever. I'd love to be invisible right about now, or to be able to just run out of the room and never come back.

I know that isn't an option, though. I don't know what role exactly my family has here, but it is more than obvious Gran is in charge. Judging by her command of the crowd, her jubilant introduction of us, she'd also be the first to track me down and drag me back.

"Malakai will be first. The rest will step behind me, an' ye will'na move in front of me under any circumstance until the ceremony is done. I need yer agreement on this."

We all agree, and Malakai moves in place as the rest of us fall back to observe what we are about to be asked to do. I know Toby and I have no idea what to expect, but I wonder if the twins have any idea what this entails. I'm just thankful I won't be the first. Glancing around as people begin to quiet, all focusing on Malakai.

He rolls his shoulders, shakes his hands out, and plants his feet. Looking over his shoulder at Gran, she simply tilts her head regally toward him. There isn't a hint of apprehension or uncertainty about him. He's confident and every movement he makes relays it. He turns back to face the pedestals and closes his eyes, reaching his hands, palms flat, towards them.

Nothing happens for a few seconds, but I know he is focusing, feeling the energy moving through his body and channeling it to where he wants it to go—his hands. It's the same technique Toby and I both used. I note he doesn't speak, no words as when Wesley showed me his magic, something Gran seemed surprised to see from us before.

Suddenly, the empty jar is shaking on its pedestal, but there is nothing coming from his hands yet. Then I see a faint almost mist streaming from his palms. It is wrapping itself around the jar, causing it to move. I'm mesmerized by it when just as quickly another stream mingles with the mist, but it branches off and swirls around the jar with the shimmering, swirling energy substance in it. This stream is a faint purple, and it twists up and around the streams of mist as it makes its way to the other jar.

I hear people around the room muttering and a few gasps. Everyone is talking excitedly. Malakai opens his eyes and sees what is going on, and his mouth drops open, causing him to lose focus, and it all goes away. He stands there staring at his hands for a moment before Gran reaches up and puts a hand on his shoulder.

"Rare, but no' unheard of, lad," she whispers. "Come now."

He turns around and walks back to stand with the three of us, his face pale.

"Toby, come an' be tested," Gran speaks softly and calmly, ignoring the surrounding chatter.

That doesn't subdue it. People are leaning across tables and around others to mutter at one another.

Toby walks up and nervously rubs his palms along his pants, looking back at Gran, then up at Dad, and back at the jars before closing his eyes and reaching out, which finally silences the spectators. The silence is almost deafening after all the chatter. The entire room seems to hold its breath.

Almost right away that same swirling energy I'd seen from him before was there, and it reached out for the jar with that same purple, shimmering energy. He held it there for what seemed like forever before Gran told him it was enough.

No double jars for Toby, but still the crowd seems excited, anxious. Gran smiles at him as he walks past her, gently patting him on the shoulder.

Wesley was next, and he also didn't look nervous at all. He strode right up and began within seconds, not waiting for Gran to nod or tell him to begin, not even looking at anyone or anything else.

Just like with Malakai, Wesley had two separate Affinity streams. The first was lightning, as I'd seen him conjure up before. The stream of energy reached around the jar with the fire swirling around inside it. The second stream was the same faint purple as his brother's and went for the same jar that both Malakai and Toby's had.

I did not know what any of it meant, but I recognized the purple energy. It was the same color as mine. I had a feeling the onlookers would have some comments about that, judging by their reactions. The whispers and noise had started again in earnest, and I could feel every bit of the tension and anxiety behind them.

Gran calls my name, and I force myself up to her. She smiles at me, no doubt trying to keep me calm.

"Ready, lass?" I knew she could sense my hesitation. I'm certain it is written plainly all over my face. It was more statement than question. I know there is no turning back, no running away.

I turn toward the jars, rubbing my hands together and shifting on my feet. Closing my eyes, I feel the energy from my core moving into my hands, and I hold it there for a long moment before reaching toward the jars.

Once I do, I immediately hear the crowd go wild, as I'd expected they would. I keep my eyes shut. I know what they are seeing. As the twins before me, the purple energy was flowing from me and around that jar.

Except mine was not a faint purple—no, mine was a deep rich shimmering purple. I hold it, waiting for Gran to speak, not used to seeing myself conjuring up mystical streams of magic enough to open my eyes without losing all focus.

"Lorali, lass...hold yer magic, an' open yer eyes, dove," she says, her voice excited.

I open my eyes and see not two, as with the twins, but four distinct streams of energy flowing from my hands. The only jar untouched was filled with dirt. I had Fire twisting around Water twisting around that familiar purple shimmer, but the kicker was the rapidly twisting stream of Air forming and weaving through it all. All four streams were weaving around one another and branching off towards their respective jars. I chuckle a little, which causes me to lose all concentration, all the energy evaporating.

I turn back towards Gran, who is looking at me like I was the Second Coming or something, and then look around the room, which I just noticed was deathly silent. Everyone was staring at me just like she was, even my parents.

"Um...was that a good thing or a bad thing?" I whisper.

"Only ye can tell us tha', lass. Only time will tell," she says, very seriously but with a barely contained glee, and turns, walking back to her seat.

She was the only one who looked happy about it. Around the room, faces were shocked, appalled, intrigued, or fearful. I couldn't help but bite my lip, wring my hands, and worry.

"The four of ye have shown yer ability. Please choose a seat. An' welcome, Guardians," Gran proclaims, having reached her seat again.

I choose to sit at the table that I was calling "Energy" with the twins and Toby. I had figured out that every jar relates to an element—Earth, Water, Air, Fire. Except I couldn't quite figure out exactly what the energy jar was about, and since I couldn't read either runes or Gaelic (I'd asked Wesley what the gold writing was), I was out of luck until someone explained it to me.

So, until then, "Energy" it was. The other people at the table (all three of them) made space for the four of us to sit next to one another, thankfully. I sit down, looking around at the variety of people...all ages, races, time periods, genders. There seemed to be no mold to fill other than 'have magic.'

The room was still eerily quiet, and almost everyone was watching all four of us, though most of them were at least attempting to be discreet about it. I could feel curiosity, a sense of wonder, but the worst was the fear I felt coming from too many of the Guardians in the room.

I didn't know near enough about any of this, what was going on, about this world, to even begin to put anyone's mind at ease.

Not theirs, and not my own. I look down at my hands, apparently capable of some scary cool stuff, and feel out of place and lost.

TWELVE

"Yer the first to 'ave four," a voice says from not far away, pulling me from my thoughts.

I look up towards the sound, and a woman not much older than me is looking at me like I am a puzzle to be solved. She is beautiful in her Victorian dress, accentuating her slim figure. Her copper skin is flawless; black hair pinned up, sparkling amber eyes shining at me. She may have found me an oddity, but she was exuding friendliness. Everything about her was open, welcoming, and warm.

"Lena," she says, thrusting her arm toward me, reaching over Malakai between us. "1885."

I take her arm as I'd seen others do, and she grasps mine firmly before letting go.

"Lorali, present day," I reply, a little amused at the sheer oddity of the introduction.

We don't have time to say anything else as my gran stands again. Whatever conversation they'd been having at the head table over now.

"Although it is no' our way to deny a person, as the Council sees it's a dark 'n troubled time," she looked over at the four of us and sighed, "a tally'll be taken on if those wi' more'n one Affinity will be accepted as Guardians."

The room erupts into cross talk, some yelling that it was not the way 'the Order' did things. Others that this should have been done long ago. Others still yelling about the lack of Guardians as it is. I hear the name Evangeline more than once. My dad stands, raising a hand, and the room settles.

"Is true tha' Evangeline held more'n one Affinity. I can'na allow ye to base yer vote on tha' alone though, as I too have more'n one."

Whispers begin going around the room, and I try to take stock of who looks surprised and who doesn't.

"There are others as well, but I will'na speak for 'em. Evangeline has clouded yer view of what those with pow'rful magics can do. I understand. But do'na hold the bairns to the fire for her sins, friends." Dad sat down to mostly overwhelming applause, though I could still see more faces than I'd have liked that look either angry or frightened.

"Liam will come an' ye'll place a white stone if yer in favor and a black if yer no'. There'll be no public shame, an' none will know how ye cast yer stone," Gran says.

Gran sits down and Grandfather stands, walking around the room with a large grey stone jar. At every table, he stops in front of each person, they place their hands on the jar and we hear a stone hitting the inside, before he moves on. He comes to our table, giving me a sad smile as he walks past. He doesn't stop in front of the twins and me, though Toby gets a vote.

I hear Grandfather telling him quietly to simply decide which stone he wants. The jar would do the rest. I guess we don't even get a say in *not* being Guardians. I don't know why it surprises me; we didn't get a say in being one either. When he receives a stone from every person in the room, except the three of us, he goes back to the Council table and sits.

Aunt Viv stands and walks around to the front of the table; picking up the jar, she calls me and the twins to stand with her.

"If there be more white than black, ye'll be added to the Order of the Guardian. If no' ye will be asked to leave the Gatherin'. Do ye understand the purpose of the vote as I've explained it to ye?" Aunt Viv asks us.

I can feel the anger coming off her as though she is about to burst with it. I had to admire her steady voice and calm face, despite the fury.

"Aye," the twins say in unison, both of their voices betraying them.They were each deeply sad and yet infuriated all at once. I wondered if it was more about a vote taking place, or the comparison to their mother.

"Yes, I understand," I reply, snark in every syllable.

How dare these arrogant jerks demand we do this without our understanding, and then have the audacity to vote on whether or not they'll actually have us? Because what? We have more than one Affinity? We don't even know what the hell that means.

Aunt Viv nods curtly and holds the jar above her head, closing her eyes. After only a few moments, a white mist swirls around her, and she opens her eyes. The room is silent, and I hear Mom cry out.

I have no doubt she was hoping it would be black. I wonder if it had been, if she'd have gotten Toby out of it as well. I am surprised at the relief I myself feel, though. I suppose I've accepted it all more than I'd realized.

Or maybe I just want to prove them wrong.

"White. We welcome our new warriors. May ye always 'ave the strength to choose the higher path instead o' the easy one, an' always 'ave the greater good in yer mind," she says, setting the jar back on the table behind her.

She then stands in front of each one of us and takes our arms, and right behind her was the rest of the Council.

We went back to our seats afterwards. I have the distinct feeling it wasn't a normal thing because they called Toby up as if it was an afterthought. Like they'd made a show of accepting us to spite the Guardians who'd challenged it. It wasn't exactly the way I wanted to be inducted into a new society of people, especially if I ever have to rely on them to have my back.

Lena was smirking, arms crossed, shaking her head as I sit back down. "Yer trouble, the lot o' ye," she says. "Knew I liked ye."

The sentiment causes Wesley to laugh and Malakai to look at her indignantly. I suppose that sums up what I know of them so far. Wesley, the more carefree, chaotic of the two; while Malakai is much more serious, mature.

"It's not like I'm trying to be trouble," I say, maybe a little too much like a 2-year-old having a tantrum, because she really laughs then. "It's not anything I can control," I argue, but it doesn't affect her amusement in the least.

"Lor, only you would complain about having *super* super powers," Toby says, rolling his eyes at me.

His reaction only serves to unsettle me more. The very last thing I would ever want is for Toby to feel jealousy towards me, or worse—resentment.

My dad stands then and addresses the Gathering, halting the conversation at our table. I glance over at Toby, concern apparent, which only makes him roll his eyes at me again before pointedly turning his head to listen.

"The Council feels it important to begin with an update on wha' we know in regards to the sealin' o' the Portals. All we've been able to determine to this poin' is that it was Evangeline tha' sealed them. We've no knowledge o' how she was able to do that or why."

He pauses to scan the room and let his words settle.

"Far as we can tell, the only period o' time we can'na travel to is the twenty years after she closed 'em. There does'na seem to be any problems goin' to times previously sealed, as though the act of sealing 'em rippled through time, but only while they were *actively* sealed. We believe it to mean she sealed 'em on the eighteenth o' November, 572. We also believe she did'na travel before they sealed, an' they opened on the fourth o' December, 592. Presumably, she herself lived through those years with 'em sealed."

He looks around the room, and surprisingly, most seem to understand what he's just said. I, however, have no clue what a word of it means.

"Anyone livin' through a time when the Portals were sealed can'na travel to the time they lived through, either. Others have been able t' travel to their sealed timelines, but they can'na reach em themselves. It's all very confusin' an we're still gatherin' information as it comes to us."

He scans the crowd again, seeming to look each person in the eye.

"If any have further information, we open the floor now for ye to come forward an' share such. If there've been any sightings of the woman, we ask that ye also share such."

He is silent as he stands there, searching the room and waiting for anyone to stand and offer information. The room is so quiet you could hear a pin drop.

Then, from the Fire table, a man stands. He has bright red hair and a bushy beard to match, and he is wearing a kilt and a long-sleeved billowy shirt, with plaid socks to match, topped off with an odd little hat. He looks like he stepped right off a postcard or out of a painting.

"I've no information for ye, Lord, but a query if ye'll allow."

Dad bows his head slowly towards the man.

"I thank ye, m'Lord," he clears his throat and walks up to the Council table, then turns to address everyone.

"We do'na know how or why Evangeline sealed the Portals, tha' much may be true. But it is also true tha' she was once one of our number. An' we all know tha' we have a duty an' a responsibility to bring her to justice for the crimes we know she has committed. No' to mention the ones she may've done without us knowin'. So I ask, brothers an' sisters—" He shifts nervously, glancing back at the Council. "Has Evangeline done enough to be labeled *saoghail*? An' face all the wrath o' this Order tha' comes with that?" His face slightly flushed, he bows his head as he waits for an answer.

I recognized the word; it was the one Malakai used, the one he said meant traitor.

I really have to ask why some words aren't in English, I think, remembering that it was likely none of these people spoke the same language as I did.

It was odd then, that certain words still came across as foreign, when I wasn't supposed to hear that after the spell. I wondered if it meant it was wearing off, or if it wasn't done right.

I feel the anger coming off Wesley like a fire raging, and I grab his hand, praying it will be enough to keep him calm. I know after the events of earlier, an outburst from any one of the three of us would be chaos. There may have been enough to vote us into the Order, but that didn't mean some wouldn't use any excuse to see us out.

I didn't need to know anyone here to know that, to feel that. He was shaking with rage, and all I could do was keep hold of him and try to pour all the calming energy I could into him. I focused solely on keeping myself calm, centered, so that maybe he would calm down as well.

"I do'na believe we have enough evidence to condemn the woman o' such at this point, Darian," Aunt Viv says quietly, though it was apparent she has opinions she wasn't voicing as well.

She looks uncomfortable, suspicious, but firm in what she said. I knew she'd argue for more evidence if she had to, no matter what conflict she had personally with that.

It was strange how much I could glean from a person by their face, their body language, just the feeling I got about them. I'd always done it; it's only now I knew it was more than being a good judge of character or being good at 'reading' people. Little did I know I was *actually* reading people all along.

"Ye can'na mean to allow her to roam free?" the man scoffed in disbelief.

"Do ye mean to *kill* a woman without a trial, Darian?" one of the Council members shouted angrily.

"Tha's quite enough, Calliope." Gran shot the woman a meaningful look, placing a hand on her arm.

"I say it is'na, Analyse. We do'na condemn a person to their death with no trial. Tha' is no' our way!" The Councilwoman stands, slamming her hands on the table.

Water began trickling from her fingertips, running across the table and dripping onto the floor in front of her.

Gasps and muttering began around the room, all eyes locked onto this woman. I could sense something more than just a need for justice coming from Calliope, though I couldn't quite place what it was. Her raven hair was loose, falling around her face in waves, blue eyes bright with rage.

"Calliope? What is this? It is'na our way to lose our tempers in discussion either," Aunt Viv warns, but I could tell she was sensing something was wrong too.

She calmly put herself between Calliope and everyone else, walking around to the front of the table to look up at her, trying to calm her.

"An' there is'na a single person callin for anyone's death. Ye know that. Ye know that is'na our way."

"I see no' a thing wrong with labeling a *saoghail* for wha' she is. Look at the damage the woman 'as caused!" Darian says passionately.

His face has gone red, flushed from the confrontation, his passionate beliefs all too apparent. I want to rush over and slap a hand across his mouth to shut him up. Did he not see how irate this woman was? How my aunt was using herself as a shield, trying to calm the situation?

Calliope turns to him suddenly, raising an arm as she does so.

"*Voro,*" she hisses, a vicious sneer on her face.

A blast of water shoots across the room, lifting him off the floor and surrounding him. Everything seems to start moving in slow motion, as though it is a dream. People bursting into action all around me. Darian seems paralyzed and unable to move, his eyes wide, every muscle stiff, shock evident.

Several Guardians try to pull him out of the column of water he is trapped in, but they aren't able to even penetrate the surface. Aunt Viv's eyes are wide, panic flitting across her face as she shoves my grandparents back—Calliope shooting another blast towards my family, barely missing the mark.

That's when I realize what I'd been feeling from Calliope. Hatred. Rage. Not in general, or at the thought of condemning a woman without proof, not from a conviction for fairness or justice.

For everyone in the room. Shit.

Just as I have the thought, I realize she's been defending Evangeline specifically...not some code of honor or integrity. Which means Evangeline is a much bigger threat than I want to admit or think possible. She has allies, or at least one, inside the Order—and they hate the Guardians with a burning passion.

It was what I imagined one would feel if they were indoctrinated into a cult, that unthinking, unequivocal hate towards others. That unwavering loyalty and obedience. I feel all of that and more flooding every sense, as though Calliope has been holding it back, just below the surface, and the dam broke—unable to hide it for a second longer.

Until that moment, Evangeline, the Portals, the past and all I'd been told was foreign, distant. I hadn't taken it as seriously as I should have. I felt the weight of every word that had been said so far about it all crash down on me. It made my blood run cold.

Lena had gone running toward Darian and was trying to reach him in the column of water, but wasn't able to break in any better than the others who'd tried. Dad was holding Calliope in the air, surrounded by lightning crackling around her.

She kept trying to shoot water through—at him and others running past—but every time she did she got one hell of a shock for the effort. It seemed to only fuel her rage more, make her efforts more frantic and irrational.

"Come on, ye can get him out o' there," Malakai declares, grabbing me by the hand and dragging me toward the column of water.

He pushes and shoves through people, a battering ram in the middle of the chaos.

"How?" I ask in shock. "I don't know what the hell I'm doing!"

"It does'na matter, ye can do it. I *know* ye can," he says, ultimately confident.

We were standing right in front of the column, and people were shooting all types of magic at it, trying to reach in, throwing things, beating their fists against it. Nothing was working. The column of water was impenetrable. I look at Darian, who was starting to struggle against the reflex to breathe, eyes darting around at the myriad of helpless Guardians.

"Jus' reach in, lass. Do'na think—jus' do it. Trust me. It'll work," Malakai says.

I look at him skeptically, unsure. He is staring at me so intently and so confidently, not a hint of doubt—so I nod, close my eyes, and reach.

I feel the barrier; it's strong, but I can feel the cracks in it too. I focus on where I feel the cracks and imagine them growing wider and wider, enough to fit a hand through. I can feel the icy water and don't dare open my eyes in case I distract myself and lose my chance to save this man; the memory of the terror in his eyes driving me onward.

I feel Darian grab my hand and focus on my goal—pulling him out alive. I focus all my energy on the task at hand, pulling with every ounce of strength and will I have in me.

I really shouldn't have put quite so much emphasis on the pulling, because Darian ended up over my head behind me, and everyone within a 5-foot radius ends up drenched in icy cold water. At least Darian was breathing, and the column of water was gone.

Everyone was staring at me, and Calliope was screaming (I'd bet money she was heavily cursing my existence) in Gaelic. I choose to ignore the psychopath. Dad seems to have her well enough contained for the moment and instead turn to check on Darian.

"Are you okay? Are you hurt; you didn't break anything did you? Should we call a doctor?" I fire at him, gently bending his arms, legs, searching for any evidence of injury.

Coughing, he waves me back a bit as he sits up, staring at me in an odd way. "Lass, ye do'na even know what ye did, do ye?" he asks, disbelief apparent.

I just look at him, confused. This isn't exactly the kind of reaction I was expecting. It wasn't just him, either. All around us people were gazing on with looks of shock and admiration in equal measure. The only people in the room who don't look surprised are Gran and Malakai, but neither of them makes a move to intervene.

"Ye broke a spell made by another. An' no' just any other. One of the Council. Only the most powerful sit on the Council, lass. What ye did was near impossible, an' yer no' even trained."

Pulling himself up on his feet, he clasps a meaty hand on my shoulder.

"I thank ye for my life an' am ever in yer debt. One day ye'll understand what ye did here today, an' why so many will either fear ye or die for ye. Help us all, ye may be the key to finally stoppin' tha' *saoghail* once an' for all."

He quietly holds his arm out to me and grasps my forearm in his, then touches his forehead to mine briefly.

"Ye have a good heart, lass. Do'na let anythin' change that. Yer heart'll be the thing tha' keeps ye from goin' down the path Evangeline went down. Do'na let the darkness take ye," he whispers, before pulling away and giving me a supportive smile.

Turning, he walks out of the hall, leaving me standing there wondering what exactly it all means.

The only thing that I really understand is that I'm different, even among different, and it's not a great feeling. I never really fit in at school with other kids, except Isobel. To be facing the same ostracizing and judgement even here makes me feel a little hopeless and defeated.

A loud bang startles me, and I turn to see Gran and Dad standing over a now subdued Calliope. Mom is hovering in the background, and Aunt Viv is actively calming the Guardians surrounding them. Gran nods firmly, and with a look filled with remorse, waves a hand toward Calliope.

She's huddled in on herself on the ground, like a cornered animal. No longer trying to shoot off magic, but there is a crazed and wild look to her. Two large men step forward, lifting her onto her feet and walking out of the room with her.

"Gran? Where are they taking her?" I ask, closing the distance between us.

"A prison o' sorts. She'll 'ave a trial. But no' this night," she says sadly.

The Guardians are beginning to settle back into their seats, and Gran shoots me a sad smile before heading towards her own. I walk back to my table with more questions than when the night began, and I have a feeling they will answer almost none of them before it was over.

"We will hold Calliope in Eldria while we prepare for a trial. Notice'll be sent to those who wan' to attend." Gran looks very sad, glancing toward the now empty chair. "We've bound her pow'r, so she'll no longer be a harm to anyone. As for Evangeline, there'll no' be any orders t' kill her. Tha' should be known without my havin' to give it voice; we all *know* it is'na our way," she chastises, obviously amazed at the insinuation.

"We can'na allow her to go free, though. She is t' be captured as quickly as can happen. Defend yerself if ye have to, but only so far as ye have to do so." Gran looks down at the Guardians and waits for any response or outbursts.

I get the distinct feeling it isn't a common occurrence, and Calliope's outburst has further implications I'm not quite grasping.

"Are there any further questions or information regardin' Evangeline?" she finally poses to the room.

No one offers another word on the subject. Honestly, I think everyone is still reeling from the incident with Calliope. I'm sure it wasn't every day a council member went rogue like that. It seems to have taken over the entire event.

"Very well. There's one other piece o' business we need t' cover before we're done for the evenin'. I'll allow Vivienne to bring it to ye," Gran says and sits as Aunt Viv stands from her seat.

She moves swiftly and gracefully around the table to address the Guardians. No hint of uncertainty or distress about her.

I have to admit, I was kind of into how the men didn't seem to say much. I wasn't too clear on the flow of power or whatever, but it was interesting to see the men take a backseat while the women ran things for once. Especially in an ancient order of Portal Guardians that have magic and travel through time in Portals. I would have bet it was a more patriarchal system than it obviously was, based solely on the history I knew.

Maybe the history books didn't know half as much as they thought they did, I muse to myself.

"As well ye know, our numbers are less wi' every generation. O' the eight Scotland Portals, only the Galloway line has a modern Guardian. Magic in this time is all but *sàmhach-*. Dormant. An' what is'na is in practice by modern day fools who've no' a clue what they're doin'. The dormancy of magic in this time requires action from us all." She folds her hands together and straightens, authority clear in every move. "An' for this reason the council asks ye all to help us locate yer descendants. If yer line has'na lasted into present time, we ask for a Guardian, t'be sent to guard the Portals here. We can'na allow a Portal to be left vulnerable again." She allows the words to settle, keeping her head high and gaze fixed.

"Vivienne, surely ye don' mean ye'd take our children." A woman at the Earth table stands.

She has long, black hair perfectly seated across her shoulders and down her back in waves. She is dressed like a picture I'd seen of a girl in the 1930s except with one of those sash things most of my family had on. Her gown is akin to old Hollywood Glam, some sort of silky material in a rich blue, tailored to hug her body and yet flowing from her at the same time. Her elbow-length gloves cover hands that are steepled in front of her on the table, resting just under a face full of concern.

"Aye. Tha' is what I'm sayin'. I was barely 25 when I came t' do my duty, Saerenna. An' younger still the first time I was called from me family to defend the Portals. Do'na forget who nor wha' I have sacrificed for this Order. An' do'na forget the danger I faced at a younger age than yer bairns," she lectures, locking eyes with the woman. "But ye've a brother an a sister as well. An' unmarried the both of 'em. Yer children do'na need to be the ones to make the sacrifice."

Aunt Viv refused to look away from the woman, and they seemed to have a battle of wills for a moment. It wasn't long until Saerenna bowed her head once and frowned before taking her seat, but offering no more argument.

"Does anyone else have an objection they'd like t' raise?" Aunt Viv says, raising a brow and looking around the room.

She was openly daring anyone to go against her in that moment. Frankly, she was downright intimidating, and I was unsurprised the silence was so complete you could almost hear their hearts beating.

No one spoke against her, and several actually hung their heads as if ashamed. I wondered what exactly my aunt was referring to when she said she'd sacrificed for the Order and why so many Guardians were shamed into silence by it. What or who could she have possibly been forced to give up? What could have been taken from her?

"Well, then. Those o' ye that can find yer descendants will have two weeks t' do so. If ye can'na bring them here by then, ye'll bring a trained Guardian or a Potential." She looks around the room once more. "Ye can bring more'n one if ye like, an' if untrained, they'll be trained. We do'na ask o' ye what is'na required. Or wha' we have no' sacrificed before ye, in an effort to spare ye from doin' the same."

Aunt Viv goes back to her seat, and the room suddenly feels very heavy. I could feel the weight of sadness and obligation like a blanket over every Guardian. It seems my family wasn't the only one hoping the Portals would remain sealed, the only ones mourning their opening.

"There is one las' thing, if I may." Saerenna stands again, addressing the Council. She is glancing from the Council towards our table and back again, waiting for permission to continue.

"Aye, Saerenna, what is it?" Dad asks, encouragement and support on his face.

"Jus' after the Portals sealed, this was left on my door. It had the twins' names on it, Council," she explains, holding up a small velvet pouch. "I don' know why it was left with me, but I kept it. I did'na even know who the names belonged to until tonight."

She walks over to our table and stands in front of us, Wesley and Malakai on either side of me. Wesley was leaning slightly forward, eager to know what she had, while Malakai sat stiffly, showing no interest at all.

"I opened it once, t'see what was in it. I knew right away what it was." She dumps two rings into the palm of her hand from the pouch. "They're no' dangerous, do'na worry," she says, holding them out to the twins.

Wesley practically lunges for one, examining it from every angle excitedly. Malakai studies it for a moment, realizing his only real option is to take it, and carefully picks it up without really looking at it. He holds it in his palm, resting on the table in front of him, his discomfort painfully on display.

They were identical silver rings, the head of a dragon on top, the body of the dragon making up the band. The eyes were made of two perfectly cut emeralds. The rings actually looked almost identical to the brooch Aunt Viv was wearing. Wesley slid his on, making it look as though the dragon was wound around his finger, head perched just under his knuckle, keeping watch.

"They're bonded, the rings. An' warded for protection," Saerenna discloses. "Ye'll feel if the other needs ye, or if there's danger. Might be more to it, as I've not seen a set before. Only read about 'em. I did check 'em for dark magic an' there is'na any. They're clean. Safe to wear."

"Thank you. Yer kind to have kept them safe." Wesley smiles sweetly at her.

"Aye, yer a good woman to 'ave brought 'em to us. Thank ye," Malakai agrees, though his smile is forced.

Saerenna bows her head and returns to her seat.

Malakai studies the ring more closely then, but still makes no move to put it on.

"If there is'na any further business, we can end the Gatherin here. There's food through to the dinin' hall or ye can rest if ye prefer. Yer all welcome t' stay as long as ye need, an' of course in a fortnight we'll see ye again to sort ou' the Portals. Blessed be all of ye," Grandfather says as he stands and takes Gran's hand, leading her out towards the dining room.

It would take a lot of getting used to, the formality of it all, especially the authority of my own family, and the distance it seemed to create as I watched them leave.

Thirteen

The Council dispersed right away, which meant my entire family save Mom, Toby, and I. Mom followed behind Dad as soon as he walked out. I know there had to be some kind of protocol to follow, but it still felt really odd for none of our family members to have acknowledged Toby or me. Since it seemed we were on our own, I chose to check in with Toby myself.

"Hey, bud. You okay?" I ask, placing a hand on his shoulder.

He hadn't said a word since the vote, or even looked my direction. I wasn't feeling any anger off him, but a lot of confusion. It had to be a lot for a fourteen-year-old boy to take in.

"Yeah. Yeah. I'm okay," he says, absently.

Looking over at me, his asks, "Do you think we'll ever go home, Lor?" His eyes are sad.

"I don't know, Tob, I really don't." I sigh, allowing myself a moment to be sad as well.

I still hadn't answered a single call from Isobel, and she'd started calling about every hour on the hour this morning. I knew I'd have to come up with something at some point.

"Well, that really sucks. My girlfriend is gonna be so peeved," he says, resting a cheek in his hand.

"Wait. What?" I scoff, stunned.

"Oh, yeah, girlfriend," he says. "Guess we just broke up, though, huh? Since I really don't think we *are* going back anytime soon." His attitude is nonchalant, he is so like Mom in that way. Nothing flusters them, nothing rattles their perfect mask of calm—not for long, anyway.

"Toby. Don't think that way. Yeah, so we have to travel. But like, it doesn't mean we can't just come back to the day after tomorrow or whatever, right?"

"Ach. Lass. Ye'll no be goin back to yer life before," Wes says quietly, slowly shaking his head and refusing to look me in the eye.

"Excuse me," I say loudly, "but I don't really think that's your call, now is it?"

"He'd have the right of it, though, lass," Malakai chimes in. "Yer a Guardian now. We did say yer life is'na yer own any longer, no?" Looking me directly in the eye, as if in challenge, so very different from his brother.

Toby chooses that moment to push his chair back and run full force out of the room. I shoot one scathing look at the boys and stand to go after my brother, hoping I could undo the damage they just did.

"Wonderful time for the two of you to finally agree on something," I snap, giving them both a nasty look as I stalk haughtily out of the room.

I push past guests and try desperately to find my brother in the crowds, only to find him chatting up Lena, the girl we met a little while ago. I'll be damned if he didn't look, for all the world, just as happy as ever.

Must've gotten that trait from Mom, I think again, sighing.

"Oh aye, once the Portals closed, we made do," Lena explains to Toby. "I've known I was a Guardian since I were a wee one, haven' I?" She laughs, comfortable and confident, even after the craziness.

"Hi there," I say, smiling. "Do you mind if I steal Toby away for a minute?"

Grabbing my brother by the arm, pulling him toward the sitting room. Okay, maybe I got a little of Mom's demeanor too when it's necessary.

"Well, that was rude!" he says, pulling his arm out of my grasp but following, all the same.

"Yeah, well, so was running out on me like that," I snipe back.

"Oh lay off, Lor. You had plenty of company." He huffs as he throws himself into his favorite chair by the fireplace.

"Toby," I start, reaching a hand to touch his hair as he yanks out of my reach. "Toby, come on. You're all that matters right now," I plead, truly concerned at his ever shifting mood.

"Really? Am I, Lor? *Am I*?" he snaps, refusing to look my way still.

"Toby. What is going on? I know it's a lot," I start.

"Yeah, it *is* a lot. Not that anyone is gonna care, because I'm not the one with multiple Affinities or whatever." He picks at the arm of the chair, flicking off imaginary dust.

"That's what you're upset about? Seriously?" I demand, offended. "Over something I have zero control over."

"It doesn't matter," he mumbles, crossing his arms and sulking.

I crouch down in front of him and wait until he gives in and glances at me. "Yeah, Tob, it *does* matter. We've only got each other right now," I say. "And I need to know you're gonna talk to me when you're upset, or this is going to be so much harder than it already is."

"Really?" he asks, turning fully toward me now. "Cause I think I'm pretty much going to get ignored because I'm not special."

"Not *special*? Toby!" I cry. "You have freaking *magic*!" I grin up at him, feeling his jealousy fade a little.

Okay, maybe I am being a tiny bit condescending, but if he wants to act like a child...well. You get placated like one.

"Well, yeah, but you have more." He pouts, and I hate the jealousy I can feel from him.

"No, just different. Not more, at least I don't think," I reassure, wanting nothing more than to put us on even footing, and feeling a little guilty at trying to treat him like a toddler who dropped their ice cream.

"Well, if I ca—" Malakai begins, but is interrupted by Aunt Viv waltzing in.

"Now that is quite enough o' this now," she says, smiling down at Toby and me. "It's about time ye had a meetin with the Council, I think."

She reaches a hand to both of us, pulling us to our feet. As we pass Malakai, I can see Wesley standing a few feet behind him, and notice Aunt Viv nod her head down the hall, indicating they should follow us. It doesn't take long to realize we are headed for Grandfather's study. A room I have never once seen the inside of.

As we get close, the huge double wooden doors swing open, and I can see Dad on the other side of them, holding them open for us. He gives me a quick smile as I pass by, getting my first look into the room.

The study is definitely masculine. Lots of wood and leather, and I can smell tobacco in the air. Funny, I have never seen anyone in my family smoke anything, ever. I turn to my left and see the source of the smell in Darian, standing by a window, puffing on a pipe. He nods his head to me and turns back to the window. I hear the doors shut behind me, and it feels suddenly as though the air is 10 times thicker around us.

Gran is sitting in a chair next to a massive mahogany desk with Grandfather sitting behind it, shuffling some papers around. I can't tell if he's actually busy or just trying to appear that way. Mom stands from a bench under a window across the room and rushes to pull Toby and me into her arms.

"Oh, my babies," she sighs into my hair. "I would have given anything to save you from all this," she says, pulling back.

I can see tears in her eyes as she looks from me to my brother, a hand to each of our faces. Dad comes up behind her and places a hand on her shoulder. She leans into him, dropping her arms to hold on to our hands. The look on the faces of our parents is striking, and very new. I've never seen them worried. Not really. Not like this.

Gran clears her throat and rises gracefully out of her chair. Mom and Dad both shift protectively behind us, and we all face her.

"To our newest Guardians, Fàilte." She smiles at the four of us. "Please, allow me t' introduce ye to the rest o' the Council."

She motions an arm to three people standing off to the side, and they all step forward.

"Rowan and Dean, twins, and members of this Council. 1432," she says, and a man and woman step forward, reaching out to grasp arms with each of us, a smile on their faces.

"Tis an honor to meet the next generation of Guardians, an Galloway line at that," the woman says with a smile, "I'd be Rowan, an this here's me brother Dean."

The man nods his head and smiles genuinely.

"An here is Elizabeth, member of this Council. 1976," Gran states, then turns to Darian, urging him forward. "O' course ye've met Darian already. The newest member of this Council. 1800."

Both Elizabeth and Darian nod briefly, and I can feel the relief in the room, as well as the tension. It doesn't take a telepath to know they're all preoccupied with thoughts of Calliope right now.

"Now that's done, would ye all please sit. We've still a lot to discuss this night, an I can feel the hour getting late."

As everyone finds their seats, it is obvious the four new Guardians are expected to sit on the couch together, surrounded by the Council. I raise my hand and look warily around the room, which is met by chuckles from most.

"Aye, girl, no need ta raise yer hand, ye can simply say yer piece," Dad says, amused.

"Okay. Well, um, I guess I'd like to know what that meant back there... I mean. I know, I know. It's our Affinities or whatever. But what does it mean? I can figure out that I've got Water, Fire, and Air. Malakai has Air, Wesley Fire, but what was the last one? What is it that Toby has? Well, that all of us have?" I blurt out quickly.

"Well done, lass," Grandfather says, standing and walking around to the front of his desk. "Ye've the right of it, a good job identifyin' the elements. Now, as for the last. That'd be Spirit," he sighs, rubbing a hand across his neck.

"Spirit, Force, Pure Magics is really what it is," Aunt Viv chimes in, looking at us with an excitement in her eyes. "An we've no seen it in young ones in many a year."

"Aye, me brother was the last as far as we know," Gran says.

"But, Gran, there were a couple people at the Spirit table," Toby points out.

"Ye're no wrong, lad. There were, but they'd be Undefined. They've not got actual Spirit Affinity," she explains.

"Undefined? What does that even mean?" I ask.

"It means they've no true Affinity. They hold magics, but not enough connection to any one element or Affinity to test," Wesley mutters.

"Then how are they Guardians? Isn't that like, the only test?" I blurt out.

Darian chuckles, and Rowan steps forward.

"Ach, lass. Ye've a lot o questions and a lot o misguided notions, don't ye?" she laughs. "Ye've only need to have magics to be a Guardian. Having an Affinity just means ye can initiate travel, safely."

Both Toby and I must look terribly confused, because at this point my dad puts a hand up, shushing the room, and looks to us with a reassuring smile. "I know it's a wee bit confusin' for ye now, children. We have'na gone about it the best way we coulda, to be honest." He clears his throat. "An' there will be a lot ye'll need to learn in order to truly understand what's needed to be understood."

He glances at Aunt Viv, and she nods sadly.

"We test Affinity because we've learned, ye can have magics and not be able to control the Portals. We've lost to the Portals. Aunt Viv had a twin, a girl with powerful magics, but no defined Affinity."

He looks down at the ground before he continues.

"We did'na know at first. When the Order came ta be," he nods to himself and continues, "we thought magics is all ye needed, and we were wrong."

Mom puts a hand on Dad's back and sighs heavily.

"I suppose it's time we tell you the story of the Order, and where we began," she says. "Please. Get comfortable, this is going to take a while. Even the twins won't have heard the whole of it, have they Analyse?" She turns to Gran.

"No, no, they hav'na," she admits, and I hear both boys inhale deeply in shock. I wish I felt guilty at how satisfied I felt that they, too, had things withheld from them.

Since the beginning of time, magics have been here, running through the very fabric of the Universe. Long, long ago, almost everyone could wield the magics around them. Even small children had to be taught care. A simple thought could start a fire that would rip through a village. A tantrum could level mountains, erupt volcanoes, and cause the seas to rumble.

Spells weren't as necessary back then. Many wouldn't even have known what one was—it was simply second nature, like breathing or sleeping. Magic just *was*. As it is now, not every person was *good*. Some wanted more. More power, more control. Some just wanted to hurt others.

Since magic is closely tied to a person's emotional stability, it became clear quickly that not every fire, flood, or animal attack was pure coincidence. It didn't take long before people started to notice that when certain individuals got upset, bad things began to happen around them. Today, that idea has developed into "bad luck." Some would even say they cursed the people around them.

It was neither of those things, though. It was evil, and it was intentional. Some of the more powerful, the men and women who used their magics for the good of all, they banded together to protect from these attacks. They called themselves the Order. It became their sole mission to find these evildoers, to bind their magics, and to end the suffering of innocent people. The Order fought against many, and taught others to fight as well, and so the Order grew.

Over time, it became obvious that cooperative leadership was needed, and the Council was brought into being. Together, they became the most powerful force on Earth and discovered how to bind not only one person's power, but to prevent that power from being born into their children as well. Many within the Order thought this was an abuse of their combined power, and a war broke out against the Council.

With the Order broken into two factions, chaos spread across the world. Eventually though, those on the Council who sought to control magics were captured, their magics bound, and peace reigned again. All but one. All but the one who created the Portals.

The New Council, which was led by Analyse Galloway, discovered these Portals, and the search for Lucian, the one who created the Portals, was renewed in earnest. The Council had no idea how the Portals were created, or how to use them, but knew that to find Lucian, mastery of them would be key.

They tracked him down, using the Portals he had created. Lucian was apprehended and sentenced to death, but at significant cost to the Order.

They lost several powerful potentials in the effort, and it was through that loss that we learned to test for Affinity as a measure of ability to travel. Though people with an Undefined Affinity can result in powerful magic, without an Elemental Affinity, any who tried to travel were lost.

Our Affinities are what ground us, connect us to the Earth. To ourselves. When we travel, it is our Affinity that offers us the protection to not be lost in a void—that calls us back to the element we are connected to. Without that connection, there is no link, and the travel is uncontrollable.

"I believe that'll be enough history for today, dear heart," Gran said, laying a hand on Mom's shoulder.

Every person in the room was quiet, the air heavy with loss and guilt. I look over to Aunt Viv, who sits silent and heartbroken on a window ledge. Even with the smallest understanding of my Empathic abilities, I know that loss was most personal for her.

"There's much more to that story, though, isn't there?" I ask quietly of the assembled Council.

"Aye. Much more t' be told, but not today," Gran replies with a sad smile.

"So you're the leader of the Order, Gran?" Toby pipes in.

Leave it to him to be more concerned about who runs things than with the magnitude of the knowledge Mom just threw at us.

"Ach, Toby," Dad admonishes, "Maybe we go over peckin order another time, eh, son?"

"No, it's a'right lad," Grandfather steps forward, "Aye, tis true yer Gran is the head of the Order, and now's as good a time as any to explain how the Council runs to the bairns."

He nods, as if agreeing with himself.

"The Council sits eight of the most powerful and prominent members of the Order, four from Clan Galloway, and four that have proven themselves a mind for justice and equality," he says, leaning against his desk. "Yer Mam and Da share the responsibilities of one Galloway seat, which is why yer Mam is allowed in these meetin's."

I look over to my parents; the question forming in my head, but Aunt Viv answers it before I have time to speak it.

"Yer parents wouldna have remained in the Order unless the both of em could have a say in its runnin'. Not with two bairns they knew could be pulled in ta the fight," she says without turning from the window.

"It was somethin' we agreed ta when you were born, Lor. Though now I suppose we should invite the rest o' the Council to have a say in that as well, now we can meet again," Dad says, looking around the room at the other Council members.

A chorus of "ayes" and other murmurs of agreement erupt from around the room. It feels like the Council members are more concerned with the day's events than whether or not my family gets an extra seat.

"After what the girl did for me today, I do'na care if there be twelve of ya on this Council, so long as she's trained proper," Darian grumbles out, smiling at me.

I acted off pure instinct, but I know I've made an ally for life in him today. I also know instinctively, my life from here on out will be dictated by these people, and I'm not sure *that's* a reality I can accept.

Aunt Viv turns to me quickly at that and subtly shakes her head, a clear sign I need to keep that thought to myself. From what I know of Evangeline, I think it's best I not make waves, at least not right now. Not until I know and understand more, not until I don't undeniably link myself with her in their minds without meaning to—and I can't avoid that without the complete story.

I lean against the arm of the couch we're sitting on and place my head in my hand. I feel like I should pinch myself. This whole thing feels so unreal. For the second time today, I feel absolutely lost.

"I know it's a lot to take in, sweetie, and we are here for any questions you have, but maybe right now you four should go and relax." Mom walks over and runs a hand across my hair. "It's been an endless day already." She looks over to my dad, as if to encourage him to agree with her.

"Aye, it's best the young ones take a bit o' break." He nods, looking around at the other Council members.

Malakai stands and walks out of the room without saying a word, and I can't tell if he's upset or simply following orders. Wesley stands, bows at the waist to the assembled Council, and follows after his twin.

My brother and I look at each other for a moment, then at our parents, who seem very eager to have us out of the room for some reason.

"Cards?" I ask him with a smile, and he just nods and stands to leave.

As we walk out of the room, a thought hits me, and I can't help myself. I lay a hand on the frame and speak loudly, my back turned to them as I gather my courage. "Mom, if it was common for children to have outbursts, and Toby and I have this Affinity..." I turn and face them, wanting to see their reactions as I ask what I need to know. "Why didn't we ever have an outburst? How could you have hidden it from us this long without a single incident?"

Aunt Viv averts her gaze to the floor halfway through the question. Mom's face drains of color, Dad looking as if I've hit him.

"Well?" I demand, *knowing* the shame I'm feeling is not my own, but theirs. The anger swells inside me as I see the other Council members shift to distance themselves from us.

"The tea. It was the tea, Lorali. Any time you got upset, whenever we had something to tell you we thought would be upsetting. That special blend we always have on hand. It dampened your ability to connect with whatever powers you might have." Mom somehow manages to look me in the eye, stating the facts without much emotion.

"Since you had yet to actually use your powers, they were already somewhat dormant. It didn't take a lot to ensure things remained calm. I doubt it would do much now you have awakened them."

I clench my fists by my side, take a deep breath to try and calm myself.

"Ye must know we did everythin' we did to protect ye both, dove. Ye've no real idea the danger it coulda put ye in." Dad moves to reach out to me, but I stop him with a hard look and terse shake of my head.

"I get that you did what you thought best." I take a shaky breath; I *will not* lose control. "Did you ever stop to think the long term effects these lies would have on our ability to trust you might be a factor later on?"

I turn and pull the doors closed behind us, denying anyone a chance to respond. I can already hear my parents start quietly making a case for why we need more time, sadness and defeat in their voices. More time for what, I am entirely unsure, and I don't know if I want to know anymore. It seems the more answers I get, the more excuses I have to make to myself. The more allowances I have to make. How much more before I have none left?

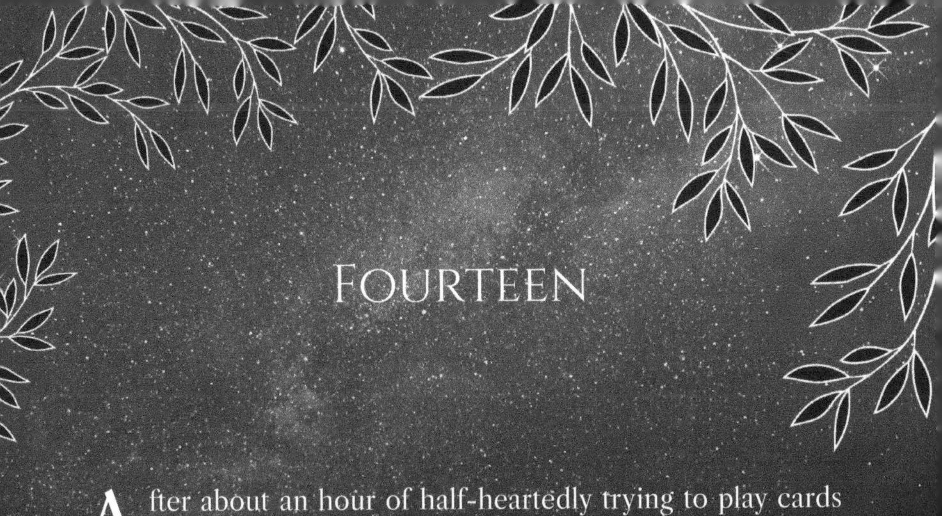

FOURTEEN

After about an hour of half-heartedly trying to play cards with Toby, we both decide its best if we have some alone time to process the day's events. While Toby went off to God knows where, I decide a midnight snack would be just the thing. Walking through the halls of the house, I run into a few Guardians lingering, some engaged in hushed conversations, others on their way to bed for the night or outside for a walk under the surprisingly clear night sky. No one seems too keen on stopping to chat, and I am unbelievably thankful for it.

As I round the corner to the kitchen, a wave of extreme sadness washes over me like I have never felt before. Hurrying my steps, I make it to the door before I hear my Aunt Viv and Uncle Seamus whispering rapidly. Most of the time, I'd have turned around and left them to their privacy, but something tells me I'm needed tonight.

Next to the kitchen island stands my aunt and uncle, tears running down Aunt Viv's face and Seamus looking confused and hurt. As Aunt Viv sees me, Uncle Seamus turns and walks out the door into the night, without even looking in my direction. I guess their conversation was over, anyway.

Aunt Viv simply crumples onto the stone floor, totally and utterly defeated. I rush over and throw an arm around her shoulders.

"Aunt Viv!" I cry, the power of her sadness overwhelming me completely as I, too, start to weep. "Oh, Aunt Viv. Surely it can't be that bad?" I plead with her.

"He can'na trust me now, can he?" She sniffs breathlessly. "Says he has'na a clue who he married. An' how could I no' tell him all this time?" Her head goes down, beautiful curls falling into her face and hiding her from view.

I take a beat, compose myself as best I can with her emotions battering at me. "Uncle Seamus will come around, you'll see. I know he will," I try to reassure her.

"Oh, Lor, my sweet dove. Aye. I know he will forgive me; I *know* how he loves me." She sighs, wiping a hand down her face. "But the real question, do I be deservin' of it?" She looks up at me with eyes that betray how vulnerable she is right now.

"Of course you do!" I grab her up in the biggest hug, my head on top of her hair. "If I can forgive all of you, hiding who and what I am my entire life, if I can understand..." I trail off.

Well damn, I have forgiven them, haven't I? I hadn't even realized I was no longer angry with my family for all the secrets kept, all the lies told.

Viv barks out a laugh, leans back, and looks me dead in the eye. She's a sight, tears streaking down, a mixture of surprise, heartbreak, and disbelief on her beautiful face.

"Well then. I admit I did'na expect yer forgiveness near so quick either, lass." She sighs and pulls herself up to her feet, reaching a hand to help me up.

"Yeah. I guess I do forgive you all. Truly." I look out at the full moon. "I'm not happy about any of it, for sure."

I look back at Aunt Viv for emphasis. Some part of me wanting her to understand it really isn't that simple.

"I'm not *happy*, but I understand. I believe you all did what you thought was best under impossible circumstances."

She nods, pulling back her last bit of composure to herself like armor. No longer a huddled mess on the floor, looking every bit a hardened warrior. Not a hint of emotion on her face now.

"I honestly don't know that I would have done it any different, in my parents' shoes," I admit, barely able to force the words out.

"Ye have to know, lass, they only wanted t' protect ye and Toby. We all did." She brushes a strand of hair from my face. "I may have thought ye deserved to know more'n ye did, but even I would'na have told ye the whole of it unless I had to." Aunt Viv putters around the kitchen, sadness still flowing off her, but determination to fight just as present.

"Why *didn't* you tell Uncle Seamus anything, Aunt Viv?" I ask quietly.

"Oh, dove." She stops and looks over at me for a second, pulling out the supplies for her famous cocoa. "There's still s'much ye do'na know," she sighs heavily, "Have a seat, we'll have us a good cuppa cocoa, and I'll tell ye the story of how I ended up this side o' the Portal in the first place."

I pull out one of the stools lining the other side of the island and settle in for what I can already tell is going to be a heartbreaking story.

"Evangeline was one o' the Council, she was. Once upon a time. A good one, at that." She fires up the stove and starts mixing in ingredients. "She was yer Gran's strongest ally in the beginnin'. Without her I dunno that we'd have stopped Lucian at all, that be the truth of it. But somethin' changed her, and not a soul knows what did it. She threatened to seal the Portals, said it was necessary. Pregnant with the twins, she were, though none knew it then. She and yer Gran, well, they started disagreein' on how the Council worked. Who should have the pow'r and who should'na. Course, that's what set the whole war off to begin with, ye ken?"

She pours two steaming mugs of cocoa and sits next to me with a sigh.

"Yer Gran, she did'na want to bind anyone's power. Not ever again. Said it was'na the place of the Order or the Council to decide who to be takin' the gift from. Not to mention, bindin' the powers of children yet to come? It did'na set right with most. And we had the Portals now, had to be watched, did'na they? Guardians were already growin' thin. Between the persecution o' witches and the bindin' of power. We had hurt people, denyin' them their gifts."

She shakes her head, looking vacantly at the stars for a long moment.

"Some o' those bairns the Council had bound before their birth, some of 'em were hunted down. Slaughtered, as witches. Magic woulda saved 'em. They shouldna have died, an' that hung over me Mam's head. Knowin' the Order was responsible, even if she had put a stop to it. She did try to go back an' undo what they'd done. Lucian destroyed any record of who they'd bound, though, ye see. Twas impossible for her to track 'em all down."

She sighs heavily, slumping subtly over her mug.

"Evangeline, she thought that 'cause there were less who had the gift, well, thought that's what gave her multiple Affinities didn't she? Her and the few others who showed more'n one. Yer Father, and several others. Course we only just started understandin' Affinity then. Everythin' was just theory and speculation. But Eva, she was certain. If fewer people had the gift, it had to find an outlet in those who did. Thought it was nature's way of releasing the magics, she did. Maybe 'twas the pregnancy, maybe the twins' father, but somethin' changed in her. She no longer wanted fairness; she wanted to feel powerful. Protected. She did'na want anyone to be able to hurt her, or her bairn."

She drifts off and simply stares for several long, quiet minutes.

"Aunt Viv?" I ask, resting a hand on her arm.

She shakes her head as if to clear her thoughts, then gives me a sad smile. "None o' that mattered much to me right then. Rosalynn was lost, that was me twin. Rosalynn. I was mighty angry, and sad, too. I found meself a good, kind man. I wanted to settle in, no' be dealin with the Order anymore. I do'na know exactly what happened after that night Eva let the Council know she was strikin' out on her own, ashamed I am to say I would'na even speak of magics. Not even to me Mam. Then one day I woke and he was gone, me husband."

She pats my arm lightly at my sharp gasp, hand over my mouth and eyes wide.

"Aye, married that man, I did. What I did'na know was he was'na mine at all. I said I did'na want a thing to do with magics, and I meant that. Blocked me own gift, wanted a quiet life, with a good man; last thing I wanted was t'know what was in his head. What a fool I was."

She stands, puts her mug in the sink, and turns back to me, one hip leaning against the edge.

"We can'na be certain, but I think he was the twins' father. He was good at hidin' his true nature, that's for sure. Took off after Eva, not long after we heard she was expecting twins. First I'd even heard of her expectin' at all, to be true. I do'na think he knew before then, either. He was odd that night, before he vanished. Went to bed alone, he said he was'na feelin' well. I shoulda known, never shoulda blocked meself from knowin'."

She huffs, shakes her head, and looks at me with pure rage in her eyes.

"It did'na take long for me Mam to figure they'd known each other, that he'd used a Portal. He said he did'na even have magics," she scoffs.

"Well, I vowed to never make that mistake again. Went right through the Portal, landed here, met Stuart. He was takin care o' the land, the Portal here. We did'na have any living relatives here, did we? Could'na have done as the Portals sealed with us on this side, though we did'na know that was the reason then.

"The Council set him up to care for the Estate. Should we need it, or should we have descendants after all. We chased 'em both for a long while. Then the Portals started closing, a few at a time at first. Just a few left, an the family decided yer Gran would stay behind, protectin' the past, in case she came back. The rest came here, to the last time either one of the *saoghail* was seen."

Aunt Viv walks over to the window, throws it open, and takes a deep breath.

"We hoped they would'na all close, ye know. We did'na think she'd be so daft as to pen herself in. But that's what she did. Dropped those boys on Mam's step, an she vanished. Portals all sealed that night. Mam got us a message, etched it right in the stone of the house. Not a one o' us ever thought we'd no be able to get back. That was 20 years ago now."

She looks back at me, tilts her head, and studies me a moment.

"I told meself I would'na fall in love. Lost too much, too many. I did'na want that for me life again. Seamus deserved more than I gave him. I shoulda told him, at least, that I could pick up some of his thoughts. Maybe no' the whole of it, but I told him nothin', Lor. Not a thing. An' by the time I loved him, well, then I was scared he'd run away from me, ye ken?"

"Aunt Viv..." I start, feeling a desperate need to defend her, but she puts up a hand and shakes her head.

"No, dove, I made a mess o' it for sure. I tell ye now, and maybe ye'll make less a mess than I have. Ye should know how much ye can lose. I did'na, nor did I know how dangerous it can be to trust the wrong person."

She walks towards me and wraps her arms around me.

"Just ye be more careful than I was, lass. An' do'na let yer heartbreak deny who ye are. What ye have, it is truly a gift, even if it does'na feel that way sometimes. Listen, an' remember what I said here tonight, an' do'na ever think to cut yerself off from yer magics."

She releases me and gives me a quick pat on the head.

"Now, I think it's time I track down me husband, and ye should get some rest, too. There'll be plenty o' time to dredge up all o' the sordid past. I've given ye enough to digest for now."

I stand up, hug her fiercely, and begin to walk out of the kitchen. "I love you, Aunt Viv," I say, turning at the door.

"Oh, I love ye with me whole heart, dove," she says, smiling at me, and walks out the door into the night.

Malakai is leaning against the wall by my bedroom door as I walk up to it, looking entirely too good at way too late an hour. Mom always says nothing good ever happens after midnight, and it's probably closer to 2AM at this point. He's wearing normal clothes, at least.

Someone must have given him some modern clothing at some point, though I can only guess as to who. *He certainly knows how to make a pair of sweats and a T-shirt look good*, I think before reminding myself, again, that nothing good ever happens past midnight.

He stands straight as he sees me, and *honestly*, would it kill the guy to smile or look at all like there's anything to be happy about in the world? I guess he did get a lot of information today, same as the rest of us. That and his only family is his twin brother, who he really seems to dislike. To be fair, they seem to really dislike each other.

"Lorali, do ye know what hour of night it is? Is it common for ye to be up and about alone this late?" He huffs at me.

Okay, yep. I'm going to have a problem with this attitude he has regarding women.

"Um, *excuse* the hell out of me," I bark out, crossing my arms and giving him a very pointed look through narrowed eyes.

"Whoa, there, lass," he says and holds up both hands, palms forward. "I did'na mean anything by it. Just that ye can cause some worry if yer not in yer bed this late," he adds hastily, obviously regretting the previous tack.

He drags a hand over his long hair. "Are ye alright, then?" he asks and seems genuinely concerned with the answer.

"Yeah, I'm fine," I say, opening the door to my room and walking through. "I just don't appreciate a complete stranger acting as if he has *any* right to know where I am at *any* hour, since I'm perfectly capable of making my own decisions on where I should be and when," I chastise, not willing to let him off the hook that easily. "Are you coming in or what?" I ask, turning and seeing him standing unsure in the doorway.

I could really laugh at the hesitation as he tries to decide what to do. Normally, I would not be inviting a guy I just met into my room this late—or maybe at all—but I have a point to prove.

"I..." He shifts from one foot to another. "I should come back in the morn," he says, turning toward the hallway.

I reach out and grab his arm, pulling him into the room and closing the door behind him. "Oh come off it, caveman." I laugh. "You obviously have something you want to talk about or you wouldn't be here in the first place. It's fine."

I goad him further, trying to silence the voice in the back of my head that says it's a dumb idea to invite a hot guy into your room in the middle of the night.

"Aye, but it's not right, me being in yer room this late—an with no chaperone," he attempts to argue, going so far as to place a hand on the doorknob.

"Oh, please stop it. I don't know exactly when you come from, but *please*. This is 2018. If I want a guy in my room, I can have a guy in my room." I roll my eyes and sit on the window seat by my bed. "It's not like we're naked or something, and even if we were, that's my choice, too," I say haughtily.

Okay, I may have gone a bit far with that one, and I think he might just have a heart attack right there. I am not, however, backing down on this one. I don't care if he's from 1092 or 1952, I am a modern woman, and I will not be told what to do by some backwards-thinking old man.

I laugh out loud at that.

"An' just what's so funny to ye then?" he asks, both indignant and confused all at once.

"Nothing," I sigh. "Just. I thought of you as an old man, is all. When really you're basically the same age I am. It's just the way you're thinking," I explain.

Immediately, I know I've made a mistake by the look of horror on his face.

"No. I am not reading your mind." I roll my eyes again. "*Or* your emotions. Actually, you have those on pretty tight lockdown. I can't pick up a thing from you."

I see him visibly relax a little.

"I just meant, the whole 'its not proper' crap. We don't think that way anymore. Not when the girl is an adult," I try again. "It's not like unmarried women in this time need a chaperone. We don't," I further explain, frustrated at his confusion.

"Ah. I see," he says. "So yer a woman grown then? And in this time that means ye do'na need permission to be alone with a man?" He seems really flustered.

It would be endearing if it wasn't so irritating.

"That's right," I confirm. "Also, I can be in a room alone with a man and it can be totally innocent. So don't get any ideas," I blurt out, realizing I may have been giving him other ideas.

"I did'na—"

"Alright, alright. Sorry. Obviously, we're having a bit of a miscommunication here. Just sit, please."

He sits in the chair I pulled into the middle of the room earlier that day. Seems like days and days ago now.

"Now, what is it you needed to talk to me about in the middle of the night, Malakai?" I ask, with maybe a little too much sweetness in my tone.

"I was only walkin, hard to sleep after all that happened today." He stops, weighing what to say next. "I...I did'na feel ye in yer room." He looks down at the floor. "So I waited, to make sure ye were alright."

"Feel me?" I question. "What in the actual hell does that even mean, *feel* me?"

"I was'na even standing there long—"

"Malakai," I say firmly, standing and putting my hands on my hips. "What. Does. That. Mean?" I fix him with my best 'I mean business' stare.

"Ye have an energy bout ye, that's all," he says. "I did'na mean to notice it, I can'na help it."

"Like an Empath?" I ask, curious, more than disturbed by his description now.

"Aye, it's alike," he says. "I can'na feel yer emotions, as such. I can feel yer energy. It does'na happen with everyone, but yers? Yers I can feel across the room," he states, looking at me.

"Uh. Well. Alright then." I pace, trying to make the pieces fit. "So, like, I'm an Empath, right?"

He nods.

"Right, and Aunt Viv, she is an Empath *and* a telepath—"

"Oh Gods. She is'na," he says, standing and knocking over the chair, a scared look on his face.

"Got something to hide?" I ask teasingly and then grow serious as he pales.

"I...I hav'ta go now—" he says, rushing the door.

I get there first and bodily block him from it. No way is he just running away, not when I have questions he may have answers to. "Oh, no, cowboy. I don't think so," I say, placing my hand flat on his chest.

My vision goes hazy, and I feel a little dizzy, when suddenly I can see a meadow. It is full of flowers, and a little boy is running toward me, wooden sword flailing.

"Kai!" he says. "Kai! Come and see what Lyse made!" He giggles and turns to run the other way.

Malakai backs up like I just hit him, rubbing his head and looking at me like I'm the scariest thing he's ever seen.

"Wha—what was that?" I ask softly, taking a step toward him.

He steps back defensively and holds out a hand. "Yer no' just an Empath, Lorali Galloway, that's what *that* was," he replies, keeping space between us. "Yer much, much more'n that." His voice carries both fear and awe.

"Oh, come on. You did that," I plead.

Haven't I had enough shocks and surprises for one day?

"Lass, I did'na." Shaking his head, he plops the chair back upright, standing behind it as if it were a shield.

From me.

Great. Now someone else fears me.

"Malakai—" I start, reaching out again.

"Lorali, please, do'na." He shakes his head slowly. "Me memories are me own, an' I share them as I want; do'na try to take them again."

"*What?*" I practically shriek. "Take them? Oh, come *on*, that is not a thing!"

He says nothing, as if he's done arguing with me.

"Take your memories?" I ask, a little scared myself now. "People can actually do that?"

I sit back down on the window seat, giving him the space he clearly needs.

"Please, whatever you think I did, I didn't mean to do it. I don't even know what just happened."

That's the phrase leaving my mouth as my door bursts open. Both of my parents, my aunt, brother, and Gran all bursting in like I just screamed bloody murder. From the look on my dad's face, the only one who's going to be screaming is Malakai.

Fifteen

"Dad!" I jump up and plant myself between my family and Malakai.

"Jasper." Mom puts a hand on his arm, her tone holding a warning.

"That was a mite quick, was'n it?" Gran asks, chuckling and shaking her head, gaze fixed amused on Malakai.

"Lor, how come there's a boy in your room in the middle of the night?" Toby asks accusingly. "And why'd you yell for me? And why could I hear it in my head? I thought you were in *trouble*." He crosses his arms and pouts a little.

"I didn't, you dork," I snipe at Toby. "Did you have a bad dream or something?" I ask.

"Alright. First, let's all be glad Lor is alright," Mom says, trying to calm the assembled family in my room. "I heard you yell too, baby. Toby came running in our room and said you were in trouble. Then Gran came flying down the hall too. Are you sure you're alright, love?"

Malakai shifts on his feet.

"We'll get to why you're here in my daughter's room in the middle of the night in a minute, young man."

Mom points a perfectly manicured finger at Malakai, who has the nerve to look ashamed.

"I'm not a child, guys, jeez," I complain, doing a little pouting myself now. I'm both embarrassed and infuriated by their

Dad only levels me with a look that clearly says I am so screwed. Mom looks indignant, and Toby looks at me like I just got caught doing more than talking to a boy. Gran, at least, still looks highly amused.

"Oh. come on!" I yell, throwing my hands in the air.

"Lor, we will discuss that later," Dad warns, obviously mad. "Right now I'd like to know why Toby, yer mother, and Gran all heard ye yell for help."

His eyes are firmly fixed on Malakai, as though he's done something horrible, and Dad is simply waiting for the confirmation. It's not lost on me that he's a little hurt *he* didn't hear me too.

"I didn't!" I say. "I don't know *what* you all heard, but I am perfectly *fine*!"

Malakai clears his throat, stepping forward just a little, but keeping his distance from my parents. "I think I know," he starts, "why ye all heard her cry out to ye." He hesitates, shifting on his feet in what I now recognize is his way of showing discomfort or reluctance.

"Oh, out with it, lad," Gran demands. "I would like to sleep at some point, an' I need to know everything is alright here to do so."

"She's as pow'rful as ye are, Lyse," he says. "She can Pull."

Gran gasps, hand to her mouth. Dad looks like someone just stole the air out of the room, and Mom sways a bit before slumping onto my bed.

"That's...that isn't possible," Mom stutters. "Jasper, that's not possible."

She looks at him pleadingly. He reaches out, taking her hand, and looks to Gran.

"Mam?" he says, confusion and fear in his voice.

"What the hell is everyone *talking* about?" I demand. "And why does everyone look like someone just died?"

Gran lays a trembling hand on my shoulder. "Ye best sit, lass. I've some questions for ye, and then ye'll get answers."

Her face tells me I won't have any other choice, so I sit, reluctantly, on the bed next to Mom and wait for everyone else to take a seat. Malakai starts to walk to the door, and Gran puts a hand out to stop him.

"Ye'll sit down right where ye were, lad, I've not finished with ye yet."

She points to the chair in the middle of the room, and he reluctantly turns to sit in it, defeated. I'm sure he was hoping to make an escape while my family was focused on me and whatever he just revealed to them. I shoot him a nasty look at the betrayal, which he has the decency to look slightly shamed by.

"Alright, lass. Now I just want ye to close yer eyes and breathe in. Slowly, that's it," Gran says, voice calm and soothing. "I'm gonna move yer hand now, dove."

She grabs my hand, and I can feel her moving it up higher than where I am sitting.

"Just stay relaxed, now," she says.

I feel the warmth of her forehead under my hand, and again I feel dizzy. Though my eyes are closed, it's as if my vision is covered in a thin haze. It's no longer the dark world behind my eyelids, but a hazy vision instead.

I'm sitting on the ground, snow covering all I can see. I feel a terrible, heart-wrenching sadness, and I can feel tears falling quickly down my cheeks. I scream once, as loud as I possibly can, and pound my fists on the ground in front of me, head falling forward as I double over.

Suddenly, I'm warm again and can feel the bed beneath me, my hand cold from being pulled off Gran's forehead. My eyes fly open, and Gran looks shaken and sad.

"Gran?" I ask, choking back tears that aren't my own.

She sits back on the bed, pats my hand softly, and wipes a tear from her own cheek.

"Gran, what was that?"

"A memory, lass." She sighs, wringing her hands. "Mine, to be clear."

"Oh, Gran." I feel so horrible. Like I lived it myself, and I know without asking—it's the moment she knew the Portal was closed, and her family was on the other side. It's disorienting and confusing. I *remember* it, as though I lived it myself.

"It's alright, dove. That was long ago, and it did'na last forever, now did it?" She smiles sadly, patting my hand.

I fling myself into her arms and hold on as tight as I can. No one else in the room says a word, though I'm certain Mom can feel the sadness flowing from me. I don't know how to hold it back from her, and she reaches out to stroke my hair.

Slowly, Gran pulls back and puts herself up as straight as she can, giving me a smile. "Well then. One thing to do, I suppose." She looks over at Dad, who looks as if he's just been told I'm dying. "They'll not be goin anywhere until I've taught her how to only Pull when she means to."

Dad nods, a mask of indifference settling over his stricken gaze. Mom still looks horrified; Malakai is quiet and brooding but not looking at any of us.

"Anyone wanna tell me what everyone's so upset about?" Toby says, a little too loudly.

I look over, and he's fidgeting with the blanket on my bed, looking between the family in the room.

Suddenly, I hear a loud *bang* right under my window. Everyone jumps up, Dad putting himself between us and the window.

"Well, that's a sight," he says and lets out a long breath, moving out of the way.

Just outside, there's an entire window full of various animals, all looking agitated and like they want to get in.

"What the fu—"

"Lorali!"

"Oh. Sorry..." I have the decency to look shamed. "Uh, I did not do that. I swear," I claim. "I know I don't always know when I do stuff, but I think I'd know—"

"I did it," Toby says in awe, putting a hand up to the glass.

Several of the animals howl, caw, and otherwise acknowledge him, some bumping their noses against my window.

"I just, I thought how much I'd like to go outside and watch the animals and..." he tries to explain.

"Have t' admit, Tob, even I can'na call that many at once," Aunt Viv pipes in proudly, "an' definitely not before I trained that gift."

Toby grins up at Aunt Viv and reaches to open the window. Dad catches his hand before he turns the latch. "Ach, lad. Ye'll be havin em all in yer sister's bed if ye do that," he laughs.

"Aye, just tell them to go for now, lad," Aunt Viv says. "Ye can come out with me in the morn and we'll see what ye've got then, huh?" She ruffles his hair and grins.

It's then that Wesley rushes in, breathing heavily from running. He takes one look around, glares at Malakai, and spins on a heel, slamming my door behind him. Well, shit. I get up to follow him, and Gran stops me.

"I'll deal with him, lass. It's entirely too late an hour for ye to go chasin that lad down." She turns and quietly leaves the room.

Unfortunately, my dad seems to remember it's really late, and I was alone with Malakai. He turns to him with barely contained rage and stomps the few steps to close the distance between them.

I can't even hope to understand the rapid Gaelic they're firing off and look to Mom for help.

"Alright, love. I think the boy understands." Mom slides an arm through Dad's, pulling him back a step gently. I take a breath to speak, and Mom just shakes her head once at me. I guess I can argue the point with my parents later. Definitely when Toby is not present.

"I'll jus' be goin' then," Malakai says quietly, looking at the ground and going for the door.

"Malakai," I say. "Can we talk tomorrow?"

He only nods, without meeting my gaze, and walks out of the room.

Toby gets up, playfully punches me on the arm, laughs, and walks out too. "Glad you're not dying, sis," he says as he walks toward his own room, yawning.

I turn and face my parents, wondering if we are going to have this conversation right now, after all.

Dad looks disappointed in me, then seems to shake it off before speaking. "It's been a long day, Lor. We can talk tomorrow." He kisses me on the top of my head. "I love you, bug."

I hug him hard and reach an arm out to my Mom, who joins us for a sweet embrace. No matter how weird and crazy this thing gets, at least I've got my parents on my side. Always.

The sun streaming in on my face wakes me, telling me I overslept in a big way. I roll, throwing the blankets over my face with a groan. Reaching for my phone, I make a promise to myself that I will call Isobel today. At some point. I should talk to Mom and try to figure out what I'll even say to her. She's definitely going to know something's up. I never let her go to voicemail. Especially not for days on end.

Ugh. 8 missed calls, 4 texts, and 14 instant messages. All Isobel.

Damn it.

I toss my phone back down on the bed, not even wanting to look at the stupid thing anymore. I wonder if she'd buy me losing my phone...or maybe if I say I broke it? That's believable; she'll know I had to go into Glasgow to get it fixed. Maybe I can just use Mom's phone to call, then I can say it isn't fixed yet, buy me a little more time.

This is so stupid, I think, throwing off the blankets and flipping over the edge of the bed, feet hitting the floor.

I have never lied to Isobel; I don't lie to anyone, really. I am not excited to start now. I've always been big on being able to be honest with people, and if you can't...well, maybe you shouldn't have those people around. Where does that sentiment leave me now, that I can't be honest with anyone outside this house?

I shower as quickly as possible, throw on the comfiest sweats and sweatshirt I can find, and slide into my fuzzy slippers. I don't even bother to dry my hair before heading to the kitchen to find some food. I don't run in to anyone on the way, which either means most of the Guardians have left, or there's a meeting going on I wasn't invited to. Either way, I don't care. I'd rather deal with as few people as is feasible right this second, anyway.

I grab a piece of banana bread off the counter, make myself a gigantic cup of coffee, and head into the dining room. I walk in and can't help the smile that jumps out, seeing Aunt Viv and Uncle Seamus sitting at the table, her head on his shoulder and a warm, loving energy coming from them both. I clear my throat so they know I am in the room, and Aunt Viv chuckles quietly.

"I coulda heard ye comin a mile away, dove." She stands, hugs me, and pulls out a chair across the table from them. "Have a sit and enjoy yer breakfast."

Uncle Seamus smiles at me. "Mornin, lass."

I sit and look between the two of them for a second. "This is all I needed for a good morning today." I grin. "I just knew everything was going to work out with you two."

"Aye, yer a smart one, aren't ye?" Uncle Seamus chuckles. "Just needed a bit o' time with it, didn't I?" He looks over at Aunt Viv, running a hand up and down her back. "Tis not everyday ye find yer wife knows what yer thinkin' afore ye do."

"You're amazing, Uncle Seamus," I croon, grinning over a bite of banana bread.

"Ach, lass, dinnae be givin' praise undeserved." He shakes his head. "What kinda man would I be if I walked away from me wife over somethin' she can'na help? She is who she is, is'n she? I loved her afore I knew. Why would I not now?"

He looks so sincere, so full of love, I feel a little emotional about it.

"I'm just sorry I reacted the way I did. Ye should know it was'na what she can do had me upset," he explains. "I could'na understand why she'd not trust me with it til now." He sighs heavily, shakes his head. "I shoulda known she had her reasons, and no' let me pride rule over me heart. The gifts ye all have, they're not to be shamed of, ye ken, lass?"

His gaze bores into me, as if it's the most important thing in the world I know he means what he says.

"Oh, Seamus," Aunt Viv cups his face in her hand, "ye had every right to be upset. I shoulda told ye long ago."

He shakes his head. "No, *mo chridhe*, yer allowed to tell me what ye will in yer own time." He glances at me, then back at Aunt Viv. "I shoulda let ye explain the whole of it before I made me mind up."

I sigh, leaning my head against my hand, admiring the love between them. The fact, even after finding all of this out, they can love with such trust and understanding between them, is so beautiful to witness. Uncle Seamus has always been held in my highest regard, but now? Now he's akin to a saint in my eyes.

"Don't ye settle for less when the time comes for ye, lass." Aunt Viv levels me with a serious stare. "Don't ye forget that lovin' a person, even marryin' a person, does'na entitle ye to anything they can'na or are not ready to give." She reaches out and grabs my hand in both of hers. "Sharin' yer heart with another does'na mean ye can'na still be yer own person just the same."

I know she's not only referring to her current marriage. The warning she's giving is more 'never change who you are' than it is anything else.

"Aye, lass." Uncle Seamus looks at me intently again. "Genuine love will'na demand ye to give what ye can'na."

"Well, truer words were never spoken, Seamus." Mom beams as she walks into the room, a steaming mug of coffee in her hand. "Good morning, bug," she says, dropping a kiss on my hair and pulling out the seat next to me. "Seems we're having very serious breakfast conversation."

"Just explainin' why even a secret so big as mine is'na enough to send my Seamus runnin for the hills." Aunt Viv chuckles.

"Ahhh..." She nods. "I never doubted you once, Seamus." Mom grins at him.

He blushes and stands up from the table, kissing Aunt Viv. "Time for work, it is," he states and walks out of the room, leaving the three of us laughing at the table.

"Never been a man to take much praise," Aunt Viv says. "I ought to go find Toby meself, learn how far he can push his connection with the animals."

Pushing her way from the table, she follows behind her husband, leaving Mom and I quietly sipping coffee.

"How are you doing this morning, Lor?" she turns to me and asks. "We haven't really had any time to talk since we got here and the bottom kind of fell out."

I nod, taking a minute to give some real thought to my answer, knowing she won't take a simple 'I'm fine' this time. "Overall, I guess I'm doing okay. It's a lot to take in, and I have probably a million questions when I think about it." I sigh and take a sip of my coffee. "I know my whole life just changed, in a big way, but I don't think I've really processed that yet, ya know?"

Mom nods but says nothing.

"I can tell people are a little scared of me, some are anyway, and I don't really get that. I mean, everyone here has some kind of superpower, so I guess I don't see why they'd have any reason to be scared."

I pause and look over at Mom, who's throwing off wave after wave of anxiety.

"Honestly, now that I know I'm an Empath, it's so easy to tell all that anxiety is not mine at all."

I pick at the crumbs from my bread.

"I won't lie and say I'm not still a little mad you couldn't have at least told me that much. Do you have any idea how hard that has been? I really thought I had some problem or something, that I couldn't even understand my own emotions half the time. They weren't even *my* emotions." I stop, knowing anything more will only lead to me yelling. As frustrated as I am with my parents, I'm trying so hard to understand they did the best they could. I really don't want this to turn into me telling her what an awful choice she made.

"Sweetheart," Mom begins. "I really didn't know. You've always been so calm. I had no idea you were dealing with that. I didn't think you *were* an Empath, though maybe I should have."

She sighs.

"I don't think I wanted to see it. I know what I went through, being an Empath, before I had a handle on it."

She wipes a tear away from her cheek.

"I *never* wanted this for you," she whispers, the guilt all too apparent on her face and in her voice.

I know she's done the best she could, and I'm not a child anymore. My parents are human, they aren't infallible or without their own hang-ups and issues.

"Why do we even have these things? I mean, I know it's genetic or whatever. But, where did it come from? If magic has been around forever, why don't more people *know* about it?" The questions tumble from my mouth. "Is this like, gift from God type stuff? Am I gonna see a freaking unicorn in the woods? Like what's even real now?" I blurt out, unable to control it now I've started.

"Oh boy. Okay. Jumping right in, huh?" Mom rubs a hand over her forehead. "Where does magic come from? Well, that I don't know exactly, it's always been. A gift from God isn't a bad way to look at it; that's how I see it." She hesitates, biting her lip and looking unsure. Very out of character for Mom. "I don't want to get into the theology of it all, because honestly, I just don't know. I think we've got a lot of stories from a lot of cultures, and I will go so far as to say I believe God—a Creator—exists. Now's as good a time as any to tell you we *know* Angels do."

She takes a deep breath and continues before I can interrupt.

"Everyone's heard of Merlin. Wizard, myth, advisor to Arthur." She nods, as if in encouragement to herself to continue. "What people don't know is he was real, he existed. He's your ancestor, he's Gran's father," she proclaims, finally looking me in the eye.

"Wait, what?" I barely manage to squeak out. I can*not* have heard her right.

"He's an Angel. And no, I've never met him. He disappeared a long, long time ago. Long before I met your father," she rushes out, knowing if she slows down, I'll never let her finish. "It's why Gran is the head of the Order, why she's so powerful, and very likely why you have the type of gifts you have. Why it will make some people scared of you," she finishes, folding her hands on the table and waiting for me to respond.

Leave it to Mom to drop that kind of bombshell and then act as if it's all perfectly fine and normal. Just another Tuesday morning.

"So what on Earth does that make *me*, then?" I ask.

"It very well might make you immortal, Lor. We just don't know," she says. Her eyes are full of unshed tears, fear and hope falling off her in equal measure.

"Immortal?" I gasp. "Like, live forever?" I can't wrap my head around the thought. "What about Dad? Toby? Gran?" My chest tightens. "Mom, what about *you*?"

She shakes her head, and a tear escapes down her cheek. I feel as though someone just ripped my heart out of my body.

SIXTEEN

"Let's go take a walk, Lor." Mom wipes her eyes, pulling herself together. "I could use the fresh air, and I think it'll do you some good as well."

I nod, unable to say anything at all right now. My universe is spinning, everything I thought I knew now clattering around in my head with this new reality.

We walk through the big double doors from the dining room and out onto the pavers of the patio in silence, lost in our own thoughts. I inhale deeply, happy for the fresh mountain air. I take a moment to close my eyes and simply revel in the crisp morning.

Without saying a word, we set off in a direction away from the house, where we are unlikely to run into other people. I don't really know how long we wander along like that, not saying anything, but taking comfort in the other's presence just the same.

"I'm pretty sure unicorns aren't real, but you may want to ask Aunt Viv or Gran about it," Mom says, finally breaking the silence.

Absolutely serious.

I can't help but stop in my tracks and laugh uncontrollably. Mom looks at me for a second, and then she, too, starts laughing. It's just the thing we needed to break us out of the melancholy that has been drowning us.

"Oh, Mom," I say between giggles. "I love you."

She grins at me, wrapping me in a hug as her laughter dies out. We stand there a minute before I pull back.

"Mom, thank you." I say, studying her face. "I know none of this is easy on you, either."

"Oh, baby," she says, moving a strand of hair from my face. "I'll be just fine, as long as you're alright." She sits on the ground, wrapping her arms around her bent knees, her chin on her arms.

I settle down next to her, picking at the grass poking out of the snow. I know there's more she wants to say.

"So I guess we should have a discussion about that boy," she starts, suddenly.

Shit. Not what I expected her to want to talk about. Wonderful.

"Mom," I protest.

"No, Lorali, you need to hear me out here." She waves a hand at me. "I know you're not a child anymore, and we trust you to make your own decisions." She looks over at me with a small smile. "Really, we do. That doesn't mean we aren't going to have a reaction to a boy in your room in the middle of the night. Especially not the first time it happens," she says pointedly. "And I cannot promise you that your father will be as calm about this as I am."

"Mom," I stop her. "It wasn't even like that, anyway!" I exclaim in frustration. "Even if it *were* like that, which *it wasn't*, I'm practically nineteen; I can make those choices for myself," I say, indignantly.

"Lorali. Please understand how difficult that thought has to be for your dad, especially," she pleads. "It's not an easy thought for me, either, you know. It's a hard thing to watch your child become an adult."

"Yeah, Mom, I get it. But still. You've gotta have a talk with Dad. He can't act like that. It's *my* choice," I grumble at her.

"He'll get there, honey. Be patient, and understanding," she repeats, rubbing my back like she did when I was little and throwing a fit.

"Alright, you win," I give in, mumbling. "It wasn't even like that, anyway."

"I know. Emotions were running a tad high. It was already a hell of a day without thinking you were in trouble, only to find you alone with a boy." She nudges me with her shoulder, obviously trying to lighten the mood.

"I get that, I guess. I still don't know why or how you heard me call for help. I wasn't even thinking I needed help."

"Gran says that when you're Pulling someone else's memories, it can allow your own emotions to go a little wild," Mom explains calmly. "I think you just didn't understand what was happening, and subconsciously you called out for your family."

"Oh." I think about it for a minute. "Yeah, that does kind of make sense. Malakai was really upset about it too, and that kind of freaked me out a little to be honest."

"I can't imagine it was expected by either of you," she agrees.

"Understatement of the century." I laugh. "Gran can teach me to control that, though, right?" I ask seriously.

"Yes, love, she can." She smiles at me reassuringly. "There's probably more you can do, things we haven't thought about. Just try to take it slow, yeah? We'll figure it out as we go."

I sigh heavily and nod. The past few days really starting to sink in.

"Ready to go back?" she asks. "I know you've got more questions, but I think little bits at a time is best for now. Give you some time to think things through before we throw more at you?"

"Okay, I'd like to go find the twins, anyway. I think Wes is mad."

"I love your big heart," she says, standing and helping me to my feet. "But if he's mad that his brother was in your room or that he wasn't a part of all of us being there, honey." She shakes her head, looking me in the eye. "That is not your problem, and you owe him no explanations."

I nod, knowing she's right, but still feeling bad. "I just don't want to cause any more problems with them, Mom."

"Oh baby, that's also not something you can control, and you are not responsible for their feelings."

I can tell she'd like to say a lot more, but she holds back.

Seventeen

My mom is big on letting me make my own choices, and about learning from your mistakes. I also know she's worried about my relationship with the twins. For her to have given any warning about how I interact with them is huge.

She hasn't given me advice on how to handle my friendships since I was about eight years old and had a fight with Isobel over sidewalk chalk. To be fair, I haven't really needed her advice since then. Mom only ever stepped in when *I* was the one who needed to change. If I didn't understand by now that *"The only thing in this world that you can control, Lor, is yourself,"* well then, I'd probably never learn that lesson. Thankfully, I learned it at eight.

I caught on pretty quickly how to deal with conflict and how to set boundaries. Both of my parents taught us the importance of setting and respecting boundaries from the time we could speak, but I know she thinks I'm ignoring my own now. Maybe I am. I'm not operating at my best right now with all the added stress, for sure.

I decide to go grab my journal instead of seeking out anyone just then, to get a better grasp on how I'm thinking and feeling about everything. It has always helped me to write out the more complex situations in my life; it helps me to stay level-headed and really understand how I'm reacting to them, and how I can improve that reaction.

I pull my journal out of my backpack and settle in to write it head out to find Wes and Malakai; it's time we had a chat. Before I find either of them, though, I find Toby in the sitting room, engrossed in conversation with a beautiful girl I don't recognize.

"Lor!" he says happily, waving me over. "Come and meet Julia!"

The girl—Julia, I assume—stands and smoothes out the legs of her jeans with her hands, smiling brightly at me. She has absolutely gorgeous, silky smooth, jet black hair, high cheekbones, and the sweetest brown eyes.

"Hi!" she says enthusiastically. "You must be Lorali; I'm Julia." Holding out her hand, she waits for me to respond.

I shake it and smile back. I like the sunshine-y energy coming from her. "Hi, Julia." I grin.

"Julia just got here; she's from Seattle!" Toby explains. "Can you believe it? We could've just used the Portals instead of getting on a plane for an entire day!" He laughs.

"You..." I look over to Julia, perplexed. "You came here through a Portal?"

"Yeah," she beams, "when your mom called and asked for the journals, I just popped right on over!"

"Wait, but I thought you could only go through time?"

"Oh, gosh. No!" She looks sweetly bemused. "Sure, you can use them to move through time, but once you know how to use them, you can go to any other Portal as long as you know where it is you want to go."

"Oh," I say, speechless.

"She brought these really old journals too," Toby rushes on. "Mom gave them to her to study 'cause her family watches the Seattle Portal, but now that we know everything, she had Julia bring them here for us."

"Journals?" I ask.

"Oh!" Julia blushes. "Yes! They're with your mom now, but they belong to your family." She sits delicately back on the chair across from Toby.

I sit down on the arm of Toby's chair, stunned.

"They were written by your great, great, great uncles on your mom's side I think." She looks between Toby and me, obviously unsure what to say to my reaction.

"Sorry," I say, shaking my head. "I just. I guess I didn't realize Mom's family were Guardians too."

"Oh, should I have not said?" She looks at Toby, concerned.

"Nah, it's fine," he assures her. "Lor is just being a drama queen."

"Toby!" I smack his arm. "I am not!"

He laughs, holding his arm. "Chill, sis!" he says. "No need to get all worked up about it."

I wonder silently how much Mom and Dad have filled Toby in. He is taking everything in stride, and significantly better than I am, though I would never, ever tell him that.

"I'm not worked up," I argue, crossing my arms over my chest and glaring at him.

"Whatever," he says, rolling his eyes, "anyway, Julia was telling me how she homeschools and that she had her Affinity test when she was like eight. Can you imagine, Lor? She's known her whole life!" He looks at her with a kind of awe. "Even though the Portals have been closed, she was trained how to use them, and her parents even let her come here all by herself!"

I study the girl more closely; she has to be closer to Toby's age than mine. I can't even imagine Toby traveling by himself, and I'm shocked she could do it so quickly alone.

"It's really not that hard, using the Portals," she says, nodding. "My dad trained me how to do it while they were still sealed. We went through yesterday together. Just a brief trip, to make sure I was okay after we got the call about the journals, and here I am!"

"It has to take more than just knowing how to do it, though, right?" I ask her.

"Not really," she replies sweetly. "Just know the spell, and know where and when you want to go."

"There's a spell?" Toby asks excitedly.

"Yeah, you just stand in front of it, say *Imperium Porta*, hold your destination in your mind, and step through."

"That's...it?" I ask, amazed. Everyone made this sound so dangerous and difficult.

"Basically," is her cheery reply. "I mean, never without knowing you've got an Affinity first, but sure, once you know that, it's easy. Mine is Earth, so I ground myself and...well, you really just walk through."

"Whoa," I hear Toby quietly say next to me.

"Yeah," I agree, "Whoa."

I shake my head, thinking they should both have a little more wariness about the whole thing.

"Can't things go wrong, though?" I ask pointedly. "I mean, even with an Affinity defined, couldn't you end up in trouble?"

"I don't think so," she says, frowning slightly. "My dad didn't say anything about it, and he definitely would have warned me."

"Huh," is all I can muster to say. It's not that I doubt what she's saying; she's entirely genuine. It's just, well, the Council seemed like there was a lot more to be afraid of with the Portals. Is it really *that* simple, as long as you've got an Affinity?

"Julia, you wanna go see the horses?" Toby asks excitedly. "I can even call some deer if you want to see some."

"Sure," she answers. "I'd love to see that!"

They stand, wave at me, and walk out of the room. Julia makes a point of telling me it was nice to meet me on her way. I smile and nod, but am too lost in thought to properly reply. Everyone made it seem so dangerous to travel when we were talking last night.

They said Aunt Viv had a twin who was killed trying to travel. Or lost. Honestly, I don't know if that means killed or not. I'm learning that the specific words they use can mean a lot more than I'd ever think they did. I don't like the feeling that anyone is giving that much thought to their wording, in order to not be forthcoming.

I get up to find someone to ask when I run right into Wesley. Again. That's a dangerous habit I really need to get out of.

"*Oh...*" I stumble, flustered. "I'm so sorry."

He has a hand on my elbow, looking at me with an intriguing mixture of amusement and frustration. "Do ye never look to see where yer goin', then?"

"I—"

"It's a'right, lass. I was a wee bit distracted meself." He smiles and walks to sit in a chair next to the one I just jumped out of. I sit, because honestly I need to speak with him, and he clearly wants the company.

"You okay?" I ask, concerned.

He smiles at me and stares without speaking.

"What?" I rub a hand over my face, thinking I must have something on it.

"Yer brow wrinkles just so when yer worried about another person. I was wonderin' if anyone else noticed."

"Um...I don't—" I've never been so flustered in my life.

"Ye need not be worried over me." He gazes into the fireplace, suddenly serious. "Been a long time since I needed anyone to."

"Wes," I begin, reaching out to put a hand on his arm. "Of course I'll worry. You're my friend. It kind of comes with the territory."

"Even after me temper tantrum?" He sighs. "I should'na have stormed out of yer room that way. I thought ye were in trouble and was overtired. It will'na happen again."

"Was that an apology?" I asked, amused.

He nods, still not looking in my direction. I wonder if he's used to people giving up on him so easily that he expects me to stay angry. That's basically what he's just alluded to.

Really, the whole mopey, self-pity thing should have me running the other way, and usually it would. Guess when you've got very few people you can talk to, the rules change a bit. Besides, I really don't believe he's a bad guy, just maybe a little lost.

"Accepted." I sigh, leaning back in my chair. "Now why don't you tell me what's got you so distracted?"

He finally meets my gaze, and I can't help but see the little boy he once was, full of hope and happiness, behind those sad eyes. It's knowledge I shouldn't have, but I do—and it changes the way I see him.

Catching Malakai's memory of him was an accident, but I'd be lying if I said I wasn't a little thankful for it. One day I'd really like to know what changed him so drastically.

"I do'na deserve yer forgiveness," he whispers.

"Well, that seems like a decision for me to make, doesn't it?"

"I'll do me best to not require it again."

"Wes, we all make mistakes. A good friend can accept us even when we aren't at our best." Frustrated, I stand and put my hands on my hips, facing him. "And if you haven't had a friend like that, well then, you haven't had a decent friend before now, and I suggest you get used to my way of doing things. Heaven knows I'll have bad days too and need the same from you."

I pace in front of the fireplace. Sad and more than just a little angry that he could think a single not-so-great reaction could make me think any less of him.

It's offensive, really. I'm not so easily swayed.

"Usually, before I make up my mind about a person's actions, I have a conversation about it first. At least. We haven't even seen each other much less spoken." I fix him with a stare. "You may not know me well yet, but why would you think I'd just not want to talk to you?"

"I can see I've upset ye, I am sorry." He hangs his head and adds quietly, "I've not had many friends."

"Well, you do now," I say and plop back down in my seat, all the frustration washing away.

I've never been all that great at holding onto emotions like that; it's just so much work to stay mad. Life is much easier when things are calm. Not that I can't get mad, or sad, or frustrated—and stay that way—I just would rather not if I can help it.

Geez, maybe I am like Mom after all, I think in disbelief.

We sit there in silence, listening to the fire crackle, lost in our own thoughts for a long while.

Suddenly, Wesley stands and moves in front of me, holding out his hand. "Come on, then, let's get out o' this house for a bit."

I reach out, let him pull me out of the chair, and tuck my hand into his arm. I can't help but try to hide the grin a little and nudge him with my shoulder teasingly. "Fine, but let's steer clear of Toby." I would rather not see him flirting with Julia again. It's unnerving.

The sun is hidden behind clouds today, but it isn't raining, which is really wonderful. The snow is still crisp and clean. The perks of having a ton of land and not a lot of people, I suppose. I complain a lot about coming here every year, but it really is the most beautiful place for Christmas.

I look up at Wesley and wonder if he has ever been anywhere else. I know he's obviously traveled here. I'm uncertain how long the Portals have been open, but I doubt he's really gone far in terms of geography.

We walk, chatting and laughing about silly little things, just enjoying the day and each other's company. When we get near the place I first ran into him, we turn off towards the trees. I don't know that anyone else should be coming through the Portal, but I would really rather just hang out with Wes right now. It's nice to just talk and laugh and not have to worry about the next thing someone is going to drop in my lap.

"Would ye like to sit and talk a bit? I can build ye a fire," he asks as we walk into a cozy little meadow between the trees.

"Yeah, that would be nice." I smile. "But can I try making a fire with magic?"

"I suppose ye do have the ability," he teases.

"I might need your help, actually. I've never tried it before."

"Well, first let's gather some wood, or yer gonna have me carryin' ye home tryin' to keep it goin' with just yer magics," he says, already starting to grab branches.

I may not want to have any new information thrown at me, but the thought of doing my own magic is thrilling. We quickly build a little stack of branches and twigs, even pulling a large log over to sit on.

"It's not very different from when ye tried calling yer pow'r that first time," he explains. "Yer just gonna make sure ye focus on fire and hold yer hands out, with the wood between 'em."

I hover my hands over the wood and close my eyes.

"Try to picture the flames there between yer hands, feel the heat of it," he says quietly. "When yer ready, say *ignis,* an' let it flow from ye."

I think of the fireplace in the sitting room; the flames dancing around over the wood, the warmth of it on my face. I can feel a warmth growing in my hands, a tingling sensation that is so intense it's all I can focus on.

"*Ignis,*" I whisper.

I feel a blast of heat and then Wesley's arms around my waist, yanking me backward. He throws me into the snow, knocking the wind out of me when he lands right on top of me. I can't see, my cheek is pressed firmly into the snow, and I think at least half my face is covered by it, and Wes hasn't shifted in a good 10 seconds. I worry that he's knocked out on top of me somehow.

"Wes," I manage to force the air out.

"Oh, sorry." He shifts, pulling me up with him. "Ye should probably not try to use Fire again for the moment." He points over to the stack we'd made, that is now nothing more than ash.

Well...damn.

I sink down onto the log that was, thankfully, behind me when I tried to start the fire. Wes is already busy throwing more branches into the burned circle, glancing at me every few seconds but saying nothing.

"Is that...um...should that have happened?" I ask. I already know the answer, but I still need to hear it.

He fusses with the stack of wood a moment, lights it, before he turns to me. "It should'na be that surprising, honestly." He shakes his head, sitting next to me. "Ye could call up pow'r without help, focusin it with a spell...I should'a known better."

"Wesley, you are not responsible for every damn thing," I say hotly. "In case I missed something, you're what? A year or two older than I am? Stop being so hard on yourself." I kick out at the snow, sending it floating around my boot. "Especially in regard to me," I emphasize. "I am not your responsibility, and I was the one who asked for your help to begin with. It *was* stupid, but only because Gran already told me to be careful. *I* didn't listen."

"I am near to 21," he says defensively. "And I may not be much older than ye, but I've had years of trainin' under Lyse. I should'a known." Shaking his head, he sighs and looks over at me.

I don't know if I will ever fully understand what came over me in that exact moment in time. As if I was moving through water, I reach up and brush a stray lock out of his face, my gaze darting between his eyes and his mouth. Before I know it, I have his face in my hands and my lips on his.

I feel his entire body tense. His hands fly up to grab my wrists and push me back. My eyes fly open to see his eyes wide with shock, mouth hanging open. And what do I do? Lean in and kiss him again, my hands up, wrists still in his grip.

Wesley jumps up, dropping my hands and backing several steps away. "Lorali," he starts.

"Oh, God." I cover my face with my hands and shake my head. "I'm so sorry," I say, though I'm not sure he can hear me with my face currently shoved into my palms and my head down. "I don't know why I did that."

I hear his footsteps as he walks to where I sit, completely humiliated. Before he can say anything, I jump up and start walking toward the house, away from him.

"Lorali," he calls, hurrying to catch me.

I ignore him, so utterly embarrassed I could have disappeared right then.

"Damn it all," he says, grabbing my elbow and swinging me around, lifting my face with his other hand under my chin. "I thought ye had to have a conversation afore ye jumped to conclusions?" he asked, searching my face.

I groan in frustration and embarrassment, turning my head away from him and out of his hand. "I don't think we really need to talk about that. Your reaction was pretty clear." I pull back again, only to have both his arms around me, pulling me to him.

"Hell with it, then," he concedes, a hand going to the back of my head as he leans down and kisses me.

Stunned, for a minute I just stand there, before my arms go around his neck, and I give in to the most exquisite kiss I have ever had. Not that I have had many, but no one has ever done it like this.

One hand still cradling the back of my head, his other snakes up my back, pressing me in closer as his tongue darts across my lower lip. He groans, then pulls back and looks down at me.

My hands slide down his shoulders and rest gently on his chest, breathless and dazed. His eyes suddenly dart to the side, and he jumps back guiltily. I look to the right, and there at the edge of the trees is Malakai, looking furious.

"Did'na take ye long, did it *bràthair*?" he spits out venomously.

I look between the two, both seemingly ready to beat the other one into the ground. Stepping into their line of vision, I clear my throat and put up my hands. "Whatever issues the two of you have, I am *not* an object to be fought over," I say firmly, walking towards Malakai. "You want to be disappointed, fine, but my choice in whom I spend my time with is *mine*."

I stop in front of him, hands on my hips and glaring him down. The fury is real, and I am reveling in it at the moment.

"Did ye even stop to think whether it be *his* feelings—" he hurls at me, pointing an accusing finger at his brother, "or yer own before ye made tha' choice, Lor?" He turns on a heel and stomps off back in the direction of the house.

I stand there, stunned at his attitude and the accusation. I look back at Wesley, who looks pale and ashamed, staring off after Malakai.

"You can't...*possibly*...think that was all you," I choke out, taking a step toward him as he takes a step back, his hands going up in front of him. The rejection and the assumption only serve to fuel the rage I'm feeling.

"Aye," his voice trembles. "Why do ye think I did'na kiss ye back the first time?" Sighing, he runs a hand over his face. "I should'na have let that happen."

"Wes," I start, reaching a hand toward him. I am trying so hard to maintain composure, when all I want to do is lash out.

How dare he.

"No, he's the right of it, Lorali." He stops me again, keeping me at a distance. "Can ye be *sure* it's you wanted that kiss?" He searches my face, and seeing my confusion, firmly nods his head. "Right. Then please do'na try to kiss me again until ye do know."

He motions toward the house briefly but refuses to look at me. I'm so stunned, I do the only thing I can think of and turn to walk away.

The walk back to the house is tense, and neither of us says a single word the entire way. Once we reach the door, Wes turns and walks back toward the river, only nodding in my direction before leaving me there. I open the door quietly and make my way to my room as quickly as I can, hoping I don't run in to anyone.

Luckily, I don't see any of my family as I make my way through the house. I do catch a glimpse of Malakai as I walk down the hall to my room—running the last few steps and refusing to meet his eyes as I slam the bedroom door shut. Resting my head against the door, I listen as his footsteps stop in front of my door, hesitating. He keeps moving down the hall. It's the last straw for me, and I can't help it when I smack the door as hard as I can.

No longer able to stand on my own feet, I rotate and slide my back down the door, bringing my knees to my chest and wrapping my arms around them as I hit the floor. I stare off into space for a second, just trying to get my thoughts under control enough to even have a coherent one.

It's futile, and all I can do is focus on the emotion of it all, this time all my own, I know. I lay my head on my folded arms and let the heartache and anger wash over me, again and again, tears falling silently, chest aching. My body poised tightly, wanting desperately to lash out and having no outlet to do so.

Rationally, somewhere in the part of my brain that's still functioning, I know this is an overreaction. I know, logically, that I'm having this overwhelming emotional experience because of all that's been thrown at me the past few days. Logic isn't doing a lot for me right now though, as I roll onto my side on the floor, arms still wrapped around me.

I look up to the bed and think how much more comfortable I'd be there, I but can't find the strength to get even that far. The sadness overtaking the rage, I simply allow it to wash over me, wracking my body as tears soak my face.

Between silent sobs I hear my door slam open, my Mom gasp. I don't hear a word she says, but feel Dad's arms lift me and put me on the bed, Mom stroking my hair back and making soothing noises. A part of me feels silly and guilty.

Why can't I just snap out of this?

I feel as though I'm a million miles away, the rational part of me, anyway. Totally helpless to what's physically happening. Instead, I just lay there and cry myself into exhaustion, falling asleep without even acknowledging my parents once.

I do hear the storm outside, though, as violent and wild as my emotions tonight. The last thought I have before succumbing to numbing sleep is that I wish I could just release all my feelings into the wind and rain, scream my pain like thunder and lightning, and be done with it all.

Eighteen

I am walking through a meadow full of wildflowers. I recognize it; it's the same one I saw in Malakai's memories. That feels like a lifetime ago, now. I reach down, running my hand along the tops of the flowers, inhale the purest air I've ever smelled. The sadness I felt still there, but more relaxed now than I was.

"Hello there, gorgeous," a voice says, arms wrapping around my waist from behind. "What are ye doin out here by yer lonesome then?"

I stiffen, turning halfway to tell him off, then realize it's a dream. I wonder why *this* dream tonight, of all nights. I look up into Malakai's emerald eyes, smiling down at me. Sure as hell beats the disappointment I saw there the last time.

"What's wrong now, lass?" He brushes hair from my face and looks at me intently. "Ye were just fine a moment ago. What has ye so melancholy now?"

I look up at him and marvel at how concerned and attentive dream Malakai is. So, so different from aloof, cold, real life Malakai. I shake my head, smiling, and turn the rest of the way to completely face him.

I suppose in my dreams, I can make him behave any way I'd like, and why lie to myself? I'd love it if he treated me this way in real life.

"Nothing, just lost in thought is all," I lie, smiling sweetly at my subconscious version of the man I've had several

"I do miss this meadow," he sighs, kissing my forehead before taking my hand and leading me further into the flowers. I allow myself the indulgence of his hand on mine, his attention and care. "Wesley and I never had a single bad day here. I only wish we could'a stayed that way."

"You'll work through this, Kai. You're not just brothers, you're twins," I say, squeezing his hand. It feels nice to use the nickname I've called him only inside my head out loud. Something I would never do in real life, he'd probably lecture me if I tried. Here, I can give in to the fantasies I won't allow myself while awake.

"Ach. Some fences can'na be mended, *bràthair* or no'," he says sadly, shaking his head. "Let's not allow dark thoughts to make us sad. Not here," he proclaims, whirling me back into his arms. "I can think o' much better ways to pass the time." He grins wickedly and pulls me closer. Heat rockets through me, his body deliciously pressed against mine.

"Can you?" I ask, giggling. *What harm is there in indulging myself here?*

"Aye, and talk o' me brother is not on that list."

He traces a hand down my face, along my collarbone. My breath hitches, and my eyes flutter closed. I hear him chuckle and feel his lips kissing a path along my collarbone, up my neck. My head falls ever so slightly back, allowing him freer access.

Well, I guess subconsciously it is Malakai I'm thinking of.

I don't want to think too much about what that might mean in regards to the day's events.

I grasp his head in my hands and pull his face to mine. He looks at me for just a second before his mouth crashes into mine, his hands in my hair. He kisses me fiercely, then sinks us onto the ground, a hand at my waist and one still in my hair.

I pull back a little, both of us kneeling on the mossy ground, looking up into his face. Dear Heaven Above, now *that* was a kiss. I'd do a lot to be kissed like that again, by him. I lean forward, intending to do exactly that.

"Ye are the most beautiful woman, Lor," he says, a finger tracing my cheek.

I timidly place my hands on his shoulders, pushing him back into the flowers, and am rewarded with a chuckle. He pulls me down, and I find myself kissing him with more passion than I've ever felt before. We roll until his chest is halfway across mine, and I feel his hand creep up my torso. I gasp and slightly shift to allow his hand to drift up to my breast.

I hear him groan, his hand instead going behind my neck, his lips moving from my mouth to my collarbone as my head falls back. A shiver of electricity runs from his lips to my core, and I can't help the moan that escapes my lips.

My hands bury themselves in his hair as I pull him as close to me as I can. He obliges me, a hand sliding under my shirt to my waist, the fabric bunching underneath me as it slides up. His mouth trailing down to meet his hand now on my breast, my back arching to meet him. He pulls back, looking down at me, and I whine in protest, pulling at him, my eyes still half closed.

He chuckles, then sighs. "Lovely as ye are, I think I'd rather wait for reality. Even if it ne'er comes," he says, as he sits back, looking at me sadly.

It's as effective as ice water over my head. "Seriously?" I push myself up. "Even in a damned dream I get rejected?" I say in disbelief.

Malakai shoots to his feet, looking absolutely terrified. "What?" he asks, in shock.

"Oh, *whatever*," I say, standing and brushing myself off, furious. "I can't even let myself have *this*?"

"Lorali?" he demands, grabbing my arm.

"No. I'm the milkman." I wrench my arm from him and spin around. "Ugh. How the hell do I end a stupid dream?" I ask out loud, looking around. I'm not usually quite so lucid when I dream, and I've never had to think about ending one. Typically, they are much more pleasant.

"Lorali," he says firmly. "Lorali, are you dreaming?"

"Duh," I say without even looking back. "And I have to say, this is the worst dream ever. Good going, brain," I huff. "Can't even escape my problems asleep now."

I turn toward him, arms crossed. Except he looks really, really livid.

"Whoa," I say, holding up my hands. "Alright, yeah, calm down, dream Malakai."

What does it mean when you dream up new rejection? Maybe I need a therapist.

"I am not a figment o' *yer dream*, Lorali," he spits out, enraged.

"What?" I say, horrified, my eyes going wide, heart pounding in terror. "This is a dream," I gasp, confused.

He only shakes his head, storms up to me, and says, "I suggest ye wake the hell up *now*, lass." His green eyes looking down at me are full of irritation.

I shoot up in my bed, gasping. My whole body is shaking, and I look over to the armchair pulled by my bed where Mom is asleep. There's the smallest light coming through my windows, letting me know it isn't quite dawn yet.

My heart is pounding, my breath shaky as I throw the covers off me and gently touch the cold floor with my bare feet. I sit there for a minute, just trying to get myself under control before walking quietly into my bathroom, careful not to wake Mom.

I close the bathroom door and lean over the sink, turning on the tap. I shake my head and splash some water onto my face, then stare at my reflection in the mirror. I can see the dark circles under my puffy eyes from my crying jag last night, but otherwise I look like myself, I think. I decide a hot shower, some clean clothes, and a little self-care is exactly what I need right now, and turn on the shower.

Thankfully, I have a clean set of sweats and a nice, baggy sweatshirt already folded on the counter, so I don't have to go back into my room and worry about waking my mom. I'm certain she needs the sleep. Knowing her, she stayed up half the night watching me sleep and worrying about me.

I can't blame her. I all but had an entire nervous breakdown. Then that damned dream. Ugh. My mind could've been nice enough to allow me to find some solace there, but *no*. I have to dream up a scenario in which Malakai rejects me too.

One twin just wasn't enough.

I step into the shower and let the water wash over me, soaking my hair and enjoying the warmth. I wonder again about what that dream was, and what it could have meant. Surely I didn't actually meet *real Malakai* in my dreams, right?

It had to have been just my own weird subconscious crap pouring into my dreams. I've heard people talk about Astral Projection; I do live in Tacoma after all. Lots of hippy, dippy, new age, witchy stuff—as Isobel would say—out there.

A lot of my friends have talked about that stuff over the years. More than one has dabbled in it. My dad explained lucid dreaming when I was about 10 years old because I was having nightmares.

Actually - *even for a lucid dream, that was really weird,* I admit to myself. Usually, I have more control.

I turn off the shower and wrap myself in a towel, pulling out my brush and hair dryer. As I dry my hair, I try to remember if I have ever heard of anyone actually interacting with another person in their dreams. Honestly, I don't think I ever have. That couldn't have been what actually happened.

It had to have been my subconscious trying to deal with everything that happened yesterday, sort out my feelings and all that. Firmly deciding that is exactly what actually happened, I pull on my clothes and decide against putting on any makeup after all. I take a deep, calming breath before opening the door to my room, knowing my mom is awake and waiting on me to come out.

I step through the door, and Mom is standing right there, waiting to pull me into a smothering hug. I can feel how anxious and worried she is, and I just hug her back tightly. She pulls back, holding me at arm's length and looking me over.

"I'm okay, Mom, really," I assure her. "I just got overwhelmed, that's all."

"Oh, love," she says, holding my face in her hands as she searches my eyes. "I am so sorry. We should have made sure you were actually processing everything."

She looks down guiltily. Neither of us really knows how to react, as I've never actually had a total meltdown before.

"I never, *ever* wanted you to have to deal with any of this. I think I took for granted how well you seemed to be handling it all."

"Mom, really, it's my own fault. I didn't take the time to deal, ya know?" I smile at her, trying to put her at ease. "I just needed to let it out and get some sleep. Promise."

A knock sounds on my door, and I stiffen a little, causing my mom to study me a little more closely. Before she can question it, I slip from her grip and walk to open the door, hoping desperately it isn't either of the twins.

"Well, lass, ye've made a mess o' it now, have'n ye?" Gran says, exasperated, as she glides past me into my room.

"Gran?" I ask, closing the door and facing her.

"Do'na ye Gran me," she says sternly. "We've got to get this under control 'afore ye do more damage than can be managed."

"Lyse?" Mom says concerned. "What's going on?"

"Yer girl is out o' control is what's goin' on, Cadence," Gran replies, shaking her head. "An I'm here to make sure she gets a handle on it, I am. Pullin' people's memories and walkin' into their dreams." She turns to my mom and pats her hand.

"*No*," I manage, a shaking hand covering my mouth as I fall into the chair Mom slept in.

"Oh, aye, lass." Gran sits on the edge of my bed and fixes me with a serious stare. "Do'na worry now, there are things we can do to make sure ye do'na keep invadin' into people's heads."

"Oh, *no*." I put my head in my hands, trembling. "Oh, please, *please* tell me that was just a dream."

"I could, but it would be a lie, lass," Gran says, more sympathetic now. "An I do'na lie."

"How did you—" I ask.

"Malakai came bangin on me door he did," she confirms. "Said if we did'na get ye under control, he'd go home until we could."

"*No*," I groan, horrified. "I didn't even know I could *do* that! I didn't know anyone could!" I look frantically between them, searching for the assurance I know they can't give.

"Ach, ye've called yer pow'r to wake up, and I shoulda known better than to think it would'na cause chaos," she huffs. Standing, she looks down at me regally. "Now there's no time to be feelin' sorry for yerself. Malakai is a grown lad, and he knows this is'na yer fault. It is time to take responsibility for it, though, and learn to use it only when ye mean to."

She brushes a hand over my hair lovingly, apologetically.

"I'll admit to some fault in this. Had a mind to let ye work it out yerself, see what pow'r ye might have. Was damned foolish of me, it was. I should'a known ye would be a pow'r to rival me Da's."

"Yeah, yeah, okay," I say, stunned but determined to fix this. I'll figure out how to look Malakai in the eye ever again later. "What do I need to do?"

"I think a bit o' my tactics and a bit o' yer Mam's will be best." She nods, looking over at Mom. "Cadence, why don' ye start by tellin' her how ye manage?"

Mom looks between Gran and me for a moment before nodding her head and sitting down on the bed, facing me. "First, you're going to want to get comfortable, and close your eyes," she instructs. "Now, I want you to focus on the feelings coming at you. Not your own feelings, just at what you're feeling around you from other people."

I close my eyes, taking a breath, and try to identify any emotions or feelings that aren't mine. I think I can feel some anxiety pushing in at me, but I am anxious myself, so I don't really know. I sigh in frustration and pop my eyes open. "Mom, how do I even know what's someone else's and what's mine?"

She opens her eyes, leans her head to the side, and thinks for a minute. "Well, okay, imagine that you just got something you really, really wanted. Got it?" she asks, and I nod. "Okay, so focus on how that makes you feel, really hone in on it, try and make it the strongest thing you're feeling."

I nod, eyes closed.

"Now, try to hold on to that, but also see if you can sense anything else, any emotion that's fainter, probably something totally opposite of what you're feeling."

I try to feel anything else, and I get a faint wave of anxiety, sadness. "Got it," I say.

"Now, can you feel how it's different? For me, it always feels almost like other people's feelings are pushing in at me, my own kind of push outward, if that makes sense," she explains.

"Oh!" I shout, suddenly understanding. "Yeah, oh *wow*. That's actually really obvious now," I say, surprised.

I can feel how Mom's anxiety, her sadness, is pushing in at me, fainter and a little detached. I try again to see if I can feel anything else and get the tiniest hint of pride, but it vanishes just as quickly.

"Stop tryin' to search for it now, lass. That's a lesson for another day," Gran pipes in, slightly amused.

I know without asking, the pride was hers.

"Okay, now, you need to remember what that difference feels like. Sometimes other people can have emotions so strong, it almost feels like your own," Mom cautions, as if I didn't already know that. "It's going to take some effort for a while, but you can block out other people. I want you to envision a wall, or a moat, or whatever image feels right, picture it surrounding you, nothing in or out without permission," she explains.

I think of the river behind the house, how swift it is, how deep. No one is crossing that without a boat. I picture myself standing on an island in the center of it, where nothing can reach me. For good measure, I picture a shield of pure energy, purple like my Spirit Afinity, and anything that tries to get through gets zapped.

I can see the emotion flowing toward me and see the sparks as it hits the shield.

"Very good, Lor!" Mom commends. "I can't feel anything coming off her, can you, Lyse?"

"Not a thing," Gran exclaims proudly.

I open my eyes and look at them, both smiling and looking proud. I sit a little straighter, realizing I feel less overwhelmed suddenly, and let out a small sigh of relief. "Oh," I mutter, "oh wow."

Gran nods, understanding. "Ye need to focus on keeping that up all the time, lass," she says. "An' that might be a little difficult at first. It does become second nature, ye just need to be aware of yerself."

"Is that it?" I ask, looking at Mom.

"That's all I can show you. I don't know if that's enough though." She sighs, looking at Gran. "She's much stronger than I am."

"It should be plenty as far as when she's awake." Gran frowns, looking around the room. "Is there anything ye wear all the time, lass? A trinket or anything?"

I shake my head; I used to have a bracelet I wore all the time, but I left it at home.

Gran reaches into her collar, pulling out a gorgeous Amulet. It looks just like the one Aunt Viv had on at the Gathering, except smaller and on a chain. She pulls it over her head and holds it towards me.

"Lyse, no," Mom chokes out, horrified.

"This was me Da's," she says quietly, completely ignoring Mom's protests. "It's already covered in protection spells, an will keep ye from using whatever pow'r ye've got without intendin' to do so."

"Lyse, please, don't do this. At least let me get Jasper, *please,*" Mom begs, her voice cracking, standing to leave.

"Tis time, lass. Sorry I am for it, but it can'na be helped. It'll protect her, ye know it will," Gran chides and holds it out for me to take.

I glance at my mother, who looks lost and helpless. She stifles a cry with a hand to her mouth and gives the briefest of nods.

I gently take the Amulet, about the size of the palm of my hand, and gasp at the rush the second it touches my skin. The power of it is so strong, even I can feel it. I sit there a minute, just looking at it, and notice it has tiny emeralds for eyes, just like Aunt Viv's brooch—these seem to sparkle slightly, almost shimmering.

The metal is a warm reddish gold color, and as I hold it, I can feel it warm against my skin. Along the edges of its body I can make out little markings.

Runes maybe?

A tingling between my eyes is the last thing I am aware of before I'm suddenly above an odd scene, an unnoticed observer.

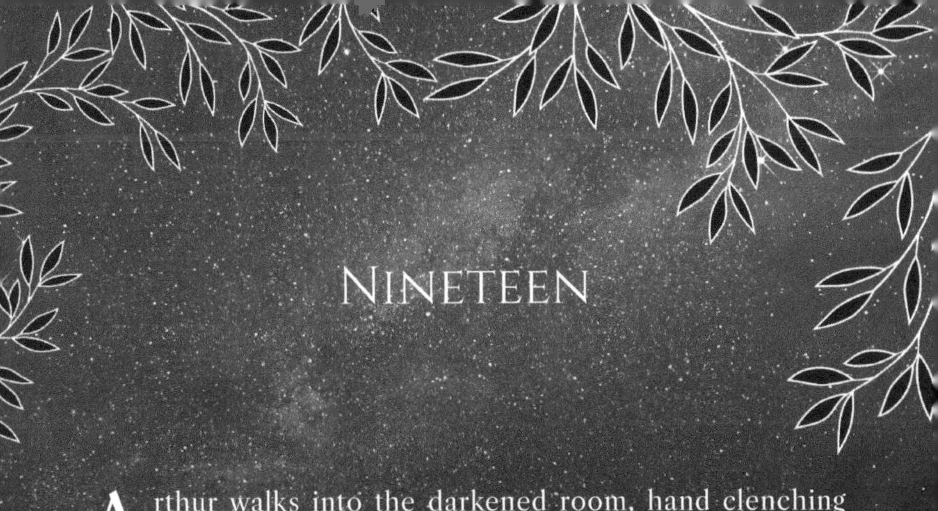

Nineteen

Arthur walks into the darkened room, hand clenching against the cool metal. As worried as he is about Merlin's erratic behavior, the paranoia, the secrecy—he could never betray him. Merlin has been his life-long friend, his strongest ally, his protector.

No, he trusts Merlin implicitly. It doesn't matter what the others say, how they advise him to sever ties. Merlin had been their salvation, whether or not they ever knew of it.

All he asks for is a piece of metal, really, Arthur rationalizes to himself. *A piece of metal and most of my magic, but that's alright long as it protects his line. They'll need every bit of it if the Oracle has it right.*

"Arthur! Hurry now, hurry. I have'na got much time." Merlin rushes around the piles of stones, tools, crystals and gems lying in piles haphazardly between tables. As he comes to Arthur, he reaches out and squeezes his shoulder, absently grinning at him—though it doesn't quite reach his eyes.

"Did ye manage to get it? The Pendragon Amulet?" His eyes meet Arthur's with a feverish zeal.

"Aye." Arthur lifts his hand, opening it to reveal a dragon made of copper glinting in the scarce light.

"Ach! That's it my boy! That's it!" Merlin slaps him on the shoulder, then gently lifts the dragon in both hands.

Turning it, examining it, he shuffles over to the fire crackling in the corner of the room. As he passes by a low table, a hand darts out to grab a pair of emeralds. Without glancing back, he waves at Arthur, motioning him to follow. "I'll need ye to help with the incantation, lad. Just as we practiced."

Arthur reaches Merlin's side as Merlin sets the objects down along a ledge in front of the fire, next to a chunk of gold. Raising his arms, a bright light flashes as he creates a barrier between them and the outside world.

"We've not much time, lad. Just as we practiced now, aye?" he asks as Arthur nods emphatically.

Merlin's hands begin to move in a pattern Arthur can't identify, the copper dragon lifting into the air in front of him. The gold slowly lifts into the air as well, until the two are almost touching, suspended above the fire. Arthur watches, enthralled, as the two begin to meld into one, the shape of the dragon never compromised or changed.

He knew, of course, what would happen. They'd gone over the process hundreds of times in the past moon. To see it happening, to watch the copper slowly glow from within as it became a deeper, warmer color. It was the most beautiful magic he'd seen in his life.

"*Annuo,*" Arthur offers, his hands going up as he wraps Air around the Amulet to cool it. "*In Aeternam.*"

I give my consent to bind our magics for eternity.

Merlin is consumed in his own incantations. The language he speaks flowing like a song from his lips, the Ancient Ones lending their powers to the process. Arthur can feel their presence like a heavy mist, pressing in, moving through everything.

A woman's face emerges from the fire, her dark hair swirling around her face. Arthur doesn't need to see her face to know who she is. The Lady Morgainne. "*Annuo,*" she reluctantly offers, her face a mask of annoyance and defeat. "*In Aeternam.*"

The words barely leave her lips as an unbearable heat sweeps over him, the gems embedding themselves into the Amulet to serve as eyes. A barely visible stream of purple light emerges from each of their chests, meeting and intertwining around the

Amulet. Merlin attempts to cover a gasp as his chest lurches forward with the amount of power leaving his body.

Morgainne screams, her head flung back as she agonizes. Only Arthur is left standing. What little power he had been given was pulled away with hardly any notice. The two Divine beings in obviously more distress, as their very existence relies on the power within them. Arthur can see an outlining shimmer, the suggestion of wings, fluctuate in and out of sight behind them.

"It is done," the Lady snarls before vanishing from sight once more.

Merlin falls against Arthur, grasping the newly created object in his hand. In his weakened state, the barrier he erected to protect them comes down in a flash of light. "Ye must find her, Arthur. Analyse must have it, or all we've fought for is lost. Go now, lad. Go now," Merlin whispers, pushing away from Arthur to slump against the wall.

"I'll do as ye ask, Merlin. Please, protect yourself while I'm gone," he begs, standing and rushing out.

The Amulet in his hand pulses once before quieting, the magic given it acknowledging a goodbye to its former home. Merlin, overcome with a great sense of loss, sobs loudly as Arthur vanishes from sight.

Swaying slightly, Gran grasps my forearm and whispers softly enough I know Mom doesn't hear, "Say nothing of what ye saw, dove."

"Gran, are you sure?" I ask, raising my eyes to look at her. She looks wistful and thoughtful, but not upset.

"Aye, child. Ye could'na even touch it if it was'na meant to be yers. It's time to hand it down." Smiling sweetly, she stands and takes it, pulling the shimmering chain over my head. "Tuck it into yer clothes now, dove. No one needs know ye've got it yet."

I look over at Mom, who is eerily quiet, and see that she's got tears in her eyes. "Mom?" I ask, reaching out to her.

She shakes her head, patting my hand but saying nothing.

"Oh now, come, lass." Gran wags a finger at Mom. "Ye knew it would be one o' them, and after seein' her Affinity, an hearin from Wesley what she can do with a spell..." She sighs and pats Mom's shoulder. "Ye had to know, truly, it was always goin' to be her."

It takes all my willpower not to demand they explain what they're talking about, but I know I'll likely learn more by letting it play out. All of this is somehow connected to what I saw when I took the Amulet.

I don't understand why Gran wants my silence about it, when I have so many questions. Surely Mom knows how it was created, and why would that need to be a secret, anyway? There is so much I do not know.

"Honestly, I hoped we'd never have to find out," Mom says in a stony voice, her face a mask of fury.

"Aye, love, I would have stayed forever if it meant keeping the bairns from havin' to pick up the sword themselves," Gran admits, melting into the window seat.

"Oh, Lyse. You know that's not..." Mom starts, the fury rushing away at the realization of her words. She looks horrified at herself now instead.

"Oh now, it is, Cadence, and ye know it. An' that's perfectly natural. We always want to protect our babes." Gran looks over to me, vulnerable, then seems to draw within herself before standing. "Lorali, I meant what I said, no one needs know ye've been handed the Amulet. Not yet. Yer parents, yer family, that's all; not even the twins need know now. Do ye understand?" she demands, forcefully.

"Yes, Gran," I agree, nodding. "But why? What does having it mean?" I finally ask.

"It means yer Merlin's heir, dove." She takes my hand, squeezing it. "It means ye'll live with a target on yer back, an' the mantle of leadership on yer shoulders."

Gran turns, looking out the window wistfully.

"It means yer gonna be hard to kill, ye'll age slower than most, an' ye'll have more pow'r in ye than anyone has a right to. Yer born of Angels, dove, with all their pow'r and none of their guidance." She sighs, turning back to me, the betrayal evident in her voice. "Ye can'na tell by lookin' at me, lass, that it's been 298 years since me birth. Me Da was Merlin, me Mam the Lady Morgainne." She holds up a hand at my gasp, urging me to let her finish.

Silencing me again from speaking of what I've seen.

"The stories ye heard of em were nothin but stories. Aye, a grain o' truth that they were pow'rful and helped to save a land from evil. What the stories do'na tell ye is that he was an Angel, and she half herself. Me Mam is a hard, cold woman, an does'na interfere with the affairs of the human race. Not anymore."

"So she's alive?" I ask, "And you, you're what? Immortal? Divine?"

"The truth is we do'na know. I age, grow older, but it is very slowly. I've had wounds that should 'ave killed me more than once, an not died. I did'na show in the grave here the past twenty years, but I also did'na come here in this time. I died, or I was unable to come for a reason I do'na know yet while the Portals were closed."

"What could have possibly kept you from your family? For twenty years? Is Grandfather like you? Dad? Toby?"

"Yer Granda is'na. His Mam was born of an Angel mother, a mortal father. His Da was a Guardian, but no Divine blood. He has aged slower than a mortal man, but he can be killed. He's been near to death more than once. Yer Da is more like me, though we do'na know how far that goes."

She looks regretfully over at Mom, who is sitting stiffly, a tremor in her hands. I don't particularly want to think about the implications of that statement right this moment.

"I can say wit fair certainty that ye'll be most like me, as the Amulet has chosen ye as its next bearer. There will be no tellin' with Toby until he gets older."

I look down at the Amulet, holding it gently in one hand. Such a small thing to mean so much. Such a small thing to be exuding as much power and magic as even my untrained self can feel rushing off it. "Okay. Well, what now?" I ask, looking between Mom and Gran expectantly.

"Now I think that's enough of this for one day," Mom replies. "Unfortunately, it's not up to me anymore. So, Lyse, what next?" She looks over at Gran, and even without being able to actually feel her emotions, the tension is palpable. I know without a doubt in my mind that if I could feel her emotions right now, it would be an unbearable pain.

"I think you have it, love." Gran smiles at Mom. "It's enough for now, an she will'na be goin' around usin' her pow'r without meanin to. T'morrow is soon enough to start learnin' how to use what she's got." With that she stands, kissing me on the top of my head and giving my shoulder a small squeeze, leaving my room.

It's just Mom and I, sitting awkwardly in silence. I think she's a little embarrassed at how she handled that. She's always so in control and composed, and I know she works hard to be that way. "I should probably go find your father." She stands and smoothes out her pants. "You need to eat and relax, bug. You've had a lot happen in a very short amount of time. Don't feel like you need to sort it all out in one day."

"I know, Mom." I look down at my hands, fidgeting with a hangnail.

"Don't be so hard on yourself. You can't control what you can't control. Everyone will understand that, even if it caused some uncomfortable situations."

I wonder just how much Wesley told my family yesterday, and how much she's guessed about Malakai. Even with a block in place, she's my mother, and they don't need magic to know when their child is struggling. Or to know what may or may not have happened in what I thought was a dream.

"I know you're young and impulsive, and just becoming an adult," she starts, as though she *could* read my mind. "Just...don't feel like you've got to jump into anything romantic. You've only just met them both, Lor."

She holds up a hand at my sharp intake of breath to argue with her.

"I am still your mother, and I can see the looks between you without anyone saying a thing. It's very easy to get caught up in high-stress situations, just promise to remember that."

I nod, knowing it's easier said than done. Also knowing she is making a really good point that I should actually take heed of.

"Mom—" I hesitate, but decide if I can't trust my mom to confide in at this point, who have I got? "I think I created a serious mess here. I kissed Wes yesterday."

Mom folds her arms and stares at me.

"I kissed him, and Kai saw and said it was stupid because it was probably Wes wanting the kiss and not me and then—"

"And then you walked right into one of Malakai's dreams?" She raises a perfect brow.

"Yeah. That," I say, resting my head in my hands and groaning. "It's not like I meant to. It just happened," I explain.

"I don't need to know details, but I'm going to guess the dream wasn't entirely devoid of romance?"

"Um, you could say that..."

"Oh, Lor." She kneels down in front of me, pulling my hands away from my face. "Listen to me, sweetheart. This is a complicated situation—period. Adding in romantic feelings? That's a lot to wade through. I can't tell you what to do or how to handle it. All I will say is to be true to your heart. That should be a little easier now, being able to block out other people's emotions."

"Yeah, I guess. But what if Kai was right, and that kiss *was* all Wes? He's going to be so hurt." I know I am pouting, and she hates that, but I can't help it. "I had to have wanted to kiss him on some level, right? I mean, can someone really influence you *that* much?"

"Relationships are messy. I don't know a single person who hasn't hurt or been hurt in love. That's life, bug, and that's okay. It's all about how you handle it, and as long as you aren't malicious, you've done all you can." She brushes the hair out of my face. "The only thing you can do is be honest and fair. Don't play games with other people's hearts and emotions, no more than you'd want them doing that to you."

I wrap my arms around her neck and sigh heavily. It might be a little weird, talking guys with my mom, but I know she will always help me become the best version of myself I can be. She will always try to protect me, and help me to deal with anything life throws my way.

"Thanks, Mom." I let her go, and we both stand. "I think I am gonna go get some food. Tell Dad what you have to...but maybe leave out the twins? I really am fine, and it would only freak him out more."

She laughs a little, shaking her head, and kisses my forehead before she goes off to find Dad. I really am hungry, but as much as I want people to stop worrying, I don't know if I really want to deal with either of the twins yet.

To procrastinate just a little longer, I drag out my iPad, but realize it's dead. Plugging it up to charge, I tidy up the room a bit and realize I need to just suck it up and go to the kitchen. I can't avoid the inevitable forever, and I feel like the coward I am hiding in my room like this.

Throwing my hair up into a messy bun, I grab a warm throw, wrap it around my shoulders, and head out of my room. The house is quiet, and I know that's because it's so late in the morning. Most everyone will be out and about for the day—well, except those of us visiting. We don't exactly have to go to work right now.

I wander into the kitchen and open the fridge, not really wanting to actually cook myself anything. I grab a container of Greek yogurt and find myself some dark chocolate granola to mix into it. Once I have my sort-of-healthy but still yummy breakfast, I decide eating in the sitting room by the fire sounds perfect and plop myself into the chair closest to the fire.

I love that it burns pretty continuously. Stuart keeps it going until late at night and always keeps the wood stocked close so anyone can feed it throughout the day.

Sitting with my legs pulled under me, throw pulled tight around me, I dig in and watch the flames dance. My thoughts quickly wander back to the twins and the very different intimate situations I found myself in with each of them. That kiss with Wesley, at the time, was wonderful. The problem is, now that I'm sitting here by myself thinking about it, and him, I have absolutely zero romantic feelings at all.

Sure, he's sweet, and I really enjoy spending time with him—and yeah, I definitely thought he was hot when I met him. That's the problem though, being physically attractive has never been the 'be all, end all' for me, and he really feels like a friend. I know that means Malakai was probably absolutely right about who wanted that kiss after all, but it doesn't assuage my guilt in the least.

I finish my bowl and set it on the end table next to me, wrapping myself in the blanket further. Malakai, on the other hand... He's hot; obviously, they look almost identical, but he does not feel *friendly*. I mean, yeah, I guess we could be friends. He's just not familiar like that.

I always feel just a little off balance around him, and my heart beats just a little bit faster. Which is crazy because he's *not* comfortable like Wes. He's aloof and cold and...and when he does relax a little, he's comforting and funny and smart.

Damn it. I really do have a crush on Malakai.

TWENTY

I wake up to the sound of wood being thrown onto the fire, my head resting on the high back of the chair, curled up against it. I sit up, rubbing my eyes, stretching my legs out. Dad turns from feeding the fire, a warm smile on his face.

"Good to see ye up and about, bug," he says, sitting on the edge of the fireplace, hands clasped in front of him on his knees. "I won't lie and say ye did'na scare me a bit."

"Yeah, I know, I'm so sorry Dad." I sit back and sigh. "I just got really overwhelmed, and it just all came out at once."

"Well, we can'na have that now, can we?" His head tilts to the side as he not so subtly studies me. "I know it's a lot to handle, but ye've got to be able to talk it out, cope with it, as it comes. Yer just as likely to break down as ye are to catch the house on fire with emotions outta control as all that," he says seriously, but kindly. "The storm ye had goin was bad enough to pull some o' the roof up out in the barn. Thankful I am we live so far out; I do'na think it was so bad for the village."

I bolt straight up, shocked and horrified. "Storm? Dad, that couldn't have been *me*," I plead.

He only nods, a little sad. I remember hearing a storm wailing outside, even thinking how cathartic it would be to go out and scream into it. But to create the storm myself? Without meaning to? How could anyone wield that kind of power and not know it?

"Aye, it could an' it was. Do'na beat yerself up about it too much, lass. Yer Gran has definitely done worse o're less." He chuckled a little, remembering. "No point in denyin that ye caused it, or for ye to feel guilty about it. Just be of a mind when ye start feelin' off, and learn to channel it better. Ye've a modicum o' protection from it happenin' now I hear," he confides, pointedly looking at the chain around my neck.

Stunned and unsure what to say, I just sink back, deflated. Dad has started rubbing his hands together, which I know means he has more to say.

"Isobel called yer Mam today, an ye may not like it, but we told her ye would not be comin' back after the break," he rushes, "said we had a family emergency, needed to stay an' sort it."

"Oh," I squeak out, "how mad is she at me?"

"I could'na say. She did'na seem too happy, but I think that was you not callin' to tell her yerself." He gives me a pointed look. "I know ye can'na tell her everythin' goin' on, lass, but ye've been close most of yer lives. She deserves a proper call, don' ye think?" he asks.

"Yeah, she does, Dad, I know." I pull at the edges of the blanket. "I just don't know what to tell her. It's going to be impossible to pretend I'm upset about staying at this point; she knows me too well. And it won't make sense to her that I'm *not* mad about it, and I can't tell her why—"

"Unless ye plan on never talkin' to her again, I think ye have to buck up an' tell her somethin', love."

I nod, knowing he's right, but not sure how to get myself out of that mess.

At least I graduated early.

I have enough to worry about without High School being one of them.

"It might be good to talk to her, give ye a bit o' normalcy?" he asks, gauging my reaction.

"Maybe," I concede, "I just...I have never lied to her, and now I'll have to." I look up at the ceiling. "I don't know how."

"Can't say as I'm mad ye have a hard time bein' dishonest," he chuckles, "but ye'll have to find some way to jump this hurdle. Soon."

"Well, there ye are!" Aunt Viv proclaims as she walks into the room, grinning. She walks over to me and pats my hair. "Toby's been in me ear all day, learnin' how to care for the animals, askin' a million questions." She smiles wider. "I was hopin' ye'd come an' have a chat today at some point, an here I find ye half asleep!"

I can't help but grin up at her. It's nearly impossible to be upset when Aunt Viv is in the room.

"Heard ye kissed a boy, an' to think ye did'na come and gab about it with yer favorite aunt!" She crosses her arms in front of her and gives me a mock angry stare.

"Ye did what, now?" Dad pipes in, clearly disturbed.

"Ach, stop yer whinin'. She's a woman grown, Jasper." Aunt Viv rolls her eyes.

"Aye, but—" Dad starts, only to have Aunt Viv cut him off abruptly.

"No. I'll not have ye spoilin it now, *bràthair*. Go on an' find Seamus, have a pint and whine about it to him," she demands. "It's time for a chat with me niece." She perches herself on the arm of the chair next to me, obviously dismissing her brother.

Dad stands, looks at her for a minute before walking over and kissing the top of my head. "Maybe it's best I don' know every detail," he admits, mumbling, and leaves the room.

I watch him walk out, an obvious pout on his face, defeat in his step. I almost feel bad for him. Almost. But honestly. I am grown, and I have enough to worry about without one of those things being placating my dad about my love life.

Potential love life, I correct myself.

I look up at Aunt Viv, still perched on the arm of my chair, eyebrow raised, arms crossed in front of her.

"Well," she says, simply.

I groan in protest, pulling the blanket over my face. Honestly, how dare she blurt it out in front of my dad, then demand I gossip with her about it! “Aunt Viv, really, I don’t know if I want to talk about this yet,” I mumble from behind my fortress of fleece.

“Lorali,” is all I hear in return, both stern and comforting at once.

I peek my head out of the blanket, eyes upward, sighing in defeat. It’s not like there’s a snowball’s chance in hell she’ll let it go.

“Fine,” I concede. “What do you already know?” I wrap the blanket tight around my shoulders and frown up at her. “And how do you know it, for that matter?”

She laughs and shakes her head. “Oh no, lass. You tell me from the beginnin’, and I’ve got my sources. Ones I’ll not divulge,” she says, grinning mischievously.

With nothing left to do, I tell her about the events of the last 24 hours as they pertain to Wesley and Malakai, more or less. I may have left out a few details about just *how* cozy Kai and I got in our dream world, but enough that she gets the jist.

“I can’na read ye. Yer Mam and Gran help with that?” she asks nonchalantly.

“Um...yeah,” I respond, a little confused.

She nods her head and walks over to the fireplace, nudging the logs with a poker.

“So...that’s it?” I ask. “That’s all you’re gonna say? I mean. I figured you’d have some advice, an opinion at least.” I’m a little offended her only response was to ask about my blocking. Wasn’t she the one who wanted to talk about this in the first place?

“Honestly, Lor, do ye really *need* my input here?” she asks, back still turned, adding more logs to the fire.

“It can’t hurt,” I huff, picking at my blanket again. “I’ve made a big enough mess on my own, a little advice might be nice,” I begrudgingly admit.

"Seems pretty obvious t'me, ye've got a mind for Malakai," she says, turning around and raising a brow at me. "And they've both got a mind for ye, which *is* a cluster if I do say so."

"How is that obvious?" I ask, incredulous.

"Lorali," she laughs, head back. "Wasn't Wesley's dream ye walked into, was it? An' don't be foolin' yerself thinkin' he was'na dreamin' of ye just the same. I'd put money he was, but that wasn't who ye went to, now was it?"

She walks over and settles back on the arm of my chair, putting an arm around my shoulders and pulling me against her.

"Do'na feel bad, dove. Ye kissed Wesley, but I think his brother had the right of it. It was'n ye who wanted to do the kissin', but him. And don't go bein' mad at him, neither. He tried to stop ye, did'n he?"

I nod, resting my head against her. It's not him I was upset with anyway, but myself for not guessing the truth on my own. Instead, I've kissed someone who quite obviously would like to do a lot more of just that—and I simply don't feel the same.

"He'll be upset, sure, but he'll get over it, lass. He's no wee lad to be throwin tempers because ye'd rather have his brother. Not in front of ye, anyway," she chuckles, a little sadly. "I feel for him, truly. But ye can'na make decisions about who yer with for any other reason than that's what yer heart truly wants. Believe me on that one."

Her tone is both wistful and sad, and I know she's referencing the man who left her in the middle of the night. I pull a hand out of my blanket and grab hers, giving it a squeeze. That man might very well be the twins' father. I wonder silently if they look anything like him, and if that's hard for her. I can't imagine that kind of betrayal. Even if she didn't really love him, they'd made a life.

"I know you're right. It just sucks," I admit. "I don't want to hurt anyone, and why couldn't anyone show me sooner how to block out other emotions? At least enough they didn't influence my own." I sigh.

"To be fair, I do'na think anyone expected ye'd be goin' off with either of 'em." She giggles. "Guess we all needed the reminder yer not a child anymore."

She squeezes me tight, then lets go and stands, facing me.

"Ye'll have to deal with both of 'em, but I'd probably go an' face the one whose dreams I invaded sooner than later, yeah?" She fixes me with a stare.

"Like now?" I squeak.

"Like now." She nods.

With that, she plants a swift kiss on my forehead, pulls me out of the chair while absconding with my blanket, and shoves me towards the door. I glance back to see her settling into the chair, wrapping my blanket around her shoulders.

"Thief," I grumble and head out to find Malakai.

I can hear her laughing loudly behind me.

As I head down the hallway where most of us have bedrooms, I look down at my slippers and sweats.

Maybe I should just dip into my room for a quick change of attire, I think, biting my lip.

I know it's stalling, but I decide to do it anyway.

Once inside my room, I look around at the mess I've let accumulate and start grabbing up laundry, shoes, my bag. The mess I stopped myself from using as a distraction earlier. Tossing them all on the window seat, I pull open the closet and gauge my wardrobe. I want to look put together, but not dressed up. Jeans and a warm sweater should do it. Pulling out my favorite black sweater, I close the door and throw it on the bed, add skinny jeans from the dresser. I change quickly, poking my thumbs through the holes in the cuffs of my sweater.

It's why it's my favorite. It's long, hitting me mid-thigh, with a v-neck and sleeves that cover half my hand, holes in the cuff for my thumbs to go through. It's cozy and warm, and super soft. I reach for the brown, faux leather, calf-high boots I tossed onto the window seat, pulling them on and zipping them up.

A quick check in the mirror and I'm thankful my curls have decided to behave today, though another hour of trying to tame them would've been fine as well.

Maybe I should call Isobel. She would definitely know what to say to both guys. I sigh, knowing I can't call her up and act like everything is fine. Although, maybe having a guy to talk about might make her less suspicious of why I'm not throwing a fit about staying here.

I file that away for later reference, admonishing myself for yet another stall tactic. I gather myself, taking a deep breath as I walk over and lay a hand on the doorknob. Straightening my back, I open the door and step out.

"Hey, Lor!" Toby hollers as he walks past, Julia in step beside him, both of them glued to his phone screen.

She looks up, smiles and waves, before looking back at the screen. I shake my head and roll my eyes. Even with a pretty girl, he's on his phone.

"Hey, guys!" I say instead, smiling as they ignore me, in their own world, murmuring over the phone.

Turning in the opposite direction, I make my way toward the rooms further down the hall, where each of the twins has their own suite, like mine. Toby does too, and I try not to think about the fact he just walked from that direction with Julia in tow. Reaching Malakai's door, I pause, shifting on my feet.

Raising my hand to knock, I stop midway and twirl a strand of hair instead. I have no idea what to say to him. How do you even talk to someone you made out with by accident, sort of, in a dream?

Ugh. I rub my head and stand up straight, then knock.

I stand there, waiting, picking at my fingernails anxiously. I knock again, ready to bolt if he doesn't come to this door in about five seconds. I don't get the chance; before I even finish the door opens to a disgruntled Malakai.

"Can I help ye?" he huffs as the door swings open.

I can tell he's been sleeping. For starters, he's wrapped his bottom half in a blanket. He could be naked under there for all I know. The thought heats my cheeks, and I quickly focus in on his face. His eyes are wide, mouth agape. Obviously not expecting me, then.

"Hi," I manage, clasping my hands in front of me.

"Lorali," he scrambles. "I...what are ye doin here?" he demands, stepping forward to look down the hall, forcing me a step back. "Alone? Yer alone? Why're ye here alone?"

"I wasn't aware I needed an escort," I say snidely, folding my arms, raising a brow, and daring him to question me again.

He quickly loses all confusion and looks down at me, face unreadable and cold. "Is it that kind o' visit then?" he asks, not kindly, hand going to the top of the door as he moves sideways, as if in invitation.

For a few seconds I weigh my options, debating how to handle this.

I decide to call his bluff and breeze past him into the room. I can hear his gasp of surprise as I pass him. I look around, noting the absolutely pristine condition of his room, save the comforter around his waist and the rumpled bed. I turn back to him, hand on my hip.

"You gonna close the door or stand there and gape at me?" I ask icily.

This is one dangerous game of chicken.

He cocks his head to the side, studying me, then throws his arm out to shut the door, too loudly. It's too dark, and I can barely see the smirk on his face. I wonder if I am really ready to play this little game after all. I know I'm not, when he starts sauntering toward me.

"I'm sorry," I say quietly, head going down, hands pulling on my sleeves.

He stops just before he truly invades my space, rigid. "Yer protected now?" he asks. "Analyse made it so it can'na happen again?" His voice is stiff, forced.

"Yeah," I barely manage, clearing my throat and forcing myself to look him in the eye. "Yeah, she did. It won't happen again without my meaning to."

He nods, rubbing a hand over his face.

"I really am sorry. I didn't even know—" My breath catches in my throat as he grabs my elbow and pulls me into him.

"I'm gonna kiss ye now, if ye've no problem with that?" he asks, face inches from mine.

I nod, excited and terrified.

"No, Lorali, ye tell me I can kiss ye, or I'll not," he demands, voice low.

"Yes, Malakai, I want you to kiss m—"

His mouth is on mine before I finish the word. The world explodes around me, my hand flat against his bare chest, his arm wrapped around my waist.

Oh, this is so much better than a dream.

He deepens the kiss, pressing me closer, and just as abruptly pulls away. I look up at him, confused.

"Any mind to kiss me brother, now?" he asks, searching my face for a reaction.

I push against him with both hands, angry. "Excuse me?" I yell, lost for other words.

"I'd like to know if ye want to be kissin' me, or him," he growls at me.

"You can*not* be serious!" I scream. "Do you think I'd be here kissing you if I wanted to be kissing him?"

"No, but considerin' he's at the door listenin', I thought he should know that too," he gloats, moving to the side slightly to reveal Wesley in the open doorway, hand gripping the frame.

Shit. Shit. Shit.

Wesley looks at me, Malakai, and back again, bows his head once, and closes the door as he backs out of the room.

"Damn it, Malakai!" I say, smacking his arm as I rush past him, reaching for the door.

"Do'na," he says, grabbing my hand to stop me. "Give him time, Lor," he says seriously.

"You're kidding!" I shake my head. "That was such a *cruel* thing to do, Kai!" I pull my hand back, but he holds on.

"Kai?" he asks, amused.

"Stop it," I warn. "This is not cute, or endearing."

"Ach, come now. Ye think he would'na know the second he saw me anyway?" he asks. "We may no' get on, but he's still me twin, Lor. He'd know." He shakes his head, letting my hand fall. "If ye wanna chase him, go. But it'll only lead to him shuttin' ye out. He's right pissed I was right yesterday, an' was likely comin' to hash that out as it is."

He rubs a hand over his face again, then looks at me for a moment before continuing.

"Ye can be angry with me, but believe me when I say that was the best way to handle that. Ye think me cruel, but in truth it was'na. It was either say somethin, or have him throwin' a punch at me, and I'd rather not have to knock him out for doin' it in front of ye."

I waffle between the door and his outstretched hand, unsure how to proceed. He does know Wesley better than I do, even if they pretty much hate each other.

"I still think it was cruel," I say, unconvinced.

"The cruelty happen'd the second he opened that door," he said sadly. "Better he hate me for it than you. Better he knock, but what's done is done."

He walks to the dresser, pulls out the sweats I saw him in before, and walks to the bathroom.

"Let me dress, an then let's talk?" he asks before closing the bathroom door without waiting to hear my answer.

I could leave, go and track Wes down, try to manage the situation. Except it's not mine to manage, is it? His hurt isn't mine to manage. Trying to do so would only reinforce a hope that isn't there.

I sigh heavily, sitting down on the edge of the bed, defeated. I know things will be difficult with him from here on out, but chasing after him would only make things worse for everyone.

Tears well in my eyes as I pick at the sheets on the bed. They start to fall, and I frantically wipe my face. The last thing I need is Kai seeing them and thinking God knows what, but it's too late. He's standing in the middle of the room, light spilling out behind him from the open bathroom door.

"Lor," he says, quietly.

It only makes the tears come faster, and I turn my face as I try to brush them away.

He comes up behind me, a hand on my chin, turning my face toward him. "*Mo chridhe*," he whispers, kneeling down in front of me, thumb gently sweeping across my tear-stained cheek. His other hand coming up to do the same on the other side, my face cupped in his hands now. "Alright, now," he says softly, soothingly. "Alright, ye cry if ye need to." Giving me a sweet, sad smile.

It's more than I can take, and I start crying full force, trying to turn my head from him. Instead, he stands, pulling me into his arms and sitting, holding me like a child. I lay my head on his shoulder and let myself go, clutching his shirt. His hand is on my back, making soothing strokes up and down, lips pressed against my hair.

"Would ye like it better if I went an got yer Mam? Or Lyse?" he asks quietly.

I shake my head vigorously, sitting up and wiping at my tears again.

"Aye, alright," he says, grabbing my hand and squeezing it. "I did'na mean to make it worse, now." He smiles at me again, reassuring.

I calm a little, realizing how ridiculous it is to be crying into a guy's shoulder the first chance I get. I shake my head, getting my bearings, before I stand and wipe my face. "Ugh. Sorry. Damn,

I don't know what's wrong with me!" I groan, looking at him, trying to shrug it off.

"It's alright, lass." He stands and pushes hair behind my ear, again tilting my chin up to look at him. "This is likely the first full day ye've had with yer own emotions in a bit?" he asks.

I nod, taking a steadying breath. "Yeah, yeah I guess," I admit, actually thinking about that for the first time.

"It can be overwhelmin', I know," he replies. "It gets easier, though. With time an' practice," he says confidently, smiling.

"Wait," I start, putting it together. "You're...you're an Empath!" I exclaim, and he nods, grinning. "That's why you were so hard to read!" My mouth gapes. "You could've shown me how to block it," I accuse.

"Well..." He rubs a hand across the back of his neck. "Maybe, but there's no way o' knowin if it woulda worked—" He looks unsure, off balance.

"She told you not to," I accuse. "Gran, she told you not to!"

"I did'na say—" he starts.

"You didn't have to, you're only ever evasive when we're talking about Gran." I pace, "But why?" I demand. "Why wouldn't she want—" I look over at him, clarity dawning. "She suspected I could Pull more than emotions. Like her." I wait for an answer, staring at him.

"She did'na want us interferin' with you or Toby, not after Wesley showed ye how to call up yer pow'r that first day," he mutters, shifting from one foot to another. "Said we could hinder ye, she did," he proclaims.

"And that's why you went to her when I invaded your dream, right?"

He nods.

"Son of a bitch," I mutter, plopping down on the edge of the bed again, stunned.

Malakai shifts on his feet again. It would be funny, how unsure he is, how unguarded, how different...if I wasn't feeling so used. I can't believe Gran would do that. She had to *know* how horribly wrong it could go, how much damage it could cause.

"Come on now," he pleads, hands going into his pockets. "No matter what ye may be thinkin', she does mean well, an' she's been at this a long time, Lor. She knows what she's doin', or I'd have tried to help ye sooner."

I don't think I'll get used to him sounding unsure, vulnerable anytime soon. I'm so used to the self-assured, aloof Malakai. I thought I had him pegged. Guess I was wrong. It only makes me like him more, though. I sigh, looking up at him. "I just wish her way of handling this didn't make me feel like a lab rat," I admit.

"Lab rat?" he questions.

"Lab rat," I chuckle. "It's like...an experiment. They test things out and see how the rats react, before they use them on humans."

"They do'na," he says, horrified.

"Oh, honey," I say sarcastically. "Yeah, yeah, they do. Humanity didn't get kinder as it aged," I tease.

He looks disgusted, then walks over and sits next to me, taking my hand and facing me. "Ye know I'd never do a thing to harm ye?" he asks sincerely.

"Yeah, I think I do," I nod, "I shouldn't, really I barely know you."

He looks offended.

"But yes. I somehow know you wouldn't intentionally do anything that would hurt me."

I take a minute to really study his face, brilliant green eyes, locks of hair pulled back. He's unbelievably attractive. Like, belongs on the cover of a magazine, splattered across a billboard in his undies, drool-worthy hot.

"Even so," I shake myself out of my reverie, "please promise me you won't hold back on me anymore, like on anything. I need to know I can trust you."

"Ye only need ask, I'll not hide a thing," he replies. "An' I'll gladly offer up anythin I think ye'll want or need to know. How's that?"

"Perfect." I smile and quickly kiss him before flopping backwards on the bed, arms spread out. "It can wait a bit, though. I wouldn't mind a little break from all the revelations." I sigh, "Unless there's something you think I need to know right this second?"

"No, nothin right this second." He laughs, then lays back on the bed next to me, relaxed.

We lay there, in companionable silence, and he gently takes my hand. It's peaceful and calming, my mind slowing down.

And then it hits me. I have something *he* needs to know. *Deserves* to know. Right this second.

I shoot up, pulling him up with me. "Um. There's something I should tell you, and I don't think you're going to like it." I hesitate. "But full disclosure, right?"

I look up for any sign from him, but he just looks a little confused.

"Okay..." I take a deep breath and squeeze his hand. "I think I know who your father might be," I blurt out and watch the color completely drain from his face.

Twenty-One

"I do'na care," Malakai says, standing up and turning away from me.

"You don't care?" I repeat back to him. "Are you sure? Should I have not said anything? I don't even know anything for a fact, just speculation. But I can't expect you to be honest with me and not be with you and—" I scramble.

"I said," he turns back toward me, "I do'na care. It's no difference to me." His eyes blaze. The air feels thicker.

"Malakai," I plead, "I really think you should know, even if you don't care who he is."

"Ye just said ye do'na even know if ye know who he is," he argues.

"Well, yes, but—" I start.

"Will it change anythin' between us to know?" he asks. "Will it change or affect anythin' at all here? Now?" he demands.

"I don't know," I admit, because I don't. I have no idea how it could affect his relationships with people here, with me.

"Well, is he here, then? Walkin' aroun' just not tellin' us who he is?" he barks out, angry, but not intimidating. The surrounding Air is heavy, hot, and I know it's because of him.

"No, Kai. He's not here. I've never met him; I hope I never do," I say, righteously indignant.

It stops him in his tracks, has him studying me.

"Ach." He throws his hands in the air and sits back down. "Now would be good a time as any to be able to read ye," he mutters. "I never knew him, Lor. Not him, not me Mam. They left us, went off an' never came back. Far as I'm concerned, they died. Too late now to mend those fences," he explains. "If ye think it could affect anythin' later, tell me, but do'na tell me just to do so." With that he sits stiffly, waiting for me to decide.

I take a breath, knowing I have to tell him, knowing it could be too much of a shock later. I worry that I'm pushing a subject he would rather avoid, but I'm more worried that he might find out later and be angry I didn't say anything.

Damn my family for not doing this themselves, and damn Aunt Viv for telling me at all.

"My Aunt Viv," I explain, "she was married, or had a man she lived with, whatever, before she came here." I glance over, checking to make sure he's alright. "He disappeared, the night your mother disappeared. Aunt Viv seems to think it could be him. I don't know why, just that she told me, and I didn't want to question her."

He says nothing for a few minutes, just sits there, staring straight ahead. "Right then," he says, nodding, "now I know, an I still do'na care." He looks over at me. "Is there anythin' else?" He is upset, but I appreciate the effort he is making to show me it's not *me* he's upset at, but the topic.

"No." I shake my head. "Nothing else." I look down at my hands resting in my lap, clasped together. "I'm sorry, I just, I thought if it came up later, you said if it could have any effect..." I trail off, unsure.

"Aye, that's what I said," he agrees. "An' it might, one day. Not today. So let's talk about happier things."

"Okay." I nod.

I feel completely unsure, in all honesty, but I've also never been in a relationship that even resembled anything adult. The biggest controversy I've ever had to face with a guy is what movie we'd see that weekend.

Relationship. Is that where this is going?

"Toby said yer birthday is tomorrow," he says. "I forgot to ask him how old ye'll be turnin'." He glances over at me.

"Nineteen," I say, still unsure of his change of topic.

"An still livin' with yer parents, no man waitin' to wed ye?" He chuckles, raising a brow.

I can't help but laugh. "Are you serious? Here and now, I may be an adult, but just barely," I say, between fits of giggles.

"Ah, well, lucky man I am, then, that ye are from now. Ye'd have been long wed where I'm from, and I would 'ave lost the chance to have ye for meself." He grins at me, and I know he's goading me.

"Oh, is a woman only good for marrying and keeping house in your mind?" I tease back.

"You do'na know yer Gran well if ye think I was raised to believe that." He laughs in earnest.

I flop back on the bed, feet dangling off the side, mostly relaxed again.

He leans back on an elbow, looking down at me, smiling. "Still, she'd no' be thrilled to find ye here on me bed, alone."

I roll my eyes and groan. "I do not have the time or capacity to deal with my family's hang-ups," I grumble. "I'm an adult, and I'll do what I like."

"So long as ye know there'll be a reckonin'," he sighs, "I'm quite happy to do what ye like."

I blush and am thankful for the poor lighting. A shiver runs up my spine, and Malakai sits up quickly, mistaking it for cold.

"I should light the fire," he says and walks over to the fireplace.Gathering wood from beside it, he throws it in and lights it with one of those overly long matches. "It'll be goin in just a moment," he says, and I can feel the air pick up slightly around me.

I push myself up onto my elbows to watch him, knowing he's using his Air Affinity to stoke the flames a little faster and send warm air my way. I grin a little, just because it's a really sweet thing to do.

His eyes are closed, and he's focused, muttering words under his breath I can't make out. I lay back, closing my eyes, feeling the warm air flow over me, and drift off to sleep.

When I wake, the room is warm, and I'm curled up against Malakai, who is fast asleep. I lean back slightly to watch him, the light from the fire illuminating his face. I look over his head and can see the stars behind the curtains. I can't believe I fell asleep again, or that I missed dinner. I've never slept so much in my life, and I can't help but wonder what physical toll all this magic has had on me.

If that is the cause of my need for much more sleep than I'm used to, someone is going to have to help me fix that, and soon. It could really be just the mental toll of having all this dropped on me in a few days' time.

I sit up, panicking.

Oh, no. Dinner.

We both missed it, and someone is definitely going to come looking. I shake him, causing him to bolt out of bed, immediately on guard.

"Lor?" He wakes fully. "What's wrong?" he asks, relaxing a little.

"We missed dinner," I groan, pointing to the window. My earlier 'do what I want' attitude is nowhere to be found, and I'll admit it irritates me a bit.

"Damn it all, "he mutters, crossing to the window and pulling the curtain aside. He turns to me with a horrified look on his face as a loud series of bangs hits his door. I look around the room, panicking for a second, then I remember myself and force myself to calm down.

I can make my own decisions. It's one thing to panic when my family can't see it, I'll be damned if they know I do it. I put a hand on Malakai's arm to stop him from reaching the door and shake my head.

"We haven't done a thing wrong, and we are not going to act like children caught screwing up," I proclaim, and he nods, still looking unsure but willing to follow my lead here.

I walk over, take a deep breath, and open the door with a sarcastic smile plastered across my face.

"Ah, Lorali, there ye are." Grandfather smiles, stiffly. "I'm to assume Malakai is in his own rooms at this hour?"

Malakai comes up behind me, pulling the door open further. "Aye, of course. Is there a problem, Laird?" he asks, voice full of respect.

"A situation, yes." Grandfather looks concerned, but confident. "If ye'd both please come to the sittin room. We've had a message," he says, then turns to walk away.

"A message?" I ask, looking up and behind me at Kai.

"Aye, that's what I said, lass. Quickly now."

With that he's halfway down the hall, orders given. I have had little interaction with him over the years, but it's very obvious he's a man who is used to not having to say a thing twice. Sighing heavily, I turn to grab my shoes that got kicked off by the bed. Kai is already waiting by the door, ready.

When we walk into the sitting room, my family is all there, plus Wesley, as well as Darian and Lena. Everyone is sitting, except the newly arrived Council members, who are standing facing the room in front of the fireplace.

We are the last ones to arrive, and my dad is refusing to make eye contact while Mom is rubbing his arm in consolation. Toby is grinning at me and has the audacity to give me a thumbs up sign with an exaggerated wink.

Gross.

Julia is sitting next to him, and she offers a smile without all the weirdness.

As we approach the loveseat, I glance over at Wesley seated under a window, removed from the rest. He is looking into the fire, arms crossed, sullen. Malakai squeezes my hand, and I look over and give him a small smile.

He knows I'm upset about how things played out with his brother, and I love that he can understand that despite his own relationship with Wesley. He could have reacted differently, though if he had, I don't believe we'd be spending time together now.

We sit, and Darian claps his hands in front of him, clearing his throat. "Now that we've got ye all here," he says, smiling warmly at me, "Lena and I were in Eldria, ensuring Calliope was secured, when a surprise guest appeared in the Council Chambers." He glances over at Lena nervously, and she nods grimly. "After havin' spoken to the guards, I went into the Council Chambers to access the library; I wasn't there but a moment, when the Lady Morgainne appeared, blusterin' on about needin' to see her daughter."

A collective gasp goes around the room, everyone's gaze going to Gran, who is sitting stiffly, a mask of fury on her face.

"Said she had a message, an' it could only be given directly to ye, Analyse. She'd not tell me anythin' else, just that I was to find ye and tell ye to get yerself to the Chambers immediately. Her words, not mine," he clarifies, at Gran's snort of derision. "She said she did'na have time to be waitin on ye and to use the glass to let her know ye were ready to receive her once ye arrived." He clears his throat again, gathering courage no doubt. "She said to tell ye exactly; tell her she had better not keep me waitin', an' bring the new Heir with her as well. Any more than a fortnight an' I'll go lookin' for her myself."

At that, he nods, message delivered, and bows his head as though waiting for the wrath of hell to rain down upon him.

It's silent for a few moments, all eyes on Gran, everyone in the room waiting for the ceiling to fall. Instead, she simply throws her head back and laughs. Dad groans and puts his head in his hands.

Mom and Grandfather look concerned, and Aunt Viv just rolls her eyes and walks over to the drink cart, pouring herself a hefty helping of Scotch. Darian and Lena look nervously at one another, Lena shifting on her feet and wringing her hands in front of her.

"Gran?" I say cautiously, and Malakai shakes his head at me, physically pulling me a little closer to him.

"Well!" Gran says, standing and smacking her thighs as she does so. "I suppose I should'na be surprised she'd know so quickly. Damned woman hides herself away for centuries an' then deigns us with an appearance just as a new Heir is chosen." She waves a hand in my direction, causing gasps from anyone in the room not directly related to me.

Damn it, Gran.

Malakai stiffens next to me, and I wonder if I should have told him after all, against Gran's instructions. To be fair, it hasn't crossed my mind since she said it, though at the time I did think it might be something to tell him.

"Just leave it to me mother to announce it to the bloody world, without a care for the dangers it puts us all in. A new Heir, untrained. I assume the entirety of Eldria has heard by now?" she accuses and gets nods from both Darian and Lena in confirmation.

"She wasn't exactly quiet about sharing it, Aunt Lyse. Went around yelling for you before she made her way into the Council Chambers," Lena replies.

"Aunt Lyse?" I choke.

"Ah, yes, my father is your great uncle." Lena smiles at me, explaining.

"As though that's important at this minute," Gran says dismissively, waving it off.

"Right. Sorry," I apologize. Lena shrugs and smiles again.

"Didn't really have time to tell you before," she says.

"We should discuss this privately," Mom starts, walking over to Toby and putting a hand on his shoulder.

"Ach. Ye can'na protect them from it any longer, dear," Gran says, "Me mother has seen to that," she snarls.

Dad walks over and pulls Mom into his side, glaring at Gran. "Well we know it, Mam," he admonishes. "Ye can'na blame us for wantin to."

Gran stops pacing, looking over at my parents, and deflates a little. "Aye. Yer right." She sighs. "I'd leave 'em out of it if I could, surely ye know that."

Dad nods, rubbing Mom's arm softly.

Mom just stands there, dazed and worried. After a few seconds, she stands a little straighter, more in control. "No one is going anywhere until the Guardians have returned, at any rate. We have a week, and we'll have to decide who will stay here to deal with them," Mom commands. "I won't have my daughter stepping foot in Eldria without more training, either." She nods, turning to me. "Tomorrow morning we start."

She looks to Gran, daring her to say anything to the contrary.

"Then ye best be gettin to sleep, the lot of ye. We'll meet in the hall at 6AM. Make sure ye've had yer breakfast before then," Gran confirms, taking Grandfather's hand and leaving.

Wesley jumps up quickly and disappears behind her, not allowing me the chance to try and speak to him. I sigh heavily, but say nothing.

Mom and Dad make the goodnight rounds, Dad staring Malakai down when they reach us and say goodnight, but not mentioning our relationship, or where we've been all evening. To Malakai's credit he holds his own, not looking ashamed—but remaining respectful without being cocky.

Julia and Toby leave with my parents. No doubt they want to make sure at least one of their children makes it to their own bedroom, alone. Darian and Lena both follow Aunt Viv to rooms she has for them, leaving Malakai and I to head off on our own.

Malakai holds out a hand, an odd look on his face.

"What is it?" I ask, putting my hand in his as we start to walk.

"Yer the Heir," he states simply.

"Um. About that..." I stop and turn to face him. "Gran said to tell no one. I thought about telling you, really I did. At least, I did when she said it, and I truly haven't even thought of it since. I just—" I hold my hands out and shrug. "I don't know anything about this world. About magic, Portals, the Council, and what is Eldria anyway?"

He stays quiet, letting me take my time without demanding an explanation.

"She's the head of the Council, right? So, like, all the Guardians are supposed to listen to her or something? I guess I decided she knows a hell of a lot more than I do about all this, and maybe there was a reason for her to keep it secret for now," I finish, looking up at him apologetically.

"It's why ye weren't truly angry with me, when ye found out I did the same."

I cock my head to the side, studying him. "I guess it was. I didn't think of it at the time, but yeah. I couldn't be mad at you for doing the exact same thing I was doing, could I?"

"So long as we agree certain orders must be followed." He nods, turns, and we start walking again.

Something about the way he said that makes me uneasy, but I am too scattered to focus in on it right then, so I don't.

"Seriously, though, what is Eldria? I'm not claiming to be an expert on geography, but I've definitely never heard of it," I ask again.

"It's the home of the Order, really. Ye wouldna have heard o' it before, as ye did'na know anything about the Order. It's no' a place ye can just walk to, is it?" he explains, stopping and looking down at me. "The only way ye can get there is through a Portal, more complicated than that, but it's as good an explanation as any." Taking my hand he starts walking again, and I let it drop for now. We walk in amicable silence, and then he stops at my door.

"Oh," I say, disappointed.

"Oh?" he asks.

"I..." I cross my arms and look at the ground. "It's nothing," I say, lying.

"Lor," he chuckles, "ye need to sleep; trainin' is not exactly relaxin."

"Yeah, of course," I say, still not looking up at him. "Goodnight, then." I open my door and start to walk in.

"Lorali," he huffs. "I do'na like ye any less than an hour ago," he explains.

I nod, but don't say anything, and take another step in the doorway.

"Aw, damn it all. I'm just tryin to make sure yer rested, an tryin not to make assumptions," he clarifies.

I stop and turn, looking at him finally, seeing he's at a loss here. "I guess I just thought we'd go back to your room," I admit, which earns me a smirk.

"Much as I'd like nothin' more, I do'na think yer ready for me to get used to havin' ye alone, or in me bed." He brushes my hair back, kissing me softly. "I'm in no rush here; yer entitled to yer own space."

"And if I don't want it right now?" I ask.

"Then I'd be more'n happy to keep ye company," he admits softly, "but it's to bed for us both."

I nod, knowing he's right, even if I don't want to agree. I need to be more careful about just how quickly we're moving. Mom was right to caution me, but I've never wanted to be this close to another person before. Maybe that's even more reason to tread lightly. He kisses me goodnight, promises to meet me in the morning, and watches me close my door before leaving for his own room.

I throw myself onto the bed, butterflies in my stomach despite the craziness going on, and wonder if I can meet him in my dreams on purpose this time. The thought leaves me with a stupid grin as I drift off.

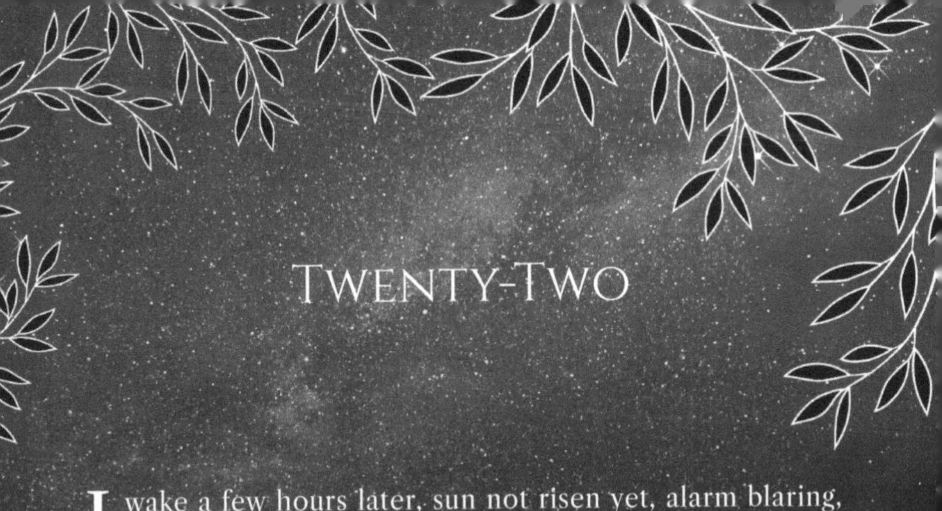

Twenty-Two

I wake a few hours later, sun not risen yet, alarm blaring, having had no dreams at all.

Bummer, I think, before getting up and starting the shower.

I go back into my room and grab my phone, throw on my most upbeat playlist, and set the volume as loud as I can. I let the spray wash over me, singing at the top of my lungs and dancing around.

I'm officially nineteen years old today. Despite the crazy, despite the danger that is almost certainly ahead of me, despite waking up at 4:30 in the damn morning to train, today is going to be a good day.

That thought in mind, I put my hair in a complicated braid to keep it out of the way for whatever training is going to entail, and some mascara just because I like it. I walk into my room wrapped in a towel, pull out my leggings, a sports bra, and a long-sleeved workout shirt. I get dressed and top it off with runners, and just as I am about to pick up my phone to scroll, there's a knock at my door.

Malakai

I can't help the silly grin that appears.

I take one last look in the mirror, adjusting my shirt, and go to the door. Except it isn't Malakai. It's my little family, and the genuine smile that brings to my face makes my chest feel all warm and fuzzy.

"Happy Birthday, love!" Mom sings, with Dad and Toby

She's holding a plate of crepes—my traditional Birthday Morning Breakfast—with one lit candle poked into the top one. I open the door to let them in, tears glistening in my eyes and a goofy smile on my face. I should have expected this, but I'm glad I didn't.

The surprise of it, even under the circumstances we are facing, makes it all the more special. There is nothing quite like knowing you're truly loved, and showing up at my door this early with crepes, Mom had to have gotten up at 3 in the morning to bake—well, if that isn't love I don't know what is.

As they walk in, they start a roaring rendition of the birthday song and stop just inside the room for me to blow my candle out. I close my eyes, wishing only for more happy moments like this, and blow. It's a cheesy birthday wish, but it's truly what my heart desires.

I open my eyes to see Mom dabbing at hers and Dad smiling proudly, an arm thrown over her shoulders. Toby jumps onto my bed, grinning, and pulls a fork out of his pocket. "Let's eat!" he exclaims loudly.

Dad pulls the chair next to the bed, Mom and I sit next to Toby, and we dig in. Usually, this would be done at the breakfast table downstairs, with the rest of the family in attendance, but I think Mom and Dad wanted a moment with us away from it all. Especially considering the situation and the uncertainty of what may happen tomorrow.

"Mmmmmm," I manage over a mouthful of Nutella and strawberry stuffed crepe, "This is so good!" I grin over at Mom, who smiles back at me.

"Not with your mouth full, Lorali," she admonishes. "You may be an adult, but I did teach you better," she teases, laughing at me.

"Sorry," I say, after swallowing the last bite.

"We wanted ye to have this before everything kicked off this mornin'," Dad says, holding out a small wrapped package.

I grin and jump a little in anticipation as I take it and rip into the paper. Inside is a velvet box, lined with satin, and sitting on it is the most beautiful ring I've ever seen. It's an emerald, surrounded by tiny little diamonds in a halo. I gasp, a hand to my mouth, as I look up at my parents. They're both smiling, happy, but I can see the hint of sadness behind it.

"Oh, it's beautiful!" I say, throwing my arms around them both in a huge hug. "Thank you so much!"

"It's an heirloom," Mom explains. "It's been in my family for as long as anyone can remember, and I've saved it for your 20th birthday since the day I found out you were a girl. I thought it may serve you better just a tad earlier," she finishes wistfully, giving my hand a squeeze before letting go and nodding for me to try it on.

Of course, it is a perfect fit. It sparkles and catches the firelight wonderfully and makes me feel warm and safe, like a cool day wrapped up in a blanket and reading on my front porch back home.

"Oh!" I say, startled. "It's magic!" I look up wide-eyed at Mom, who smiles and nods.

"Yes, I may have cooked up a little enchantment to make you feel calm, safe."

"Oh, Mom," I say, tears threatening again as I pull her in for another hug.

"It'll help when you start training today, as an Empath, and as Merlin's Heir," she whispers in my ear, squeezing me to her a little tighter for the briefest of seconds before letting me go.

I sit back, happy tears sitting on my cheeks, and just take in the picture of my family, all happy and together. I want to remember this moment, and this feeling, forever.

"Oh, don't be such a sap," Toby teases, kicking at my leg.

To get back at him, I pull him into a crushing hug. "Aw, Tob, what's the matter?" I tease. "Don't you know how much I *love* you?" I finish, giggling as he squirms to get free.

"Whatever, weirdo," he shoots back as he manages to wriggle under my arm and away from me.

"Alright, you two," Dad chides in his most Dad voice, as a faint knock sounds at my door.

My heart catches a little, realizing that is definitely Malakai, and I try to hide the ridiculous grin from my family.

"Come on, let's leave Lor to her guest," Mom says, gathering up the mess from my Birthday Crepes, and shooting Dad a warning look.

I get up and walk them over, hugging Dad as Mom opens the door and greets Malakai. She turns and hugs me again, then grabs Dad by the arm, probably making sure he doesn't try to stay and chaperone.

"See you in 10 minutes, Lorali," Dad warns, and they leave Malakai and me standing in the doorway.

"Hi," I say, smiling.

"Hello," he grins, holding out a small bouquet of wildflowers, "I do b'lieve it's yer birthday."

I smile wider, taking the flowers and standing on tiptoe to kiss his cheek. "Thank you."

I turn and place the flowers in the vase by my bed, no doubt thought up by Aunt Viv. I'm grateful she had the foresight to do so. I'd have never thought to have an empty vase sitting in a bedroom.

"Where did you manage to find these in December?" I ask, teasing.

"A man has his ways, lass," he jokes back, grinning.

"So Aunt Viv's greenhouse, then?" I poke, enjoying the banter.

Instead of answering, he simply kisses the top of my hair and chuckles. "Ready?" he asks, arm out for me to take.

I nod, slip my hand through the crook of his elbow, and we head off to the Great Hall. I doubt my actual readiness, but I put on my bravest, most confident facade despite that.

Twenty-Three

In complete contrast to the last time we all met here, the room is now virtually empty. There are a few oversized chairs placed strategically around the edges of the room and several dozen mats like you'd see in a school gym on the floor. In addition to my family, Julia, Wesley, Darian, and Lena are all milling around.

Some stand in small groups chatting, while others are stretching or sipping water. Gran strides over to me, face stern. I expect her to lecture me on being the last to show up, but instead she smiles when she gets close and puts her hands on her hips to study me.

"Ye do'na seem all that different than ye did a few hours ago." She tilts her head to the side, considering. "Funny how nothin' truly changes year to year, isn't it?" She laughs, pulling me in for a hug. "Happy Birthday, dove. Won't make me go any easier on ye today, though!" she says as she waves me forward, walking back toward the center of the room.

Malakai is laughing quietly beside me, and I'm not sure if I want to laugh or if I'm too stunned. Gran has a definite way of making me feel just off balance enough to never know what to expect next from her. I don't have long to think about it, as Gran reaches the center of the room and raises her arms high above her head.

A deafening crack echoes around us, wind whipping around the room. It takes a minute for me to realize Gran is the cause, and suddenly her voice is all around me at once.

"We'll begin simply. Form two lines in front of me, one behind the other."

As everyone scrambles to reach the middle of the room and line ourselves up, I catch a glimpse of Wesley, who walks as far away from me as he can while still following instructions. I manage to situate myself between Toby and Malakai, Mom and Dad just behind us. At least I'll be surrounded by those I'm closest to.

Once we're all where she wants us, Gran stops the wind and studies the group for a moment, nodding. "While I've no doubt there'll be somethin' for each of ye to learn during these trainin's, truly we're here for Lorali and Toby. They're the only ones who've not had any trainin' up until now, so we'll divide an' conquer."

She grabs Toby and me by the hand, pulling us out of the group to stand next to her.

"Toby has a Spirit Affinity, which we can'na really help much with, but we know a thing or two, especially with the twins here. He's also Zoolingual, as well as bein' an animal Empath. If ye've got any zoological gifts, please come an' stand over here with Toby, if ye don't, come stand with Lorali."

Gran stays where she is, as Wesley, Aunt Viv, Stuart, and Grandfather all walk over to Toby. The rest of the crowd simply shifts to one side.

"Liam, why don't ye take control of our Toby's trainin', and I'll handle Lorali here?" she asks and gets agreement from Grandfather.

That group walks to the other side of the room and starts listening to him speak, so I turn back to Gran.

"Well, we've got an awful lot of ground to cover with Lorali, so we might as well split into smaller groups." She looks around again, studying everyone. "I think we'll start by gettin' her Empathic abilities in check, an' for that we'll need Malakai, Cadence, and myself. Vivienne would be useful, but seein' as she has the strongest zoological abilities, I think she'd best stay with Toby for now."

As she speaks, Mom and Malakai both break off and come stand on the other side of her.

"The rest of ye should get together an' discuss how best to help her channel an use her Affinities. Any questions?"

No one seems to have any, so she tells them to go coordinate, leaving me alone with her, Mom, and Malakai.

"Right. Yer Mam and I have shown ye how to differentiate between others' emotions and yer own, an how to shield yerself. I think it best ye learn to allow emotion through that shield, but not so much it overpowers ye."

"Analyse, it took me decades to master that," Mom protests.

"She does'na have decades," Gran counters, "she's got barely a week, an' she'll need to practice constantly until then."

"I mastered it in a year," Malakai adds. "I think I can help her to shorten that time."

I can feel the shock on my face at his admission, and it likely mirrors what I see on my mom's.

"A year?" she asks, eyes wide.

"Aye," Malakai says, nodding. "I was a precocious child, an' did'na want Lyse in my head so much," he explains, which causes both he and Gran to chuckle softly. The admission should come off as egotistical, but somehow he succeeds in making it endearing.

"He did learn it quickly, Cadence," Gran reassures. "With almost none o' my help, too." She smiles at him like a proud mother.

"Well, alright then. I'm going to go and sit in one of those comfy chairs you've got in here, in that case, and watch my children," Mom says, gliding gracefully to the side of the room, choosing a chair that will give her a clear view of both Toby and me. Gran looks between us, then nods as if deciding Mom has a great idea and walks off to join her.

Malakai turns to me, smiling.

"Looks like it's you and me." He grins wider. "It's too bad we've an audience," he teases, causing me to laugh loudly. He sits on the floor, looking up at me and waiting for me to sit, too. I do, and he shifts around a little. "Get comfortable as ye can, an' then I need ye to tell me how you're blockin now."

I cross my legs and settle in for a long day. I explain to him what I learned from Mom and Gran, my little island in the river and the Spirit shield I envisioned.

"Ah, I think our Spirit Affinity makes it easier for us to control other magics," he says. "Yer likely shieldin' so efficiently because yer using it without knowin' yer doin it. I think it's how I mastered my Empathtic abilities so quickly, where it took yer Mam much longer," he explains quietly. "Yer Affinity is a grounding force, stabilizing. It's why ye can'na travel without one; ye need an anchor, a tether. Spirit is the most rare; only Gabriel had it until us, an' he's bound to his own time."

"Is *that* his name?" I interrupt. "My uncle? His name's Gabriel?"

"Aye, it is." He nods. "He can'na travel, but he was a good mentor to me an Wesley when yer Gran realized we had Affinity for Spirit as well."

He looks over at Gran, as if she can hear us from where she is and might interrupt at any second. As intently as she is focused on us, she very well may.

"We can talk more about him later, if ye like. For now, let's focus on controllin' yer Empathic abilities."

I nod, glancing over at Gran and Mom.

"Now, as I said, yer usin' Spirit to block out all emotions and keep yer own emotions from pushin' out onto others, even those who are'na Empaths themselves. Ye can keep the shield up to prevent yerself from sharin' yer own emotions. We won't need to do much there except maybe teach ye how to do it when ye want to be doin it."

He pauses, and I can see the wheels turning in his head. Shifting nervously, he looks over at Gran again before settling on me, face serious.

"Ye know how ye met me in me dreams?" he asks.

Shocked, I let out a groan of embarrassment. It's not a topic I'd like to discuss in a room full of other people, who could potentially use their own magic to eavesdrop if they wanted.

"No, no. Do'na go shyin away from it." He puts a hand on my knee, reassuring me. "We're gonna use that, but I'm gonna tell ye how to find me on the Astral Plane intentionally. I just need to go an tell Lyse afore we start."

He stands, walking over to Gran, who raises an eyebrow at him before he even takes a step. Mom stands as soon as she sees him, wringing her hands, worried something hasn't worked or there's a problem. I know the look.

Once he reaches them, he nods at Mom and says something, and she gasps. Gran just raises her eyebrow higher and tilts her head at him. They all speak for a minute and then he's turning back to me, grim-faced but determined.

He reaches me and holds out his hand, which I take, and he pulls me to my feet.

"We're goin somewhere we won't have an audience," he explains. "Yer rooms or mine?" he asks softly as we leave the room.

I notice Wesley watching us as we leave and barely manage to prevent myself from walking over and chewing him out. I can't give him a timetable for when or how he deals with this. It doesn't mean I'm not frustrated with him despite it.

"Lor?" Malakai asks, stopping in the hall.

"Sorry. Um, let's go to your room. Mine's a mess, and I'd have to find at least 3 devices to silence to make sure we didn't get interrupted by a ringing phone or messenger app."

He looks at me perplexed, likely because he's never used an app in his entire life, but then turns and walks towards his room.

Once there, he closes the door, fans the fire with a nice gust of Air, and walks over to the dresser. He opens a drawer and pulls out several candles, a bowl with something in it, and a box of matches. He sets up the candles around the bed, lights whatever is in the bowl, and sets the matches on the nightstand.

"Right. Now we're gonna lay down, and I'm gonna walk ye through reaching the Astral Plane. Just close yer eyes, and listen to my voice." He holds my hand as I step over a candle, and we lie side by side on top of the comforter.

I close my eyes and wait.

"I'm gonna start by countin' down from 100. I want ye to breathe in for 4 counts, then out for 3. Ready?" he asks.

"Yeah, I think so," I reply.

He starts counting, and slowly I can feel my breath settling into a rhythm; it's calming, this focused breathing. I relax and let his voice wash over me. Every so often he gives a simple instruction like 'relax your neck' or 'sink into the bed.' It's nice, the kind of calm you feel as you drift off for a nap, or when you're getting a massage. That edge of awareness, right before you fall asleep.

"Now, I want ye to envision a blank space. There's flat ground, but nothin' around ye, no grass, no walls or trees, just a space that fades into dark on the edges. Imagine floating down onto that surface, and meet me there."

"Whoa," I say, suddenly in a void-like space, glass floor under me, almost like a prism with the way the colors shift through it.

The area where I'm standing is bright, but there are no walls, just a gradual fade into blackness the further it is from where I am standing. I feel a hand on my shoulder and whip around, arms raised, startled.

"There now," Malakai laughs, "No need to do violence, *mo chridhe.*"

He's smiling at me, just standing in this space he's created.

"This," he says, holding out his arms, "is the Astral Plane. Far as we can tell, it's the space between our world an' the next. It can be a dangerous place, if yer not protected, so I want ye to picture that Spirit shield o' yers, and place it around the edges, where the light starts to fade. Can ye do that?"

"I can try." I close my eyes, holding the picture of where we are in my head, and like when I was working with my mom, I picture that purple energy around us, just where the light starts to fade away.

"Good! That's wonderful, Lor!"

I can hear the excitement and approval in his voice, and I open my eyes. I can see the shimmering purple energy around us, and it is beautiful. "Wow," I breathe, stepping closer to the boundary I have created. I reach a hand out, think better of it, and glance over at Malakai.

"Go ahead," he nods, "It's yer own magick. It will'na hurt ye. I would'na go around playin' with someone else's though."

I reach out, and even before I touch it, the energy reaches out for me, a small tendril pulling away from the wall of it and meeting my hand. It's a feeling that is overwhelming, powerful, but also calming and peaceful. I giggle, and the place where my skin meets Spirit grows a little warmer, a little more vibrant.

"It's respondin' to ye. This is actually a good way to show ye how yer magick is affected by yer own emotions." He walks over, smiling. "If ye weren't happy, it would react in a different way. With me, the color dulls, the energy gets too hot. At least with Spirit. It'll be different with every Elemental Affinity, and maybe a little different from person to person," he explains, walking back toward the center of the space.

"I want ye to come over here, an' we are gonna try somethin I think will help you to be able to protect yerself without shutting off yer Empathy. It's an important skill to have, an' it'll help ye know who yer enemies are."

I reluctantly pull away from my Spirit wall and go to stand in front of him. Thoughts of Aunt Viv race through my head, knowing what she went through because she decided she didn't want her gifts anymore. It's been nice knowing the emotions

I've been feeling are entirely my own, but at the same time I'm unbelievably grateful I won't have to continue that way.

Especially not with Morgainne now demanding an audience, and Evangeline somewhere out there on the loose. Calliope's attack floats to mind, and I shiver a little at what might have happened or how I might have reacted if I hadn't known what she was feeling. The Empathy gives me an edge, one I know I'll need as Heir. Even if I don't fully understand that title yet.

"What if my enemies are Empaths too? Wouldn't they be able to just block out what they didn't want me to know?" I ask.

"Aye. They would, not just Empaths either; anyone is capable of shieldin' themselves from bein' read, so it's a thing to keep in mind. Just because yer not gettin' any negative energy from a person does'na mean they do'na have any toward ye. If ye can'na feel anythin' from a person, it's likely they do'na want ye to, though some just enjoy their privacy. It's not always easy to tell."

He takes my hands and rolls his shoulders, which I mimic.

"Now, I want ye to focus on the shield ye made for yerself. Picture it in yer mind. I'm gonna throw some emotions at ye; can ye see em bouncin away?" he asks.

I nod, eyes closed.

"Good. Now I want ye to focus on the intention of yer shield. Ye've told it to block all outside influence right now. I want ye to focus on allowin' it through when I say to, but ye need to tag it somehow. Make it recognizable as comin' from someone else."

I open my eyes, frowning at him. "Tag it? What does that mean? How do you tag emotion?" I ask, bewildered.

"Think of somethin' material. Like yer shoes. Ye have different ones for different things, right?" I nod, still confused. "Well, now imagine if they all smelled different based on what they were for," he explains.

"So like if my runners smelled like apples and my heels smelled like wet dog?" I joke. It's a ridiculous concept, but I think I get the point he's making.

"Uh." He frowns. "Aye, that could work. With my shield, other emotions come through, but they leave a taste behind, like I ate a sour fruit," he tries to clarify.

"Wait. You actually somehow associate other people's emotions to a physical taste? Like you can really taste it when they come through?" I ask, awed.

"Aye. It took me almost a year, but I figured out that it was my Spirit Affinity I was usin' to block it all out so easy, an so I figured if I could focus on makin' it recognizable, I would'na be fooled into thinkin' they were me own. I could sense others around me again without it overpowerin' me," he says, like it's the most natural thing in the world. I nod and close my eyes again.

I think about what he's told me, and it's almost like working with Spirit is working with something intelligent. Like a sophisticated algorithm, set to learn and predict your interactions with it. I see what he means by focusing on what you want it to do. You don't really need to monitor or supervise it once it's in place. I haven't had to check my shield since I put it up, and it's held just fine.

Maybe all the Affinities are like that, but I'm not sure since I haven't worked with them, and I somehow doubt it based off Mom's warning that I would have to focus on shielding. Neither she nor Gran have a Spirit Affinity, so I suppose they wouldn't know.

I can see energy hitting the shield, being zapped as it hits. I focus on the energy of the shield, how it feels protective, like a solid barrier. I reach out to it, allowing it to reach back. When I make contact, I smile, then think of allowing that outside energy to slip through, not enough to be overwhelming but enough to get a sense for the feeling.

I allow the affection Malakai is sending to me to wash over me for a minute. I can still remember what Mom said about it being pushed at me. I can still tell the difference right now, but I know Malakai has a reason for telling me to "tag" it somehow.

I decide a smell might be best. Smell is a strong trigger for memory, and it might help me to be cognizant of the warnings he's given me today. I don't want a smell I might think is just natural; I need something distinct but not overpowering. I settle on a brilliant idea.

I'll tag anything coming at me by both smell and sensation. I focus on how it feels when I make contact with that Spirit energy, that tingling feeling when it hits my fingertips, and focus on the electric smell of it.

"I think I have it," I say, eyes still closed. "Send me something strong."

A wave of pride sweeps over me, and even though I've pulled my hand back away from the shield, it feels like I am still touching it. My eyes fly open, and I'm grinning.

"Well?" he asks.

"I've got it!" I exclaim, then explain to him what I've done. "It's like anything that isn't mine...it's like I'm touching the shield. It can come through, but it's really easy to tell it isn't my emotion now." I clap my hands and bounce a little, too excited to stay still.

"Brilliant," he says, looking at me in awe. "Ye've just manipulated the shield. It's bloody brilliant." He stands back, considering. "Ye haven't tagged anything at all, ye've just made it so ye can interact with what ye've made."

I nod, excited and pretty damn proud of myself. Suddenly, I stop and stare at Malakai, an idea forming. I wonder if I could identify people by the emotions I feel from them.

"What is it?" he asks, voice dripping with concern as he puts a hand on my arm, eyes scanning the area around us quickly.

"Oh, no," I say quickly. "Nothing's wrong. I just thought..." I hesitate, working it through before I try to explain it to him. "I thought, maybe, if I can figure out a way to identify *who* the emotion is coming from, not just that it's coming from someone else other than myself. Obviously it would only work with people I know already; it'd be pretty hard to do that if I don't know the person, but..."

I trail off, considering. Almost as soon as the idea fully forms and is out of my mouth, I can feel that Spirit shield around his energy coming at me. If I focus on it, I can feel a tug toward him.

"Aye, ye can—" he starts.

"*Yes*! There! If I focus on it, I can kind of trace its path!" I interrupt, clapping my hands together.

Malakai opens his mouth, closes it, shakes his head, and chuckles. "Ye do'na even need me to teach ye a thing," he proclaims. "That's what I wanted to show ye in here," he says, waving an arm around him, "how to focus in on me energy to find me. Every person has a unique energy, an aura, personal to them. It's a bit more than emotion, but not too far a leap ye should'na be able to figure it out."

"Oh, yeah, I see what you mean." I say, familiarizing myself with exactly how his energy feels to me. It's warm, inviting, open. "Kind of like getting a feel for a person. Before I knew I could do all this. Except better, because it's actually accurate." I laugh.

"Mostly, it will be. Ye'll find a few who can hide their true selves well, though. Ye need to be wary of it," he warns.

"Okay." I smile as he pulls me into his arms and wraps them around my waist. I lay my head against his chest, content. I know caution is an important aspect of all this, but right now I want to focus on the positives.

"Yer truly a wonder, Lorali Galloway," he says softly into my hair. He holds me out at arm's length, affection on his face.

"Time to go back to the real world, isn't it?" I ask, pouting.

"Aye," he says. "Close yer eyes and open em back there."

I open my eyes and sit up, propping myself up on my elbows on the bed. Malakai is already getting up, blowing out candles and gathering up the supplies he laid out before we started. It feels like we were gone for hours, but a quick look at the candles tells me it wasn't long at all.

Damn.

That means plenty of time for other training.

"What is all that for?" I ask, pushing myself to the edge of the bed and dangling my feet as I watch him.

"The candles are spelled for protection, makes a kind o' barrier from intruders," he explains, placing them on top of the dresser. "This," he holds out the bowl that's still smoking a little, "is a blend o' herbs to ground me. Air, my other Affinity, carries smell. Yer Affinity can ground ye in just about any situation, but especially important when yer travelin' around other planes or goin' through the Portals."

He uses a pestle to stamp out the remaining embers before setting it on the dresser too.

"That is different for everyone, dependin' on yer Affinity. An ye don't need to focus on it when yer travelin the Portals, but on the Astral Plane, ye need to focus yer groundin' on somethin'."

I hop off the bed, standing and stretching my arms over my head. "I feel like there's a million aspects to every little thing, and I'm never going to learn them all," I admit.

"There is a bit to know, but ye've a natural talent for figurin it all out." He turns from the dresser and grins at me. "Already yer usin' Spirit in a way I think Gabriel would be impressed with. He'll not let me hear the end of it when he meets ye. We spent years trainin' with him an' never thought to use it in the way ye're doin."

I saunter over to where he's leaning against the dresser, putting my hands against his chest and leaning in close. "Well, I am amazing," I tease, looking at him under my lashes.

He grunts and pulls me against him with a hand at the small of my back, a shiver running up my spine. "Ye'll get no argument from me," he whispers before capturing my mouth with his.

Just as I sink into the kiss, all hell breaks loose as the door behind us crashes against the wall, Malakai twisting us around so he's between me and the chaos.

TWENTY-FOUR

My face is plastered against Malakai's chest, his arms a vice around my body as the ground rumbles under our feet. I can't see anything in this position, but with my newly gained control, I can feel both rage and fear coming from whoever just burst in here. I realize that person is Aunt Viv just as Malakai's tense muscles relax a fraction and he allows me to pull myself away enough to glance around his massive frame.

"Find Toby, an get em the hell outta here, Malakai. Use the Portal, get em home," she says, rushing over to us as Malakai races to look out the doorway. "Ye'll have to show her how to travel the second ye get outta here. She and Toby both. They need to be able to use the Portals at any time."

"What's happening?" I yell, both confused and frustrated.

"We're under attack, dove." She stops, putting a hand to my cheek. "We knew they'd come eventually; they just came sooner than we'd like. An' now ye need to get outta here, get someplace they do'na know to look."

She looks frantically around the room, then goes to the window and yanks it open. As she pokes her head out, I can visibly see her shoulders relax slightly, and she starts waving her hand at someone I can't see.

I run over and see Toby sprinting towards the window. "Lor!" he yells, face pale, looking dazed.

I feel Malakai grab me by the waist and haul me over the windowsill, where I grab onto the frame and stop myself. "Stop!" I scream, turning to look back into the room. "Aunt Viv, where are my parents? What's going on? I'm not leaving without you all."

"Lorali Brigit, you will go and take your brother right this second. Yer no' ready to face this, an' I'll have no argument about it," she snaps, fixing me with a look I have never seen on her face before.

It is enough to make my blood run cold.

"But..." I start, but don't get to finish as Malakai jumps up and takes me out the window with him.

Without a word, he grabs my elbow as we land and starts running toward the river, where I know the Portal is. Toby questions nothing and is running right beside us. I try to dig my heels in, stop and turn around, demand answers from Aunt Viv. But Malakai's grip is too firm, and all I can manage is a glance over my shoulder.

Aunt Viv is nowhere to be seen through that open window, just a curtain fluttering in the breeze.

We reach the river more quickly than I'd like, and Malakai stops abruptly in the spot where I first met Wesley. He gives me a stern look, then releases my arm, which I rub while shooting him a nasty look right back.

Toby is panting, hands on his knees doubled over, looking up at me with wide eyes. "I know what you're thinking, Lor. But we gotta go. We gotta go right now," he says frantically, standing up and clutching his side.

"This is gonna be a little rough, but ye'll be fine. Take my hands and walk with me when I move. Got it?" Malakai demands.

Toby nods his head enthusiastically while I cross my arms in defiance.

"Lorali. We can fight about it later, but right now I'm doin what yer aunt has asked of me. Hate me later," Malakai pleads.

I nod, looking over at Toby.

*I can't put him in dange*r, I think.

"Put a hand on me arms, both of ye, an *do not* let go," Malakai instructs, closing his eyes and taking a deep breath.

A loud boom ricochets from behind us. Glancing back I see a massive cloud of dust flying through the air above the tree line, near where the kitchen is.

Malakai grabs my hand tighter. I can *feel* him willing me to do what I'm asked. "*Imperium Porta,*" he whispers, and the air in front of us seems to shimmer.

He looks over at each of us in turn, a determined look on his face, then takes a step. I lift my foot, ensure Toby is following along, and then jump back as they walk through the Portal. I hear Malakai's cursing as the air snaps in front of me and the shimmering fades.

I turn and run back towards the house, sprinting towards the kitchen when I'm knocked off my feet by a blast of wind. Groaning, the breath knocked out of me, I roll onto my back and put a hand to my chest.

Malakai's furious face is above me, his arms grabbing me around the waist as he hoists me over his shoulder in a firefighter's carry. I watch the house fade off into the distance again as he runs for the Portal. I didn't even make it far enough to see if the kitchen was still there. Not even stopping fully as he activates it, Malakai jumps through with me on his shoulder.

It's almost instantaneous, the travel itself, but leaves my skin feeling tingly—as though ice water was dumped all over me.

"Malakai!" I screech, hitting his back with my fists.

"No, Lorali," he says, coldly, and walks over to where my brother is sitting against a tree trunk. He sets me on my feet, harshly, and looks over at Toby. "I hav'na a clue where we are. Ye need to get us to yer house," he says, as Toby stands and wipes his pants.

Malakai is busy whispering phrases I don't understand, making the air around the Portal and us feel thick, charged.

"Um, yeah. Okay," Toby responds, looking around.

His gaze lands on me for a split second before he looks away and clears his throat. I can feel the anger toward me, the disbelief at my antics. I cross my arms, frustrated tears on my cheeks, pissed that even Toby won't acknowledge me. I know he doesn't know how to get home; he needs my help.

"If we—" I start, but Malakai holds up a hand without looking in my direction.

"Are we far? How long will it take to get there, Toby?" he asks.

"I don't..." He looks around the wooded area. "I'm not really sure where we are, to be honest. Dad told me the Portal was near Seattle, but he didn't say where exactly." He kicks at a rock with his toe, looking at the ground, face flushing. His anger gives way to embarrassment and frustration.

"Then we walk, figure it out, and we get ye home as quick as we can." He turns and fixes me with a glare. "Can ye follow us, or do I have to carry ye the whole way?"

Without answering, I throw my hands to my sides, fists balled, and start walking in the direction I think will take us somewhere I can recognize. I don't look back to see what they're doing. I can hear their footsteps behind me, so I assume they are following.

We walk like that: me stomping ahead with them behind me for a bit before I calm down enough to realize my phone is in my pocket.

I roll my eyes, stopping and pulling it out to check Maps. This is why Mom always tells us 'it's perfectly normal to have strong feelings when you're in a tense situation, but if you want to get through it without problems, best to keep a calm head until it's over.' If I'd been able to do just that, I probably wouldn't have the two of them treating me like I'm a toddler in time out right now.

"Son of a..." I exclaim, groaning at my phone before turning to them. "We're in Point Defiance," I say, bewildered.

"But that's not Seattle," Toby says. "We're basically in our backyard."

"Yeah," I agree. "Yeah, I know. And I know how to get home too," I say, dreading what I have to do next and totally unsure how I'll handle it. "Isobel lives five minutes away." I look at Toby, who nods.

"Well, call her!" he says excitedly, no doubt ready to get home where we're relatively safe.

"Call her and say what exactly?" I demand, more of Malakai than Toby. "How do I explain that we were in Scotland, but hey, we're back, and I haven't spoken to you since we left, and I can't explain how or why we're back, but be a pal and give us a lift home?" I bark out a laugh at the ridiculousness of it all. "Oh, and don't mind the 6'4" caveman here with us; I can't tell you anything about why I haven't told you all about him or why I can't now?" I collapse onto the ground, crossing my legs and putting my head in my hands with a groan. "We have to tell her something, and I don't know what to say!" I mumble.

"Didn't Dad tell her we had a family emergency? Just tell her we came back to pack some stuff up," Toby supplies.

"And we ended up here with no car how, exactly?" I demand. I know he's trying to be helpful, but right now I am so frustrated, I can't bring myself to coddle him.

"Is there a reason we can'na walk?" Malakai asks condescendingly.

"Oh, sure," I say sarcastically, standing and walking toward him. "We can absolutely walk for God knows how long to get across town and to our house. It's only a half an hour drive, how long could that take?" I yell at him.

"Lor," Toby puts himself between us, putting a hand on my shoulder. "Stop. He's probably never even been in a car, or seen a city like Tacoma. You're not being very pleasant."

Damn it.

He's right, and now I look like an even bigger jerk.

"Okay. Fine." I sigh, "You're right." I lift my phone, and then it hits me. "Wait, Toby, do you have your wallet?"

He nods, pulling it out of his pocket.

"Still have the debit card Mom gave you?" I ask.

"Uber!" he says, pulling out the card and showing it to me.

I quickly open the app, order the car, and breathe a sigh of relief that I don't have to make explanations I can't actually explain to Isobel. Not today, anyway. "Okay, it'll be here in ten minutes. We're a five-minute walk from the trailhead. Let's go," I say, starting off toward the meet-up point.

The ride is quiet, and Malakai looks completely lost the entire time, staring out the window at the city. Probably the first modern city he's ever seen. I take the time to self-reflect and find myself feeling more than a little ashamed at what I've put him through today. When we pull up to the house, I thank the driver and rush up the steps. I have never been so happy to be home.

#

After having left a million voicemails and texts on my parents' and Aunt Viv's phones, and after a much needed shower, I walk back downstairs where Toby and Malakai are talking quietly on the couch. I take a beat to gather myself, knowing it's beyond time for me to apologize to the both of them.

"Hey, Tob, can I have a minute?" I ask, glancing toward Malakai.

"Yeah, sure," he says, looking awkwardly between Malakai and me as he stands. "I could use a shower anyway, and I'm kind of beat. Just, um, let me know if you hear from Mom and Dad?"

I nod in agreement, and he leaves me alone to face Malakai, who hasn't acknowledged my existence since we got here.

"I'm sorry," I admit. "I thought I could help, and I wanted Toby safe."

He snorts, shaking his head but saying nothing.

"Look, I knew you'd keep him safe, but my parents—"

"Are seasoned Guardians who can handle themselves without havin' to worry about protectin' ye," he points out, standing. "Do ye have any idea what danger ye put em in tryin' to go back? If ye'd have been able to find em, in the middle of battle? Then what? Ye'd distract em and maybe kill both 'em *and* yerself?" he booms, harsh but honest. "Not to mention the danger leavin yer brother alone while I came back to stop ye? This is'na a game,

Lorali; ye've no control over yer magics, an ye've no business goin in like ye have!"

Every point he makes feels like a ton of bricks hitting me, and even though I know he's right, it makes me angry. I have never been good at handling being helpless.

"That's my family!" I yell, voice cracking. "I saved Darian, didn't I? I could've helped!"

"No!" He grasps my arms gently, but not allowing me to ignore him. "No, ye'd have killed yer Mam, and ye'd never forgive yerself."

"You don't know that!" I scream, pushing him away. Whatever understanding I had of his position ripped away by the statement.

"I do," he says, sadly. "I do because ye told me yerself."

"What?" I manage, my heart a weight in my chest. I know he's trying to make a point, but this is going way too far.

"Ye came to me, before ye met me now." He sighs, throwing his hands up. "Ye came to me the day before I left for the Gatherin'. Ye told me not to let ye get away from me, that if I did, yer Mam would be killed," he admits reluctantly, eyes remorseful.

I grab the back of a chair. My stomach revolting. "No," I whisper, bile in the back of my throat. "*No*, you're lying."

"I did'na know when, or how, but ye told me yerself that there'd come a time when yer family was attacked. Ye told me how when ye went to help, when they saw ye, it was enough a distraction she was killed," he reiterates, completely genuine.

Shaking my head, a hand to my mouth, I run to the bathroom and dry heave, tears running down my face. When my body stops trying to expel the contents of my stomach, I sink to the floor, sobs wracking my body. I feel a hand on my back and shove at it blindly. The weight of what I almost caused too much for me to comprehend.

I feel myself lifted off the floor, cradled in Malakai's arms as he walks back to the couch, sits down without letting me go.

"Lor!" I hear Toby racing down the stairs, hear him come to an abrupt halt next to us. "Lor! Lor!"

He reaches out and shakes my arm. I can both hear and feel the terror in his voice.

"What's wrong?" he demands. "What's wrong with her?"

"It's alright, Toby. She'll be alright. Let her get it out," I hear Malakai assure him.

"No, what happened? Is it Mom and Dad?" Toby's voice shakes as he asks.

"We've not heard from em yet, lad. She's just had a bit o' shock is all. Let me handle it, huh?" Malakai soothes him.

I can feel the fear pulsing off my brother, hear him sinking down next to the couch. And that's how we stay, Malakai holding me in his arms, Toby sitting on the floor beside us, as I allow my pain to wash over me.

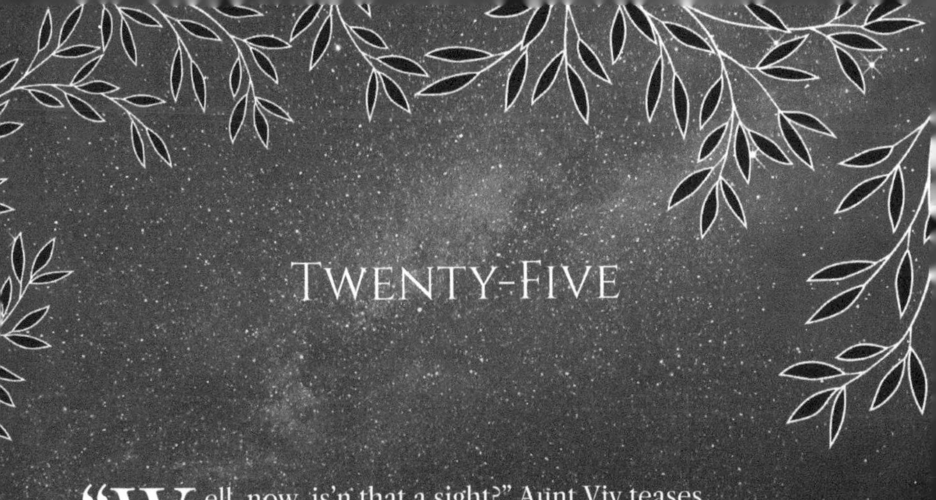

Twenty-Five

"Well, now, is'n that a sight?" Aunt Viv teases.

I shoot up off the couch, launching myself at her. At some point, all three of us passed out as we were. Toby is right behind me, wrapping his arms around us both.

"Alright, now. Everythin' is gonna be just fine, doves," she coos, squeezing us both.

I pull back, looking at her face, feeling the hesitation and wariness in her she isn't speaking. "Aunt Viv, where's Mom and Dad?" I ask, skipping the pleasantries.

She shoos us both over to the couches, gently demanding we calm down and sit. Malakai is standing off to the side and goes to leave, but she tells him to stay. Sitting in the chair by the couch, she smiles at us sweetly and explains what happened. "Yer parents are both back at the Manor. Yer Da will be fine, but he can'na travel right now. Took a bit of a blast, he did."

I gasp, and Toby jumps to his feet.

"Now, do'na go over reactin'. He'll be just fine, as I said. I promise, but we could'na call ye up. The battle messed with the energy 'round the place an none of the signals are goin' through at the moment. So I told yer Mam to stay, an I came here knowin' ye'd be out o' yer mids with worry."

"Was anyone else hurt?" I ask, clasping my hands together.

"Are ye all settled in? No injuries or whatnot to report here, is there?" she asks, looking over to Malakai. I notice the redirection, and want to press her, but they don't give me a

"Nothin' to report. We have'na been here long," he says, looking over at me.

Oh, we are definitely having a conversation later.

"Good. It seems ye've gotten some sleep. Have ye tried travelin yet?" she demands.

"No, um, we haven't really had the opportunity," I explain.

"Right. Well, now's a good a time as any. Ye've only been gone a few hours, but yer parents did'na think it wise to linger." She stands, rubbing her hands together. "All ye really need to know is where yer goin, an when. Focus on it, an say the words. There's not a lot to tell ye other than that. Ye just have to do it, not much practicin' for it, but ye can go through the motions here. Then we'll go to the Portal." She motions impatiently for Toby and me to stand.

"What, like pretend we're at the Portal? Right now?" I ask, incredulous. "What's the rush? You haven't told us—"

"Lorali, I need ye to just cooperate right now. I know it is'na easy for ye, but I just need ye to do as yer told. I'll explain more later, but we can'na stay here long, an' I need to *know* ye can travel if ye have to," she interrupts.

Toby clears his throat, closes his eyes, and says the spell to open the Portal. He's never been comfortable with conflict, and I know it's his way of diverting from it. Nothing happens, of course, but Aunt Viv looks pleased. She gives me a pointed look, and I roll my eyes, but decide to appease her.

I close my eyes, think of getting back to my parents. "*Imperium Porta,*" I whisper and open my eyes.

In the middle of my living room, the air shimmers.

"Lor!" Aunt Viv and Toby both exclaim. Malakai jumps in front of me and looks frantically at Aunt Viv.

"Stay. Here," she warns and walks through.

The air returns to normal and a second later shimmers again as she steps through, the Portal closing behind her.

"Well. Looks like we've now got a Portal in yer living room," she states, eerily calm.

"Aunt Viv—" I begin, but she cuts me off.

"Nothin' to be done about it now. I do'na know how ye did it, so I can'na explain it to ye. Fact is ye have, and ye can. It's not necessarily a bad thing, dove. But let's no' go round tellin just anyone yet."

"Did you know?" I demand, spinning toward Malakai.

"Ach now, lass, how would he?" Aunt Viv waves a hand dismissively. "At least this'll save us some time. Go on now, pack some warm clothes, and hurry. There's some things to say before we go. We'll not be goin' straight home, so pack what ye'd need for a trip. Toby, stay behind, I wanna see if ye can use this Portal," she commands, shoving me gently toward the stairs while Malakai sits down on the couch to wait.

"We're talking about this later, Malakai," I warn over my shoulder, resigning myself to the fact I need to follow Aunt Viv's lead.

For now.

I rush into my parents' room to find an old duffle I know Mom has shoved in the top of her closet and take it into my room to start throwing stuff in. As I unzip it, I notice a piece of paper laying in the bottom of the canvas bag. I pick it up, see "*Kids*" scrawled across the front in Mom's handwriting.

I grapple for a second, then set it gently on my bed to take down and open with Toby before rushing around the room, gathering all of the warm clothes I can shove into the bag, along with a pair of hiking boots.

I pass Toby on the way to the bathroom. "I'll grab extra toiletries for you, do you have a bag?" I yell at him without stopping.

"Yeah, I've got it, thanks, Lor," he shouts back.

I grab a pack of extra toothbrushes Mom stashed under the sink, an unopened box of toothpaste, an old face wash I shoved under there at some point, and extra deodorant. I have never been so happy that Mom likes to shop in bulk. I even manage to find some discount shampoo and conditioner. Not great, or what I would prefer, but my good stuff is currently in Scotland.

Hauling the bag back into my room, I toss in a couple notebooks and pens for good measure and zip it shut before grabbing the note and heading downstairs.

Of course Toby beat me down. He probably threw a couple sweatshirts and joggers in a bag and called it good.

"Did you at least grab shoes, Tobe?" I chide.

"Yes, *Mom*," he says sarcastically. "I even grabbed the sleeping bags and a tent from the garage." He motions over to a pile of camping gear on the floor.

"Will we actually need that?" I ask, afraid of the answer.

"Not that I can see, but it helps to be prepared." Aunt Viv beams approval at Toby. I roll my eyes.

Great, I think.

"OK, well, before you start, Aunt Viv, I found this in the old duffle I grabbed," I say, holding out the note. "It's addressed to Toby and me, so I figured we should read it together," I explain.

I open the folded paper and begin to read.

My dears,

If you've found the note, and I am not with you to intercept it, something has probably gone haywire along the way. Whatever has caused your dad and I to be separated from you, know that we are doing everything we can to remedy that as soon as humanly possible. We didn't expect to be coming home, so I can only assume you've come back running from something else, which means the Manor is off the table. I pray you've learned to use the Portals by now, and if not you can call Raymond Nguyen; he's the head of the Washington based Guardians while we are away. You'll find his number in the address book on my desk; make sure you take that with you, as you may need it. Any contact designated in purple ink is a Guardian, and trustworthy.

Once you are confident in your ability to travel, I want you to go to South Carolina. Your Uncle Zack is a Guardian, and the Portal is located in his backyard. You must call him first. He has enough protection spells around his house that you'd be blasted to Siberia trying to get in uninvited. Don't worry, he is aware that if anything goes wrong, you're to go there first, and will be thrilled to see you. He will also be helpful in teaching you to control your magics, should that still be an issue.

Do not trust anyone you do not know, or I have not cleared in my book. Guardians are not the only Magic Users in the world, and there are people looking for you that would not hesitate to do you harm. Please protect each other. I promise you, we will get to you as soon as we can. I love you both with my whole heart. Stay safe, and be smart and cautious.

Love,

Mom

"Well then, not much I need to tell ye. Seems she's covered it herself," Aunt Viv responds, picking up a sleeping bag and the tent. "Everyone grab a bag. I've already rung Zack, and he knows we're comin. Best no' to keep him waitin' too long."

Toby and I exchange a look, both of us a little off balance over the whole thing. Regardless, we each grab a bag and look to Aunt Viv.

"Lor, why don't ye open the Portal? We'll need to be quick, as they do'na stay open long. Toby right behind her, and then Malakai. I'll come through shortly; I need to place some protections on the house now there's a Portal in the middle of it."

She motions for us to form an orderly line, handing off her sleeping bag to Malakai. It would be funny if it wasn't so serious, Aunt Viv arranging us in a tidy row. The woman is the most disorganized and spontaneous human being I've ever met.

She hugs both Toby and me, kissing us on the top of the head. "Do'na worry, doves. I'll be right behind ye, and Malakai is more'n capable of protectin' ye if needs be." She smiles reassuringly at us, then steps back out of the way. "Hurry now," she says.

Not having any other choice, I take a breath and focus on Uncle Zack's. I haven't been there in a few years, but I remember it well enough. Picturing his backyard since that's where Mom said the Portal was, I focus and take a breath.

"*Imperium Porta,*" I call out, intent this time on going where I'm meant to.

Taking one last glance at Aunt Viv, I face the Portal and step through. That icy cold washes over me again, and then I'm smelling crisp mountain air. I walk about five feet and turn around quickly, watching as Toby and Malakai come through, then watch as the air settles and the Portal closes behind us.

A pang of anxiety hits me as it does, wishing Aunt Viv had come with us and cursing myself for opening a new Portal in our living room. I'm still anxious to find out if Malakai knew I could do it, and why he didn't stop me if he did.

"Well, it's about time y'all showed up! Viv called me 'bout two hours ago! Long time to be sittin out on the back porch in December," I hear Uncle Zack's southern twang call out behind us, followed by his feet hitting the steps into the yard.

"Uncle Zack!" Toby calls out, his face breaking into a wide smile as he drops his bags and runs towards the house.

Twenty-Six

I drop what I'm carrying, spinning around to greet my uncle, trying to beat Toby to it. Toby and I always raced each other out of the car when we came to visit, trying to get to him first. It was a silly game Uncle Zack started. Whoever got there first got picked up and spun around. Then he would pretend we were so big, we exhausted him and he couldn't lift the other, so we'd get an affectionate noogie that made our hair stand up.

It was a game Uncle Zack probably didn't intend to follow us as we grew, but it's become a tradition now, no matter how old we get. Especially since it's been a few years since we've visited.

Today, despite his head start, I beat out Toby and get lifted off my feet and spun around.

"Aw! No fair! She runs all the time!" he protests as his hair is mussed, and we all laugh.

He's not wrong. I do have an advantage. It is perfectly normal for me to run two or three miles a day at home.

"No one's stopping you from going with me! Probably do you some good to exercise regularly," I respond. "Uncle Zack, I'd like you to meet Malakai," I say, standing a little straighter and waving Malakai forward. "He's a Guardian from Scotland," I explain, intentionally leaving out the 'friend' label, or any other label for that matter. I haven't figured out what he is to me, and I don't want to put my foot in my mouth here.

The two reach out and shake hands. Uncle Zack as friendly as

"Nice to meet ya, bud!" he exclaims, grinning. "Why don't y'all come on in the house and let's get ya settled in," he says as he grabs my duffle and sleeping bag. "It's not much, but there's enough space for all of ya, and I've got some deer in the crockpot."

I chuckle a little at Uncle Zack's humility in saying the house isn't much. It's a two-story McMansion with a finished basement, complete with a whopping one hundred forty-five acres of land, a hunting cabin, and every luxury you could ever want.

The man has every state-of-the-art tech thing ever created and spends enormous amounts of money keeping everything top of the line. You could probably cook dinner via app, or at least preheat the oven. Frankly, I'm surprised he's still using a crockpot.

He turns and walks in the house, shutting down the complaint I was about to make about him carrying all my stuff. Rolling my eyes and huffing, I grab Toby's sleeping bag and follow him in, the boys trailing behind me. Walking straight into the living room, he points to the corner and addresses them.

"Y'all can just toss your stuff over there. Couch pulls out into a bed. Not the most comfortable thing in the world, but it'll do. If ya can't both fit on it, I got a cot I can pull in here. I'll probably just grab it. Malakai's a bigger guy than your Aunt Viv warned me bout."

Without looking back, he turns and walks off down the hallway, towards the back of the house. Since he is still hauling my stuff around, I know he means for me to follow him. He's a man used to having those around him follow in his wake.

That sounds much more menacing than it is when it comes to him. He's the sweetest guy you'll ever meet, he's just used to being in charge. More than that, he's used to people *wanting* him in charge.

"Lor, this here's your room. Bathroom's in the same place," he says, opening the door and setting my bags on the queen bed.

"Uncle Zack, what's wrong with the upstairs?" I ask, knowing there are 3 more rooms up there because we've stayed in them before. There's also the finished basement with a pool table, a futon, an office and its own full bath.

"Nothing wrong with upstairs, just don't want you kids outta my sight this trip," he says, shrugging his shoulders and fixing me with a 'go ahead and argue with me' stare.

"You could at least let Malakai have a room. I get me and Toby. We don't know a thing about our magic yet, but Malakai? He's got it, my Gran trained him. He's the one who's been helping me get a hold of it," I reason.

"Yeah," he snorts, "I'm not lettin' that boy roam around unchecked. Not after what I heard from your folks. No, ma'am, not in *my* house."

"Uncle Zack!" My mouth drops open, arms crossed.

"Nuh-uh, young lady. I don't care how adult you think you are. We ain't havin' none of that round here. Not if I have a say, and look at that. I do! Huh!" He chuckles, walking out of the room as he pats me on the shoulder, eyes never leaving mine and grin never fading.

I have half a mind to go sleep outside, except it's almost January in Upstate South Carolina and 20 degrees once that sun goes down. That and bugs, and whatever other wildlife is crawling around the woods. I'd probably end up with an opossum or a deer in my bag with me. I physically shudder at the thought of it.

Uncle Zack lives in Pumpkintown, SC. It is as middle of nowhere as it gets, close to the North Carolina state line, up in the mountains. Well, what the East Coast calls mountains, anyway. It's a highly debated issue between my uncle and me, whether anything on this side of the country qualifies as more than a foothill.

I know they're really mountains, but it's much more fun to watch him get all riled up about it. I've been known to shoot off a text to him of Rainier with the caption 'In case you forgot what mountains really look like.'

"Maybe we can take a stroll through the hills later!" I shout through the open door at him, just because I'm feeling ornery.

"I don't know about no hills, but we can go climb a mountain if ya like!" he shouts back, and I can't help but laugh at the predictability.

I open my duffle and pull out my hiking boots, thinking a little exploration would actually be a pleasant distraction while waiting on Aunt Viv. When I've got them on and head back to the living room to see if Malakai wants to join me, I see Uncle Zack sitting on the edge of the couch, talking to him.

"Now them right there are some good boots. Lucky I had an extra pair in the truck," he's explaining, and I see Malakai is bouncing from left to right, testing out the feel of my Uncle's boots.

He probably mentioned a walk himself, and no way will Uncle Zack let anyone walk out of his house with runners on if he can help it. He's got at least fifteen pairs of those stupid boots, in a variety of sizes—both men and women's. I think it's because my dad went out once and broke a toe kicking a rock or something equally silly. I forget the exact story.

The fact remains, no one walks out of Uncle Zack's house without a fresh pair of sturdy—and expensive—hiking boots; as state-of-the art as anything else in his house. The pair I'm wearing are ones he sent me last year for my birthday, hardly used, but I have no doubt he'll find some reason they need replacing.

What you can't tell from his laidback, Southern Redneck demeanor is that my uncle is *filthy* rich. He invented some app when smart phones got big, made a boatload of money, and then sold it for even more. That's, of course, on top of the money he and Mom inherited from their parents.

Now he runs a 'recreational park,' which really translates to a place he and his buddies can ride 4-wheelers and dirt bikes any time they want. He doesn't really 'run' it so much as own it, since he almost never works it himself. He provides several dozen jobs for the locals, though.

"Hey," I announce myself before he starts making Malakai try on his waders next. "Where's Toby run off to?" I ask.

"Oh, he's down in the basement with the Xbox. Said he hadn't played since y'all left home, and didn't know when he'd get a chance after y'all go," he replies without looking my way.

"Okay, um, well, I thought a hike might clear my head. Malakai, wanna tag along?"

"Lemme just get my jacket, I'll come with ya," Uncle Zack says, already walking off to his room.

"Come on!" I say, grabbing Malakai by the arm and rushing to the back door.

We manage to make it off the deck before Uncle Zack catches us. "Now hold on a minute, I said I'd come," he huffs at me.

"Uncle Zack, you can't leave Toby alone. I'll take Malakai, and we'll stick to the east side of the property," I reason. "Besides, don't you have a roast going?"

"Now you see here, young lady—" he starts.

"No, *you* see here, Uncle Zack. I am not only a grown woman, I'm apparently a hunted one," I cut him off, exasperated. "I will respect you, and your house. I'll follow your rules and whatever you've got in your head about protecting me and my honor or whatever other backwards nonsense you're thinking. But I need you to have a little trust here, too. I have some things I need to discuss with Malakai, and I'd rather do that in private, if you don't mind. It's not long before it's dark here; I'll be back before the sun is down."

"Well, ain't you just a chip off the ole block," he responds, laughing. "If you ain't your momma's child through and through. Coulda been her twenty years ago, standin' there tellin me off like that."

He shakes his head, throwing his hands up.

"Well, go on then. But y'all be back here in an hour, or I'm comin lookin for ya, and it won't be pretty when I find ya neither," he says, turning and going back in the house.

"Ye've really gotta learn to respect yer elders, Lorali," Malakai admonishes. "Ye can disagree without bein' rude to em."

"Oh, not you too." I roll my eyes. "Come on," I say and start walking toward the tree line.

Malakai sighs heavily but catches up to me quickly. I head toward the lake, which is really a gargantuan man-made pond, but Uncle Zack is very adamant it's a fishing lake. It's not very far from the house but private enough and out of sight of the house. Given my curfew, we can't go far if I want to actually have a discussion, and I very much *do* want to have a discussion.

We reach the lake in silence, Malakai beside me but definitely giving me some space. I'm not sure if he's still angry with me for trying to ditch him at the Portal, or reluctant to have this conversation. I sit down on the bank, leaning back on my hands and just enjoying the view for a second.

"So," I begin, looking over at Malakai, who sat down and started throwing pebbles and rocks into the water. "I suppose you'd better start at the beginning, and tell me exactly what happened before I met you at the Manor." I raise a brow and cock my head to the side.

"Aye," he clears his throat. "Guess I knew ye'd be wantin more answers than I gave ye."

"You think?" I ask.

"I understand why yer angry, Lorali, but ye've gotta understand that ye told me yerself I was'na to tell ye a thing bout it until I had to," he pleads, looking extremely concerned. "Ye came to see me, before I even knew who ye were. I do'na know how ye even found me to tell ye true. Or I did'na, until ye came into me dream. Ye must've figured it's a place I like to go, 'cause that's where ye found me..." he hesitates, glancing over at me.

"Well, go on," I encourage.

"Right." He nods, pulling apart a blade of grass in his hands. "Ye were a mess when ye found me, launched right into me arms ye did. Almost knocked me off me feet, as I wasn'a expectin' a beautiful stranger to throw herself at me. Ye must've realized I woud'na know ye yet, but ye just started talkin'. In that fast way ye have, just talkin away without lettin' me say a word to ye."

"Right, but what did I say?" I demand, frustration seeping through despite my efforts to stay calm.

"I do'na want to tell ye too much, Lor. I do'na want to mess anythin' up. It gets tricky when ye start jumpin in timelines; it can have consequences," he hedges.

"I think it's a little late for that now, isn't it? I mean, I came to you because I got my mom killed. That didn't happen now, so what else could there be?"

"I do'na believe ye came to me right away." He sighs. "Ye knew too much to have done."

"What do you mean I 'knew too much'?"

"Yer magics, Lor. Ye had a lot of control over yer magics."

"I could open new Portals," I say, but it's not really a question.

"Aye," he admits. "There's a new one right in the meadow. I could'na even tell Lyse it was there. Not when I did'na understand what was goin' on."

"But *is it* there?" I ask. "A new Portal, I mean. I never actually went there, so is there even one there now?"

"I do'na know." He sighs heavily again. "I guess there might no' be."

"Okay, so you knew I could open new Portals, but there is obviously more that you aren't telling me."

"Lorali, I only wanna tell ye what I must. That's what ye told me to do, an' that's what I intend to do."

"Was I alone?" I ask quietly.

He nods, but doesn't add anything else.

"Why would I have been alone?" I ponder out loud, the thought bothering me. "Where was Toby? Aunt Viv? Any of my family? Surely they'd have wanted to help me fix my mom's death."

"Likely because no one woulda let ye do it had ye told them," he supplies.

"Which is why you haven't told anyone. Because it shouldn't have happened," I conclude.

"Aye, it would'na have been a good idea to tell anyone. They'd have told me to let it play out as it was meant to, an' I could'na do it. I promised ye I'd stop ye, an' ye can'na tell anyone either. There's consequences for this, serious ones."

"Yeah, but it didn't even happen now, right?"

"It does'na matter. There'd be consequences. Yer Merlin's Heir, so they might be inclined to be lenient with ye, but I am not. I am simply a Guardian, which might still get me some leniency. But I'm also Evangeline's son, an' sure there are those that would rather I were'na roamin' free."

"I see," I say, feeling even more guilty now that I know he's done something he knows could land him in a lot of hot water with the Order.

"I made the decision, Lorali. I coulda made a different one. I chose to do as ye asked, knowin' what the consequences could be."

"I'm sorry."

"There's no need to be. I'd do it again, given the chance. I knew even then, I'd do anythin' ye asked of me," he admits.

I look at him for a minute, not really knowing what to say. All I can really do at this point is to ensure I don't become the person who would take such a risk, the person who would put someone I care about in danger.

"Ye can get it under control, ye know. An' may the Gods help us all when ye do, because yer the most powerful Guardian there has been. Even Lyse could'na match ye if it came to it. I shoulda guessed then ye'd be the Heir."

"I don't know that I want it," I admit, for the first time, out loud. "If everyone I love wasn't involved in this mess, I'd have run for the hills a long time ago."

"No, ye would'na have. Ye may have wanted to, but ye'd not have left innocent people to be hurt, an' well ye know it," he challenges, absolutely certain.

"Maybe," I hesitate, rubbing my forehead, "Maybe. It doesn't really matter now, does it?"

"I know ye've got a lot on yer mind, a lot yer responsible for now. Do'na ever forget that yer not alone in it. Ye'll have me by yer side, and ye'd have had me even if ye had chosen me brother instead, or if yer done with me now."

"Malakai."

"Do'na say anythin ye can'na stand by, Lorali. I know yer angry with me, an I do'na expect ye to pretend yer not. Do'na make a pledge now ye regret later."

"Malakai, I'm not saying I'll marry you. Or that I know what will happen a week from now, or a year. But I do know I want to see where this could go, and I'm not angry with you. I'm angry with myself."

"Why would ye be angry at yerself?" he asks, shock evident.

"Oh, I don't know, maybe because I put you in danger? Because I apparently became some version of myself where I would do that? Because I made a stupid, immature decision that killed my mom and set me on that path to begin with?"

"Be gentler with yerself, *mo chridhe.* Ye have no idea what led to yer decision, trust it was the best one ye could make. It is never stupid to try an' protect the ones we love."

"Is there anything else I should know? Any massive revelations that might be easier to handle now rather than waiting for me to figure it out on my own?"

"Ach, Lorali. There is nothin' more I can tell ye safely."

"But there's more."

"Aye."

"Then tell me. I told you not to tell me unless you had to. Now I am telling you that you have to. The logic is flawless."

"Yer not bein' fair here."

"Is any of this fair?"

"Lor—"

"No. Seriously. None of this is fair. Not *one bit* of it. Did you know I was accepted to college? A fantastic one. I was going to be a surgeon. A doctor. Do you really think that is ever going to happen now? Because I don't. I'll probably never see Isobel again. I haven't spoken to her since we got to Scotland."

I clench my fists tightly, ready to explode.

"She's my best friend. I've known her since I was a little kid, my whole life! I had a plan, Malakai, a *good* one. Now I have no idea what will happen tomorrow, and my entire life has been uprooted. With zero warning, might I add. So don't tell me I'm not fair, because nothing is fair!" I jump up, throwing a rock into the lake, and let loose a frustrated scream into the sky.

"That scream'll have yer uncle here in five seconds, so I'll tell ye this. Ye can share memory, not just Pull it from others. It's why I was so shocked when ye Pulled mine. I do'na know of any other Guardian who can do both. One or the other, but never both. Ye wanna know why I trust ye, why I have no problems followin' yer lead? That'd be why. I've seen what ye can be, what *we* can be."

He walks over, pulling me into his arms, resting his head on top of mine.

"I have seen what we can be, Lorali. I have seen what ye could have gone through, an' what was prevented by followin' yer lead. Now do'na ask me anymore, because I'll not share it. Do'na even think of tryin to Pull it outta me head yerself, either."

"I would never—" I protest, pulling back to look him in the eye.

"I know. I know ye would never. I wanted to remind ye of it." He smiles gently at me, cupping my cheek in his hand.

"Now you're gonna back away real slow, and then Lor is gonna explain why she just screamed loud enough to wake the dead, or we are gonna have ourselves a real big problem, bud," Uncle Zack orders, a few feet away, literal flames flickering along his arms.

"Zack, she's fine," Aunt Viv says, panting behind him. "Dear, if yer gonna scream like that, may wanna do it far enough afield that it does'na scare us out o' our wits next time..."

"Aunt Viv!" I exclaim, running over and hugging her. My relief at her being here, safe, is huge.

"Oh now. Did I not tell ye I'd be right behind?" she says, hugging me back.

"Now what the *hell* were you hollerin' about, girl?" Uncle Zack demands, still obviously annoyed and unconvinced it had nothing to do with Malakai. Flames smaller now, but still visible.

"Haven't you ever just had to yell, Uncle Zack?" I chuckle. "Very therapeutic. 10/10 would recommend."

"Next time give a warning. Like to give me a damn heart attack." He shakes his head, still eyeing Malakai suspiciously. "Bout time y'all came on back anyhow. Dinner's bout done." The flames disappear entirely, but there is still an intense energy around him.

Maybe I shouldn't have screamed.

Any thought of spending more time with Malakai is now vanished.

He waits for us to start moving before situating himself between Malakai and me as we walk back. Aunt Viv loops an arm through mine and chuckles.

"He's a bit angry that I've messed with his room assignments. Ye'll be happy to know we all have one now. Ridiculous man," she whispers conspiratorially.

"I heard that! I haven't agreed to nothin', so don't go thinkin you've got your way now," he argues, obviously offended.

"What do ye think yer sister would have to say about the way yer behavin, Zack? Do'na think she will'na come take ye to task as soon as she can, or that I will'na give her a full report when I see her next."

He shoots her a disgruntled look, but keeps walking without responding. Back at the house, we have to wait by the tree line for him to take down some of his wards before we can go inside. I may not know a lot about magic yet, but the fact it took him a full five minutes is impressive.

Especially since we walked this way out here, and he came running out to rescue me. Somehow he threw them up quickly, while running to me—ven though they're harder to take down. I make a mental note to ask him about them later. If he can show me, it will likely come in handy at some point.

Toby is sitting at the kitchen table, eating a bowl of ice cream when we walk in. "Told ya she was just being *dramatic*," he says between spoonfuls.

"Now don't you go ruinin' your supper," Uncle Zack responds, scooping up the bowl and rinsing the ice cream Toby wasn't quick enough to eat down the drain. "Bunch a heathens, that's what you are," he says, teasing.

Toby's response is to bang his fists on the table and yell in his best caveman voice about ice cream before running off to the basement again.

"Is there anything I can help with?" I ask as Uncle Zack starts pulling out dishes and silverware.

"Naw, you just go on now and wash up. I'll have this done before ya know it," he replies, shooing us all out of the kitchen. "We'll eat in the dining room like civilized people if y'all think ya can manage it."

"Malakai, Lor, if ye'll come with me, we can get these rooms situated before we sit down to eat." Aunt Viv grins at Uncle Zack's murderous glare. "An' after dinner we can all sit down an' have a civilized conversation about how we treat independent women in this family."

"Now you see here, missy!" Uncle Zack hollers behind us as we are led by the arm out of the kitchen.

My aunt and uncle have only met a handful of times I am aware of, but their dynamic is more like siblings than they have even with my parents—their actual siblings.

"Oh shut yer gob, tyrant!" Aunt Viv shoots back, laughing. "Now then, Malakai, seein' as ye don't have anything with ye, why don't ye go an' grab up Lor's bag for me, an' meet us upstairs."

As he walks off to do just that, we head up the beautiful walnut staircase to the second floor.

"Aunt Viv, it's really fine. I don't mind being downstairs. Uncle Zack is going to have a heart attack over this."

"Ach, he will'na. Safer for ye to be off the ground level, anyway. An' I'd much rather be down there, closer to the kitchen." She grins conspiratorially. "Toby's already moved down to the basement for the duration, so ye just pick a room ye like and be done with it."

I walk over to the only room upstairs with an en suite bathroom, where my parents usually stay when we visit. Opening the door and flipping on the light, I can't help the heavy sigh that escapes me. I can almost see Mom sitting in the rocking chair, reading.

"Ye do know they're fine, dove," Aunt Viv reassures, rubbing a hand over my hair. "Yer Da is a warrior. He'll recover just fine, an' they'd call ye themselves if they could. Damn man fried all the tech for miles," she mutters angrily.

"Man?" I ask. We haven't actually had a second to talk about what happened, who attacked my family. Her slip reminds me of that fact.

"Aye, we'll discuss it later," she says as Malakai walks in with my duffle. "Just set it on the bed, an claim whatever room strikes yer fancy; there's two more up here."

She walks over to the window, pulling aside the curtains and looking out a minute.

"Best we get down to dinner or that man is gonna have a fit. Probably wise to give him no more cause for tantrums tonight," she says matter-of-factly and walks out without saying another word, leaving me pondering her somber mood change.

"I'll be takin the room next to ye, should there be anythin' ye need," Malakai says, interrupting my thoughts.

"Oh, yeah. Okay," I reply absentmindedly, my mind circling what 'man' Aunt Viv was referring to, and whether or not he's still on the loose.

Seeing my distraction, Malakai smiles softly and kisses my hair before going off to get settled in his own room. I have to hand it to him, he really is perfectly fine with giving me space when he thinks I need it. After the past few days, even a minute to brush my hair and rinse my face seems indulgent.

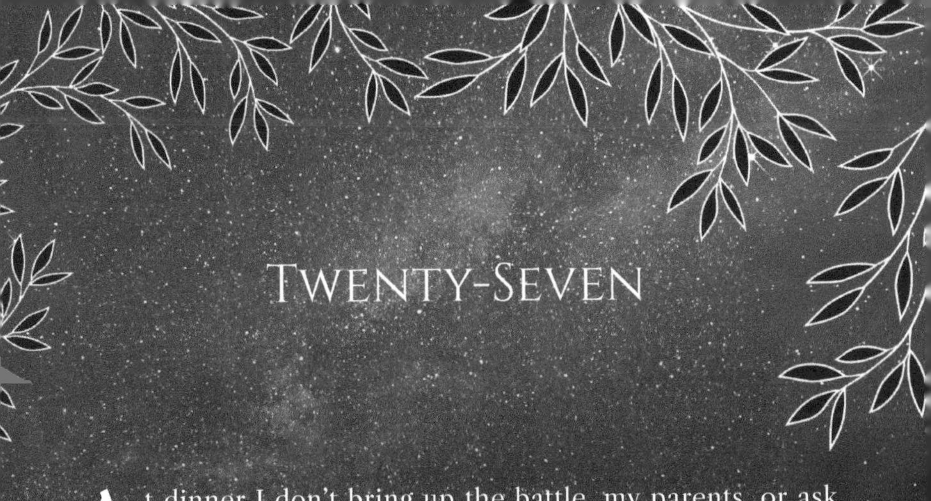

Twenty-Seven

At dinner I don't bring up the battle, my parents, or ask any other questions. It's nice to just have a meal, and I already know that everyone's alright. At least for now. That may be a copout and a crap way of dealing, but for now I'm alright with that. We spend the meal laughing, lighthearted—minus the occasional muttering Uncle Zack does about Aunt Viv 'over-riden' me in my own damn house.'

The meal was delicious and not something Toby and I, at least, are used to having. Deer is decidedly not something Mom or Dad make at home, but it was absolutely amazing tonight. It was served in a rich stew with potatoes, carrots, and I'm certain several dozen herbs and spices. Uncle Zack serves a warm, homemade apple pie for dessert with fresh cream on top that smells so good my mouth waters the second he brings it out.

"Ugh!" I mumble as my eyes roll back in my head at the decadence. "I have *missed* this!"

"Me too! Mom didn't get any baking genes at all," Toby responds around a mouth full of pie, cream dribbling down his chin. It's a wonder he doesn't permanently look like he's just lost a food fight.

"Why has it been so many years? We used to visit all the time! I don't know why we ever stopped," I say nonchalantly.

Aunt Viv and Uncle Zack glance nervously at each other.

"Alright." Setting my spoon down beside my plate with a sigh, "Spill," I demand, looking from one to the other pointedly. There goes the 'no heavy topics' portion of the evening.

"Well, ya see—" Uncle Zack glances around suspiciously.

"You're acting real sus, Uncle Zack," Toby admonishes, pointing his spoon at him, causing cream to fall onto the table. Of course, he ignores the mess and goes right back to his food.

"What is it?" I ask, folding my hands together on the table.

I spare a mournful glance at my barely touched dessert, knowing it's unlikely I'll want it after this is done. Every time I ask a question it seems to land me headfirst in more secrets, and it does little for my appetite. No matter how good the food may be.

"Well, ya know when y'all had to change to the private schools? When Jasper had to switch jobs?" he states in the form of a question.

"Yeah. That was right after our last visit. I had to have been what? Eleven? Twelve?"

Of course the two are connected, and of course I failed to put it together before now. In all fairness, there's never been a reason for me to question much in my life before now.

"Yeah, right. Well, they never really planned to do that, your parents. Jasper loved that job, had a lot of creative freedom he used to say." He picks at the crust of his pie, obviously uncomfortable. "They didn't tell y'all none a this when they told y'all about the Order?" he questions.

I shake my head, frowning.

"Damn it. Guess there's no point in keepin' secrets no more. There was an incident. Some shady character came round, askin' questions about your dad. Never did find out who he was, but it was enough to freak your parents out right good. Jasper went and signed up with a company owned by the Order next day, moved y'all to that school within a week. Never did go back in to that job, gave em a PO Box to send his stuff to."

"So, even with the Portals closed, they were worried about who might find us."

"Damn right they were! Didn't nobody know where Evangeline ended up when she closed em, coulda been anywhere, anytime. But she didn't know about your momma, didn't know about you kids. Y'all hadn't even been born when she sealed em. Wasn't just Evangeline to worry about neither; no one knows who she had on her side, or how many of em there might be."

He explains hurriedly, as though the telling of it is cathartic for him. He never was good at keeping secrets.

"After that, me and your momma talked, figured it would be best if y'all didn't come out here for a while, make sure no one could follow ya here if ya needed a safe place to scatter to one day. Far as anyone can tell, none of Evangeline's cronies ever did find out who your momma was. Which means they couldn't know who I was. But someone came lookin' after your daddy, and last thing anyone wanted was them finding out about y'all. Never did figure out who that fella was, or how he got tipped off 'bout Jasper."

"So no one thought, 'hey, might be a good idea to let the kids in on this'? You know, so we don't go leading some dangerous dude right to our house?"

"Girl. Your momma never told you don't talk to strangers? Don't bring nobody to your house without permission? I know like hell she did!" Uncle Zack rolls his eyes. "I get you're upset and are probably thinking about every shady guy you ever saw, but trust me, y'all were safe as ya could be. That school y'all go to? Principal is a Guardian. So stop your belly achin' and act like the adult ya supposedly are," he lectures, staring me down.

"Oh, Lor. You're in *trouble.*" Toby giggles, licking his fingers clean.

"Don't ya get me started on you, son. Half a mind to make ya scrub the whole dining room after you done flung your food all over. You ain't no baby anymore. Start actin' your age too."

Toby has the decency to look slightly shamed, but I know it'll change nothing. That boy is just spoiled. He'll be twenty and still eating like a toddler.

"Listen, I know y'all probably don't like bein' kept in the dark. I get that, wouldn't be none too happy about it myself. But we did what we had to do, hopin you'd never have to hear any of it. Honestly, them Portals coulda stay closed for a century, all we knew. Course now we know Lor here can make em, so. Who the hell knows, she mighta opened one up on accident somewhere one day, and we'd have to tell y'all everything anyway."

He stands, gathering up dishes to take to the kitchen.

"Toby, you help me clean this up an we'll go out, start a fire. There's some things y'all need teachin'. I wanna see where you're at. Magically."

"We can get that goin for ye, Zack," Aunt Viv offers, rising from the table and waving at Malakai and I to come with her.

"I sure do appreciate it, but I'd like to have Lor do it. And I'd like to be there when she tries. I got a theory needs testin'."

"Alright. Well, we'll be waitin' for ye out there, then. Anythin' else ye need done?"

"Naw, think we've got it pretty well covered. Shouldn't take us long to rinse these and get the washer loaded," he replies.

"Wait one second, that's a thing that could actually happen, you think? When the Portals were sealed? I could've made one?" I ask, wheels spinning.

"Well, the *witch* couldn't seal a Portal she didn't have no knowledge of, could she?" Uncle Zack asks, obviously disappointed in the question. "Ain't no tellin' what could happen. I doubt she had the power or the thought to prevent new ones, seein' as no one thought it could be done 'fore now."

"I...guess not?" I manage, flustered.

He shakes his head at me before going about the clean up again.

Aunt Viv leads us out to the back, and we pull wooden benches over to the fire pit Uncle Zack built in the middle of the yard. It's massive, easily ten feet around, and edged by beautiful stonework he cut and carved himself. The stones have symbols and designs carved all over them, some of them I now recognize as runes, others little miniatures of the moon and stars.

There's even a triquetra or two, and the moon phases along the top. I used to love trying to remember and recite every phase on the stones when we'd visit, sitting out here with my family. In the center there are already piled several cords of wood, which is nothing out of the ordinary. He loves bonfires this time of year and has one nearly every night, even if he doesn't have company. I can't count how many times we've called him on video chat and he's been out here 'thinkin' bout life and enjoyin' the fire'.

I'm a little nervous about what Uncle Zack meant by having me start the fire. He probably means with magic, and I can't help glancing over at Malakai repeatedly, knowing the last time I tried to use Fire, I kissed his brother. Not to mention almost blew us both up. Either way, it was bad. I also know the connection isn't lost on Malakai, either.

Whether or not it's bothering him is anyone's guess, though. Aunt Viv hasn't mentioned Wesley, and I've been too afraid to ask how he's doing, or if he was injured in the attack. I know he and Malakai don't have the greatest relationship, but I don't know how he'd react if his brother was hurt, or how I would.

Chances are he's already asked Aunt Viv about him, but I didn't want to intrude or make him feel like I was by talking to him about it. I know that makes me a complete coward, and I feel terrible.

"What's got ye lookin' so glum now, dove? Ye can'na go lettin' Zack get under yer skin; half o' what he says is just rubbish, anyway," Aunt Viv prods, settling down on a bench.

I sigh and sit across from her, watching Malakai floating firewood over to sit in reserve by the pit.

"Even if it were possible, it did'na happen, so why get worked up over it now?" she asks, leaning forward and placing her chin in her hand.

"We just haven't talked about what happened, Aunt Viv. All you've said is my dad got hurt, anything electrical is on the fritz, and that there was a man that attacked. I'm worried about everyone, and I'd like to know that whoever attacked us was caught. That everyone back in Scotland is safe. At least from the ones who attacked us, for now."

"Can we just take the night, dove? I know ye want yer questions answered, an' I promise ye I will do just that. Right now, ye need to focus on what ye need to learn. Until ye do, there's nothin' ye can do about any of it." She sighs heavily and gives me a sad smile, straightening in her seat. "Can ye trust me that everyone is gonna be alright? An' that I am doin' the best I can to help ye in every way I can? There'll be time enough for chattin' once ye've learned enough for any of it to make a difference to ye. Otherwise yer just gonna be distracted, an it'll show in yer trainin' here."

She leans forward, elbows on her knees as she gazes over at Malakai, a hard look in her eyes.

"This is why we train our Guardians from birth. Why we do'na keep their pow'r from em. See how much control he's got?" she asks, frustrated. "Ye should have just as much. I never liked not tellin' ye. We knew it'd be either yerself or yer brother who'd become the Heir. If we'd just been honest from the beginnin', ye would'na be hidin' out here now, crammin years o' learnin' into as few days as ye can. Dangerous, that's what it is." She stands, starts pacing back and forth in front of the bench.

Malakai walks over and sits next to me, having not only loaded the pit with even more wood, but left a sizeable stack within reach as well.

"We do'na even know what yer capable of. Ye can create a Portal without even meanin' to. Do ye know how impossible that is? We could'na figure out how the original Portals were created, how it'd be even possible! There's no tellin' how powerful ye might be, how long it'll take to train ye properly. Do'na think for a secon' Morgainne will'na try to use that to her advantage, either. Blasted woman is up to no good, same as ever."

"Alright now, Vivi. You're gonna scare these youngins half to death if ya keep it up." Uncle Zack walks up, putting a hand on Aunt Viv's shoulder and smiling at her, though the smile doesn't reach the regret in his eyes. "Things ain't quite the way we'd like em, but there ain't nothin' we can't overcome long as we're workin together." He helps her take a seat, then sits down next to her.

Toby is right behind him, jumping off the porch steps, arms loaded down with smore's supplies. How in the world he can even think about eating after dinner and dessert is beyond me, and it makes me giggle.

Uncle Zack looks back, takes in the scene, and chuckles himself. "Alright now, you just set all that down an' have a seat. Good thing I got so many benches, there'd be no space for ya."

Toby grins, dumping his goodies on the bench next to him and sprawling out himself. Uncle Zack is right; Toby and his food require their very own bench.

"Now, Lor, Viv done told me about how ya tried to start a forest fire back at the Manor. I want ya to do exactly what ya did then, but I want ya to focus in on exactly what ya want. Don't just think ya need a fire. How big do ya want the fire? How much fire do ya need to get that wood goin? Then, and *only* then, ya say the spell for it. Can ya handle that?"

"I can try, but you might want to stand back. This did not go well last time."

"I think Malakai can handle makin' sure we don't get too singed, can't ya?" Uncle Zack asks, tilting his head.

The question is part challenge, part curiosity. I have a feeling he's testing out more than one theory, but I keep it to myself.

"Should'na be a problem," Malakai agrees and looks at me. "Whenever yer ready."

I take a deep breath, glancing over at Toby who is leaning way too close to the stacked wood for my comfort and watching me intently. Trusting Malakai to not allow my brother to be burned alive, I move forward. I decide to kneel next to the fire pit and close my eyes to block out any distraction.

Remembering my uncle's instructions, I picture a fire in my mind. Not just fire though, I picture what it's like to have just started a fire intentionally, without magic. I think about the first flames in the fireplace, the glow from a new fire just brought to life.

Focusing every thought on that first flame, I exhale and hold my hands out toward the woodpile in front of me.

"*Ignis,*" I say, while keeping in my mind that I only want to *start* the fire.

"Yes!" I hear Toby hoot, and I open my eyes.

Sure enough, I've got a fire going without burning everything to ash. I sit back on my heels, smiling, and look up at Malakai as he puts a hand on my shoulder, grinning down at me. The flames are dancing around the bottom of the woodpile, not engulfing everything flammable. A marked improvement from my last attempt.

"Not bad," Uncle Zack admits, leaning back and folding his arms. "Now put it out," he challenges, studying me.

"Um, okay. How do I do that?" I fire back at him.

"Same way ya made it. The fire belongs to ya, kid. Call it back."

I furrow my brow, putting my hands out towards the flames. I concentrate on trying to make it stop, for the flames to go out. Nothing happens.

"I said call it back, not stare at it. Magic is all about intent, Lor. Ya gotta know what ya want, and ya gotta know how to get it. Did anyone tell ya how magic works?"

"I don't—"

"I take that as a *no*. Listen, when ya made that Portal in your livin' room...did ya mean to do it?"

"No. How could I? I didn't even know it was possible."

"You're lyin' to yourself. Think about it. Were ya tryin' to practice how to open a Portal, or were ya tryin' to make one? Tryin to get to your parents, maybe?"

"I..." I sit back, astonished as it hits me. "I wanted to get back to my parents," I admit.

"There ya go!" he yells, pointing a finger at me triumphantly. "Magic is about intent. That's how all this works, why control is so important. Your momma told me you caused one hell of a storm back in Scotland 'cause ya couldn't get a handle on your emotions. Why do ya think that is? 'Cause *Magic* equals *intent*!"

He stands, fire running along his arms again, holding them out to the fire.

I watch in awe as the flames from the fire I created reach out to meet the ones on his arms, the whole of them moving to run along his arms until there is nothing but singed logs left. He's totally focused inward, moving his arms in a circling motion in front of him, until the flames gather between his hands, forming a swirling ball of fire hanging in the air.

"Whoa!" Toby exclaims, and I can't help the gasp that escapes my lips.

"I want ya to notice I didn't have to say no spell, or do anything fancy or extra. It's all about intent. I knew what I wanted, and I did it. I coulda used a spell, and do when I want some extra oomph, but I don't need one for every little thing. You're *connected* to the Fire, to your magic. Both of ya. All ya need to do is have the control and willpower to make it do what ya want it to," he says, pushing towards the fire with his arms until the flames are back on the logs, crackling away at them.

"Now see, I just let it go. If there hadn't been anything to burn, it woulda just gone out, cause it's not bein' fed by magic anymore. It's like that with anything. Any Affinity, any magic."

He plunks himself down on the bench, throwing his arms out beside him.

"Exhaustin' though, if ya let it be. Ya gotta know your limits here. Thing is, magic requires energy. That energy is comin' from you, and if you ain't careful? Whoooo buddy. I seen your momma plumb pass out not payin' attention."

"Aye, ye must be aware of yer own energy when doin' magics. An if yer usin' an element that can be released, like Fire, ye must be sure ye've untethered from it when ye do. Otherwise it'll just drain ye," Aunt Viv adds, solemnly.

"So we don't need a spell at all? Why teach it that way then?" I ask.

"A spell can help ya focus your energy, your magic. We use em to teach youngins 'cause it gives em a specific parameter. Usually. Didn't work quite so well with you, Lor." Uncle Zack chuckles, shaking his head. "They shoulda guessed you'd be packin too much of a punch to focus it like that without understandin' what exactly you're doin'."

"Wesley is'na the best at gaugin' pow'r. Never has done," Malakai accuses.

"Kai," I say, laying a hand on his arm. "He was trying to be helpful."

He softens a little at my use of the nickname, but I can tell he's not fully let that situation go. That probably has more to do with that damned kiss than Wesley trying to help me harness my magic.

"No matter. We can show ya how to use em without putting such a punch behind em, can't we, Viv?" Uncle Zack grins at her, causing her to roll her eyes at him.

"Some things are best done that way, so, aye. Basics like startin' a fire? Causin' a breeze or makin' a flower grow? We do typically save that for trainin', until a person can get a feel for what they're usin'. What ye need to learn now is groundin'. It can help to sustain a longer use of magic without drainin' yer own energy."

"Grounding?" Toby asks, leaning forward again.

"Aye, ye can ground to yer Affinity, like we do when we travel. Ye've already been told about that, an there is'na much thinkin about it involved there. Yer always connected to yer Affinity, an you can use that as an energy source as well. Fire creates its own energy, same as Water, Air, Earth," she explains, picking up a handful of soil. "Every element carries with it an energy of its own, is capable of creatin' more. Ye wanna be careful, now, not to deplete its energy same as yer own. If ye can'na sustain the magic an ye can'na use the energy it creates, that's when groundin is handy."

She lets the soil fall back between her fingers, sitting up straight again.

"Malakai, ye'll have to be the one to show em how; yer unique. Ye've all got an Affinity for Spirit. It can be an infinite source of energy for ye, if ye know how to use it. I gather me uncle showed ye how to do so afore ye came here?" she asks, raising an eyebrow.

"Aye, he did. I do'na think they're ready for it. It can be dangerous, an' I do'na know that I can show em how to keep it from overwhelmin' em," he admits, hanging his head as if he's let us down.

"Malakai, were ye shown how to control it or not?" she demands, standing.

"Aye but—"

"Then yer the only one to show em. We do'na have the luxury of sendin' em to me uncle now, an there's no tellin' when we might. For *this moment*, we're safe. No one knows o' this place, an there's not a soul who'd think to find em here. I've no doubt Gabriel told ye how to avoid any dangers?"

"Aye, he did..." Malakai admits, obviously still not comfortable with the idea.

"Then ye'll just have to teach em the same as he taught ye. I do'na mean to be cavalier about it, but I can'na help them here. Yer the only one who can. You and yer brother, but we can'na bring him here right now."

"No. I can do it; Wesley is'na any good at teachin' Lorali, as he's shown enough."

Uncle Zack snorts at that, shaking his head. "Trouble in paradise, kids?" he drawls out sarcastically.

"Stop it," I spit out, glancing over at Malakai, who's jaw is clenched tight.

"I'm just sayin'," he says, shrugging his shoulders. "If he's got a problem with his brother bein' 'round ya, sounds to me like he's got some control issues."

"Or maybe that's a complicated situation you know nothing about," I snap back defensively.

"Alright now." Aunt Viv puts her hands up between us. "Settle down. Zack, ye really are puttin' yer foot in yer mouth here. I'd love to let ye go on doin' just that, but we've all got quite enough on the plate without ye tramplin' through this one."

She gets up, walks over to Malakai, and places a hand on his shoulder.

"I did'na mean to pour salt on the wound, lad. What happened with Wesley was unfortunate, but I do'na believe it was intentional, and neither should ye. That's all I'll say on it, as it's a matter between ye. I trust ye to show em what they need to know, an keep em safe," Aunt Viv reassures.

"What can I do with Spirit? I mean, I know I've got cool stuff with animals and all." Toby shifts in his seat, cautious. "Lor has all these Affinities, and that's great, really." He smiles over at me. "But other than just make a really cool light ball, what good is it?" he finishes quietly, looking dejected.

My heart aches a little for him, hating that he feels at all inferior because he doesn't have more than Spirit. He should be thrilled, considering how rare it is, but all he sees is his one Affinity to my four—and it makes me angry for him.

"Oh, Toby." Aunt Viv walks over, crouching down in front of him. "Spirit is one o' the greatest gifts we've got. Ye can create spells, protections, it's a force to be reckon'd with in battle, it is. We've only been focusin' on yer sister because we can'na help ye with it. It's a rare and pow'rful Affinity; the four of ye are the largest group of any generation to be so blessed."

"Spirit's pure magic there, bud. I dunno its limits, or if there even *are* any, 'cause I ain't never met anyone who had it. Bet your ass it's powerful, though. Lucky for ya, Malakai can show ya a thing or two," Uncle Zack adds.

"Yeah?" Toby asks, looking excitedly to Malakai.

"It would be an honor to show ye what I know," he agrees, solemnly.

"Awesome!" Toby jumps up, excited. "Not just that grounding stuff though, right?"

"I think we should make a start of it there, but there's more to learn. The groundin' bit is important so ye do'na push it too far, though. So ye gotta learn it first an' well," Malakai tells him, an amused grin on his face.

My heart swells at how amazing he's being to my little brother, and I grin myself.

"Deal!" he says, settling back against the bench and picking up a chocolate bar.

"Guess that's settled, then," Uncle Zack proclaims. "Lor, I'd like ya to try again with the fire. Call it back, an' remember what I said about intent. Once ya got that down, the rest is a piece a cake."

I nod and reach out towards the fire again. I think about all he's said tonight, focusing not on putting it out, but on calling it back in. Eyes closed, I can feel the warmth of the fire on my fingertips as I concentrate. I hear Aunt Viv gasp, and I fling my eyes open to make sure I'm not lighting the house on fire or something.

What I see is magnificent. The fire is licking my fingertips, just as I pictured in my head, almost like I'm absorbing it back into myself. I grin and focus more on pulling the fire away from the pit, feel the rush as that energy is transferring back to me. It's like a jolt of espresso hitting my system, every nerve in my body zinging.

"That's it, girl! You got it!" Uncle Zack hoots, slapping his leg. "You got it!"

I grin wider and focus on the flames now flickering on my fingertips. I admit to showing off a bit, making the flames dance higher, pulling them back, dancing across the backs of my hands before I focus on putting it out entirely. Absorbing all that energy, I feel like I could run a marathon, it's exhilarating.

I sink back on the bench, staring wide-eyed at my hands. My leg bounces with pent-up energy, and I have to keep myself from jumping around.

"I get it! Is it the same for any element?"

"It is, far as I can tell. I'm not quite as gifted as you may be, only one Affinity for me. I've trained my share o' youngins, though, and it sure seems the principle is the same 'cross the board. Same as anything, once ya know how it works, the rest is just icin' on the cake."

"So you're saying the only thing we really have to do is to know what we want to do, and just...do it?" Toby asks.

I can see the wheels spinning in his head, and I shift in my seat, wondering what he's plotting.

"That's about right," Uncle Zack confirms.

"Huh..." Toby stands, putting his hands in front of him, and suddenly the firepit is full of purple flames.

"Toby!" I jump up, clapping. I'm thrilled for him and don't try to hide it.

"How'd ye—" Aunt Viv is sitting forward on the bench, knuckles white and hands grasping the edge.

"Son of a..." Uncle Zack's eyes are wide, arms limp by his side.

It's Malakai's reaction that is the strangest. He doesn't say a word, just stares at Toby for a second, then walks over and puts a hand through the flames. Nodding, he closes his eyes and says something under his breath I can't make out, and the flames are gone.

"Malakai?" I ask when he doesn't open his eyes or move for a few seconds.

I jump to my feet when he still doesn't answer and put a hand on his shoulder.

Suddenly, his eyes open and there's an eerie purple glow to them. Aunt Viv jumps up, pulling me back as he opens his mouth to speak.

'Bound by Three are We
Guardians All,
And Magic released.
The Lady waits,
The Wizard bound,
Anoint the Heir
Where Angels roamed.
Handfast her to Dragons,
A Union strong.
Beware the Crone
With Raven's song.
Claim The Spirit,
Heed our Call.
Become the Lock
That fits the Key.'

"Malakai! Malakai!" I scream, yanking out of my aunt's grasp as he crumples to the ground. Throwing myself on the ground by his side, I pull him into my arms. "Malakai!" I tilt my face up, tears streaming down my face, and find my aunt hovering over us. "Why won't he answer me? Aunt Viv, what's wrong with him?" I scream, frantic.

This can't be happening. It isn't happening.

She shakes her head, eyes wide and full of worry.

I turn back to Malakai, putting a hand to his cheek, begging him to wake up. Rain starts falling heavily, lightning shooting across the sky constantly. I start to shake him violently, my heart crushing under the weight of the panic I feel.

Come on, Kai. Wake up. Wake up, please. I can't do this without you.

"Lor, I have to get him in the house, hun. Come on now, let me take him in." Uncle Zack is kneeling down in front of us, hands disappearing under Malakai, lifting him out of my arms.

I want to cling to him; I want to force him to open his eyes and stop all this. Instead I sit there, dumbfounded, watching as my uncle takes him from me.

"Viv," he says, as he stands and rushes into the house, Malakai still quiet in his grasp.

"Come now, dove. In we go," she says, gently helping me to my feet as the rain drenches us. I look up and see Toby, a horrified look plastered across his face, color drained away.

Oh no. Toby. The thought flickers across my mind before I am consumed again by the way Kai crumpled to the ground, as though his body was no more than paper, no longer able to hold its own weight.

"I didn't—" he stammers, stricken.

"Hurry now, Toby, run an' open the door for yer uncle," I hear her command.

I should be more concerned about Toby. Somewhere, under the shock and the pain, I know that. He's going to be devastated.

What if Malakai doesn't ever wake up? That makes me gag, leaning over onto my hands unable to withstand the idea.

Aunt Viv grabs me under the arms, pulling me off the ground. She leads me into the house, the rain so heavy I can't see more than a foot ahead of where we walk. Every step I take, the mud sucking my shoes down, making the movement even more difficult.

I want to sink down into the dirt. Lie on the wet soil, let it suck me under. So much has gone wrong. So much has changed.

Once we get inside, my numb mind focuses enough for me to sprint into my uncle's room, where he's laid Malakai on the bed. I sit next to him, taking his hand and reassuring myself slightly, watching the rise and fall of his chest.

He isn't dead, Lorali. He isn't dead.

It isn't enough to pull me from the darkest corners of my own mind. The overwhelming helplessness and despair. First Dad, whom I have no actual information about—and now Kai.

At some point, Aunt Viv tries to convince me to change out of my sopping wet clothes, but I refuse to move. I hear Toby come in, sit in the rocking chair across from the bed. They continue to move around me, but it's as though I'm underwater, their existence a muffled, far off sound. Aunt Viv convinces Uncle Zack to move him upstairs to my room, saying something about it being safer off the main floor.

Someone gently guides me up behind them; it must be Toby. Somewhere under all the reactions, I know it's not fair that he has to step up and care for me.

Uncle Zack comes in and forces me to take something, wash it down with water. I don't care enough to ask what it is, my eyes never leaving Malakai's sleeping form.

As my sluggish mind realizes it must have been a sedative and I drift off into darkness, I barely catch hushed tones around me. Normally, I would be livid. Instead, I'm panicked.

What if something happens while I'm sleeping?

"I had to do somethin', Viv! She's got such a storm brewin', she'll flood the river. If that girl don't get a hold of herself, she's gonna hurt someone. Isn't this what that damned Amulet was supposed to prevent?"

"Ach. I know, Zack. I just do'na think druggin' her was the best way to handle it. The Amulet only goes so far. She's more pow'rful than even it is."

How? How can the Amulet not be enough? I saw it made. I know it has the power of three extremely powerful and important people. That power is imbued into it. I can't possibly be overpowering it; I can't have that much power and not know how to help him.

It's the last thing my muddled brain can think before I succumb to the darkness closing in.

About Author

J L Casten is an avid reader, addicted to coffee in all its forms, Mom to 4 lovely kiddos and 5 ornery fur babies.

She lives in the foothills of the Blue Ridge Mountains with her husband and kids, though she misses the Pacific Northwest and its wonders.

She is a Disabled Army Veteran, who loved her job as a Medic, but is quite content as the eccentric Author she has become.

She has lived all over the US as well as Germany (twice) and is most at home in the mountains surrounded by trees.

Follow her and get all the latest news and releases by subscribing to the blog at www.jlcasten.com

ACKNOWLEDGMENTS

This book has been years in the making, and I can hardly believe it is a reality now. I am so very thankful for everyone who had a hand in this. When I started writing I had no idea it would become what it has, but I am overjoyed at the end result. I have found my passion and my purpose again, and I will happily write all the rest of my days.

To my family who tolerated the long nights, all day writing sprints, editing endlessly, and of course my frustration at all of the things that go along with creating a book. I love you, you are my entire world and every time I wanted to throw my laptop and give up, you kept me going. I hope I have been a good example for you, that you can live your dreams- even if it's hard sometimes. I only ever want you to be happy, and to live a life of passion- chasing after the things everyone else tells you are out of your reach. Never let anyone talk you out of chasing your dreams. Not even me.

To Julie, my first cheerleader, my first rival, my first partner in crime. I love you more than you will ever know, my sister. Thank you for encouraging me, for reading the roughest of rough drafts, and for answering my FaceTime so I could cry to you from 8 hours away about how hard it all was.

To Jackie, I will always mourn all those years we missed, but I am so damned thankful we found each other. Thank you for being the first person to finish the very first draft. Thank you for telling me how wonderful it was even when it had so much work to be done.

To Jessica, thank you. Thank you for being there for so many years, for growing up with me, for pushing me to make this book what I wanted it to be. You believed in me when I didn't think I could make it happen, pushed me to get uncomfortable, and this was the result. I love you to the moon and back, dear friend.

To Shay, I could not have created such a beautiful book without you. Thank you for holding my hand, for checking my work, for catching all the million little flaws so I could be proud of the finished product. Here is to us, becoming household names and best-selling authors. I hope you realize you are stuck with me for life now.

To all of my early readers, thank you. A million times, thank you. You were the first to set eyes on this book, the first to give me feedback and help me to see my story from a reader's perspective. You have no idea how absolutely invaluable each of you has been. Thank you for helping me to create this world, these characters, this story. You made me believe I could.

As cheesy and ridiculous as it sounds- Thank You to all the Authors of TikTok. Thank you for creating a place where we could all gather, despite a pandemic, despite any distances, where we built a community and uplifted one another. Truly, there are some amazing individuals on that app- and I am so very thankful for each of you. Sometimes you were all that stood between me and a significant emotional event.

Lightning Source UK Ltd.
Milton Keynes UK
UKHW010636090522
402703UK00001B/70